CROWNING KEYS

To those who just want to be happy…

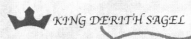
KING DERITH SAGEL

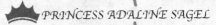
PRINCESS ADALINE SAGEL

CAPTAIN BRUTIS — CAPTAIN CARTER

CAPTAIN MARC — CAPTAIN REMND

CAPTAIN CAMILLA

LIEUTENANT MAX

LIEUTENANT LINX

LIEUTENANT FIONA

LIEUTENANT TREVOR

LIEUTENANT WES

LIEUTENANT HANK

LIEUTENANT JACKE

LIEUTENANT PAULE

LIEUTENANT KEN

LIEUTENANT ALEXANDER

PRINCE COOPER SAGEL

COMMANDER CRYMM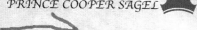

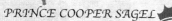

CAPTAIN   CAPTAIN   CAPTAIN   CAPTAIN   CAPTAIN
AUGUSTUS DANIEL   JULIUS   SABRINA   RUFUS

               LIEUTENANT   LIEUTENANT
LIEUTENANT   GREY   BAXTER
   LUIS

            LIEUTENANT
             BRENDA

            LIEUTENANT
             VINELLE

Part 1: The Arrival

Chapter 1

Forty-one, forty-two, forty-three.

My eyes trace the last tile on the floor and I fight the urge to count them all again. *Don't fall back into old habits.* I rip my eyes up from the floor.

The bare mattress chills my legs through my black pants. I lean back against the cinder block wall and stare across the naked room. The backpack and sword I carried here are tossed to the side. There's a small desk in the right corner of the room with drawers I haven't had the energy to investigate. In the far left corner, a tall skinny mirror hangs, and I'm actually terrified to step in front of it.

Cold white tiles stretch across the room, making it seem awfully bright. The wall across from me is made up of three large panes of glass with a half circle window above them. Outside, the sun has reached what I would say is about noon, maybe a little before. The blue ocean ripples in the distance, just beyond the wall that encloses all of Libertas. My room has a gorgeous view, but on this island, I have a hard time believing there is a bad view.

My hair is dried and full of saltwater. I haven't been motivated to change out of my clothes, even though I was presented with clean ones days ago. I don't want to accept this. I don't want this new world or this new life. It was hard enough the first time my life changed paths when I was thrown in prison, and then it changed a second time when I escaped the prison. I don't need this third life change. I don't want the life that has been prepared for me here in Libertas.

We've been on this island for about three days now, but I haven't left my room. I just sit here and try to deny this world where my father lives and my mother is forgotten and left behind on Dather. A few people come to check on me and bring me food throughout the day. They even bring by some bedding and offer to prep it for me every night, but I refuse to move or to talk to them. They've mentioned my father has requested to see me multiple times, but Linda has told him to give me space.

"Come on Adaline, open the door." Alexander's voice finally breaks through the barricades I had on my mind from the world outside these walls. "Adaline."

Alexander stops by my room multiple times during the day to see if I'll let him in. Reluctantly, this time, I get up and approach the metal door. We all get temporary rooms that share the same long hall here in the castle until they prepare our living quarters. Surprisingly, we ended up being a little ahead of schedule. Lucky us.

"What's up with you?" Alexander immediately questions me when I pull the door open.

I don't answer. Instead, I turn my back to him and sit back down on the bare mattress.

"Are you not happy your father is alive?"

I look at Alexander for a long time before finally saying, "It's easier to forgive a dead man." It's the first thing I've said since we arrived.

"What does that mean?" Alexander asks under his breath, and he takes a seat next to me. His eyes scan the room and me, taking in the disastrous state we're in.

"It means I was able to forgive him for abandoning me, and being responsible for my mother and Titus dying, because he was dead. It didn't do any good to go on hating someone who was dead. Now he's not dead but my mother and Titus are. That's not fair," I say flatly, sounding like a child.

"You didn't even give him a chance. You don't even know his side of the story," Alexander says.

"You really think he's going to have a good reason for the murder of my mother and little brother?" I ask, shocked.

"No, but I honestly don't think he knew they were going to die. You didn't see how confused he looked when he didn't see them with us after you stormed off." We both fall silent as I try to fight the fact that Alexander could be right. "You need to talk to him," Alexander says in a soft voice. "Especially with what's happened with Molly."

I can feel my hands tighten into fists and tears brim my eyes at how frustrating it is for me to try and give him a second chance. I know they have Molly locked up here, still trying to figure out what

King Renon's motives were for leaving her as bait in those tunnels. And I fell for it. I brought her here and he knew I would do that. I feel Alexander push his hand into mine and squeeze it tightly. "It's a good thing that your father's alive. You know it is."

"Have you forgiven your father?" I ask him and my angry eyes flip to meet his.

"What do you mean?" Alexander begins to backpedal.

"Your father, George, left you alone in a castle ruled by a brother who tried to kill you when you were a baby. He and my father let Marin suffer on the old Libertas for seven years," I begin to list off and Alexander's face hardens.

"I have forgiven him," Alexander says and I shake my head.

"You're just telling yourself that. It's not that easy, is it?" I turn back to him and he's quiet, contemplating the truth I'm speaking.

"I'm at least trying to forgive him," Alexander says and I don't know how to respond to that. "My father, mother, and I sat down the night we got here and talked, Adaline. It didn't fix everything they did to each other or me, but we are taking the right steps."

"So they know you're aware King Renon is your brother?" I ask defensively. "What about how Molly is your sister?"

"We did talk about it," Alexander says, and I'm surprised. "My father told my mother I knew."

"I bet she was angry he told you without her there," I say and think about how Marin must have reacted.

"She was upset at first, but it was a small detail compared to what Molly announced," Alexander says as he remembers how much his life has changed in the last couple of days.

"So does Molly know you're her brother?" I ask gently.

Alexander shakes his head. "No, and we agreed to not tell anyone else right now. My parents don't even know that I told you." His eyes land on mine, begging me to agree to keep his secret.

"I won't tell anyone," I agree and Alexander relaxes next to me. "But you can't live in this secret forever. They are about to start a rebellion against *your* brother. I think the rest of Libertas should know that."

"I understand, but it just doesn't feel like it's the right time," Alexander says sheepishly. "Now stop deflecting the conversation away from you and your father," Alexander says and nudges my shoulder.

He says it lightheartedly, but it makes my stomach turn. I can feel his eyes burning into the side of my face and reluctantly I lift my eyes to meet his.

"I'm not going to see him," I say through a tight throat.

Alexander's head falls. "I figured you'd say that."

I watch as he rises from the mattress and moves to the open door of my room. He leans his head out and exchanges a hushed conversation. My heart picks up; nervous about who could be standing outside these walls. I knew I shouldn't have let him in, but before I can get up and seal myself back in my room of solitude, Cooper walks in. Alexander slips out into the hall and closes the door behind him.

"So, you'll let Alexander in, but not your older brother?" Cooper asks me. He walks to the window, shoving his hands into his pockets.

"Because I know you're on our father's side," I say dryly, and apparently so is Alexander.

"Mother would want you to forgive him."

He says the words so matter-of-factly they take me by surprise. My heart clenches in my chest.

"You have no idea what she would want," I say, but stop myself from getting lost in my anger. I spent seven years with her in a prison cell under King Renon's castle. I, more than anyone, know what she had to go through because my father left us.

"Adaline," he drops his voice, so gentle in comparison to my anger.

"How can you forgive him for leaving you in the woods?" I ask.

"Because I understand it was for the greater good of our world. I found you and I helped bring you to Libertas. You can fulfill your destiny now." His words bleed with passion, but I see the light falter in his eyes.

I stand and cross to him. "Don't lie to me and tell me you aren't even the tinniest bit upset that you didn't get a normal childhood. He ripped our family apart."

Cooper presses his mouth into a thin line. "Sometimes," he admits and heaves a sigh. "But I know this is bigger than me and him. It's so much more than that. Whether you forgive him or not, you have to come out of this room at some point. Father needs us to start working together. He wants you to come meet with him now."

In a matter of seconds, Cooper has lit the reality of this on fire. I was brought here as a piece in a prophecy to free the gifted. I have a role to play here. I don't think I will ever forgive my father, but I do want to try and save what I can of this tattered family.

"Will you come with me?" I ask quietly.

"Of course," he says. We leave my room and walk into the hallway that branches off from the foyer we were in the other day. First, I'll talk to my father, and then I need to figure out what is going to be done about Molly.

We walk back through the hall, now empty and deathly silent except for our footsteps against the white marble floors. I look up to the double grand staircase, and the moment from days ago when I saw my father for the first time in seven years replays in my mind, his words still echoing.

"We've got a lot of catching up to do," he had said.

"Father?" my small voice choked out.

Then, he had seen Molly, and when she said she was King Renon's sister my stomach hit the floor. I turned slowly seeing the shock set on everyone's face. I brought her here, it was my fault. I felt my heart quicken with everyone waiting to see what would happen next, and for a second I wasn't sure what to do. So I ran. I ran away from everyone. Linda found me sitting outside the castle and walked me to my room.

"Are you okay?" Cooper asks, laying a soft hand on my wrist.

"What?" I ask, and realize I had gotten lost in the memory for a second. "Yeah, I'm fine," I say and we walk up the staircase. At the top, two grand doors are propped open. We both walk in and I look around the elegant room. It seems to be a den. There is a large wooden desk in the back of the room with two enormous windows behind it. Some sort of seal is carved into the front of the desk and I can only assume it must be the emblem for Libertas. It's a mix of all the gifted symbols. *Very fitting.* There is a set of chairs in front of the desk and two couches in the corner of the room, but the most amazing aspect are the rows and rows of bookshelves. There have to be hundreds of books in here.

"Adaline?" My father's voice comes out broken and I snap my head from the books to him. He walks in from a room that's connected to the den.

"You wanted to see me," I say and can hardly recognize my voice.

"Do you want to sit?" my father asks as he lowers himself into the chair behind the desk.

I look to Cooper, letting him lead me. He nods and we walk and sit across from our father.

We sit here in awkward silence until finally, he says, "I'm so sorry."

I can feel the tears coming again. I look away from him and say, "Yeah, well, that doesn't change what's happened."

"I didn't know they were going to die, Adaline," he almost whispers.

"That's not going to bring them back!" I yell and cut him off. "Nothing's going to bring them back."

"I know, and trust me, I'd give everything I have to get them back," my father says, leaning forward on the desk.

"Mother knew," I say and look down to the floor. "I could tell she knew the day they came to take us to the prison, and the day they came to kill her, but she wouldn't let me save them."

"That's not your fault," Cooper says, putting a hand on my shoulder.

I squeeze my eyes tight because I know that I don't only blame my father for killing my mother and Titus. I also blame myself. I shouldn't have let them die. I should have done something. I had this gift of an enhanced sense of sight and I did nothing.

"I should have saved them," I squeeze out, and finally, for the first time, I accept the blame I've been trying to push on my father.

"Adaline, no one is to blame for their deaths. There are things that are set in people's lives. We can't change that," my father says, and he gets up and moves around the desk. When his cold hand rests on my arm, I flinch back from him.

"Don't," I snap. "I don't want you to comfort me."

My father's eyes sadden. I pull my tears back and wipe the ones that escaped off my cheeks.

"I didn't come here to make amends. I'm not here to forgive you. Cooper said you wanted to see me. If this isn't about the war you've been master mindedly planning my entire life, then I'll go."

"I want to make this right," he says, still trying to reason with me.

"Tell me about the rebellion," I say shortly. I have no interest in hearing about anything else right now.

"I wanted to be the one to explain it to you and Alexander," my father says. He moves back to his chair on the other side of the desk.

"Mio thought you were dead, so he told us," I say, still keeping my voice flat.

"Yes," my father says, nodding. "We are moving toward a rebellion to free all the gifted, and give justice to those that are gone."

"Mio told me that Alexander and I are supposed to play an important role in this rebellion," I say, hoping my father can shed some light on the mystery.

"This rebellion has been on pause, waiting for you to arrive. There's a prophecy that refers to you both as the saviors, but we'll discuss this later," my father says. "I assume you're about to have more important matters to attend to."

I turn over my shoulder and see Linda enter the den. "The council is ready to discuss the residency of your group."

"I've got some work to do here, being the King of Libertas is no small task," my father says.

"You're the king?" I ask. Suddenly him at the desk with the seal in this den clicks the pieces in place. I knew my father was of some importance to Libertas and, I guess this den is grand enough to be for a king, but I just see him as my father.

"I am. I'll tell you about it later, but you both should follow Linda to the council room," my father says.

Cooper and I leave with Linda and head back down the marble staircase and deeper into the castle. At the end of the main hallway, two guards stand at attention, flanking a wooden double door. The wooden doors take me by surprise, as everything else in the castle is marble and rough stone.

"This council room has seen the arrival of every single person in Libertas," Linda tells us. Both of the guards pull the doors open, and we see that the entire council room is crowded with people. "This room is the oldest thing on Libertas, and is completely refurbished from the original council room that was built on the old Libertas."

As we walk into the historic room, I feel the weight of all the past councils land on me. Inside, there are rows and rows of wooden pews. We walk in and I notice that there is a balcony of another twenty or so rows above us that are also filled with unfamiliar faces.

"Everyone wanted to be here for your arrival," I hear Linda whisper in my ear as she leads us down the center aisle.

Along the left side of the room, twelve citizens are sitting in a huddled group. At the front, there is a podium with an older man sitting behind it. An empty stand is placed next to him.

I notice Mio and Cinder in the first row and see that the rest of the group is here. My eyes scan down their familiar faces. Toby is here, as well as James, Albert, and Essie. Alexander and Zavy sit together at the end of the front pew, whispering back and forth.

Alexander's mother, Marin, is absent, but I remember she's been helping move the gifted to Libertas for a long time. I'm sure she has already been approved for residency here.

Then, my eyes land on Molly.

"Adaline," her young voice calls to me. She stands and slides out of the pew. "I've been asking to come see you," she begins to explain and I kneel to her level. I notice she looks much healthier than a couple of days ago and I wonder what kind of medicine they have been giving her.

"I thought they had you in a holding room," I say and glance back to Linda.

"Her residency is in question as well. She is a part of your group," Linda says and disgust bleeds from the comment. I catch her roll her eyes, clearly frustrated with me for bringing Molly here.

I remember when my memories were returned to me at Cooper's camp, and I'm sure the last few days have been very confusing for her. Just like for me, the journey was real for her and the relationships she built with me and my group were true. But King Renon had to have planted her there for a reason, and if she jeopardizes this rebellion it will land on my shoulders.

"I swear I don't know why he sent me here. I'm not trying to hurt anyone, I promise," she pleads to me and I hear Linda let out an exhausted sigh.

"She's been saying that nonstop since you arrived. Let the Council decide if she should stay and then we'll see what information we can get out of her," Linda's bitter voice rings as she turns to leave the council room.

I look at Molly's frightened eyes and I believe her. She's just a child. She's not responsible for what her brother did.

"Do you want to go back?" I ask Molly and her eyes shift. It's probably the first time someone thought to ask her what she wanted instead of treating her like the enemy or a spy.

"No, I want to stay with you," she says softly. "My brother." She lets the air hang heavy for a moment before continuing, "He's horrible. I don't want to be sent back to him or that castle. He scares me." Her voice begins to shake and I lay a gentle hand on her shoulder.

"It's okay, Molly. I will fight for you to be able to stay," I say and I motion for her to sit back with the group.

I don't know what King Renon's motives were, but I swore to protect her and keep her safe. If that means fighting for her to stay in Libertas, then that's what I'm going to do.

Chapter 2

I take my seat in the wooden pew, next to Alexander, and the crowd around us whispers about our arrival. I assume some of them probably take note of my horrid appearance, including Mio who fires me a judgmental glance. It screams that I need to get a hold of myself.

The old man behind the podium lifts a wooden gavel and pounds it against the stand. Everyone surrounding us rises, so we do as well. "This council is now in session. We will begin by calling each potential resident to the stand to hear why he or she should be given a chance to reside here. First, we want to hear about the journey from Adaline."

Everyone sits back down and I'm escorted to the smaller stand at the front of the room.

"Just start from the beginning," he urges me.

"All right. Well, I guess it began when my mother and younger brother passed away on my last day in the prison," I start to tell the story.

"Approximately how long ago was that, Ms. Sagel?" a voice asks from the group at the side of the room.

The old man next to me turns and explains, "They get to ask questions throughout your statement. Please answer them truthfully."

I swallow and search for the answer. "I'm not sure. I guess it's been longer than a week." I pause and it registers that my mother and brother have been dead for over a week. Time keeps moving forward without them.

The person who asked the question nods for me to continue my story, but my eyes keep wandering over all the judging faces in the room, and it's getting to be too much. I don't know any of these people, why should I share any of this information with them? I wish I hadn't left the privacy of my bare room. But then my eyes land on Alexander's. I hold his green stare and pretend that he's the only person in the room.

"I knew I needed to try and escape, even though they were gone," I say, picking up where I left off. "Before they took my mother she told me I was a Force Lifter. So, I used my gift to get out of my cell and out of the castle."

I pause for a second, remembering the mysterious guard that night who helped me escape, who I never did get to thank.

"Then, I met Alexander outside of the castle. He was working as a guard there on night duty. Together, we fled into the woods and tried to stay hidden from Paylon and his search party."

"You fled with someone who was working for King Renon?" another individual asks from the front row of the group.

"Well, not exactly," I stammer. "I had fallen while I was running from Paylon. Alexander found me and carried me away from the castle," I explain and her confused face pushes me further. "It's complicated. My mother had altered his memories so he would think he knew me from when we were kids. He saved me because he thought that's who I was, and I went with him because I thought that was who he was."

"So at this point, you both have no idea what your true connections are. You were just running for your life and he was trying to save his friend?" she asks, trying to suck out every detail.

"That would be correct," I say.

The door at the back of the council room opens and my father walks in with Alexander's father and mother behind him. I watch as they take a seat in the back of the room. Seeing George reminds me of the letter he had left Alexander.

"Alexander had a note from his father saying that Alexander needed to help me escape when the time was right," I add. "So, Alexander and I made our way deeper into the woods and continued to Libertas. That's when we ran into Zavy and Toby. They had fled from Garth to live in the forest rather than the prison. We teamed up and decided to come out here together, since this is a place for fleeing gifted. After some setbacks with Paylon, we eventually all came together at Sard and sailed here.

The journey on the ocean went smoothly until the eels in the ocean attacked us. They destroyed our ships, but I was able to teleport us to an island that we were just off the shore of. Not everyone made it though," I say, and my voice cracks.

I imagine the faces of those who were lost at sea. I didn't move quick enough before they drowned. A piece of my heart lingers with each one of them.

"We're sorry for your loss, Adaline," the old man next to me says.

I realize I've been silent for a while. Tears fill the eyes of my group in front of me. *Finish, Adaline. Finish the story and then you can go sit down.*

"We later learned that we had washed up onto the old Libertas, and that's where we found Marin," I say, forcing myself to continue. "She had been stranded there for seven years, and together we were able to reconstruct our boats and get back on the ocean. Then, a couple of days ago, we arrived at the docks and were escorted here."

Immediately question after question starts flying at me from the twelve individuals sitting along the side of the room.

The older man hammers into his stand yelling, "Order, order in the Council Room." When the room finally falls silent he continues, "Each juror will get their turn to ask a question starting at the top. Remember, we have many other individuals to hear from today."

A thin man with long brown hair speaks first, "If you had to pick a member that arrived with you today, excluding those with gifts, that aided you the most in your journey, who would it be?"

I pause, startled for a second at the stupidity of his question. "There isn't one person who helped more than another," I say, insulted that he wants me to choose. "Each person contributed something to the journey, and without any of them we wouldn't have made it here."

"But who helped the most?"

I still don't answer, and I hold his stare.

"Okay, so they all helped. I'll acknowledge that, just who helped you, personally, the most."

I drop my eyes from his and scan over the group of people I arrived with.

"Cooper," I say without an explanation.

The next juror, a young lady with thin blonde hair asks, "How so?"

"Because he made all the pieces fit," I say shortly until the next juror asks me to explain so I continue. "By being able to fill in all the parts of my past. I always felt like I was missing something, and when we came upon him in the woods, it was like everything had finally clicked back into place." The room falls quiet now that I have answered their question in full, even if I didn't want to.

"That is all Ms. Sagel," I hear the old man's small voice say next to me, dismissing me from the stand. I rise and make my way back to my seat in the pew.

"Alexander, we'd like to hear from you next," the old man motions for him to rise. He slowly leaves my side and takes my place up front.

"Please tell us how the journey was for you," he instructs Alexander.

"Adaline explained it well enough," Alexander tries to dismiss the need for his story, but the jury isn't so quick to let him go. Since

Alexander doesn't have anything new to add, the jury takes to asking questions instead.

"Can you tell us more about the letter you found from your father? That's when this all began for you," the same lady who asked me why I chose Cooper speaks first.

"I awoke one morning and my father was gone," Alexander says and his eyes hold his father's gaze from the back of the room. "I had found a note under his pillow that told me to help Adaline escape."

"And your memories had been altered to believe Adaline was your childhood friend?" the same lady asks and Alexander nods his head.

"Yes, I've spent the last two years with those memories in my head as I grew up and started working at the castle." Alexander thinks back to all that time he had spent thinking and caring for a girl he didn't truly know.

"And what happened when your memories were restored?" The first man who had asked me a question speaks up. "What were the memories that were returned to you?"

I watch as Alexander's eyes dance around the room. He seems to stiffen in the chair and I hold my breath. I know what Alexander's true memories are, but I don't know how this jury will react to the truth.

"Just your typical childhood memories," Alexander says. "Memories of school and friends I had. Nights with my family and holidays. I didn't live a very glamorous life before all of this."

He lied.

My eyes scan the jury and the rest of the room, but no one seems to question his answer. His eyes land on me, begging me to let him keep his secret. I feel the weight of his actions settle on my shoulders. Alexander is not only keeping his past a secret, but now he's lying about it. This is just going to make it that much harder for him to come clean in the future, but I realize he must never intend to.

"Do you wish to add anything else to the description of the journey to Libertas?" the old man asks Alexander once the jury agrees that they don't have any further questions.

"I do not," Alexander says simply and hurries back down to the pew. He slides in next to me and the muscles in his body are still tense from the interrogation. Without speaking, I slide my hand into his and hold it tightly. I feel his heart pounding through our grasp. I squeeze his hand three times, and then a pause. Just like I used to do with my little brother, Titus, to calm him down.

"All right. Then let's begin with each candidate's review. We'll start with you, Mio." Everyone shifts in the room and I feel as though the judgment they turned toward Alexander and I has doubled for the non-gifted members.

Mio rises and makes his way to the stand. The old man then says, "Just simply tell us why you think we should let you stay here."

My mind starts to wander from the scene around me, and I begin to block it all out again.

This is bizarre.

I can tell, just by looking at the faces of the jurors, that they don't think any of these people are worthy of staying here on their island.

As if, since they don't have a gift, they are somehow beneath us. I stare down at the wooden floorboards beneath my worn black leather boots and tune out everything going on around me.

Group member after group member gets up and gives their list of reasons as to why they want to stay, but I don't hear any of them, and neither do the jurors.

"Molly, you're next," the old man's voice breaks through my mind's barricade. My head snaps up and I watch as tiny Molly makes her way up to the empty chair. "Why should you get to stay?"

"Because I want to," her small voice says and there's a huff of laughter from the jury.

"How did you help in bringing our saviors home?" one of the quieter jurors asks. He leans forward, resting his arms on the wooden beam in front of him.

Molly is quiet for a moment as she thinks back to the journey here. "Adaline saved me, really," Molly says and her young eyes land on me. "She found me in the tunnels and rescued me."

"But that was a trap your brother had planted," the same guy interrupts. I had left that out of my statement, but clearly word has already gotten out.

"I don't know why I was there," Molly begins to stammer and hushed voices begin to break out around us.

The old man raises his hand and quiets the room. "This is not an interrogation about King Renon's plans against us. This is simply a residency council for members of the traveling group," the man clarifies and glances down at Molly. "Just tell them what you did that should earn you your residency here."

Molly scans the jury's stone faces and says, "I took care of Adaline when she was hurt after teleporting us to the island." She looks to me and gives a small smile. She's right, she did take a turn watching over me. The jury turns to me and looks for my response so I nod, agreeing with what she had said.

"That's all Molly, you can return to your group," the man says, dismissing her.

He turns and releases the jurors to go and make their decision. I feel the irritation build up at how demeaning they have all been toward the non-gifted.

"Wait!"

The room falls silent and all eyes move to me.

"Is there something you'd wish to add?" the man behind the podium asks me, and his old eyes of wisdom peer down.

"I just need you all to understand that every single person sitting here with me deserves, and is worthy, of getting to stay here. Mio, he was our guide. I'd still be circling the forest if it weren't for him." I pause and swallow, begging the nerves to stay down.

"Cinder, she was the brain behind the operation. Without her, I'd have starved to death because I didn't know what was safe to eat. Cooper, he was my missing piece. Essie kept us all clothed. Albert and James cooked all the food we ate and reconstructed the boats that brought me here, and Molly," I say, my eyes meeting hers. "She was the one who kept me from falling into an endless spiral of depression. They're my family now, all of them," I finish and turn back to the jurors, but their faces seem unfazed.

"Just know that without any of them, there is no me, and there is no key," I say, holding up my arm to show the jury the birthmark Mio had revealed to me on the boat.

I see small hints of fear flick across some of their faces, and I know I've struck something, but I might have gone too far.

Chapter 3

"Hey," Alexander whispers in my ear, nudging me off his shoulder. My heavy eyelids fall open and I realize I must have dozed off while waiting. "The jury is coming back in."

I sit up and scan the faces of all the jury members, each looking tired, empty, and somewhat sad. Alexander tightens his grip on my hand and we wait for them to announce their decision.

One of the jurors steps to the center of the room with a folded piece of paper. His cold eyes land on me for a second before he drops them to his list. The room falls silent as he unfolds the decision on who gets to stay. He doesn't look up, and starts to instruct the group from the sheet in his hands.

"We have made a list of the candidates who have qualified to stay in Libertas. In order to accept your place here in Libertas, all individuals who have qualified must also agree to serve alongside us during the rebellion."

I nod, agreeing it's only fair they help defend the place that gives them freedom.

"When I call your name, please come forward and sign your

agreement to serve us, and stay standing here in the front. First, we want to honor Mio Sanders." I exhale at the sound of our leader's name. I can see the relief on Mio's face. He stands, moves to the front of the room, and signs his agreement on the stand. He turns to face us, tears welling in his eyes, and it's the first time I've seen him be vulnerable.

"Cinder Campbell," he says, continuing the list and it keeps going on and on. "Cooper Sagel, Essie Jane, Albert Brown, James Young, Zavy Lane, Toby Lane, Alexander Thompson, and finally Adaline Sagel." I rise and make my way to the front stand, and pick up the pen lying next to the piece of parchment. My eyes scan down the long list of names of those who have traveled with me, and I feel nothing but relief. I scribble my name down beneath Alexander's and then turn to face the crowd again.

That's when my eyes land on Molly, tears and fear quickly welling up in her eyes. How could I have missed her name on the list? The man who announced all of our names is calling for our congratulations. Everyone who came to watch, stands and applauds our achievement, but I've become so numb I can't even acknowledge them.

"What do you plan to do with Molly?" I hear Alexander's deep voice yell over the crowd. At the sound of his voice, they all fall silent.

A nervous sweat starts to break out on the man who called our names. "The jury has decided that Libertas is an unsafe environment for kids, now that a rebellion is being planned."

"And the children currently living in Libertas?" my broken voice chokes out. "Where do you plan to send them?"

The man starts to stumble over his explanation as the weight of the judgmental crowd lands on his shoulders. "Arrangements have been made for those children to move into underground bunkers until the rebellion is complete."

"And Molly can't stay with them?" I push and start to move toward him.

The man turns and gives a questioning look to the rest of the jury. An older woman stands and says, "I don't believe we should have to give up any space down there to kids who don't belong here. The quarters will be tight as it is. Besides, her kind is the reason we had to leave Dather in the first place. You're lucky any of you got picked."

It dawns on me that they aren't letting the non-gifted stay for extra support in the war. They want them to be another target, hoping they will die before their own gifted have to. They didn't sign a service document, they signed a death certificate. The jury doesn't want Molly to stay because she won't go to war. She'll actually live off their resources, and they will seek no benefit. At the lady's remark, a commotion breaks out among the rest of the jury; some supporting her and some admitting that the non-gifted are innocent.

"Order." The old man hammers into his stand, causing the room to fall silent again. I turn to him and see his eyes are trained at something in the back of the Council Room. I spin and see my father slowly making his way to us.

"Clearly, the jury wasn't truly decided," the older man says, giving a disapproving glance their way. "The decision will move forward to King Derith."

Everyone in the room rises and bows toward the center aisle as he passes. My father is stiff and formal. It's the first time I think I may see hints of a king in him. As he walks, the medals on his uniform clink together, the only sound in the hall. For some reason, the idea of having him decide Molly's fate, is more terrifying than having the jurors decide. Just a couple of days ago, he was outraged that I had brought her here. I know his visions showed that Molly being here would be bad, but maybe his visions were wrong. Maybe we can change them.

"Please," I whisper when he reaches the front of the room. My eyes study his face, trying to read his expression. "I need her."

He considers my words carefully and offers the flash of a small smile before turning to acknowledge the crowd.

"Molly has earned her residency here just like everyone else from the traveling team." My father's voice is even and clear. There is no mistaking his decision. I want to thank him, but then he continues. "However, we will still conduct an investigation to see if she is a threat to us. If we discover that her presence here could cost us the victory in this war, she will be removed. This council meeting is now over, you are all dismissed."

Most seem to agree with my father, but some truly want nothing to do with the non-gifted, especially one that is the sister to King Renon.

Everyone stands and mumbles to one another as they exit the Council Room. Molly instantly comes running up to me and throws her arms around my waist. "I'm going to be okay?" she asks into my side.

"Yeah, you're going to be just fine," I say as I run my hand over her thin hair. I don't know what kind of investigation my father plans on having, but I know, deep down, that Molly can't possibly be a threat.

Molly steps back from me and looks up to my father. "Thank you, your Highness." She drops into a very low curtsy.

"You're welcome, Molly. I do need you to come with me for some more questioning," my father says gently.

Molly nods tentatively and the two of them leave the Council Room. I'd follow, but Linda is charging me, her stride very determined.

Linda reaches me and says, "I need you, Alexander, Zavy, and Toby to come with me."

"Where are we going?" Alexander asks as we make our way out of the Council Room and down a side hall of the castle.

"Training for the rebellion must begin immediately. We don't know how much time we have until King Renon sends his army out here," Linda says as we turn and start heading down a steep, wide staircase, going deep underground.

"So what exactly does our training entail?" I ask curiously.

"Well, first we need to figure out what gifts you have," Linda says flatly.

"What are you talking about? We know what gifts we have," I say confused.

"No, we know what gifts you think you have. None of you have been tested, is that correct?" Linda asks, stopping at the bottom of the staircase. She turns to meet our eyes. We all nod our heads in agreement and she turns back around, heading deeper down the hall. "Then we will test you all, and find out what gifts you have."

We all reluctantly continue to follow her through the twist and turns of the underground hallways. Finally, we come up to a room on our right that has a long window that allows us to peer inside. There are a couple rows of chairs, and most of them are filled with other kids our age or younger. We enter the room and all eyes flip to us. Almost immediately, the kids stand and come to attention. I didn't think Linda held such high authority here until I realize they are all looking at me. "Relax," I hear Linda huff beneath her breath, and the kids sit back down.

"You can wait here. An official will come and get you when it's your turn to be tested," Linda says, motioning to a couple of empty seats among the group. I take a seat next to Alexander, and a younger girl with light brown hair.

"Are you nervous?" I ask and turn to her. She looks up at me, shocked that I am speaking to her. "You don't have to treat me like I'm anyone special. I'm just like you," I say lightly.

"You're our savior," she says in a high voice.

"Oh, I wouldn't say that," I brush off. "I mean I'm just as lost as the rest of us here," I say. I can see a sense of worry rush across her face. I try to put myself in her shoes. How would I feel if the one I had been told would save me admitted to being completely lost? "I mean, I'm going to help all of us. I'll figure this out," I say to reassure her.

She relaxes back into her seat and wraps her arms around her waist. "Yeah I'm a little nervous," she admits, answering my question.

"What is the test?" I ask her, trying to get a grasp on what I'm getting thrown into.

"It's kind of complicated," she begins hesitantly. "I'm one of the last in my class to be tested. I waited as long as they would let me. They tried to prepare us in school, but I'm not sure I understood it all that well. Basically, they hook up a bunch of sensors to your body, and then they will read different situations to you or show you them on a screen, and then your body reacts. They'll document how you react and that should explain what gift you have. I don't explain it very well, I'm sorry," she says sheepishly.

"No that's okay, I think I understand," I say.

Suddenly, a tall thin woman with short blond hair comes through a sealed door that was hidden in the wall. "Will the following people please stand and come with me. Erik," she begins and a thin boy from the back of the room stands up. "Rebecca, Peter, and Jennie."

The girl beside me takes in a sharp breath at the sound of her name being called last. I give her a tight squeeze on the hand. She looks at me, and in her eyes I can tell she is thanking me. Either for reassuring her or for being the savior in the rebellion.

Once all of them have walked into the other room and the door closes behind them, another door opens to our right, and this time, a tall balding man steps out and says, "Will the following people please stand and come with me. Adaline, Zavy, Toby, and Alexander."

Together, the four of us stand and make our way through the door and into a tiled hallway that is dimly lit. Halfway down the hall, we come to a stop at a door to our left. The man leading us puts a piece of paper in a folder attached to the door and says, "Zavy you may wait in here." I watch as Zavy enters the room, and the man swings the door shut. He continues walking down the hall until he comes to another door. Here he drops off Toby, and then Alexander.

When Alexander enters his room, he looks back to me, his green eyes lock with mine, and then the door to his room closes, separating us. Finally, I am the last one to get assigned a room at the end of the hall. "You may wait in here," the man says, his grey eyes scanning me.

Without saying a word, I enter the room, and he closes the door behind me. At my movement, the lights flicker on above me. I have to squint until my eyes readjust to the dim lighting. An eerie silence settles over the room, and a chill creeps through me. The only thing in the room is a simple metal chair in the center. I walk over to it and am about to sit, when a door to my right slides open.

"Good afternoon, Ms. Adaline. How are you doing today?" a man says in a strong voice. He is reading over a glowing piece of metal in his hands and is wearing a long white coat. He looks up from his device when I don't respond.

"I'm fine," I say, my voice harsh.

"Good. All right, please come here and stand on this tile," he says. I walk over to him and stand on a tile that is colored black, while the rest of the floor is an odd blue-grey. When I step on the tile a screen lights up on the wall with the number *110*.

"What's that mean?" I ask and look to him.

"That," he begins as he taps on his device, "is how much you weigh. And this," he says, tapping the number on the wall. I watch as it changes to *5'6*, "Is how tall you are."

"Did I pass?" I ask and look to him.

"Pass?" he questions. "You aren't being tested on height and weight," he says and laughs. "It's just protocol. We will use this to monitor how your body is performing. But if you were being tested, I'd say we'd have a problem with that weight."

"Why?" I ask, worried.

"Well, it's simply unhealthy for a girl at sixteen to be that malnourished. I know you didn't have a choice in that, since you grew up in the prison back in Garth, but you will need to start eating better here."

I nod and he motions for me to go take a seat in the chair. "I'm not exactly sure what I'm supposed to do," I admit as I lower myself onto cool metal.

"Don't worry. I'll help you through it. You don't have to do much. It's all up to your brain and instinct."

He walks over to me and starts to fasten restraints to my wrists and ankles to keep me in the chair.

"Is that necessary?" I ask, looking at him bewildered that I'm being locked in the chair.

"For my safety, it is. Once we put you under, there's no telling how you'll react." He then walks over to the wall behind me. I turn my head over my shoulder and watch as he touches a spot on the wall. It slides open revealing a large monitor and a set of white cords. He grabs the white cords and unravels them. He walks back over to me and starts to explain. "These are sensors. We place them along the nerves in your arms, legs, and head. It'll allow us to read the signal your brain is sending to the rest of your body."

He sticks the final two sensors on either side of my head. "This might sting just a little," he says, and I watch as he pulls out a needle from the pocket of his coat. It's filled with a clear liquid. "It's just going to interfere with your ability to think."

I give him a questioning look, so he explains further. "Like if you were, to say, in battle. You would be trying to think whether to fight or maybe run away, but this keeps you from doing that. Instead, you always go with your first instinct." Suddenly there's a sharp prick at the side of my neck and I cringe. "There, that didn't hurt too bad," the man says, but his voice has already grown distant. My vision becomes fuzzy, and the last thing I think of before going under, are the papers I saw back in Sard. The ones in the abandoned building that were about the gifted and the testing process, and then the room goes black.

Chapter 4

My eyes shoot open, my heart rate rocketing. I'm lying on my side with my face pressed in the dirt. My fingers grasp the soft, dark earth as I take in deep breaths to steady my heart rate. I sit myself up and scan my surroundings. I seem to be sitting in the middle of the forest. I rub the side of my neck where a strange stinging sensation is. I can't recall why I'm here.

Suddenly, off in the distance, I can make out the sound of feet smacking against the ground. "She's up ahead," I hear a man say. I jump to my feet and spin around the clearing, trying to figure out where their voices are coming from. Then, a group of guards charges into the clearing. I recognize their uniforms as those from the castle. I realize that they aren't wearing the green rocked necklaces that keep them immune to my gift, so I instantly freeze them with my enhanced sense of sight.

As always, they do as I see. I lift their swords to their necks and kill them without giving it a second thought. They all fall to the ground, their crimson blood staining the pure white fabric. Then I hear his voice.

"Adaline!" he yells.

It's Alexander.

I hear his voice yell again, "Adaline, help!" Without thinking, I start running in the direction of his voice. I stumble through the underbrush of the forest until I run into a clearing with a large lake.

"Adaline!" I hear him cry again. It sounds as though his voice is coming from in the water. Instantly, I take the water and lift it from the earth, leaving a damp crater underneath. There are two steel doors at the bottom of the hole and I know that's where his voice must be coming from.

While balancing the water in the air above me, I run down into the crater and heave the doors open. I can barely make out a set of stairs that leads down into the darkness. I start down the stairs, close the doors behind me, and drop the water back into its place. I squeeze my eyes shut and when I open them again, the staircase is visible in an eerie green light. I take off down the stairs, two at a time, and once I'm at the bottom all I can see is a long stretch of the empty hall. I sprint down it. My heart pounds in my chest. Every breath hurts, stabbing me deep in my lungs. But I keep running. After a while, a large door comes into view. When I reach it, I lean in and look through the small window encased in it.

A yellow light glows through the window. Once my eyes adjust, I start to make out the horrific scene on the other side. There's a pit in the other underground room with bubbling molten lava. Alexander is tied above the lava by a slim rope, and the only thing keeping him up, is Paylon on the other end.

I step back from the door and I don't even bother trying to force it open. Instead, I simply see myself on the other side and teleport through.

"Alexander!" I scream to him. I try to teleport him from the rope to me, but it's not working. No matter how hard I try to use my gift, it's no use. I can't do it.

"You're too weak, Adaline," Paylon yells to me. "You're too weak to save him." My eyes meet Paylon's and a sly smile spreads across his face. I watch Paylon let go of the rope and Alexander falls through the air.

"No!" I scream and run to the edge of the hole. I fall on my stomach, extending my arms out to him. His hands grab mine as he falls past and we hold onto each other tight.

"I've got you!" I yell, but as hard as I try, I can't pull him from the crater. "I don't understand. Why can't I save you?" I scream to him. I try as hard as I can to get my gift to work. To get anything to work.

Alexander says simply, "I'm your weakness."

"What?" I yell to him over the sound of the bubbling lava.

"You can't save me, because I'm your weakness," he says and he loosens his grip.

"Don't let go, Alexander," I choke out, tears forming in my eyes.

"I have to let go," he says and he releases his hand from mine. I watch as he falls into the earth below. I clench my eyes shut and let out a hysterical scream.

"Adaline!" I hear a strong deep voice yell over mine. I stop screaming and my eyes fly open, tears running down my cheeks. My fingers are clenching the cold metal arms of the chair. A cool sweat rolls on my neck. I take in deep breaths of dry air, and try to stop my heart from exploding.

"You're okay, Adaline. The simulation is over," the doctor tells me.

"Did I pass the test? What did that all mean? I don't understand, what just happened?" I ask, the words running out of my mouth.

"Slow down, Adaline," he says, trying to calm me. "I'm not certified to discuss your results. We'll move you to a different room and another doctor will come and talk to you about your results," he says as he unfastens the restraints on my legs and wrists. "Follow me."

I rise from the chair and gently massage my wrists. I'm silently led out of the testing room and into the room across the hall. This room has white tiled floors and instead of a metal chair, there's a different contraption in the center of the room. It resembles something like a small bed that is slightly propped up. There's a desk across from the bed with a metal tablet, similar to the one the previous doctor had used. The wall behind the desk is one giant black screen.

"You can have a seat and wait in here," he says, motioning to the bed. "Dr. Riley will be in shortly to discuss your test."

I hoist myself up on the piece of parchment that runs down the leather bed. The doctor turns to exit the room and as the door clicks behind him, another one swings open behind me.

"Hello. I'm Dr. Riley," a young voice says. I nod, scanning his appearance. He is wearing a similar white coat but is much younger, twenty or so. "Your test results were quite interesting," he adds as he walks over and takes a seat at the desk. He clicks a button on the monitor and the tablet lights up.

He begins tapping on the screen and I ask, "What do you mean?"

"Well," he starts, "what results did you expect to get? The test was supposed to confirm what gift you have. So, what should it have said?" he asks me. He stops tapping his screen and turns to stare at me.

"Well, a Force Lifter," I answer. "Is that what it said?"

"Nope," he says. Dr. Riley clicks a button on the monitor and the giant screen on the wall behind him lights up. Graphs with colorful lines project up on the screen. Two labels appear in the far corner.

Name: Sagel, Adaline

Gift: Alterken

"What's an Alterken?" I ask, the word sounding foreign on my tongue.

"It's complicated," he says. "We've never seen anyone have results like these. I'll do my best to explain it. We'll start with your test. Let's walk through it," he says, clicking on one of the graphs with colorful squiggly lines. "These are the waves from your brain to certain parts of your body. So, the test began with what? What was the first thing you encountered under the simulation?"

"Dirt," I say remembering how the test began. "When I opened my eyes I was lying in the dirt."

"Okay. Here, on this graph, the first line that spikes is the orange line, which is associated with the sense of touch. So, first your brain sent signals to your hands to analyze what you were touching." He stops, looking to see how these words affect me. "Did you know where you were?" he adds.

"The woods," I say.

"Which woods?" he asks.

"The ones I was in on Dather," I say confidently.

"How do you know that? Was there something there that you recognized?" Dr. Riley questions.

"No," I say, confused. *How did I know?* "I just knew."

"Okay, we'll move on," he says. "What happened next?"

"Next, I heard guards running to get me. I heard them talking about me," I say, trying to analyze my test.

"And the next color to spike was green, which is connected to your sense of hearing." He pauses again like he's waiting for me to say something, but I don't know what he wants from me. Of course I'd use my sense of hearing when listening. That's not new.

"Next?" he asks.

"Next, they came into the clearing and I used my gift to freeze and kill them," I say.

"Right. Okay the next color to spike was," he draws out his words.

"Yellow. Let me guess, that's for sense of sight," I say, remembering the yellow painted symbol for an enhanced sense of sight in the tunnels under Sard. I begin to connect the symbols and their colors to the graph in front of me and feel the pieces starting to align.

"Correct," Dr. Riley nods. "What happened next, Adaline?"

"I heard Alexander's voice screaming for help," I say. A creeping pain courses through me. I look up to the graph and confirm that the green line spiked again. "And then I ran, following his voice." I scan the screen and see the green and orange lines spike together. "And then the water. I raised it." Yellow joins the spikes on the graph. I notice that brown is also spiked. "What's brown?" I ask, forgetting what I had seen in the tunnels.

"Brown is your sense of taste," he says simply. Right, the brown symbol of a mouth. His eyes scan my face, trying to figure out if I understand.

"I didn't taste anything," I say confused.

"But you did. You breathed in the air through your mouth. Do you remember that?" Dr. Riley squints his eyes, further examining me and my reactions.

I think for a minute. "I had just run, so I was tired. Yes, I was breathing through my mouth. What did I taste in the air?" I ask.

"Did it taste salty?" Dr. Riley asks.

"No it didn't taste like anything," I say.

"You were trying to test if the water in the pond was freshwater or saltwater." Dr. Riley rises and goes to point to the graph. "When the green wave spiked, those guards were miles away, but you could hear them clearly. It spikes again when you hear Alexander. He's not only miles away, but he's also underground."

Dr. Riley's voice raises and he begins to talk faster and faster, getting more and more excited. "Then, you're running and your sense of touch spikes because you're barefoot. You were tracking Alexander. Red spikes for his smell, touch spikes for his path, sound spikes for his voice. Then, the water. Next, underground, sight spikes with night vision." He pauses and I recall the eerie green sight I had underground.

Dr. Riley continues, "Then you're running again, tracking, until you find him. You didn't touch the door, you transported through it." I notice sight is spiked. "It's not only spiked because you teleported, but you saw the thermal properties of the door. Had you touched it, you would have seared your hand right off. But you knew, you could see it."

"And then I couldn't save Alexander!" I shout over him. "I can do literally everything, but I couldn't save him. Why?" I ask as flashes of Alexander falling into the lava below plays in my head.

"Well, he said it himself," Dr. Riley says softly. "He's your weakness." He pauses, letting is words crush inside of me, and then continues. "Alexander's the one you love most, so your gift won't work on him."

"I saved him once before though," I say, remembering the time in the woods. I transported us both out of Paylon's camp.

"Do you love him more now than you did then?" Dr. Riley asks.

"Well, I actually know who he is now. My memories were still altered then," I say, understanding.

"Heart versus mind, Adaline," Dr. Riley says. "The ones we love most will always be our biggest weakness. They will always be the ones who have the power to hurt us the most."

"So I can't use my gift on him?" I ask.

"If you continue to grow the feelings you have for him, then yes," he confirms.

"And if I stop loving him?" I ask and my voice grows very soft.

"Then, you could save him." Dr. Riley nods, trying to be gentle with me.

"Is this weakness something everyone has?" I ask, confused about this new information.

"No, you and Alexander are a special case," Dr. Riley says, choosing his words carefully.

"What gift do I have?" I ask Dr. Riley, finally ready for the answer. I look over the colorful chart and take it all in.

"You're an Alterken," Dr. Riley says, the word becoming more familiar each time. "All of your senses are enhanced."

"Can you explain how my mother, a Future Holder, didn't know this?" I ask, not able to believe my results.

"She probably did. Maybe she thought one gift was enough for you to teach yourself. But also, she may not have known exactly what you are." Dr. Riley pauses, his words making me feel like a mutation. "We've never seen someone with these results. You're the first Alterken. You're special, Adaline," Dr. Riley says again. I glance down to the key birthmark on my wrist, a constant reminder of how special I really am.

"So what's next?" I ask softly.

"Next is training. Commander Crymm wants you to attend daily training lessons to learn how to master your gift, and how to lead a squad of your own. Once you're ready, I'm sure that means the rebellion will begin." Dr. Riley looks up and sees the skeptical look on my face. "Well, it's all unknown. I don't actually know their plans. Some people want to stay here and live out their lives while you protect us. Others want you to use your gift to fight and take back Dather."

"What do you want, Dr. Riley?" I ask.

Dr. Riley pauses for a long time. He moves back to his desk and begins to close out of the testing screens until the monitor on the wall fades back to black. "I want to live," he finally says and looks at me. "We've never been attacked here. I think we should stay. Hide here. Live safely."

I simply nod my head in response because I'm not sure what the best move is. I don't feel like I really have a say either. It sounds like the ruler of Libertas might already have a plan for me. My father, I remind myself, is the ruler of Libertas. *He already has a plan for me. Another plan.* There's always a plan, it seems, and it's never one I get to make myself.

Chapter 5

When I get back to the waiting room, I see Toby and Zavy have already returned from their testing. I take a seat next to Zavy and we are quiet for a moment before I ask how her test went.

"Fine," she responds shortly. "It confirmed I have an enhanced sense of hearing. It was kind of scary, though. It felt extremely real," she adds as she rubs her hands together. "Did you die in yours?" Zavy asks, looking up at me for the first time.

"No," I say. "Alexander did though. I couldn't save him," I admit and silence falls between us. I turn it back to her test and I ask, "You died in your test?"

"Yeah, my doctor said that's normal. He said that means I don't have the gift that would have saved me," Zavy explains as the test replays in her head.

I watch her rub her wrists while stuck in thought.

"I hope Alexander's test is going all right," Zavy adds softly.

I nod, my own test still playing back to me. I'm about to break the silence again, when the door to the testing hallway slides open and Alexander steps out. His face is drained of color and there's a slight sweat on his forehead. His vibrant green eyes lock with mine and he swallows hard. I wonder what happened in his test. I wonder if he had to watch me die like I had to watch him. Am I his weakness?

Zavy suddenly stands and hurries across the room to meet Alexander. She whispers something to him, the presence of the others waiting to be tested forcing her to keep her voice down. Alexander says something back to her, and her flushed face looks at me and then back to him. He presses his lips together and the two of them cross the room and take a seat on either side of me. Without speaking or looking at each other, he takes my hand in his and squeezes it tightly. A moment later Linda returns.

"Follow me back to your quarters please," she instructs.

Alexander lets my hand drop, and I wish he wouldn't. After finding out my love for Alexander would keep me from saving him, it feels an awful lot like goodbye. We stand and follow Linda out into the hall.

"What's next?" I ask, coming in step with Linda. I'm starting to feel like I'm just being herded around my father's castle, like I'm some kind of doll Libertas is prepping for battle.

"Your Welcome Ceremony," Linda says very matter-of-fact. "You'll have new garments to change into back in your quarters. Please do so." She pauses, looking down at my sun-dried coral top I received back in Sard. It has a slight salty aroma from both the ocean and my sweat. Linda continues, "We need to present you to the public and try to get everyone to trust you. Some of Libertas's most fine help will come to style you for the big event. There will be a short parade through the town, and then we'll end back here at the castle where we will have a feast with only the most highly ranked of Libertas and those who will be joining you in the fight."

"We can't have a parade," I gawk and stop in the hallway. Linda turns slowly, clearly annoyed with me for holding her up.

"And why not?" she asks.

"Because we need to figure out what's going to happen to Molly. Have you even tried to talk to her?" I ask, frustrated at how Libertas has been handling our arrival. Molly is King Renon's sister. That should be more important than residency councils or Welcome Parades.

"Yes, we had our commander interrogate her while you were being tested," Linda says harshly. Like I am a child questioning an adult.

"And?" I push her for more information. I watch as her mouth sets in a thin line. "I want to see her, now."

"She's still in her interrogation," Linda begins to backpedal.

"Then take me there. I want to help them figure out what's going on," I command.

Linda gives the idea a quick thought and then rolls her eyes. "Fine, we have some time before the festivities begin. I will bring you to her." Linda breaks off from the main underground hall and leads us all into a steel room.

There are two rows of chairs facing a large pane of glass. I walk up to the window and see Molly is sitting at a metal table on the other side. My father and another woman sit across from Molly. The other woman must be the commander that Linda was referring to. She has white hair braided up into a tight knot on the top of her head. Her eyes are a misty blue and her skin is a ghost white. She's dressed in a stiff military uniform, its light blue fabric cleanly pressed.

"Who's that?" Zavy asks.

"That would be the Commander of the Army, Commander Crymm," Linda says and she takes a seat in one of the chairs in the back row.

I remember Dr. Riley saying that Commander Crymm would be heading our training. My blood burns at the thought of having to train under her. She looks about as cutthroat and intense as it gets. Zavy, Alexander, and Toby take a seat in the front row of chairs to watch the interrogation, but I stay rooted by the pane of glass.

"You said your brother kept you locked up," Commander Crymm says, reviewing some notes she has scribbled in front of her. "How often did you see him?"

"Pretty often. He'd come and sit with me. He'd read me books and eat dinner with me almost every day," Molly says.

"Can you explain where he kept you locked up?" my father asks and he lifts a pencil to his notes.

"It was my room in the castle. There were lots of toys and my bed. I had a closet full of clothes. Oh, and my window looked out over Garth." Molly's description sounds far from a prison cell.

"He just locked you in your room?" Commander Crymm confirms and Molly nods.

"But he would never let me leave," Molly says and her voice

grows angry. "I begged and begged him. I even tried to escape and go down into the city. I screamed from my window but no one ever heard me."

"Why wouldn't he let you leave?" my father asks and his eyes narrow into curious slits.

"He said I killed my mother, so I wasn't allowed to leave," Molly says softly.

Alexander stands and leans closer to the glass when she says this. My eyes flip from Molly to him and I read his tense expression after hearing how his real mother died.

"He said I was going to have to be a secret sister so that no one would know the person who killed the Queen was still alive."

"Your mother died when you were born," Commander Crymm says and she jots it down with the rest of her notes.

Slowly, the pieces begin to fit for me as they do for Commander Crymm. Molly's mother died in childbirth. King Renon ordered for her to be locked away and kept as a secret to punish her.

"Molly, you didn't kill anyone," my father says softly.

"That's what my servants always said," Molly agrees and her use of the word *servants* reminds me again that she is royalty.

"I want to ask her some questions," I say and turn to Linda.

"You can't, Adaline. Let your father and Commander Crymm do their jobs," Linda lectures.

I turn back to the glass and simply teleport my way into the other room. I don't need Linda telling me what I can and can't do. One second I'm in the viewing room, and the next, I'm under the bright white lights of the interrogation room.

"Adaline," Molly says, shocked when I appear in the room.

The metal door to my left rips open and Linda rushes in. "I told her not to come in," Linda says.

"It's fine," my father says. "She's the closest to Molly. Maybe she can help us."

"Molly," I say and lean against the table she's sitting at. "We need to know why your brother put you in those tunnels. Do you remember anything from the last night you were at the castle?"

"I don't, I already told them," Molly says and her voice grows more upset.

"Try again," I say gently and calm her. "Close your eyes and try to walk through the last night in the castle." Molly closes her eyes and takes in a deep breath. "Tell us what you see."

"I'm sitting in my room," Molly begins to say after a moment. "I was sitting at the table, waiting for my brother to come for dinner."

My father and Commander Crymm start to take notes as Molly walks us through her last time at the castle. I know how hard it can be to recall memories after they've been restored. She has the memories; she just needs to unlock them.

"He entered the room and seemed really upset," Molly says as more of the memory comes back to her. "No, not upset, nervous maybe. I asked him what we were having for dinner and he said I wasn't going to be eating tonight." Molly pauses and lets silence fill the room. I imagine the pause in her story is being filled with King Renon's words to her.

"He told me I had to seem like I was starving when Adaline found me."

My back stiffens at the thought of my name coming from his mouth. My father and Commander Crymm pause their pencils before jotting down the information.

"He told me I was going to get to leave the castle finally, and I had asked if this means I'm not in trouble for our mother dying," Molly says and her voice grows upset. "He said he didn't want to keep me locked up anymore, but knew I couldn't live in Garth where everyone would wonder where I came from." Molly's eyes flash open and tears roll down her cheeks. "He put me in the tunnels so you would bring me here and I could have a life of my own." Her eyes scan between our three faces, looking for how we will react to this information.

It doesn't line up. King Renon did something selfless? We thought he had planted Molly in the tunnels as a tactic to destroy the rebellion. Could he have just wanted to give her a second chance to live somewhere else?

"That doesn't make sense," Commander Crymm says the words we are all thinking. "King Renon wouldn't do something like this if it didn't benefit himself."

"That's all he told me," Molly says and wipes her eyes. "After that, he put in the false memories and placed me in the tunnels with the other girls."

"Did you actually know those other girls?" I ask.

Molly shakes her head. "I didn't know anyone except my brother

60

and my servants. He just put them in the tunnel so I would blend in."

"So four innocent children were kidnapped from their families. Their parents don't even know that they have died," my father says, shaking his head. "That sounds more like King Renon."

"He sent you to a nation that's trying to rebel against him," Commander Crymm says. "You can't have a life of your own here if we're just trying to take back Dather."

"He said I would find my second chance, he didn't explain anything else," Molly says.

"I believe her," I say after a wave of silences passes through the room.

"I agree, it makes sense," my father says, scanning over his notes. "Not that he would do something selfless, but that you would need to leave Dather in order to start a new life."

"For now, we can close the interrogation on that," Commander Crymm says and she stands from the table.

"So I'm free to stay?" Molly asks.

"You are free to stay and start this new life, Molly. You shouldn't be defined by your family. You were honest with us and we respect that honesty," Commander Crymm says.

"I think that means it's time for the Welcome Parade," my father says and Linda exhales with relief.

"I need to get you back to your quarters right now if we're going to make it on time," Linda says and waves me from the room. Molly and I follow her, and Alexander, Zavy, and Toby fall in step with us. Linda leads us back to our rooms at a brisk pace, trying to make up for the lost time in her strict schedule. As we walk back to our rooms Linda is sure to remind us multiple times that we are on schedule. The purpose of this Welcome Parade is to introduce us to the people of Libertas. These are the people that will be rebelling against King Renon and we need them to trust us.

We arrive at our quarters and I'm ushered back into the white tiled room I was in earlier. The door clicks behind me and I'm left in silence. My footsteps echo as I walk across the marble floor to the now made bed in the corner. Laid on the end, is a deep royal blue dress. It's made of a very soft velvet. I hold it up, my fingers curling into the soft fur. It has long sleeves and a deep neckline. It looks short; maybe knee length.

I'll be perceived as rich, royal, young, and innocent. I'm far from every one of those things.

I clean up in the small bathroom attached to my room, finally washing the clumps of saltwater out of my hair and dried skin off my arms. While my test results still hang over me and the idea of a parade seems daunting, being clean helps me feel a little better.

I change into the dress, and my first thought is that I've never worn something so expensive before. It stretches and pulls at my skin, feeling suffocating. I've been dreading looking in the mirror for days, but with a ceremony to get ready for, I have more motivation to do it. I move to the tall skinny mirror in the corner of the room and finally step in front of it.

Short brown pieces of my hair stick out around my face. My eyes are their normal vibrant brilliance but are accompanied by dried red splotches on my face. The dress hugs my stomach and flares out over my knees.

All of these luxuries make me sick. Images of my mother and brother's dead bodies flash in the mirror, followed by Codian and all the other gifted who are imprisoned by King Renon. Why am I being paraded around? We need to save them. I shouldn't be wearing a dress, I need armor and training. We need to go save these people. My breaths come quick and I push my bare back up against the white wall, its cold touch crawling over my skin. I know it's all coming; the training and fighting. I have to do this to get the trust of the people in Libertas.

I look up to one of the ceiling lights, its harsh rays hurting my eyes. I squint and try my hardest to tell what temperature it is. That was one of the things I did in my test, but nothing comes to me. I blink hard and my vision is filled with black circles. I take the end of my dress in my hand and try to pull as much information as I can from it, like Alexander can do, like I'm supposed to be able to do, right? But nothing comes to me.

My eyes flutter up and land on the door to my room. Alexander is just one room down from mine and I can't help but wonder if I should tell him about my test. I want to know about his test, but I can't ask him without explaining mine. Am I his weakness too? I guess if he cares about me as much as I care about him I would be. I'm torn between wanting to know and not wanting to know.

As I contemplate this, I slowly find myself moving toward the door. My hand lands on the cold, round knob. I breathe in and am about to twist it open when the door to my room flies back from me. Three young girls, all with long blonde hair braided back, file around me. They are wearing dark blue shirts and pants that seem to be a thin material, like some sort of nurse scrub I remember seeing some medical personnel wear at the castle. The dark blue matches the blue of my dress and I'm starting to understand that blue may be the color of Libertas. I drop my hand and turn to face them.

"Hello, Ms. Sagel," one starts to say and the three take a low bow.

"Please, just call me Adaline," I interrupt.

"Yes of course," another adds. "We are here to get you prepared for the celebration tonight. Please, have a seat," the middle of the three says as she gestures toward the chair in the corner of the room by the desk. I walk over quietly and listen to them whisper about me. I catch something about what to do with my hair. One asks who cut it so poorly, taking note of the jagged ends. The other tries to figure out which color to put on my face that will complement the dress, but still bring out the green in my eyes. Finally, I turn back to them and give a small smile.

"My apologies," the first girl says. "We're about ready to start. It may take longer than we originally planned."

The three move closer and begin opening the drawers in the desk that I had no interest in earlier. They hold mirrors, a pair of scissors, and a brush. Each of the three girls grabs an item and circles around me.

"You don't mind if we fix your hair by giving it a little trim, right?" her soft voice asks as politely as she can, trying to hide the disgust she has for how it looks.

I exhale and say, "Oh, please fix what I messed up."

"Oh, I'm sorry, Ms. Sagel," she begins stuttering, clearly embarrassed for herself.

"Adaline," I correct.

"I didn't mean to insult you," she continues to stammer.

"It's okay, really," I say, and the three look at each other, passing the blame. First, they untangle my wet hair and run a brush through the damp strands. One of the girls works her hands through my hair and I feel it soften and become dry.

She catches my puzzled expression and says, "Dry and straightened now." She gives a small smile and adds, "I have an enhanced sense of touch, Ms. Sagel. I'm a Transformer. It's one of my many tricks."

Then, I feel the girl with the scissors grab a chunk of my hair and lift it. I suck in a breath, hoping I still look somewhat like myself when she's done, and then I hear the snip of the scissors. She continues to snip away and I watch her meticulous small hands work in the handheld mirror that the girl in front of me holds. I exhale when I realize she's keeping the overall cut the same and is just cleaning up the edges. When she's done the other girl with the brush pulls it through my hair. I watch as the loose dark brown pieces flutter to the ground.

Next, the girl who had the scissors takes a piece of my hair and wraps it around her hand. She squeezes and holds it for a moment. I feel an odd rush of heat coming from her hand. Out of instinct, I flinch. "Hold still," she gently scolds, and then she releases my hair. I watch as it falls into a gentle spiral.

"How'd you do that?" I exclaim, amazed by her ability.

"Enhanced sense of touch. I'm also a Transformer. I can send heat through my skin, or cool to the touch," she says without missing a beat. While she works on curling my hair in the back, I take a small piece in the front and twirl it around my finger. I tell my finger to burn with heat, but every time I let the hair fall it lays limp.

I glance at the girl with the hot hands in the small mirror and ask, "Can you teach me how to do that?" This causes her to stop in the middle of twisting my hair. Her light green eyes meet mine in the mirror.

"I'm sure I misheard you, Ms. Sagel. You have an enhanced sense of sight, right? You can't do this," she says slowly. "At the trial this morning, that's what you said, right? A Force Lifter?"

I drop my eyes from her gaze and say, "Yes, I'm sorry." I try to cover up my question. It dawns on me I'm not sure what all I'm allowed to tell anyone about my gift. Dr. Riley said it was the first time he'd ever seen these results. I'm different. People don't trust different, and I'm supposed to be getting everyone to trust me.

They fall back into a silent rhythm as she finishes transforming my hair. Once she's done, the girl with the brush looks at the curls and I watch her twist them into a braided crown, leaving a few pieces down. Carefully, the two work together to pin my hair into place. Then, the girl who had been holding the mirror puts it down and opens the only other drawer on the desk. Inside is a soft, pink bag. She places it on the counter and unbuckles the latch on it.

"I'll do your makeup now," she says. She pulls out a small round dish and removes the cap. Inside is a pale powder. She takes the brush and dips it in. I recall watching my mother put on makeup once. I was so young then. She was sitting at a desk similar to this one. I remember she was pregnant with Titus at the time because she had to sit a bit back from the desk. I watched as she gently brushed the powder over her cheeks.

I remember asking what she was doing and she smiled down at me. "I'm making myself look pretty."

"Can you make me look pretty too?" I asked eagerly.

"You're already beautiful, Adaline," she said softly as she went back to putting the powder on her nose.

"Why are you putting it on?" I ask, taking a seat next to her feet.

"Your father is taking me out to dinner tonight. We met fifteen years ago today," she said into the mirror as she finished powdering her face.

"Fifteen years?" eight-year-old me asked, amazed. "That's a long time."

"Well, your father and I love each other very much. We'll always be together." She paused for a moment and added, "For forever."

"Are you okay?"

My eyes flutter to the voice replacing my mother's, and I see the blonde girl holding the brush is looking at me, concerned. My wet eyes threaten to release the tears, but I pull them back.

"Yes, I'm fine. I was just thinking about my mother." I drop my eyes and close them while she brushes the powder over my face.

"Are you okay with this color?" I open my eyes and see she is holding out a gold shimmering powder. "It'll bring out the gold flakes in your eyes."

"It's beautiful," I say flatly and close my eyes again. Her cool hand lands under my chin and she tilts my head up before brushing the powder on my eyelids.

"Keep your eyes closed and try not to move," the girl instructs.

I feel a cool liquid slide across my eyelids and feel it quickly drying, like paint. After a moment, she asks me to open my eyes and to look up. I do, and she starts brushing a deep black paste onto my lashes. When she finishes, she steps back and looks at my face, but never in my eyes. She tilts her head, taking in every inch of my face like I'm a piece of artwork. That's all they want the people of Libertas to see tonight, anyway. A pretty painted face of their supposed savior. Not Adaline. No one gets to see me.

"Almost done, just a few finishing touches," she mumbles under her breath. She finishes by brushing a warm pink powder on my cheeks and a deep red paste on my lips. "There, all done. You look beautiful Ms. Sagel."

"Can I see?" I ask cautiously. I've never had makeup on before. The girl retrieves the mirror and steps in front of me. I take in a sharp breath. I look just like my mother did that night. The tears threaten to return so I drop my gaze from the mirror to my interlocked fingers and breathe out. "Beautiful."

The girls move quickly and return everything they were using back into the drawers of the desk. Before leaving, one of them returns to me with gold strapped shoes.

"You can put these on and Linda will be down to escort you to the ceremony soon." She nods her head and quietly dismisses herself from the room, closing the door behind her.

I take the gold shoes, slide my feet under the straps, and gently buckle them at the ankle. I walk around the room and find myself eventually stopping in front of the long mirror in the corner. I look flawless. The dress's sleeves and my painted face hide my skin's red blotches from the sun. Not a single strand of my hair is out of place. I lift my hand and touch the symmetric curls and notice the dress is perfectly tailored so the sleeve stops right at my birthmark.

The key birthmark reflects back to me. I have been prophesized to be the literal key in this rebellion. Tonight is only the beginning. I will gain the trust of these people, and I will lead them to dethrone King Renon. The beautiful girl staring back at me looks more than capable of that, but that's not me. Beneath the makeup, perfect hair, and velvet gown, I'm just a scrawny prisoner. I'm a fugitive trying to survive. I'm not a leader and I'm not a savior, but I need to become that. I will become that.

Chapter 6

I hear my door click open and turn to see Linda lean in. She looks more exhausted than when she dropped me off nearly an hour ago. I guess she's been busy getting the final things in order for tonight's events. My stomach tightens at the thought of being in front of thousands of people I don't know. Since I was isolated in prison for so long, I'm naturally a shy and reserved person.

"You look beautiful. Follow me," Linda says. She pushes the door wider and I catch a glimpse of Alexander pacing out in the hall.

I exit my room and scan Alexander, my breath catching in my throat. He looks unbelievably handsome. After living in the woods for days. I'm caught off guard by his vibrant, tan skin and styled golden hair. They have him in a crisply pressed, dark blue suit with a gold undershirt that is buttoned up to his collar. We match perfectly. His eyes land on me and he instantly stops pacing, as if he's caught in a trance.

Linda breaks our frozen minds and says, "This way you two."

She heads toward the front of the castle, but Alexander grabs my wrist and puts his lips beneath my curls.

"We need to talk later," he whispers. Alexander pulls away and I catch a glimpse of serious pain and worry, maybe even anger, in his eyes.

He lets go of my arm and begins to follow Linda. I can only assume this has to do with his test. We've talked before, about needing to stay friends no matter what our feelings may be, but he knows now how much more dangerous it is if we continue to fall for each other. But tonight I'm not Adaline. Libertas has painted me up as a picture-perfect savior and asked that I stand alongside my partner, companion, and lover, Alexander. They want the people to look at us as the couple who will save them, so I get to be her today. I get to be the image they want, the savior who can openly love Alexander and not have to worry about our gifts or our destinies.

I pick up my pace and catch up to Alexander and Linda. We stop outside the main doors of the castle where we entered days earlier. Except now, a large golden chariot sits in the entranceway with two elegant white horses tied to its front and red roses tied along its sides. This Welcome Ceremony will be anything but subtle.

Linda turns quick on her heels and looks at us both. "Okay, quick rules for tonight. The people need to trust you. Smile, wave, let them know you're human and that you are here to save them. The people also need to love you. So we need to paint you both as a pair. Hold hands, act like you are happily joined together, and finally, the people need to believe you." She stops and gestures at the two of us who have clearly grown colder to one another since our tests. "This needs to be believable. We have enough to worry about on our end with training you and starting this rebellion. We don't need to be worried about whether or not these people trust you and will follow you. Is that clear?" she asks us, her voice more commanding than I remember her being earlier today.

Alexander and I take our places on the chariot, and I see a young soldier sitting on the ledge between us and the horses. I assume he must be able to use his gift to control the horses and I'm reminded Zavy has the same gift, a Communicator. I notice Zavy and the rest of my traveling group aren't here with us and I ask Linda why.

"You two are the saviors. This parade is for you. They will join you at the dinner after the parade," she says, brushing off my concern. "Get ready, it's almost showtime."

We both nod our heads, fully understanding that this is supposed to be just an act. We are supposed to be playing the characters they've painted us into. But if this were just an act my heart wouldn't flutter when Linda has Alexander lock his fingers in mine, and my breath wouldn't catch in my throat when we're told to stand closer together, our arms brushing slightly, and my eyes wouldn't fill with longing when I catch his glance.

Two guards pull open the marble doors of the palace and the large crowd outside the castle begins to roar with cheers and applause.

I underestimated what Linda prepared for our arrival. The sea of people stretches as far as I can see, screaming and clapping their hands. Above their heads, bright fiery sparks explode in the sunset, blue and green vibrant rays falling through the clouds. Triumphant trumpets blare over the cheering, signaling the parade is beginning.

"Grab on," the young soldier controlling the horses says. Alexander and I take our free hands and grab the edge of the chariot. As we pull through the grand doors and into the setting sun, we are transformed into our characters. *Adaline and Alexander, the saviors of the gifted.*

"Remember, it's just an act," Alexander whispers in my ear as we roll onto the stone path. The pain and anger flashes in his eyes and I nod, understanding. We both turn out to the crowd and smile and wave to all of the unfamiliar faces of Libertas. The boy controls the horses and they begin to parade away from the castle and down the street. From up on the hill, I can see the long winding path of the parade route leading all the way down into the heart of the city.

In front of us, dancers in outfits draped in feathers perform as we follow them on the parade route. A band is in front of them, their music sending flourishing joy through my veins. Banners with our names on it hang overhead, gold confetti falling from the sky as we roll along. It is the grandest thing I have ever seen.

The people already love us, so it makes our jobs easier. Especially the kids. They look to us like superheroes, and I realize we are to most of them. They grew up being told stories of us, learning the prophecy in school I'm sure.

A couple of rows back I catch a few individuals who don't clap. Not so naïve to trust a prophecy about two proclaimed saviors. One girl, with pixie blonde hair, looks at me, her eyes scanning my body. She's judging to see if I'm what I'm sure I've been hyped up to be. A guy on the other side, his muscles bulging from his shirt, seems to care less, unfazed by what we mean to the rebellion. A couple of rows ahead I catch another unimpressed girl turn away, her red hair flipping over her shoulder, not interested in our parade.

As we near the end of our route, I see a large platform has been set up in the middle of the town square. My father sits on a large golden throne, his form still looking like a haunting image of my dreams. When he sees us rolling in, he stands and joins the others in applause. We pull up next to the stage and are escorted down from the wagon. We take our places in the two smaller thrones next to my father's. The applause die down as my father begins to command the area.

"Hello, and welcome to our savior's celebration," his voice booms loudly.

Someone with a gift is amplifying his voice so we all can hear. I scan the town square and can't help but fall in love with it. Very detailed and colorful stones fit together to create the cobblestone walkways. The small shops are draped with wooden signs with the words *bakery*, *clothes*, and *tools* engraved on them. They are basic signs that hang on the stores' doors, and I love how simple it is.

The applause begins to die down again and my father continues, "My beloved daughter, Adaline, and her companion, Alexander, have finally arrived. We are one step closer to returning to our rightful home. Dather will once again be a safe place for the gifted to live." He pauses and the crowd cheers and whistles.

I try to keep my focus on the people in the crowd and the scene in front of me. I keep my gaze adverted from my father as much as possible, knowing it's easier to keep the scowl off my face if I don't look at him. The sight of him with a crown on his head makes me nauseous.

My father continues, "I'd like to invite both Adaline and Alexander up now to speak to you all."

My father turns to us and smiles. The crowd continues to cheer, but it all becomes muffled and blurred. The blood begins to pump faster, pounding in my ears. I can't talk to all of these people. It's one thing to parade in front of them, but it's another to speak to them. Alexander's face swims into view as he stands above me. He stretches out his hand to help me up. I take it and stand on wobbly legs, but I hope no one notices.

Alexander doesn't miss a beat and reads my fear. "I can talk if you want," he whispers to me, knowing he's truly better with words than I am.

We take our places in the center of the stage and the whole city falls silent, their eager ears ready to hang on every word we're going to say. I even catch the pixie girl, the muscular man, and the redhead stop and give us their attention.

"Hello," Alexander starts. "Many of you know us as your saviors, but few of you know us as Alexander or Adaline. But we are just like you. We are defined as different in the words of King Renon, wanted for our gifts. Our future was destined to be imprisoned and used for these gifts. But we are here to be free and to fight to help free everyone like us. To protect us." They erupt in cheers, but I catch those three and they aren't impressed. They don't believe. Alexander turns to head back to our seats but I'm stuck, *frozen.*

"I'd like to say something," my small voice breaks.

Again the city falls silent at my command.

"We have all lost someone in this journey to freedom," I say, and flashes of those who I've seen die go through my mind.

I watch as many people hang their heads, remembering the ones they have lost.

With a shaky voice I continue. "I lost my mother and brother early in my journey. They never got to make it to this freedom. I watched those imprisoned for their gifts rather take their own life than go another day under that torture. We are here, and we are free, but someone like us is suffering, trapped inside their own body and being controlled by the retched king."

I think back to my conversation with Dr. Riley. I had asked him if he thought we should hide or fight. Now I know what the right answer is, and I need to convince people like Dr. Riley to understand too.

"We can't sit here and be free while others who deserve this freedom are suffering on Dather. I've been here less than a week and all I can think about is, every minute we're here, someone is being imprisoned. Stand by us so we can save them, but either way, I will be going and fighting for them."

I stop and see these three, but I can't read their faces. They seem a bit more pleased. The rest of the crowd explodes in cheers. My father ushers Alexander and me back off of the stage, and onto our wagon with the two horses.

"Stand and follow our saviors into the rebellion," my father's voice roars.

The wagon starts to pull back up to the castle, and as we roll forward the crowd files in behind us. They march with us back up to the castle. The wagon bumps along the road, and Alexander's hand grabs mine, and I steady myself. I look to him and he gives me a soft reassuring smile. He thinks we did a good job, and I hope he's right.

When we make it up to the castle, Alexander and I are escorted from the wagon and into a nearby room while everyone else files into the grand ballroom where the rest of the celebration will take place. Linda tells us to wait here, and we'll have our own grand entrance shortly. She turns and clicks the warm brown door in place. My eyes scan the room around us. It seems to be a quiet sitting area. There's a lush blue carpet that runs under my feet. It has white and gold patterns pressed along the edges. There's also a beautiful crystal chandelier that hangs above two couches that sit on either side of a glass table.

Along the walls are rows and rows of books. Alexander begins walking past them, reading and running his fingers along their spines, and I'm sure he's pulling information from them. I move across the room, my gold flat shoes sinking into the carpet, and take a seat on one of the couches. I notice that the material of the couch is the same as my dress, a very soft and rich blue velvet.

I clear my throat and break our silence. "Do you want to tell me what you wanted to talk about?" I ask cautiously. It seems so strange that just this morning we were so close, but somehow that test has changed everything. Alexander nods and takes a seat next to me on the couch. He sits with his arms on his knees, hunched over.

"What were your test results?" he asks bluntly.

"Alterken," I say. Alexander nods his head and I ask, even though I feel I know his answer, "What were your test results?"

"Alterken," he says, and I don't feel very surprised. Ever since our matching birthmarks were revealed, Alexander and I seem to be more and more alike.

"We're a danger to each other," Alexander says, his voice growing harsh.

"Our gifts won't work if we keep falling for the other," I say softly.

"How can I fall in love with you knowing that it means I can't protect you?" Alexander asks and his shiny green eyes meet mine.

"What if I don't need you to protect me?" I ask, searching his eyes.

He simply shakes his head. "Adaline, I will spend my whole life always protecting you. I know we talked before, about not falling for the other because our future was unknown, but now we know. There is a Libertas. We made it here. We are about to lead this rebellion against the largest army in the world, and if I admit and start to love you, I can't save you in this war." His warm, strong hands wrap around mine. "I need to be able to save you. I can't be your weakness."

It's a conversation we've had before. Our relationship has felt like a swirling whirlpool the last couple of days. It's been floating around and around the drain, but still holding on. I was still having hope for us. But there's no avoiding this, and now I feel us going down the drain. As hard as I try not to cry, my eyes fill with tears because he's right. I want to protect him. The odds of surviving this war aren't good, and I would never forgive myself if he died because I was his weakness.

"What about after the rebellion?" I ask softly.

"We have to survive it first," he says, squeezing my hands and I nod gently. "Hey," he says, his voice growing lighter and he cups his hand on my cheek. "There were some pretty sharp looking guys in the crowd tonight. I bet they'd all be happy to be with you."

I laugh and the tears fall. He wipes them away and gently kisses my forehead. My heart explodes at the gesture.

"I'm still by your side, always," he whispers.

I hear the door behind us click open and Linda's high-pitched voice rings in. "All right, it's time for your grand entrance." Alexander pushes himself off the couch and walks toward the door. Linda puts a hand out to stop him and adds, "Remember, happy pairing." I let out an exhausted breath, stand, and follow them down the hall to the ballroom.

Chapter 7

The large doors to the ballroom are sealed shut, but I can hear the commotion of the crowd on the other side with royal music playing. The song seems to fade out and Linda tells us to get in position. Alexander takes his spot next to me, and I place a tentative hand on his arm.

"Are you nervous?" Alexander asks me, and it feels like he's trying to push past the conversation we just had. I look up and scan his familiar face, his green eyes truly caring if I'm okay.

"I don't like crowds all that much," I admit. I don't want that last conversation with Alexander to make it awkward for us, I care too much about him. "I've been isolated most of my life."

Alexander nods and stands up straighter. "You're not doing this alone. I'm here with you," he says and I lean against him for more support.

The two guards, on either side of the doors, grab onto the golden handles. I take in a deep breath as they pull the doors open. Again, the cheers ring out and are deafening. Slowly, we walk in and take the time to smile and wave at those who came to support us. My heart beats hard in my chest but I try not to let them know, and after a minute, I start to get used to all the eyes on me.

It helps that Alexander is here to take some of the attention. He helps keep me moving forward and I realize how much more suited he is for the role of the savior. He's spent his whole life training to serve. It's easy for him to smile and engage with the crowd, and they all love him. His gestures come off as warm and welcoming. He truly looks so happy to be the savior. I look like a frightened cat, not sure if I can trust my own shadow. I remind myself that I'm not Adaline tonight. I have been painted into the savior I need to become, and it gives me the confidence I need to try and be her for the night.

There's a large stage set up on the opposite side of the room. A wooden table is placed on it with three chairs sitting behind it. We are led up onto the stage and seated on either side of the throne in the center. My father walks out, takes his place there, and orders for the meal to be served.

I look out and notice the round tables are lined across the sides of the room. Everyone moves to take their seats and I see that each table is cloaked with a different color fabric.

"Sorted by gifts," my father says, noticing I'm staring at the tables. He begins to assign each enhanced sense with a color. "Sight is yellow, touch is orange, hearing is green, taste is brown, and smell is red."

"Oh yes, from my test. I remember," I say shortly.

My eyes fall and see our table has a royal blue cloth running down its center. Blue, for the royalty of Libertas. Over in the corner, I see tables draped in white. My eyes scan those tables and I'm overcome with relief when I see the faces of my traveling group. Mio, Cinder, Cooper, all of them are here. Even Molly. They have cleaned up and are in nice evening attire. Libertas didn't provide them with anything as elegant as my clothing, but I'm just glad they're here. I find Alexander's mother at a table cloaked in orange and his father at one that's cloaked in yellow. They are beaming, and it's obvious how proud they are of their son.

Out of the corner of my eye, I catch people begin to file into the room in black and white outfits, carrying food similar to when we were in Sard. A steaming plate is laid in front of me, and my mouth waters at the scent. It seems to be chicken covered in cheese, a white sauce, and a crunchy crumble on top. It looks delicious, a warm, flavorful steam rising off the plate. Served on the side are bright green pieces of broccoli and orange carrots. Tentatively, I pick up the silverware that I've recently learned how to use, and devour the meal.

It's just as mesmerizing as the meatloaf I had in Sard, but in an entirely different way. It's full of flavor and herbs. Delicately seasoned with ingredients that explode on my tongue. I had them send meals to my room the last few days, since I refused to leave, but they were usually already cold and not nearly as extravagant.

Once I finish eating, I go back to scanning the room. I'm surprised by how many people have come out for our arrival. I find the girl from the testing room this morning, Jennie. She's sitting at a table cloaked in brown, enhanced sense of taste. She is grinning from ear to ear, laughing with the girl sitting next to her. I'm glad she found her place. I'm glad her test results gave her a home and didn't lead her to feeling more alone. The servers return and collect our empty plates, and music begins to fill the room again. I scan for its source and in the back corner of the ballroom are a large variety of instruments, but no players behind them.

"Enhanced hearing," my father says over the sound. "They manipulate us to hear the music. The instruments are really just decoration."

My eyes flip from the instruments to my father. He is beaming, joy radiating in his eyes. I force my lips into a small smile and give a soft nod. It's so hard to look at him, let alone talk to him. I turn my gaze back to the crowd and force my stubborn anger away.

The music slows to a lovely ballroom ballad, and I don't have to ask what's next. A dance for the saviors. Of course.

Alexander rises first and steps in front of me. The corner of his mouth twitches up into a sad smile. The heartbreak of our conversation minutes ago is still raw. He offers me his hand and I accept.

I stand, keeping my eyes on his green gaze the whole time, and he leads me down to the center of the ballroom. In this moment, with the beautiful melody soaring through the banquet hall, the rest of the world fades away. It's just me and Alexander. Oh how I wish it could just be me and him.

It's now that I realize I've never danced before. Alexander must see the realization cross my face because me places his free hand on my waist, causing mine to naturally find its spot on his shoulder. I take in a shaky breath, emotions and nerves bubbling inside, and then we begin to flow together to the music.

One step to the right, then one step to the left.

My father motions for others to join us, and the floor begins to fill with bodies.

One step to the right, then one step to the left.

Alexander's grip tightens on my hand and I feel his heartbeat through our tight grasp. I know interactions like this will be limited as we try to separate our feelings from each other. So, I memorize the feeling of his heart beating through our clasped hands, the rustic smell of his tan skin, the feeling of his eyes tracing me, and his soft blonde hair brushing against the side of my face as I lean into him.

The beautiful melody fades and a new one takes its place.

"May I interrupt," a cool voice breaks over Alexander's shoulder.

I pull back and see a tall, lanky boy in a simple black suit. There are hints of yellow on his shirt and I assume it pairs him to his gift. There's also a simple gold medal with a yellow tie pinned on the right side of his jacket.

"Of course," Alexander says and steps aside.

The gentleman steps toward me and I place my right hand in his and my left hand on his shoulder.

"It's so great to finally meet you, Ms. Adaline," he says smoothly. His buzzed brown hair spikes ever so slightly.

"And you are?" I question my eyes scanning his.

"Max," he says.

"Well, yes, it's nice to meet you. Thank you for your support tonight," I say.

He laughs a little and says, "Oh, of course, but I should be thanking you for supporting me. I'm Lieutenant Max, your commander."

A cool rush of embarrassment flushes my cheeks. "Well, then you're welcome," I say lightly.

I continue to scan his young green eyes, and know he can't be much older than me, or else he'd have changed their color. The music begins to fade out again and Max drops his hands from mine and bends into a low bow out of respect, and I suppose Libertas tradition as I see the other guys on the dance floor do the same thing.

"Thank you for the dance, but I look forward to seeing you out on the training grounds tomorrow morning," he teases, his lips parting into a loose smile.

"Starting right away I see," I say, my lips matching his.

"Well, as you said, each second we wait, another gifted suffers," he says, quoting my speech from earlier.

I watch him turn and melt into the crowd and out of view. I spin around and find myself surrounded by unfamiliar faces. I shrug my way through the crowd and process the kind of person Max is. He's already a lieutenant at such a young age. He must be well respected here in Libertas and come from an important family. He did seem like someone I could trust. As usual, though, I have a hard time doing so.

When he said his rank, it quickly brought me back to the reality of this evening. We are celebrating the beginning of a rebellion. We are on the brink of war and I am expected to be the savior in this fight.

"Adaline!" A young girl calls to me.

I turn and see Molly waving her arms the air. The light purple dress they gave to her is lovely. She's sitting at a table with Cinder and Toby, the three of them eating a second round of desserts.

"You look extravagant!" Cinder gushes when I get to their table.

"Thank you, Cinder. Are you enjoying yourselves?" I ask and Toby and Molly nod excitedly.

I'm reminded how young they are. Toby is only twelve and Molly is ten. They both have so much growing up to do. I forget that sometimes.

I hope this is just the beginning of nights where they have full bellies of chocolate and nice clothes to wear. This freedom we're fighting for will surely change their entire lives.

"Have you seen Alexander?" I ask Cinder but she shakes her head. "I'm going to try and find him. You both eat more dessert for me," I tease Toby and Molly.

When I turn away from the table, I nearly run into Alexander's parents, Marin and George.

Marin immediately greets me with a tight hug. "You look so beautiful, Adaline."

"Thank you," I say, stepping back from her hug when she releases me.

George extends his hand out to me and I accept the greeting. "I think it's time we have an official introduction. I'm Alexander's father, George."

"It's nice to meet you," I say.

"Alexander's told us a lot about you and how you saved his life multiple times on the journey here," George says.

"He probably exaggerated a little," I say lightly.

"Thank you, Adaline," Marin says. Her voice is sincere and I see the emotion rise in her eyes.

"You have our deepest gratitude," George says.

Before I can say anything, the two of them excuse themselves and move around me to talk with Cinder. I find myself out of the crowd and lingering along the wall looking in. I'm used to always looking into the world around me.

Everyone seems so happy and relaxed. Don't they know some of them will be dead by the end of this rebellion? You can't have a war without death, and so many have already died. My eyes find Alexander on the corner of the floor, dancing with a girl with jet-black hair. What if he's one of the ones who dies? It's possible, I think, and I swallow hard as a nauseous wave goes through me.

Alexander spins the girl he's dancing with and I get a flash of Zavy's familiar face. I realize they haven't gotten to talk much since all our memories were restored. She was pretty closed off toward him back on our journey, not caring about him since she didn't truly know him. But now she's smiling ear to ear, dancing with him. They've both fallen under the happy, carefree curse of the island. It fits Zavy's personality, though. She loves to complain just as much as she loves to celebrate. So, if she's given a moment to be happy, she'd live it to the fullest.

I hear the music start to fade into a new melody. Many guys on the floor step back and bow to their dancing partner as Max did to me. I see Alexander has joined the Libertas culture and bends into a low bow toward Zavy. When he stands, Zavy grabs his hand and stands on her toes. I blink and catch her kiss his cheek ever so slightly. I almost miss it, and I scan the room to see if this is just another part of the Libertas culture, but it's not. I feel the heat flush my cheeks and my pulse picks up.

Zavy turns and walks away from Alexander. I see the shocked expression on his face as he looks after her, clearly transfixed by her. *Zavy and Alexander.* The thought makes the chicken from dinner turn over in my stomach. He could have anyone on this island; can he not choose my best friend? Could my best friend not choose him? Another nail in my heart, and with each blow, I feel more and more alone in this new life. I spin on my heels and race toward the nearest exit.

When I reach the grand doors of the ballroom, a guard stands at attention and stops me, "Ms. Adaline, may I ask where you're going?"

"It's getting late. I think I'll call it a night," I say coldly.

The music stops suddenly and my father appears on stage. "I'd like to welcome Alexander and my dear Adaline back on stage."

"Sorry, Ms. Adaline, but I can't let you leave. You're needed," he says and nods his head toward the stage.

I blow out a breath of frustration and make my way back across the room. I walk up the side of the stage, and I feel the heat continue to flush my face. I want to be as far away from this room as possible.

Alexander walks up the opposite side and meets my eyes. His wide smile makes me want to slap it off his face. My gaze at him could cut glass. His smile falls and he gives me a confused glance, but I don't let up on my glare. We turn to face the audience and I can't help but find Zavy. I send my burning stare into her, but she doesn't even have the decency to look at me. She can't pull her glossy eyes from Alexander, her cheeks blushing bright pink.

"Tonight, we celebrated the arrival of our saviors," my father projects. "Tomorrow, they will begin training to lead us in this rebellion. Thank you for being here to support them tonight. Thank you for fighting alongside us." The crowd applauds and begins to file out of the room. I spin on my heels and fly across the stage and down the stairs, folding myself into the crowd. I hear Alexander calling my name, but I don't stop. Once I'm out in the main hall I turn and race deeper into the castle, not entirely sure where I'm going.

Eventually, I end up back in the familiar hall that is lined with all the rooms of those who traveled with me. My blood is still pounding in my ears, my face is still flushed hot, and then I hear their voices. Zavy and Alexander echo together down the hall. I slide inside my room and quietly click the door closed behind me. I push my ear up against the crack of the door and listen.

"I had a really great time with you tonight," Zavy says.

"I'm glad we're getting to actually know each other since the whole memory flip," Alexander says politely, but his voice seems distant.

"Don't take this the wrong way," Zavy says, her voice dropping slightly. "I love Adaline to death, but sometimes she seems to have you on a leash, and I never got to talk with you before." A silence falls over the hall except for the pounding of my heart in my ears. My face burns as I try to fill their silence with what could be happening.

After a moment I hear the door to Zavy's room creak open and Alexander says, "Good night Zavy."

Another pause weighs in the air and then Zavy responds with, "Good night Alexander." Then, I hear her door click shut. Alexander's soft footsteps start to move down the hall and stop outside my door. There's a soft knock on the other side of the door and I contemplate ignoring it, but I crack it open and look up into his green eyes.

"Yes?" I ask and my voice cracks.

"Are you okay?" he asks gently.

"It's not your job to check up on me anymore," I say coldly.

"I didn't see you after that guy stepped in. I thought maybe he said something to upset you," Alexander starts to say, his voice full of concern.

"That guy is Lieutenant Max and he was a fine gentleman," I say sternly. Alexander looks at me and I add, "I'm fine, Alexander. Good night." Before he can respond I close the door and step back from it.

Let him go, Adaline. Let him make the mistake of falling for Zavy. Let him make that unforgivable mistake. But my heated temper won't cool. I grab the doorknob and rip it open. Alexander is still standing there.

"You can have anyone on this island. Don't choose my best friend," I say.

"Adaline-" he starts.

"No," I cut him off, "I don't want to hear whatever you are going to tell me about what happened tonight. I'm telling you now, don't."

Silence settles between us and Alexander stumbles on his words. "I didn't...I'm sorry." His hand lands on my wrist and I fold to the familiar warmth of his grasp, and his green eyes look deeply into mine.

"I'm here to train and I'm here to lead a rebellion. I'm not interested in any relationship conflict with you and Zavy," I say and pull my wrist from his grasp.

"Adaline, believe me when I say I am too."

I nod silently and close the door again.

I don't even bother to slip out of the dress. I lay on the mattress, under the softest blanket I've ever felt. With my gift, I flip the lights off and let the moonlight mix in the grey shadows across the floor. In the dark solitude of my room, I feel exhaustion set in.

Tomorrow is the first day of training and I'm sure it will be just as chaotic. *This is what I wanted.* I didn't want to waste time on parades and Welcome Ceremonies. I want to learn how to be an Alterken.

My eyelids feel heavy, the day's events finally catching up to my sleep-deprived body. Was the trial really just this morning? Today was my first day out of this room since we arrived here on Libertas and my life has completely spun out of control. Under the weight of emotional exhaustion, I fall into a deep sleep that is filled with dreams of Alexander and Zavy. I think I wake up twice, sick to my stomach.

Chapter 8

Light streams in the large wall of windows. My eyes crack open at the pounding on my door. I don't move to open it. I use my gift and pull it ajar. One of the girls that did my hair yesterday walks in with a pile of clothes.

"Good morning, Ms. Adaline," she says simply. "Here are your training outfits," she says and lays them down on the desk.

She notices the pajamas that were laid out are untouched and turns to see I'm still in my gown from last night. She stops herself from giving any judgment and turns and leaves.

The door clicks behind her, and I cross over to change outfits. I'm relieved to get out of the costume and character they wanted me to be. I'm ready to train and use my gift, but I'm also nervous to start learning all the new things I can do.

The outfit laid out for me is a solid, matte black jumpsuit made out of a smooth stretchy material. It slides on, and even though I'm sure it was made to be fitted to my figure it still hangs loose. It stretches down to my ankles, but the short sleeves hit just under my shoulders. I go through the drawers in the desk and take out a brush.

Gently, I run it through my loose curls and smooth them out. Inside the drawer with the brush is a pile of black ties. I take one and pull the loose curls up into a high tail.

As I'm putting away the brush, I notice a small box in the back of the drawer. I take it out and find damp cloths inside. I wipe the pristine white cloth across my face and my smudged makeup begins to erase itself from my skin. I feel more myself now, and finish off my outfit with my ankle-high leather boots from Sard. I exit my room and start to wander the halls until I run into Linda. She seems shocked to see me out of my room but thinks better of scolding me.

"Good morning," she says and nods. "Here, I'll lead you to the dining quarters. They should be serving breakfast soon."

I follow her through the halls, adding to the map in my head. I take note of where rooms and hallways are, and also where guard posts and exits are. I don't plan on ever needing to know, it's just instinct from being a prisoner for so long. We stop and turn into a bright, white tiled room and a large glass table sits in the center. Along the sides of the room are piles and piles of food.

"You can help yourself," Linda says. "The rest of your group will be here soon." Linda turns and hurries from the room.

I assume she's going to collect everyone else. I didn't want to wait and walk with them. The thought of Zavy and Alexander in the same room with me sends a wave of heat over my cheeks.

I move my attention to the food and walk over to the long stretch of delicacies. I lift the white glass plate and start to place the food on it. I try my best to identify what the foods may be. I take a scoop of eggs, some sort of meat, a crunchy piece of bread, and these small round pastries covered in a clear glaze. I grab silverware, a cup of water, and take a seat at the end of the clear table. As I sit, the door clicks open and my father walks in.

"Good morning," he says and walks over to get himself some food.

"Morning, Father," I say and we both freeze for a minute. "I never thought I'd get to say that again," I softly admit.

My mind had been so consumed with thoughts of Alexander and Zavy, I subconsciously greeted my father.

"I never thought I'd get to hear it again," he says and flashes a soft smile over his shoulders.

"Father," I say and pause.

"Yes?" he asks as he continues piling food on his plate, much more than I had taken.

"I just thought you should know, Alexander and I aren't actually a couple." The smile on his face grows.

"My daughter wants to talk about her relationship with me," he chuckles to himself.

A hot wave of embarrassment crawls across my skin and I stumble, "No, I just wanted to clear that up." I try to bring the cold edge back to my voice.

He laughs to himself again and says, "I know."

I'm reminded he's a Future Holder, like my mother. "Right, of course you know."

"I also know it's hard for you right now," he says, placing his plate across from me and taking a seat at the table. "And that's just a father's instinct."

I look up from my food. "Did you know I was an Alterken before my test results came back?"

"I had a guess. Some of my visions didn't make sense. Your gift kept changing." His brow furrows remembering the different futures he's seen with me. "I think this probably goes without saying, but don't announce that you're an Alterken today at training."

"Why not?" I ask. I don't particularly like to keep secrets.

"I don't want to startle the people with this idea. I'll make an official announcement tomorrow," my father says. "For now, we'll ease you into the training. The only person I informed was Lieutenant Max. He'll be in charge of organizing your training schedule."

The main doors swing open and our conversation falls quiet. Our entire travel team files in, all exploding in conversation. I see Cooper and Alexander lead the pack and Zavy brings up the rear, looking distant and much sadder than the gleaming girl spinning in a pretty dress from last night. I'm guessing Alexander talked to her, or maybe she overheard me yelling at him last night. Her cool green eyes catch mine. Her sad mask flips to anger, and she rips her glance from me.

My father catches the exchange and comments between mouthfuls of food, "She was never that great of a friend."

I glance at him, shocked by his blunt opinion. He's not wrong. Zavy has always been dramatic and everything was always about her, but she's the friend I had chosen.

"Your mother had a friend like her," my father adds. "They're good fun, but they make awful people to depend on."

I nod, agreeing with him. Of course, he doesn't know there were a lot of good moments with Zavy too. Years of playing together and gossiping about our classmates. We were the youngest in our class, having skipped a grade. She's always been my rock, and my father wouldn't understand that. My stomach tightens. I don't want to fight with Zavy. Maybe I can forget the kiss on the cheek ever happened.

I glance up and try to catch Zavy's attention. I watch as she grabs a scarce amount of food and takes a seat at the opposite end of the table, avoiding my gaze. The rest of the group grabs their food and fills in the other seats.

"Morning, sister." Cooper takes a seat next to me, and he makes his comment sound sarcastic.

I shoot him a glare because it's written all over his face that he must have heard about the conflict with Zavy and Alexander.

"Father," he says and gives him a slight nod of acknowledgment.

"Leave your sister alone," he says.

My heart warms at the comment, but I fight the feeling away. Even with me keeping my guard up around him, he's still trying to just be my father.

"Cooper, when they head to training bring the others to my office and we'll begin discussing our operations."

"What operations?" I ask. My father finishes his breakfast and stands to leave.

"You're responsibility is fighting this war. The non-gifted will be helping me plan it. I need to go meet with Marin and George now. Have a good first day at training." He grabs his things and leaves the room to meet with Alexander's parents.

I watch as Mio sits next to Cooper and Cinder sits across from him. "Where's Molly?" I ask, realizing she isn't here.

"With the other kids in Libertas," Cooper says softly. "She has no place with us in this war."

I nod, understanding, but I don't like the idea of her being off on her own already. I have to remind myself that my focus needs to be on training and the rebellion.

The rest of the chairs fill, except the one my father left and the one across from Zavy. I scan the room and see that Alexander is still filling his plate, taking maybe three times as much food as I did. It suddenly feels like lunch in grade school. Alexander turns and the realization crosses his face.

He'll have to choose between Zavy and me.

It's stupid because it's a chair, but Zavy and I both look at him, holding our breath and waiting for his decision. The rest of the group's conversation quiets, also interested in where this will go. Alexander exhales and walks up to the chair across from me. He places his plate down and sits quietly.

After a minute, the table returns to their conversation. I glance down to Zavy and she turns her back to us as she stands to leave the room. So much for forgetting the kiss on the cheek ever happened. Zavy storms from the room, the door rattling in its frame behind her. It's clear Zavy is mad at us, but wasn't she the one who started this?

Cooper laughs to himself and Alexander shoots him a glare.

"You're all a bunch of children," Cooper says, pointing between Alexander and me with his fork.

Alexander and I lock eyes and I say, "Or maybe we're only interested in training, and Zavy needs to stop creating drama."

Cooper nods to himself and him and Alexander fall silent as they eat their breakfast. I've already finished mine and I contemplate getting more of the glazed pastries. I notice Alexander has a pile he brought for himself. If we want the awkward tension to go away, then we need to start loosening it. I pick up a pastry from his plate and pop it into my mouth.

Shocked, he looks up from his plate. "Excuse me?" he asks as a smile splits his lips.

"They're not very good. You won't like them," I say and pop another one in my mouth.

He laughs and the tension does slip away. We're partners in this new life. Maybe at a different time, we could have been lovers, but for now, we'll be each other's protectors.

"Help yourself," he says.

He continues eating the rest of his food while I pick away at his pile of pastries. Him and Cooper exchange loose conversation about the party last night. I update Alexander on my father's instructions about keeping our actual gifts a secret for today. Once we all finish eating, Linda returns and we follow her out of the room. Cooper and the non-gifted file off from Alexander, myself, and Toby. I had forgotten he was even here, he's so quiet.

"Linda, shouldn't Toby be with the other children?" I ask

"Toby's gift is to master weapons. Don't you think that would be useful in a war?" Linda asks over her shoulder.

"But he's just a kid. He can't fight with us," I say.

"Oh, Adaline, that's not what I meant. He will only be helping teach our fighters how to use these weapons."

"Oh, I understand," I say and a silence falls over us as we walk out of a side door and exit the castle.

My eyes adjust to the sunlight and I see an extended yard of training grounds. There's a long line of colored tents that stretch down the length of the grounds. I realize each color corresponds to the gifts. Outside of the tents are roped off areas of open ground for us to practice our gift and learn hands-on combat.

Many people pair up and practice attacks with dulled swords. The clashing of the metal rings through the air. I watch a girl outside of the yellow tent practice slicing a sword through the air with only her enhanced sense of sight to control the weapon. The grip she has with just her gift is incredible. She makes it look effortless while her counter part struggles to fight off the enchanted weapon.

"Tents are classroom learning and then you'll practice your gift on the grounds," Linda says.

I notice a large ring in the center of the training grounds. It's stone edges stretching high into the sky.

"And the ring?" I ask.

"Where you test your gifts on each other," she says simply. She sees the shock on my face and says, "We have Transformers trained in healing standing by."

I notice all of the people walking around the training grounds are in similar outfits to mine, but there's a colored stripe down their sides. I realize Toby's is orange to match his gift. I see Max walking toward us in a black suit with yellow slashes down the sides. There's also a yellow collar on his shirt, the only indicator he's of a higher rank than us.

"Good morning," he says. His eyes meet mine and he gives me a small smile. Max turns to Alexander, almost like he forgot he was there, and extends his hand, "Lieutenant Max," he says. Alexander shakes his hand and I see a bit of caution in his eyes.

"I'll leave them with you, Lieutenant," Linda says as she turns and walks back toward the castle.

"All right, follow me," Max says.

He leads us behind the length of tents to keep us out of the way of others that are training. As we walk, I catch glimpses of people engaging in combat training. Groups of people flow in and out of the colorful tents. I'm overwhelmed by the sheer amount of gifted around me. The early morning air is full of energy; everyone seems to be buzzing at the excitement of training today. I do catch the wandering eyes that follow us across the training grounds.

"Everyone here has been training since birth," Max says. "You'll have a lot of ground to cover in a pretty short amount of time. Savior or not, training is hard for everyone."

We stop outside the orange tent and another lieutenant, I note by the orange collar, takes Toby.

"Adaline. Alexander," a sharp voice calls from our right.

I turn and see Commander Crymm walking toward us. Each stride is calculated and fierce. Instantly, I feel nerves flood my body. I take in a short breath and hold it, hoping it will keep my nerves down.

"Commander Crymm," Max says, stiffening his back and giving her a stiff nod.

"Welcome to the training grounds. I'll be stopping by later today to see how you are doing. Do you have any questions for me?" She tilts her head and for some reason I feel like she is already testing us.

Her white hair is slicked back into a tight knot on the top of her head. For some reason, staring at that when I answer is easier than looking into her eyes.

"No, ma'am. Lieutenant Max was just explaining everything to us."

"Good. Well, I will see you later." She turns sharply and moves on to another group of trainees. The sun reflects the medals on her light blue uniform. I wonder what the medals are for. We haven't fought in a war yet.

"That's Commander Crymm. Seems like you've already met her," Max says, loosening his posture now that she's walked away.

"She was in charge of the investigation with Molly," I explain, keeping a close eye on where she's at on the grounds. "Which tent do we go to?" I ask, noting we don't have any color on our outfits and there's no special tent set up.

Max glances over his shoulder before saying his next words. "We aren't announcing that you are both Alterkens yet."

"Because people don't trust different," I say and scan the numerous fighters around us that we are expected to lead.

"No, because your father wants to make the announcement himself. Eventually, you'll take your turn through all the tents," he says. "Today, we'll start you in the gifts you've discovered on your own. We want you to be comfortable here in the transition."

"So I'll stay here at the orange tent?" Alexander asks for his enhanced sense of touch.

"Yes, and this," Max says and gestures as another lieutenant walks out of the tent, "is Lieutenant Linx."

Lieutenant Linx is a large balding man. He has a nasty scar on the corner of his mouth and cold dark eyes.

"This way," Linx's harsh voice orders and gestures for Alexander to enter the tent. The two turn and leave, and I silently wish they wouldn't split our training up.

"So I'll be in the yellow tent today?" I ask and we begin to make our way across the training grounds.

"Correct," Max says and I note the yellow on his outfit again.

"You have an enhanced sense of sight?" I ask, glancing at his yellow collar.

"Yes, I'll be your direct lieutenant. I'm a Force Lifter," Max says.

"So let me see if I got this straight," I say as we approach the yellow tent. "There are lieutenants in each color for specific gifts under the larger sense?"

"Correct. So the lieutenant I sent Toby with specializes in

weaponry perfection under the sense of touch, while Lieutenant Linx specializes in knowledge from the sense of touch." Max sees the confusion on my face and adds, "The first lieutenant works with Aeros, and Lieutenant Linx works with Sensors."

"That's complicated," I say and laugh a bit, trying to keep all the titles to the different gifts straight in my head.

"Well, it's the human development that makes it complicated. Technically someone with an enhanced sense of touch can do all of its sub-components, like be a Sensor and an Aeros, but it's the limit of the individual's strength that stops them. It depends on how they push themselves. We're all learning here. You could go your whole life training and never master all the sub-components of your sense."

"But you're expecting me to learn all the sub-components of all the senses?" I ask, overwhelmed by the thought of it.

"You were chosen as the savior for a reason," Max says simply and we step inside the yellow tent. "Your ability to master these gifts is why. You were born able to do it." Max pauses when he realizes I've stopped listening and am in awe at the inside of the tent. It's much larger than it appeared to be from the outside. Around the edge of the tent are sections split by yellow curtains.

"Yellow for an enhanced sense of sight," Max says as he points around to the yellow tent. Then he points to one section, "Future Holders, those who use their gift to see the future." He moves his finger to the next sections. "Force Lifters, those who use their gift to control things, and that's Vision Shifters."

"Able to make things invisible," I say, remembering Mio's

brother Leo who housed us in Sard has that gift.

Max nods. His finger moves and lands on the fourth and final room and says, "Information Scanners, they use their gift to pull information from something. Such as thermal properties and materials. In enhanced sight, we have four lieutenants, one for each sub-component. As I said, I'm the lieutenant for Force Lifters, which is where you'll start," he says and we walk over to the section he had pointed to earlier. When we enter, everyone who was already here in their seats stands and bows. I assume it's for Lieutenant Max, but I feel it may have been for me as well.

"Have a seat, please," Max instructs. They do as he says and I realize the majority of people here are younger than I am by a year or two and range to much older like Lieutenant Linx, but they aren't ranked. "Training is for all ages, Adaline," Max says as he notices my staring. "You can have a seat, here, in the front."

I take a seat next to a young girl and her cheeks flush red. I assume it's from being nervous at sitting next to the savior. Max takes his place at the front of the room where a blackboard sits up on a tall stand. A white piece of chalk is raised in the air with what I assume is Max's gift. With the chalk, he writes the word *LEVITATION,* and then he says, "Can someone tell me the first step in making an object levitate?"

Step? Suddenly I feel very lost. *Don't you just do it?* The hand next to me shoots up.

"Yes, Lilliana?" Max calls.

"You breathe," she exclaims.

"Yes, that's correct," Max says and the chalk sketches *BREATHE* under the title. Hands continue to rise and more and more words are added to the list.

BREATHE IN.

SEE IT.

BREATHE OUT.

RAISE YOUR EYES.

We are then instructed to do so and are each handed a piece of chalk. I raise it easily without any of this nonsense theory, but I notice many people struggle and take many deep breaths before the chalk finally raises.

Max moves in front of me. "Adaline, try again with theory. Learning how to apply the theory now will make it easier when we move into more complex tasks."

I cut my gift off and the chalk falls to the desk. I breathe in and hold the chalk still, and as I breathe out, I raise the chalk. I look up at Max and he simply nods his head in approval. We continue to do this with many different objects and Max goes into a long lecture of physics and Newton's Law to calculate the mass and gravity so we know how much force we have to apply to the object. It's much more knowledge than I ever would have thought would be needed.

Max announces that we are a bit ahead of schedule this morning and decides he wants to lecture on invisibility, one of his personal favorite tactics in sense of sight. He explains that while his specialty is a Force Lifter, he has mastered being a Vision Shifter as well.

"It's not really making yourself invisible," Max instructs. "You camouflage yourself with your surroundings." I tilt my head trying to process the theory. "Your enhanced sense of sight takes in your surroundings and layers them around you so that others only see this and not yourself." Some of the class seems to understand, but for clarification I watch Max go invisible. He's just... *gone*. My eyes widen in shock. That can't be real. A moment later there's a thud on my desk and I jump. Max becomes visible again and I see that his fist is slammed against the top of my desk.

"Visible or invisible you are still a solid body. You can still be hit. It's important to remember what's real and what is simply a projection of camouflage when using this ability."

Chapter 9

After the first half of the day has passed, we finally break for lunch. I haven't had to sit through any kind of class since I was nine years old, and I'm not looking forward to how many other lectures I'm going to have to go through to learn how to use my gift.

Lunch is presented in a similar self-serving manner to how breakfast was. There are many round tables set up in the center of the tent with the food lined up around the edge. I take my plate and pile it with food, not sure what I grab. My head feels like it's been turned inside out after hours of theory. I sit at an empty table on the outskirt of the tent and shovel the food down, too tired to even taste it. A plate clanks down next to mine and I look up and see Max.

"May I sit here?" he asks but doesn't wait for my permission to take a seat.

"I don't know, I might get labeled as the teacher's pet," I say teasingly. Max laughs to himself and begins eating his lunch.

"Why did you decide to become a lieutenant? I ask.

"You don't become a lieutenant," he says. "You're appointed."

"Okay, so how did you get appointed?" I question again.

"Because I'm that good," he says very simply.

"Seriously," I push. "How do ranks work here in Libertas?"

"It's your first day as a student and you already want to be appointed to a lieutenant?" he teases.

"No, I just-" I start to stumble.

Max waves me off and says, "You master all the sub-components in your enhanced sense first."

"So you can do all four?" I question. I know he had just lectured about Vision Shifting and Force Lifting this morning, but I didn't think he could do them all.

He nods his head and says, "Yes, but I'm best as a Force Lifter. Then, the War Committee promotes people as roles become available. For a while, there weren't promotions because lieutenants are really just teachers, but now that we are moving toward an actual war we will need a lot more of them to lead their own troops."

I nod and say, " I understand, I was just surprised you were a lieutenant because you don't seem much older than me."

Max's cheeks flush a light pink and he says, "Yes I'm only seventeen. My father is a captain in the War Committee."

"Oh, so you already had someone on the inside," I say. "Who's in the War Committee?"

"Well, it's headed by King Derith and Commander Crymm, actually," he says and glances at me. "Then there are ten members on the committee. Two captains from each enhanced sense."

"Is your father in this group?" I ask, gesturing to the people from enhanced sense of sight.

Max nods. "We also have a small Navy Fleet and Air Force. Two or three lieutenants in each."

In my head, I try and keep the information that Max has told me straight. Everything here in Libertas is much different than I had expected. I didn't think they'd have such organized operations. I suppose that's good since we are going into a rebellion. I wonder if Alexander is feeling more comfortable in all this since he spent the last two years working in the Dather army.

Once we finish eating I ask, "So more theories now?" I'm slightly annoyed at the idea and the question comes out bitter.

"For some, yes, but not for you. Clearly you are ready to practice your gift in the performance ring."

A slight fear spreads through me and I picture the large stone circle in the center of the tents.

"Oh, I'm not sure," I say, and now lectures sound like a great idea.

"Adaline, you've already fought Paylon's army with this part of your gift. There's nothing more I can teach you about the theory of being a Force Lifter. You need to be using it."

A trumpet rings outside the tent, the command for everyone to move on from lunch. Max and I drop our dirty dishes into a bin on the edge of the table and I follow him outside of the tent. We cross to the tower of stone and I notice the other people coming to the ring are the older members here at training. I search the crowd for Alexander, but can't find him.

As we get closer to the ring I start to take in the arena. The stone walls stretch high above us and gradually come down in slabs of stadium seats. It's a much smaller version of the coliseum back on Dather. The coliseum where my mother was murdered on Parting Day, I remind myself. I hate thinking of that place and the number of people I watched die in that ring before I, myself, was at risk of being put in there.

Every week they'd make everyone in Garth fill the stands of the coliseum and we'd watch them execute more and more prisoners. They'd force us to watch with the intention of filling us with fear so we wouldn't disobey King Renon. Being in this ring awakens that same fear that was drilled into me every week I had to watch more people die. My feet feel very heavy and I can't get myself to move forward. More and more fear returns to me, and I feel like that child being dragged in to view the killings.

Max turns and sees my face has gone very white. "Are you okay?" he asks.

My words are caught in my throat and my eyes keep scanning the stone circle. As the fear creeps through my veins I feel my mind turn to the one thing it always can control, numbers. "It's Parting Day," I finally choke out, my mind convinced I'm back in Dather.

"What's Parting Day?" Max asks me and my bewildered eyes meet his.

"What do you mean? King Renon makes us go to the coliseum on Parting Day," I try and explain but the fear and anxiety continue to confuse my brain.

"Adaline," Max says and he grabs both of my shoulders, forcing me to look away from the ring and at him. I feel my mind begin to clear now that I only see his wild green eyes. "You are in Libertas. This is just the training ring."

"You were born here in Libertas, weren't you?" I ask Max softly, because I know if he had experienced the number of Parting Days that I've had to live through, he'd understand.

"Yes, I was," Max says. "I don't know what Parting Day is or what the coliseum is back on Dather, but I promise you, you are not there now."

I take in a few deep breaths and try to convince my mind that what Max is saying is true. As I step back from his grasp and look back to the stone ring, I feel better. The rest of the crowd has maneuvered around us and is heading toward the edge of the ring. There are rough stone stairs that lead up into the rows of seats. Max extends his hand and leads me up into a section of the ring.

I scan the audience around us and see that they have everyone sorted by their enhanced sense. I take a seat with the rest of the group marked in yellow. Max sits next to me and we look down into the ring where ten individuals enter and stand in the center. They are wearing similar outfits to ours, solid black with various colored stripes down the side, but in addition, they have bright collared capes around their shoulders.

"Captains?" I ask.

Max nods, making eye contact with who I assume is his father. He's a tall and extremely muscular man with thin slicked-back dark brown and grey hair. He has translucent blue eyes, which chills me even more knowing he picked the color himself. I scan the other captains and find them all equally terrifying. My blood chills when I recognize the pixie cut girl, muscles, and the redhead from the parade. They're our captains, no wonder they were so hard to convince. They're fighting alongside us. They're in charge of me and yet, I get the parade and celebration.

"All right, let's get these lessons started," Max's father's voice booms, and again I'm sure someone with a gift of enhanced hearing is amplifying his words.

"We'll pair up two different enhanced senses and you'll go until one of you says you're done. For those of you where this is your first time in the ring, it'll probably be quick." He pauses as many people begin laughing. "The goal is to get past your opponent and grab this flag."

I watch each captain pull out a flag that matches their colors. "There are no further rules." Nerves settle on the group as we realize the first fight is about to happen. "Any volunteers?"

The silence that follows doesn't reassure me that this is all that safe, but eventually a hand raises from the orange section. Enhanced sense of touch. It's not Alexander and I exhale, glad he's not stupid enough to volunteer on our first day of training. The muscular commander cloaked in orange smiles at a volunteer from his own group.

"Darin, join us." He extends his hand, his proud voice booming.

I watch as Darin stands and moves down into the circle. His bleached hair is in a short buzz. He's lean and built for fighting, the sunlight shining on his dark skin.

The pixie commander's high voice rings out next as a girl from the red quadrant stands to volunteer. "Lexi, join us!"

As she walks down the tall stone steps, she pulls her long, slick, blonde hair into a high tail. I notice a black *X* marked in ink on the olive skin at the back of her neck. She looks like she could kill you with the flip of a finger. Lethal, like a snake.

"All right, we'll have touch against smell." The captains clear the circle and the two volunteers take their spots on the edge of the ring. They first walk to the center, bow to each other, and shake hands for good sportsmanship. Then, they turn and walk back to the edge of the ring. A red flag is launched and placed at the top of the ring behind Darin, for Lexi to try and get, while an orange one is raised behind Lexi for Darin to try and get.

"The flags are more of a bonus," Max whispers in my ear under the settling air. "Most people will stop before either has gotten the flag."

There's a loud *click* in the air and the crowd cheers, *three*, and another *click*, *two*, and a final *snap*, *one*.

As the crowd screams *one*, Lexi and Darin break quickly. Darin slams his fists on the dirt and I watch as the ground whips Lexi in the air like a blanket. She falls and several large cracks follow. Darin charges at her, but she pulls herself to her broken feet. Darin suddenly kneels over coughing.

"What did she do?" I ask.

"Poison or gas. She controls what he smells. His body is going into a defensive mode." As Max says this, I watch Lexi hobble around Darin, but Darin slaps his hand on the ground again and the dirt changes to slick ice.

Lexi fumbles on her snapped ankles, unable to keep herself from sliding. Darin clears the ice on his half of the arena and begins to crawl toward his flag. The ice on Lexi's side begins to melt and turns into a patchy slush.

Darin's powers are weakening.

Lexi turns and sees that Darin has begun to move faster, running or wobbling toward the flag. I watch Lexi take in a deep breath through her nose and blow out an enormous wind, throwing Darin to the dirt. Then, she continues to blow, turning up a large dirt tornado around him.

"Stop!" I hear a weak boy's voice croak out.

Darin has called for a cease. I understand why, breathing in nothing but dirt and rock would kill him. Those clothed in red for an enhanced sense of smell jump and cheer. Lexi celebrates for a brief second before collapsing, revealing her injured ankles. A team of five, dressed in white suits, runs into the circle and they carry both Darin and Lexi out of the arena.

"Healers?" I ask and Max nods in response.

"All right," Max's father's voice booms as he re-enters the circle. "Let's get our next match up. Let's do sight," he flicks a wrist and the red flag transforms to yellow. "Against hearing." Again he flips his hand and the other flag turns green. "Any volunteers?" he asks and a wicked grin spreads on his face.

He turns to stare down the group of members from an enhanced sense of sight, and everyone squirms from his gaze. Those icy blue eyes lock on mine and I realize my hand is raised.

"Are you crazy?" Max hisses. "You aren't ready for the ring. I was joking earlier."

I look up at my hand, confused. "I didn't," I start to say and realize someone with an enhanced sense of sight is controlling me. My arm drops limp, free from their control.

"Adaline, what an ambitious surprise," Max's father says. "Please, join us."

I glance around me, looking at what I should do, but everyone is staring at me.

"Go," Max whispers, nodding toward the stone stairs that lead to the arena floor. I stand and make my way through the crowd.

"And from hearing?" Max's father's voice calls as he turns to the green section.

"I'll face her," a rough voice calls out.

Zavy.

She stands, the muscles in her neck and shoulders tensed. She moves though the crowd effortlessly. She's confident and it makes me look cowardly.

"Some new talent to grace our lesson," Max's father says, finding amusement at this pairing. Zavy and I walk to the center to bow as Darin and Lexi had done.

"Zavy, what are you doing?" I hiss, my eyes searching her stone-cold gaze.

As we drop into our bow she says, "Next time, you'll think twice before deciding who I or Alexander can have a relationship with." She pulls out of our bow sharply.

"Zavy," I say, but before I can continue she whips around and makes her way to the edge of the ring, centered under the flag I need to grab.

Reluctantly, I turn and take my place under Zavy's target; the green flag. But as she stares me down, I realize the flag is not her target. *I am.* I hadn't realized me telling Alexander not to get in a relationship with Zavy would anger her so much.

The crack of a whip rings out, signaling the crowd to begin our countdown. With each snap, my heart races faster, adrenaline coursing through my veins. Since we've arrived in Libertas, I haven't had to fight or survive. Not like I had to do on Dather. The familiar fear of being someone's target returns to me, and I feel my natural instinct to protect myself take over.

The circle and crowd ring out and when they yell *one,* I'm hit by a horrible screeching sound. My hands fly over my ears, trying to block the horrid noise, but it has no effect. I pull my hands away and they are coated in blood. She's going to leave me deaf.

My fighting instincts take over. With my gift, I flip up dirt and rocks around Zavy but she only finds it to be an irritation. I don't want to hurt her, but the screeching seems to be turning my brain to mush. I try to picture lifting Zavy into the air, but nothing happens. I can't focus enough with this horrid sound vibrating in my head.

Max's lesson swims into view. *Theory first.*

I remember the lesson and follow the steps he used on the chalk. I breathe in and exhale. I move my eyes up and watch Zavy lift into the air. Higher and higher and the screeching wavers ever so slightly, but as quickly as it wavers it punches back twice as hard. Images of Zavy and Alexander, twirling hand in hand last night, come back to me and the embarrassment, frustration, and jealously take over.

My eyes trace the perimeter of the ring and I begin to spin Zavy around the arena, faster and faster until I hope she's so sick from the spinning that she won't be able to stop me. I pull her down to the ground so hard the earth cracks below her. The screeching finally subsides.

I sprint across the circle and up the large stone stairs toward my flag. When I reach it, my hand locks around the wooden handle. I spin around, and see Zavy lying in a crater.

The green flag is in her grasp.

She pulls herself to her knees, because I'm sure the impact crushed her feet. A thick trail of blood runs down the corner of her mouth. With her pale, thin hand, she wipes it and raises her flag. The green side erupts in what I'm assuming are roaring cheers because, as the thumping of my heart subsides, I realize I can't hear a thing. When I spun her around the perimeter of the ring she must have grabbed her flag.

A wicked grin spreads across Zavy's face, overly proud of her victory, which is more from me losing my temper. My eyes dart around the arena and everyone's mouths are moving and pointing toward me. My eyes find Commander Crymm in the crowd, shaking her head disappointedly.

I drop the yellow flag and watch it fall to the ground. I stumble down the stone stairs and see the healers file toward me. We begin to make our way out of the ring and I find Alexander standing in the orange section.

He hurries down the stairs and meets me at the edge of the arena. I turn and see Zavy watching us. As I pass by Alexander, I slip my hand into his and we walk off together behind the healers. I glance over my shoulder one last time and I don't miss the smile wiped from Zavy's face.

Alexander nudges my shoulder and I look up and see his mouth is moving but I can't hear what he's trying to say.

"I can't hear anything," I try to respond but I don't know if it comes out.

The fear that crosses his face makes me think the message was clear. He reaches for the healer nearest him and I assume he's asking if they can fix my hearing. The healer nods and brushes him off. Alexander squeezes my hand in short bursts, the only way we can communicate now.

We are ushered into a white tent at the edge of the training grounds. They lead me to a long flat table and I lay on it. The healers and Alexander seem to be arguing. I think they are telling him to go back to training, but he's trying to stay here.

Out of the corner of my eye, I see Darin from the fight before mine. I assume this must the loser's tent, but seeing Alexander here with me makes me feel like I've all but lost.

Zavy has drawn the final line. There's no forgetting what she's done. Alexander aside, she jumped at the opportunity to fight me and has embarrassed me in front of the entire Libertas army. We are no longer friends.

One of the healers places a clear mask over my nose and mouth, and a gas is pushed into me. I lose consciousness almost instantly.

Chapter 10

A steady beeping pulls me from my sleep. Slowly, I sit up and take count of the tubes coming out of me. A couple of wires attached to my arms run off into the machine causing the beeping. Besides being immensely sore, there's nothing else wrong with me.

"Thought you were supposed to be our savior," a hoarse voice chokes out. I turn and see Darin still lying in his bed.

"It's different, I didn't want to kill my best friend," I say and the words *best friend* feel wrong now.

"King Renon could make his entire army look like her, then what would you do?" Darin asks, further proving his point.

"Well, I guess it doesn't matter anymore, we aren't really friends," I say and let out an exhausted sigh.

"Oh, your life is so hard," he grumbles and pulls himself into a sitting position. "Cut the schoolgirl drama out. Get your head straight and learn to fight and lead this rebellion. I've spent the last seven years of my life training for this."

"I am here for the rebellion," I say and cut him off. "I've lost too many to not see this through."

Darin considers this for a minute and seems to loosen his tense front. "This training ring, it takes some getting used to," he says, trying to lighten the conversation.

"You've been trying to understand it for seven years?" I ask.

He lets out a rough laugh. "This is one of my few losses. My biggest fear is suffocation and they know that."

"Well, I don't have time to get used to the ring. I'm going to need to redeem myself. The savior can't lose," I say and then I remember that I didn't even volunteer for it in the first place. Someone out there controlled me and volunteered me for that awful arena.

"It just means your human," Darin offers and our eyes meet for a second.

Then, the curtain in front of us is pulled open and Alexander rushes in. "Adaline, you're awake."

"I'm fine," I say and brush him off. He needs to learn he can't lose it every time I get hurt.

"You're hearings back," he says, stating the obvious. "Zavy shouldn't have fought that hard," Alexander complains.

"That's how the ring works," Darin cuts in. "You fight hard in the arena so that you can learn how to defend yourself when those attacks matter." A silence settles between us and I notice Alexander's face goes bright red.

"You can't volunteer for the ring," I say and his eyes meet mine. "We can't have both saviors losing in front of everyone."

"Well, I wouldn't lose," Alexander says and he helps me up out of the bed. "You shouldn't have volunteered either," he says softly.

He leans closer to me and helps remove the sensors and tubes on my arms.

"I didn't," I whisper so just Alexander hears. His emerald eyes flicker up and meet mine, searching for an explanation. "Someone controlled me into volunteering." My eyes dart around the room to make sure no one else could be listening. "We can't trust everyone that's here. Some are obviously testing us."

Alexander pulls back and catches Darin peering over at us. He clears his throat and says, "The healers cleared you both. You've been approved to leave." He turns back to me and adds, "You missed the rest of training for today. We're heading to dinner soon."

I stand and follow Alexander to the entrance of the tent. I pause and turn back to Darin. I don't say anything, but I let my gaze linger with him before finally stepping outside. Linda is waiting for Alexander and me at the edge of the healer's tent and she leads us back to our rooms. I give Alexander a side glance and he knows it means we need to talk in private. He nods his head, understanding.

On the way back to our rooms, Linda tells us about the dinner that the best chefs in Libertas will be preparing for us. She doesn't comment on my loss in the ring, though I'm sure everyone must know about it. Once back in my room, I wait until Linda's footsteps have silenced. I sit on the edge of my bed and let a couple of minutes pass, and then there's a soft tap on my door. I open it and let Alexander in.

"Someone was controlling you?" he blurts out as I close my door behind him.

"I'm telling you, I would never volunteer for that," I admit.

"Who would do that?" Alexander questions and his brows furrow together.

"It could have been anyone with an enhanced sense of sight. I was surrounded by them," I think out loud.

"But you didn't feel it happening?" he asks.

"No, so it must have been someone very skilled." I look up and see Alexander is shaking his head. "What? Who do you think it was?"

"I bet it was Lieutenant Max," Alexander huffs with disgust.

"No, it wasn't him," I say flatly.

"Why are you so quick to dismiss him?" Alexander asks defensively.

"Because he was shocked I had volunteered. Also, he wouldn't do that." I pause for a moment and add, "But his father might."

"Who's his father? Captain Brutis?" Alexander asks.

"Is that the one in yellow that announced training?" I ask, realizing Max never mentioned his name.

Alexander nods and argues, "Why would he want to volunteer you? He didn't volunteer me." I don't have an answer for him.

"This just means we can't trust everyone here," I say and an acknowledgment of understanding passes between us.

"I should get ready for dinner," Alexander says as he moves toward the door. "I don't think it was Captain Brutis," Alexander adds, looking back before leaving.

"I don't think it was Lieutenant Max," I say, because I know that's who Alexander is wanting to blame.

"Should we tell someone?" Alexander asks, the thought finally occurring to him.

I shake my head silently. "If we tell someone, we'll be locked up here in the castle for our protection. We can take care of ourselves," I say and our eyes meet. "We'll take care of each other."

Alexander nods and says, "Like we always do."

There's a moment of lost hope that passes between us, knowing we have to keep our feelings in line in order to protect the other.

"I'll meet you in the hall and we can walk to dinner together," Alexander says and quietly clicks my door shut.

I approach the desk in the corner of the room and see a change of clothes has been set out for dinner. It's a beautiful, bright yellow dress made out of a very soft and thin material.

I change out of my tattered training uniform, shower, and put on the yellow gown. After Alexander changes into casual jeans and a button-up we walk down to the dining room where we ate breakfast but find it empty.

"Did they say where dinner was?" I ask and glance at Alexander.

"No, I just assumed it'd be here," Alexander says.

"I think they need to give us a map of this place," I say.

"Not necessary," Linda's voice rings from behind us. "I'll guide you where you're needed, just don't wander off and we'll all stay on schedule." Her high pitch voice echoes in the hall.

It's the closest she dares to lecturing us, our ranks here are probably far above her. Linda doesn't wait for us to apologize and turns to leave, motioning for us to follow her. Linda leads us deeper than I have ever gone in the castle. This seems to be a more private section of the castle. There aren't as many guards and the extra decorations that were displayed in the front of the palace are lacking here.

We enter an elegant dining room where a royal blue carpet stretches under a dark wooden table. The entirety of our traveling group is here, including Zavy who is grinning from ear to ear as she tells the story of how she beat the proclaimed savior.

Our presence pulls a silent wave over the room. Alexander and I take our seats next to each other at the far end of the table. I sit at the edge and assume my father will take the head of the table, and my brother, Cooper, sits across from me. Linda exits the room and the table turns back to a few small conversations.

"Heard you had a tough loss today," Cooper says and I know this is his twisted way of asking if I'm okay.

"I lost in the ring more than she won," I huff, still mad at myself for letting my emotions get the best of me. "How was your day?" I ask, eager to hear what organizing a rebellion could mean.

"We made some progress," he pauses and can't seem to find the right words. "A lot of it's confidential right now." Before Cooper can say anything more, my father and Alexander's parents enter the dining room.

"My apologies, I didn't mean to keep you all waiting." My father takes his seat between his two children at the head of the table.

Alexander's parents fill in the empty chairs next to him and now the room turns their attention to the meal that is about to be served. Even though I'm sure my father has heard about my loss in the ring, he looks at me like he couldn't be me more proud.

The meal is served and the rich flavors are even better after a long day of training. As fast as the food is placed in front of us, it is eaten just as quickly. I feel like my stomach has grown meal by meal, and finishing them off seems to get easier and easier.

Linda returns and her voice rises over the dinner conversation. "We have good news! Your official living quarters have been arranged for you. I will escort you there now. We have small houses for each of you just outside the castle grounds."

Everyone stands to leave, but my father asks Cooper and I to stay back. I watch as my group goes and I feel the separation start to settle in.

"We need to catch Adaline up on the rebellion," my brother says as the door closes.

"We have to take other steps first," my father says. "We need to solidify our political grounds. I am the King of Libertas, which makes you a prince and you a princess."

He lets his words settle before he continues.

"We will have a ceremony officially giving you your titles in the next day or so, and if anything happens to me in this rebellion, Cooper, you will become their king. I need you both to learn everything you can about being in a royal family, on top of training and organizing a rebellion. Starting tomorrow night, you will each begin attending night lectures about being royal children."

We both nod, understanding our roles in this puzzle, but it's hard for me to see my father as a king, or me as a princess. Talking about the rebellion with him is much easier than the father-daughter moment he was trying to have earlier.

From a prisoner to royalty in almost two weeks. The transition here in Libertas keeps moving faster and my role in this new life keeps getting bigger.

"Okay, now about the rebellion. Adaline, you and Alexander have just over a week to learn as much as you can about your gifts," my father says.

"A week?" I interrupt.

"We have word that King Renon is organizing his troops in Dather as we speak, and they will be making their move soon. He won't come to us, not right away," my father says waving his hands. "They are securing their borders now to keep us from going in. If we wait too long, we'll miss our opportunity to infiltrate their lands."

"Why won't they come to us?" I ask.

"For many reasons," my father says. "One is that King Renon isn't interested in sending his soldiers on a voyage that could kill them. He'd want to keep as many alive as he can for when we come to them."

"Which he'll be expecting because of the prophecy?" I ask.

"If he's discovered you and Alexander are the keys mentioned in the prophecy, he knows it's only a matter of time until the rest of prophecy unfolds." My father nods thoughtfully.

"What's the other reason that he won't come here?" I ask.

"The other reason is that he couldn't find us," my father says, letting a smirk cross his face.

"What do you mean?"

"Gifted with an enhanced sense of sight work around the clock to keep the island invisible." My father studies my face, and he must know what my next question will be because he answers it. "When you sailed in, we made ourselves visible so you would know where to go. If King Renon's army were to be sailing towards us, they'd see open blue water."

"And when they got too close?" I ask, remembering how Max had explained invisibility. This island is still a solid body.

"They'd be dead before their boats could hit the wall," he says.

"So, King Renon has no idea where Libertas is?"

No wonder everyone is so relaxed here. They have no fear of ever being ambushed.

For a moment, I second-guess why we're fighting in this war. We could hide here, far from King Renon's grasp, forever. But the gifted I left behind surface in my memory. Specifically the girl, the hound that got away from Paylon, comes back to me. She had told me she was going to try and free her sister. She is fighting. This war has already started. We can't abandon the gifted back in Dather who have already begun to fight.

"Okay, so one week," I say, swallowing away the idea.

"One week," my father says and all of a sudden the weight of the rebellion seems to multiply on my shoulders. "I'll show you to your new quarters."

It's at this moment that I feel the separation from my traveling group settle in. Cooper and I are royals. Even Alexander being a key component in the rebellion can't match the important status that Cooper or myself hold.

But I remind myself that Alexander is royal by blood.

The wrong blood.

My new room here in the castle is larger than the house I used to live in on the outskirts of Garth. Off from the main entrance hall to my chambers is a sitting room filled with bookshelves and couches. The only two personal items from my old room, my bag and sword, are tucked away in the corner of the space.

Two rooms are coming off either side. One of the additional rooms holds hundreds of outfits that range from training gear to some of the most elegant gowns I've ever seen. There are even heels made of real crystals I assume. I find the navy blue dress I wore last night tucked away neatly in the closet.

The other room is my bedroom, with a bed three times the size of the mattress in the cell I was trapped in for seven years. Lush deep blue carpet stretches out over the entirety of the rooms with the exception of the final room that attaches to my bedroom. A grand bathroom all to myself. A large tub and spacious shower with more buttons than I assume I'll ever get the chance to use.

The room doesn't quite feel like mine. It feels as though I'm playing pretend and none of this is real.

I change out of the light sundress and into the most comfortable clothes I can find. I bury myself in the enormous bed, curling up deep under the covers, and I feel so small.

I'm the savior and a princess, but I just feel like a child. I'm a warrior and a murderer, but I feel frightened of my own shadow. When will any of this start to feel normal?

Part 2: The Royals

Chapter 11

When my eyes crack open and I see the early morning light bleed into my room, the first thing I think is *seven days*. Just one week until our forces make their first move. Today is one of those seven days. I can't waste it. My breakfast is brought to my room. I eat alone in the main sitting area of my chambers. I don't feel as small today. Sleep and the comforts of my room have recharged me. I get dressed in another identical training outfit as to what I wore yesterday. There's a soft knock on my door and when I answer, Linda is on the other side.

"Ready to go?" she asks and I nod.

I close the door behind me and feel my muscles tense as we walk. After the way I left training yesterday, I wonder what people have been saying about me. I feel myself build stiff walls in my brain, ready to try and be stronger today. Linda escorts me all the way out to the training grounds and I meet up with Max and Alexander.

"And the princess arrives," Max says.

I roll my eyes at the humor in his voice. I wasn't expecting that to be what people were talking about. Alexander smiles, but in his eyes

I catch him scanning me, as if somehow my future royal title may have changed me.

"What's our training schedule? I was told we don't have much time between now and the war," I say and Max nods.

"There's an announcement this morning before training commences," Max says as he leads Alexander and me toward the ring.

The lieutenants of each enhanced sense have gathered their groups of gifted and they all sit color-coordinated in the stands of the arena. Max takes Alexander and me around the base of the ring and we file through an archway, into the main arena floor. I find Cooper waiting there as well and I'm confused why he wouldn't be with the other non-gifted. My father stands in the center of the arena dirt floor, trying to quiet the crowd.

"Good morning," his voice rings, and even though I see my father in front of me, I don't recognize him in his royal outfit.

"Most of you have spent a lot of time on these grounds. Many have grown up here, training as soon as you could walk. Not everyone is born a fighter and would never choose this path," my father says, and nods of acknowledgment pass through the crowd. "As you know, the war with Dather has become a reality, and I am grateful for your services to protect our community. I am honored to fight beside you when the time comes. Our forces will begin to move out in just one week. So, train hard these next couple of days. We've brought you all together to make some important announcements."

When he says this, he turns and gestures to Cooper and me. We walk out from under the archway, and the eyes of the entire army of Libertas rests on me. Even with the hundreds of eyes peering down on me, my eyes find her's instantly. Zavy sits in the front row of the green section, leaning forward like she's watching her prey in a cage.

My least favorite thing about this ring is that, no matter where I stand, I will always have my back to someone. Defenseless, and unaware of their movements. Since losing in the ring yesterday, the fear seems to have tripled. When we walk across the dirt arena floor, my heart beats faster. I think I know what my father is about to announce, but I'm not sure it's going to be received all that well.

"Before you are Princess Adaline and Prince Cooper. They will pledge to lead us to the freedom we all want." The silence that follows is unnerving, but many people smile and nod. I assume they all expected that. When my father gestures for Alexander to step forward into the ring, I wonder if they're ready for what's next. He walks out to the center of the circle and takes his place next to me.

"We were told, and made to believe, that Adaline was a Force Lifter, and Alexander a Sensor, but their tests did not show that," my father says, using our formal gift titles.

The whispers and curious glances confirm that they didn't know this was coming.

"The test revealed that they are Alterken," he titles us.

The higher ranked personnel's eyes widen, as they know what this means, but many others, Zavy included, wait for my father to explain.

"All of Alexander and Adaline's senses are enhanced. They are capable of doing everything." My father gives a small laugh and adds, "I wouldn't expect anything less from a savior."

But most people don't share in his humor of the ironic twist. They look at us like we are something that doesn't belong. Like a lab experiment gone wrong. We are different and people don't trust different.

"Adaline and Alexander will be rotating through all of the senses to try and learn them all before we move out this time next week." My father bows his head slightly and finishes with, "That's all, your training schedule will return as normal."

With that, everyone stands and exits the ring. They make their way back to their tents, but I don't miss the exchange of questing conversations about the information they were just given. My father and Cooper return to the castle to continue their efforts on planning the war. Alexander and I meet Max and he escorts us to today's training tent.

"We are going to have to have you and Alexander rotate and train together from now on. We think it may be quicker to figure you both out at the same time," Max says and I can't help but feel like Alexander and I are a special breed of animal.

"Our main goal is to teach you all that you have the potential to do," Max continues to explain as we walk. "Just simply give you knowledge. Whatever you pick up and can do is great, but as long as you know what your possibilities are, the rest will come in time."

"So we have four more senses to cover and six days. Not much room for delays," I scoff.

"One sense a day and then we'll throw you back into the ring to test them out," Max says stiffly.

"So today?" Alexander directs.

Max continues to walk past each tent and says, "Today you'll start with sense of smell." Max stops outside of the red tent and a lieutenant from this sense steps out. "Lieutenant Luis, two new students for you." Luis scans Alexander and me before shaking our hands.

"Pleasure to meet you," Lieutenant Luis says and his words seem to come oddly slow.

"Yes, we only have one day to teach them every potential they have," Max says as he turns to leave.

Luis nods before turning and guiding us inside. The red tent is set up the same as the yellow one I was in yesterday. There are two classrooms sectioned off with red curtains and the common area for lunch is placed in the center. Luis begins to give us the layout. "Under the overall sense of smell we have two sub-components. The first is a Tracker, and the second is a Manipulator, a fighting tactic. We'll start you there."

Luis leads us into an identical classroom like the yellow tent where Max taught his lesson. Similar to then, everyone previously sitting at their desk stands and bows to Lieutenant Luis and then they take their seats again.

"We have two special guest students today," Luis's slow, deep voice pushes out and he gestures to two empty chairs in the front. Alexander and I take our seats and Luis moves behind a large desk at the front of the room.

"Today, I will be teaching you how you can use your gift in combat. Some of you may have witnessed one of our own use this tactic in the ring yesterday." He gestures to Lexi who stands and the rest of the class whistles and claps. "You can use your gift to control what your opponent smells," Luis says, continuing his lecture and Lexi takes her seat again.

"This does not mean you create the thing that matches the smell. For example, you can make them smell poison, their body will react and try to defend itself, but there is no real poison." Luis must sense my confusion and he gives another example. "Or you could make them smell a fresh batch of cookies, but they aren't really there." A couple of people laugh at the dumbed-down example. "But there's one condition," Luis says and he leans back against the desk and crosses his arms. "What is it?" he asks and the majority of the hands shoot up.

"Yes, Ally?" he calls.

"You have to know the smell," she says and Luis nods approvingly.

"You have to know what the smell is so you can inflict it. If you've never smelt freshly baked cookies," Luis says, going back to his example. "Then you can't push that smell onto someone else." I nod, understanding. It's just like teleporting. You have to know the place to be able to go there.

"Now, for the theory," Luis says and he moves toward the chalkboard and begins writing. "These are the steps. First, recall the memory where the smell originates, confirm the smell with your own sense, picture the person you want to affect, then push the scent to them," he says and actually pushes his arms out as if he were shoving someone away. "And always maintain eye contact."

"Is eye contact necessary?" I question and stop Luis's lecture. I realize I should've raised my hand and I think Lieutenant Luis debates scolding me, but decides not to at this moment.

"No, Ms. Sagel. It's not, but it helps when learning to do this skill for the first time."

"Does distance from your target matter?" Alexander asks with equally as bad manners to mine, but Luis seams to only care that we're engaged.

"Yes, you have to see them, be in their presence," Luis says and Alexander and I nod, trying to understand.

"Now to practice," Luis says. He kneels behind the desk and pulls out ten sealed containers. "Partner up." He waves at the class. Everyone turns to those sitting next to them, and of course Alexander and I stick together. Luis hands out the containers, one per group, and returns to the front of the class. "Partner one will crack open the container and take in the smell. Then, they will try to push this scent onto partner two. Partner two will try to guess what's in the container. Each container holds something different. We will rotate the dishes until everyone has tried each one. Some are harder than others," he says and smiles.

I understand now why some people go into teaching. He really enjoys sharing his knowledge. The class falls silent and no one wants to be the first to break into the exercise so Luis says, "Go ahead and get started."

I turn to Alexander and take the container in my hands. "I'll try first," I say and crack open the lid just enough for me to breathe in what's hidden inside. I'm overcome with a warm scent of pollen and I know it must be flowers. I smile because it smells like the flowers my mother and I used to pick in the fields outside our house on Dather. I close the container and look to Alexander. I try to follow the theory. First, eye contact. I've got the memory and confirmed the smell. I picture Alexander there with my mother and me, smelling and picking flowers.

"Well," Alexander says.

"I'm trying," I mumble and stare at him, holding my breath and not daring to blink.

Alexander laughs and I'm sure I look ridiculous.

"I don't think you're trying hard enough," he jokes and I let out my breath, frustrated.

"Push," Luis says from behind me. I turn and watch him push his arms out. I look back to Alexander and draw the memory back up. I breathe in, confirming the smell, and with both hands push through the air and try to send the smell to Alexander. His eyes flutter in rapid blinks and then he sneezes.

"Did you smell it?" I ask, excited like a child.

Alexander laughs and says, "Flowers, yes, I smelled it." I remove the lid and confirm he was right. This was the first time I have done something that wasn't with my enhanced sense of sight. It feels as if it wasn't real, as if these powers aren't real.

"Great work, Adaline," Luis says and then to the rest of the class he adds, "Rotate containers to the next group. This time partner two gets the container."

Alexander takes the container from the group closest to us and we pass ours along. I watch as he presses his nose up to the container, taking in the scent. I see his eyes react to it, trying to find a memory to align it with. He looks at me and breathes in. As he pushes his hands toward me I'm hit by the overpowering scent of ray berry pie; my father's favorite.

I'm instantly pulled back to being five-years-old, standing in the kitchen with my mother. Her belly is so large it could pop. She's bent over our poor excuse for an oven, pulling out the pie we'd slaved over all morning. Cooper runs around the house with one of his toy airplanes in his hand. The front door cracks open and my father enters, looking so much younger than he does now.

"Father!" I squeal and run to him. He embraces me in a tight hug and throws me up on his shoulders. He makes his way to the kitchen where the familiar ray berry pie scent seemed to always linger. Cooper runs through his path with his plane.

"I'm going to fly a plane one day," Cooper says and loops around us making zooming noises. My mother moves the pie to the table and gives my father a small kiss on the cheek.

"Happy birthday," she says, her voice so soft and eternal.

"Happy Birthday!" I scream and tighten my arms around his neck.

The memory fades as Alexander stops pushing the scent.

"Maybe I'm not doing it right," he huffs.

Tears hang at the edges of my eyes. I wasn't ready to relive that. To think about the times we were all happy together. I miss my mother so much.

"Ray berry pie," I say and a small, sad smile splits my lips, letting the warm memory fade.

Alexander looks at me, shocked, and rips off the lid to confirm it. "Yeah, how did you know?"

"You sent me it," I say and I know he's feeling just as weird about these powers as I am.

This continues, on and on, with different targets; saltwater, meats, dirt, perfume, until Luis has us stop and takes the containers back to the front of the room.

"Next, you'll learn to do it with something you can use in battle," he says simply, pulling out a final bin that is filled with a cloudy grey mist. "Smoke," he whispers. "Most of us won't get the chance to learn what poisonous gas smells like, but smoke can be just as deadly. Partner one, come up."

I walk to the front of the class with the others and Luis lets us each take in a breath of the smoke. Each person leaves coughing the scent from their lungs and I'm no exception. We return to our partners and Luis instructs us to push the thick smoke onto partner two and stop once they start showing signs of its impact.

"What if we can't find a memory with that scent?" I ask as Luis walks over to us.

"I just gave you one," Lieutenant Luis says and adds, "It doesn't need to be a real memory. You can paint one up in your imagination as long as you know what the smell is." I nod and focus on Alexander, trying to push the smoke to him. After a moment he begins coughing a little and I stop.

"Keep going, he can take more than that," Lieutenant Luis says.

I focus again and push the smoke to him. I watch Alexander's cough grow. His eyes water and he's struggling to breathe.

"Back off just a tad," Lieutenant Luis says, the excitement of teaching written all over his face.

I do, and I balance Alexander between letting him breathe and keeping the smoke heavy in his lungs.

"Good, you can stop," Lieutenant Luis says, and Alexander falls back in his chair, taking in deep breaths of fresh air. "It's important to find that balance. To hold someone in that state is just as valuable as pushing it too far. It's a great skill to utilize in the ring."

"Very nice work, Princess Adaline," a woman's voice calls from across the room.

I turn my gaze in the direction of the voice and see Commander Crymm standing in the classroom entrance. She walks up to us and I feel everyone in the room stiffen.

"You have excellent control with your gift. Remarkable on your first day of training." She stops and takes a seat next to me and Alexander. Lieutenant Luis quietly dismisses himself to go work with the other students.

"Thank you, Commander," I say, trying to find the right way to respond to her.

"I knew you were going to be a fighter when I saw how you defied Linda during Molly's interrogation," Commander Crymm says.

"I must admit, I don't follow orders very well," I say honestly.

Alexander tries to suppress a laugh. He's the only one who seems at ease with Commander Crymm here.

"Is that so?" Commander Crymm asks, her voice holding a joking tone.

Alexander nods and says, "You can't tell her to do anything."

I want to yell at Alexander for saying something like that to the Commander. Doesn't he understand that she's going to be giving us orders, and he just told her I can't follow them.

"Oh well, that's not entirely true," I say, trying to stay in the Commander's good graces. "They just have to be orders I'd agree with." I wince as I say the words. That didn't sound any better. Honestly it may have been worse.

Commander Crymm studies me for a moment. "I should tell you that defying orders from your superiors is not advised."

I quickly nod, hoping I can turn this conversation around.

Commander Crymm continues, "But don't lose that moral compass, Princess Adaline. Between you and me, sometimes the orders are wrong and they shouldn't be followed."

Her words feel heavy in my head as I think them over. She stands and watches me process what she has just said. "Like the orders King Renon has for enslaving the gifted," I finally conclude.

Commander Crymm nods. "Defying orders is at the heart of our rebellion. It's what we are doing when we start this war."

I look at Commander Crymm and she suddenly doesn't feel as scary or as stern. I have incredible respect for a woman who can lead an army against King Renon and not be terrified. But I feel like I relate to her more when I think about the fact that we're all fighting for the same thing.

"I'll let you get back to your training," Commander Crymm says, quietly dismissing herself. I watch her leave the classroom and then turn back to Alexander sharply.

"Thanks a lot," I mutter.

"What?" he asks and laughs through his gapping grin.

"Don't tell her I can't follow orders."

"She seemed to like that quality about you. I do too." Alexander sits there and gives me the look that says I should be thanking him. He showed the commander something he must have known she'd want to see in a savior.

Once the rest of the room finishes their testing, we swap and Alexander gets to push the smoke onto me, and the feeling of my lungs filling with ash is added to my list of things I hope I never have to experience again. Lieutenant Luis lets us break for lunch, but tells Alexander and me that we will need to move on to tracking soon. We fill our plates with food and eat quickly.

"What's it like being a princess?" Alexander teases me between mouthfuls of food.

"I'm not a princess yet," I correct him.

"Will they have you in royal classes?" Alexander asks and I squint, wondering how he concluded that.

"Yeah, how'd you know?" I ask.

Alexander shrugs his shoulders and says, "The kids in the castle in Garth went through it."

This makes me start to wonder how different Libertas is from Garth. Both have a king and are preparing for war. Are we really all that different, besides what makes up our blood?

"How are the quarters they placed you in?" I ask, turning the conversation away from me.

"Nice," Alexander says, swallowing his food. "We have people there that still cook and guide us around."

Lieutenant Luis walks up to our table, interrupting us. "Time to move onto tracking."

I've hardly finished my lunch, but I don't complain. I know how much we need to learn and how little time we have.

We scoop up our plates and drop them off at the edge of the tent before being handed off to another lieutenant whose specialty is tacking. My brain begins to feel more and more like the mashed vegetables from lunch as she begins to lecture.

We're both taught how to follow our sense of smell. She says it helps when we only focus on this one sense so we close our eyes, cover our ears, and just breathe. We try and guess the different scents or objects she has. After a while, we move outside and increase the distance between us and her.

It's a lot harder than this morning's lecture. Some things we get,

I'm particularly good at the flowers she has, but Alexander finds this one very difficult for him. I try my hardest to stay focused and learn as much as I can, but my mind feels somewhere else this afternoon and I think Alexander's is there too.

The Hounds that were hunting us back on Dather fill my thoughts. This was their specialty. This is what they are controlled into doing. I imagine how many people King Renon has enslaved with this gift and it leaves me feeling sick.

When we are finally released from training today I'm overcome with relief that quickly falls when I remember the royal classes I'll have to attend tonight. Everyone starts to depart, heading in the direction of their homes.

I watch as they all walk, dragging their feet from today's exhausting load. But they all smile, happy to be tired. It means they believe in what they're working towards, and so do I.

Chapter 12

Linda meets me at the edge of the training grounds and tells me she will take me back to my room to clean up before dinner and my royal classes. I turn and give Alexander a soft wave, and watch him head to where Libertas must have set up their houses. I hate to watch him leave, but I also feel a weight being lifted off my shoulders. The distance will help us, and I follow Linda back to my room.

I struggle with the shower in my new bathroom, wishing there weren't so many buttons and options. I miss the simplicity of my old home, but really, I'm missing my mother and Titus a little extra today. After I've cleaned myself up, I change into the simplest outfit I can find in the massive closet. Linda leads me to the large dining room we ate in the previous night, and I find it hollow with just Cooper and my father.

"How was your training?" my father asks as I take my seat with them.

"Good," I say simply and I begin to eat my dinner.

"What cool powers did you master today?" Cooper shoots, his tone slightly falling on the edge of jealousy.

"We trained in sense of smell," I say and Cooper's eyes narrow, trying to think of what we could do with that.

"Sounds lame," he finally concludes and goes back to eating his dinner.

"What did they teach you today?" my father asks and I wonder how much of the future he's really seen. Does he really not know or is he just making conversation? Either way, if it's training he wants to talk about, that's easy for me to do.

"We started by learning the fighting tactic of controlling what your opponent smells," I start. "Actually, one of the scents we practiced with was ray berry pie," I say, recalling the lesson.

"My favorite," my father says between mouthfuls of food.

"I know. It made me remember that time mother made it for your birthday." The words escape me before I can register what I've said. It's the first time I've talked to him about something that isn't the rebellion. I've mentioned home and my mother and one of my most treasured childhood memories. I curse myself to forgetting the wall I've built up between my father and myself.

My father's face stretches into a smile, remembering the day as clearly as I did.

"I don't remember that," Cooper mumbles.

"You were playing with your planes," I say, trying to dismiss the comment all together.

The recognition crosses Cooper's face and he tries to hide his growing smile. "That sounds right," he admits, remembering his obsession with those things. Amazed by the machines we'd only heard rumors about in school.

We continue to eat our dinner, filled with small talk about what Cooper did on his end and how the War Committee's planning for the rebellion is going, but I know all of our thoughts are with my mother now.

I miss her terribly, and I hope she'd be proud of where I am now. I guess I would know if I hadn't destroyed her journal. Cooper's words from the other day come back to me. *Mom would want you to forgive him.* I hate admitting it, but he's right. She gave her life so this plan could unfold. She believed in it until she drew her last breath, which means she believed in my father and the things he had to do to get me here.

I look between my father and Cooper, and even though my heart still feels like it has a hole for my mother and Titus's absence, my father and Cooper are what I have left of my family. I don't want to have a wall between my father and I. Maybe I can move past him abandoning me. The longer I'm here in Libertas, the more I understand the importance of his decision. I know I won't forget what he did, and I don't trust him in the slightest. But he's my father, and I'm his daughter.

Having this small bit of family here makes my heart feel as full as it can. From my mother and younger brother, to my father and older brother. I hope they never leave me.

Once we finish our dinner, we are quickly reminded that our royal lessons begin tonight. Linda takes Cooper and me to a small sitting room at the front of the castle. I recognize it from the night of the Welcome Parade where Alexander and I called off any future relationship. Linda instructs us to have a seat on the plush couch and she sits in the one across from us.

"All right, we have two nights to teach you everything you need to know to be the Prince and Princess of Libertas. Then, you will have your coronation, just in time for the war to begin a few days later," Linda says, reading off a piece of paper with a detailed outline of our schedule.

"You're going to rush to get me sworn in as the Prince of Libertas just to send me off to die?" Cooper jokes and the sour look that crosses Linda's face tells me she didn't find his remark all that funny.

"We are hurrying because this is your rightful position by blood," Linda sneers. "First, we'll discuss the history of royal families here at Libertas. You two are the first royal children we've ever had. King Ray was our first ruler. He led the very first movement out of Dather at the age of eighteen."

Linda stands and pulls a large blackboard up from the back corner of the room. I watch as she begins to draw out the tree of rulers of Libertas. First, she writes *King Ray* at the top with the dates *4934 - 4996.*

"King Ray led many journeys out of Dather and to the Old Libertas, but soon realized when he left to go back for more people, he left his island unprotected and without a leader. So, King Ray appointed Marvin Long to lead the journeys and he stayed behind on the Old Libertas to rule." Linda adds a branch for Marvin Long on the board.

"When King Ray passed, rule fell to Marvin Long," Linda says and adds the dates of King Marvin's reign, *4996-5012*.

"He lived to be over ninety?" Cooper asks, interrupting Linda's lesson. Most people don't live to be over sixty-five in Garth, yet the past rulers of Libertas have lived well beyond that.

"We used our powers for healing," Linda says and I remember how quick they worked on Darin and me after our losses in the ring.

"King Marvin is most well known for being the king that moved us from the Old Libertas to the island we now call home," Linda points out. "After King Marvin," Linda says, raising the chalk to the board. "Is your father."

Derith Sagel is scratched onto the board with the date *5012* written next to it.

"As King Ray had done, King Marvin knew he needed to take the throne and appoint someone else to lead the fleeing gifted to Libertas. So, he appointed your father to help lead the journeys out of Dather in 4996. When King Marvin passed, your father took the throne just like every leader before him," Linda says and sits back on the couch.

"Who was the next person to be appointed to help the fleeing gifted?" I ask, wondering who may have been making those journeys in my father's absence.

"No one," Linda says. "We have filled this island to the brim with as many gifted as it can hold. Your father, and many other Future

Holders, had seen a rebellion in our future. We couldn't bring in anymore gifted, so we trained and grew our community the best we could until now."

Linda pauses, scanning both Cooper and myself. Once a moment of silence passes, Linda assumes this means neither Cooper or I have any questions.

"Now for the structure of Libertas," Linda says, unrolling an aged map across the clear center table. Cooper and I both lean forward, scanning the beautiful artwork of the island.

"Libertas is split into counties by gifts." Linda points to each section on the map, identifying which kind of gifted lives there and I'm reminded of the book my father had given me about Libertas long ago. The memory that originally cued me into coming here resurfaces, and I remember the book had a similar map to the one in front of me, though not nearly as detailed.

"Each county on the island is led by two captains. Under the captains are lieutenants, each in charge of a specific type of gifted," Linda says and she begins to shuffle through some more papers.

I nod, finally hearing some familiar information. Max had already told me about the captains and lieutenants. I hadn't known that the island itself is actually divided by gifts, but I'm not surprised. Everything at training has hinted that there is a natural division between the type of gifted you are.

"You'll need to know each of them by name and their gift," Linda says, pulling out the rolled up piece of paper she was sifting for. When she unrolls it, it stretches just as wide as the map.

Linda dives into the long list of which captains and lieutenants pair with each enhanced sense and gift. Some I've already learned in training, but most I don't recognize. I find Captain Brutis and Lieutenant Max's names near the top of the list. I wonder what Max would think of me learning about him and his father. We run through the names and the history on repeat until Linda is pleased with how much we've retained.

"Good enough for tonight," she says, obviously growing impatient with Cooper and myself, and we slouch back on the couch. "We'll test what you remember tomorrow and we'll move on to what you're required to do as royal *children*." She seems to lay extra emphasis on the word children, but I don't argue with her.

She stands and ushers for us to follow her and she leads us back to our rooms. Once my door clicks behind me, I exhale and slide to the floor, so happy to let the silence surround me. I close my eyes and try to enjoy my first time to myself, but my vision is filled with images of the rebellion. Hundreds around me are dying. The horrific scene grows in my head and haunts me. The images of blood pouring across the ground like a river, the screams of people, too young to be dying in a war, ring in my ears.

And then there's this tapping, softly in the background. It sounds very out of place, foreign to the scene in my head. I open my eyes and the images and screams stop, but the tapping persists. I scan the room and can barely make out a figure on the other side of my clear balcony door, tapping on the glass. I stand and move to the double doors and crack them open, letting the refreshing night air seep in.

Alexander's soft face becomes illuminated from the lights seeping out of my room.

"Are you lost?" I ask, taking in Alexander standing on the balcony of my room.

He laughs and drops his gaze from mine. His blonde hair shifts in the breeze.

"Earlier, you were asking about the quarters they put us in. I thought, maybe, you'd want to see them."

His green eyes peer at me through his golden hair. His reply sounds like a perfectly rehearsed excuse to get to see me and I immediately blush.

"I don't think a princess is supposed to be sneaking out in the middle of the night," I say softly.

"I thought you weren't a princess yet." Alexander extends his hand out to me, gently resting his fingers on my wrist.

Everything in me says not to go. Especially when my heart jumps at his soft touch. Don't take this step back into this relationship. But his life isn't in danger right now. I don't need to be able to protect him tonight. I place my small and delicate hand into his protective grasp. I look from the balcony, to the ground below, and quickly teleport us down.

Alexander's eyes widen and he laughs. "I'll never get used to that feeling."

"You'll be able to do it yourself, soon," I say, and Alexander starts leading me from the castle.

"I hope so, I spent forever trying to climb up there," he says, and a natural laugh escapes me.

We walk down a new dirt path that winds further from the castle until a row of houses comes into view, each built identical to the ones next to it. Each house has a small plate on the door with a number carved on it.

Alexander starts to list off who is staying where, starting with Mio in the first house. Cinder is in the house marked with the number two. Essie, James, and Albert take up the next three homes. Zavy and Toby share the sixth house and lastly, Alexander's house is the seventh home.

There's a dark figure sitting on the porch next door, her green eyes peering out and her jet-black hair pulled into a high tail. Zavy watches us like a cat on the hunt. Alexander notices her and he tries to block her from my view as we walk up to his home.

It's a grand stone building with a steel door. The architecture is very similar to that of the castle. He places his hand above the knob on his door and I hear it click, unlocking to his touch, using technology I've never even dreamed up in my imagination. He pushes the door open and we walk in, letting the lights blanket over us. The marble theme from the castle continues through the home and into a grand living room with tall glass windows.

"They sure didn't hold back," I say taking in the elegant furnishings and gorgeous design.

"Yeah, so you can sleep a little better at night knowing that they aren't mistreating the rest of us." Alexander gestures wide to the large room.

I shoot him a playful glare. "I didn't forget about you all when you left the castle," I say brushing off his comment. "You're not staying with your parents?"

Alexander glances away from me and says, "No, I needed a place to myself." His voice is soft.

"You shouldn't push them away," I say, but I feel like it may not be my place.

"I'm not pushing them away," Alexander says harshly and I see the muscles in his face tense a bit. "I've been on my own for years now. That's what I'm comfortable with."

I let it go for now because the last thing I want to do is make him upset. I move around the living room and take in what Libertas has given him. Most of the shelving in the room remains bare except a few books. I'm sure Alexander has already scanned them with his gift. I pull a thin blue one off the shelf and see it is titled *Tomorrow*. I open the old book and skim the lines of text. It seems to be some kind of storybook.

"My mother had that with her," he says, his voice breaking my train of thought. "I loved that book growing up. She took it with her when she left Garth."

I smile, glad Alexander's mother thought to bring things from his childhood with her.

"Can you teach me how to scan objects?" I ask, waving the book in the air.

"You should really just read it," he says as he takes a seat on one of the soft blue couches.

I sit next to him and turn the book over in my hands. I look at the book and begin to levitate it in the air over our laps.

"I'll teach you to do this if you teach me to scan it," I say, striking up a deal.

Alexander laughs and grabs it, pulling the book from my vision's grasp.

He explains the steps and I follow. "First, you'll want to put one hand on the cover and one hand on the back. The more surface you cover with your touch the easier it is to pull the information."

I nod, sandwiching the book between my hands.

"Then, grasp the knowledge," he says simply.

I laugh lightly. "More specific, please."

He laughs and places his hands over mine. "All right, focus," he says, as if he knows my stomach twisted at the feeling of his hands on mine. *Focus Adaline.*

"Push your hands together," Alexander continues explaining.

I feel him press against my hands, increasing our force on the book.

"Focus on the feeling of the book's flat edge against your skin. Open your mind."

All my mind wants to think about is the feeling of his hands on mine. My brain tells my heart to focus on the book. I flip the switch in my head, and then there's a rush of information.

My head feels like someone is writing down the information at the speed of light. The story *Tomorrow* plays out in my head. It's the story of two brothers who try to change the world by changing tomorrow, until the eldest is sent off to fight in a war he didn't believe in. Together the eldest brother and his father leave for war. They never make it back, and the youngest has to bury both his father and brother. And then the last lines rush in. *We always planned on living today so we could change tomorrow, but now he's gone. His tomorrows are gone.*

And then silence. The writing in my head stops and I know I've pulled all the information out of the book. I look up to Alexander and see a wide smile cross his face.

"That's a horrible ending for a book," I say and he laughs when I confirm that I pulled the information. He takes the book from my hands and places it on his lap.

"All right, now hold up your end of the deal," he says, excited to learn levitation.

I begin to teach Alexander the theory that Max had taught me yesterday at training. I emphasize the breathing to be in sync with your thoughts and after a few minutes, the top of the book begins to lift slightly and then immediately falls back down.

"That was good, but you have to keep your focus," I begin. "When you see it working, use that to power you to focus even more."

Alexander nods and tries again, until slowly, and wobbly, the book rises in the air. After a second of levitating it, he drops it and exhales an exhausted breath.

"That's so much work, and it's just a book," he says, a little frustrated.

"It gets easier," I say, reassuring him. "It's like a muscle. You keep working it until you get stronger."

I take the book from Alexander and place it back on the shelf I had found it on earlier, and then I notice a small, old picture leaning up against the inside corner. I pick it up with careful fingers and look over the image of a small, blonde boy sitting on the wooden steps of a house.

"Scan the image," Alexander says, looking from me to the picture. I take my seat next to Alexander and try to pull the information from the photograph. It rushes in, but differently than the text of the book. Instead of writing, my mind plays out the memory frozen here.

"Sit still, Alexander," Marin's familiar voice rings over the camera. Alexander crawls around the stairs, more interested in the worms sinking in the dirt. Eventually, Alexander's father, George, walks into view and gingerly places Alexander on the wooden steps.

"Smile for the camera," he says as he steps out of the shot.

Alexander lets his wide, goofy grin I know so well spread across his face, and the memory stops, freezing right where the camera captured the picture.

"Did your mother have this with her too?" I ask

"Well, you should know that," Alexander says, nodding to my hand grasping the photo.

"Don't focus on the information pictured here. Instead, focus on the material. Read that," he instructs.

I focus again and this time the history of the image comes to me like the text in the book and it confirms that Alexander's mother did carry this with her every night of her trip to Libertas and even the date of the picture, June 9th, 5008, crosses into my head.

"She did," I say, but it comes out almost as a question.

"She did," Alexander confirms.

Silence fills the room and I know he must be thinking about his family, the ones who are here, and the ones who are not.

I take his hand in mine and lean my head against his shoulder. I try and comfort him, rubbing my thumb on the tough skin of his hand.

"Do you miss your mother and Titus?" Alexander asks me, his voice barely a whisper.

My thoughts, similar to Alexander's, are with my family.

"Everyday," I say softly.

We sit here like this, in the silence of his home, and I let myself dream of what it would be like if my mother and Titus were here with me. I'll always keep them close to my heart.

Alexander gently nudges me off his shoulder and my eyes fall open. I must have dozed off. Darkness still blankets the outside world, so I couldn't have been asleep for that long, but there's a tight pain in my neck, which means I've been asleep for at least a couple of hours.

"I wanted to let you sleep, but you should probably get back soon," Alexander says, his voice soft and hoarse.

I nod and stand, stretching out my stiff muscles.

"I'll walk you back," Alexander offers and I follow him out the front door.

My travel companions' homes sit dark in a row. The only signs of life are the crunch of our footsteps. Up high above us, the sky rings out with a low, enormous grumble. I feel the first wet drop hit my forehead.

"Rain," I say and laughter consumes me as the sky reels open and the sheets fall down on us. Immediately, I'm soaking wet, but it's the most relieved and relaxed I've felt since we arrived in Libertas. Alexander and I take off running toward the castle, him avoiding the puddles and me running straight for them.

"You're crazy," Alexander yells over the pelting rain.

"I just know how to have fun," I say, running past him with my arms spread wide. My wild laughter layers with the thunderous roar of the sky above.

"I love rain!" I scream to the world and splash into the nearest puddle. The sky echoes back to me and lets out another cry of thunder.

Alexander holds his hands above his head, as if that could keep him dry. I run back to him and pull his arms down to his side, forcing him to let the rain drench his blonde curls. He looks at me and a wide smile spreads, parting his lips.

Through the curtain of rain, my eyes trace his face. Wet droplets track down his cheeks, curling at the corners of his mouth.

In the bitter cold of the storm, warmth radiates from his body. Wrapping around me and crawling up my fingers that still tightly clasp his wrists.

The clouds let out another crack of thunder that mirrors my thumping heart. Alexander flinches at the sound, an excited laugh straining to be heard.

I look at Alexander, standing in the rain, laughing at me. My fingers slide down his wet wrist and I grab his hand, pulling him back into a run toward the castle. We take cover under my balcony, escaping the rain.

I turn back to Alexander, breathing deep through my wide grin. He is drenched, his hair dripping little droplets on his soft, pink cheeks.

"Do you want to come in and dry off?" I ask, gesturing up to my room.

"No, I should go back," he says, and his voice holds a little bit of disappointment.

My green eyes search his as I take in this moment. Him and I. No training or threat of death. Stupidly soaking wet. The moonlight illuminating his damp features perfectly. He takes my hand in his and gives it a light squeeze, causing butterflies to explode in my stomach.

"I'll see you tomorrow," he whispers.

I watch him turn and run back into the pouring rain until the darkness swallows him. I'm surprised hurt and sadness don't overcome me. Or that frustration at the world for keeping us apart doesn't fill my veins.

Instead, I am still as unbelievably happy as I was running through the rain, because he's alive and here. I understand now how this will all be okay. I would give up any romantic relationship with Alexander to keep him alive. I need to be able to protect him with my gift so that we can have nights like tonight. So I can dance in the rain with him.

I know my emotions are still all over the place. When it comes time to go into battle, I need to learn how to shut the feelings off. I teleport up into my room, crash onto my bed in my wet clothes, and fall back into a deep sleep.

Chapter 13

Linda wakes me the next morning, horrified to find me sleeping in my damp clothes from last night. I dismiss her and eat my breakfast before changing into another training outfit. She escorts me out to the training grounds, still lecturing me about keeping up my appearance and how I need to start acting like a princess since my coronation is tomorrow night.

Just like yesterday, Alexander and Max are waiting on the edge of the training grounds. When Alexander's eyes meet mine his cheeks flush a light red. I smile to match his growing grin.

"Which sense today?" I ask as Linda drops me off.

"Sense of hearing," Max says and he leads us toward the green tent. Alexander and I share a side glance, knowing this means a day with Zavy staring down our necks. When we reach the tent Max introduces us to Lieutenant Grey and I remember her from my royal class the night before.

"Welcome to your day of training in the sense of hearing," Lieutenant Grey says as she leads us into the green tent. "We have three subcategories here. A Communicator, a Sound Waver, and

Noise Absorber. You'll tackle the last two this morning, and communication after lunch."

We walk into one of the draped off classrooms and everyone turns to see us except one girl in the front. *Zavy*. I assume she heard us coming.

Alexander and I take our usual seats near the front and Lieutenant Grey begins to ramble on about the theory behind being a Sound Waver; how you can use it to make those around you deafly quiet. She says it's a good tactic when sneaking up on someone.

You can also make them hear a high pitch scream that will destroy your opponent, and I remember how Zavy did the same to me in the ring.

Zavy had said she was a Communicator back when we were on the same team, which means she's already started to master her other abilities.

We partner up and test the silent wave, and I find it therapeutic to blanket myself deaf to the world. Lieutenant Grey then has us try to throw music into the head of our partner. I look to Alexander and play the tune of *Stay*, the song my father sang to me the night he left, and the one we sang the first night at Cooper's camp. Then, we switch.

Alexander sends a song that I can't quite place right away. The instruments remind me of the Welcome Ceremony from the other night. Strings and flutes mix into a beautiful tune. Images of Alexander and Zavy spinning to its melody flash from my memory and I'm taken aback.

"What song were you trying to send?" I ask, anger slowly rising.

"I was just sending *Stay*, again," Alexander says.

I whip around and catch Zavy sending me a wicked grin.

"What is it?" he asks and I brush him off.

I won't engage with her. I won't let her play with my emotions.

Lieutenant Grey then switches with another lieutenant who's specialty is being a Noise Absorber. I miss her name but know it's stored somewhere in my memory.

Being a Noise Absorber is all about tracking and it's similar to tracking with smells. Alexander tends to do better than I do, though my focus seems to be elsewhere right now. We move outside and see how far we can hear. We try to move around and see if our partner can hear the path we take.

After tracking, we break for lunch and Alexander and I take our seats on the outskirts of the tent. We eat our lunch in mostly silence, letting the exhaustion from this morning's lessons settle.

The rest of the people training in sense of hearing sit around the tables in the center, with Zavy at their core. They seem to worship her. I guess the fact that she beat the savior has made her famous.

I take my fork and spear a piece of meat on my plate.

"Everything all right?" Alexander asks.

"They're acting ridiculous," I say, rolling my eyes at everyone fawning over Zavy. "I let her win more than she actually won," I say, before eating the meat and stabbing another piece. "I'd beat her if we fought again," I say more to reassure myself than Alexander.

"I'll put you to the test." I turn and see Zavy standing over my shoulders.

"Keep your ears to yourself," I spit back and turn away from her.

"You think you're all special with your multi-gifts, but I think we all know how much of an act *this* is," she says, adding emphasis on *this* and I know it's a shot at Alexander and me. I don't know who told her that Alexander and I broke off any future together. I assume maybe he did the night of the Welcome Ceremony.

The tent has fallen quiet and I'm sure everyone is listening in on our conversation. I slide my chair back and stand, my height allowing me to tower a whole head and shoulders over her.

"Show some respect to the Princess of Libertas," I say, my voice smooth, and even I convince myself I'm royalty.

Zavy steps back and her face hardens. "I don't bow to anyone," she says, her voice low. "And you're not a princess yet." She flips her hair over her shoulder as she walks away. Her last comment rings out in everyone's ears as she uses her gift to send it out. "Don't look now, our savior is trying to fool you into thinking she's royalty. I wouldn't bow to her if my life depended on it."

Everyone's eyes are on me and I feel their judgment trying to figure out if I really deserve the title I've been given.

I take my seat again and turn away from their prying eyes as my cheeks flush pink. I feel a wall of silence fall over me and I look up at Alexander who's pushing it around us.

He says his words so only I can hear. "You'll prove them all wrong, Adaline." I nod and he lets the silent blanket fall.

After lunch, another lieutenant, whose specialty is being a

Communicator, leads us to our final training room for today. She enters with a long leather rope in her hand. Whatever is on the other end sits just behind the desk at the front of the room.

"Welcome to communication training," the Lieutenant's voice rings.

I tense, not taking my eyes off what could be behind the desk.

"One of the best ways to practice communicating, is with animals." As she says this the animal on the end of her leash jumps up and its mane puffs out around its face. "This is Mindy, and you will practice communicating with her."

The giant cat tosses her head back and forth before letting out an enormous yawn, showing off her large teeth and long pink tongue. A sweat breaks out on the back of my neck. I'm sure this lieutenant can control this beast, but I don't trust it not to turn us into an afternoon snack.

"The first thing we'll do is take turns saying hello to Mindy." Suddenly the lion turns and lifts her paw in Zavy's direction. "No showing off, Zavy," the lieutenant teases.

Zavy just shrugs her off. "This one's my specialty."

I scoff under my breath. "Teacher's pet." A couple of people sitting around me laugh a little.

The lieutenant then breaks into the theory behind communicating with animals before we take our turns talking with Mindy. Some people get her to raise her paw, but most get a questioning head tilt or a large yawn.

Alexander steps up and Mindy lets out a low purr as she tilts her head down to him. Many people in the room congratulate him, but the confused look on his face makes me think he wasn't sure what he did. The lieutenant has a questioning look on her face, but doesn't say anything.

I step up next and look into Mindy's golden, wild eyes. I try to push a simple greeting toward her. I watch her eyes shrink into slants and she lets out a low growl. The room falls quiet except for someone snickering in the back.

The lieutenant steps up next to my side and says, "Try again."

I swallow and try her theory again. Mindy lets out another low growl. She pulls back the corners of her mouth to reveal her sharp teeth.

I feel the lieutenant tense next to me, but I don't dare look away from the big cat, afraid she may pounce at any given moment.

"Try again, but make sure she can only hear you," the lieutenant instructs, and I catch a jet-black ponytail flip out of the corner of my eye, and suddenly it makes sense.

Alexander didn't speak with Mindy, Zavy did, and she's doing it now, hoping it'll pounce and slit my throat before the lieutenant can step in. I take a deep breath and blanket me and Mindy in silence. Almost instantly her eyes widen and she sits back up in her poised position. As hard as Zavy may be trying to infiltrate my silent blanket, I am stronger.

Again, I push out a greeting to Mindy and a warm, smooth voice fills my head. "Hello, Adaline," Mindy says as she lifts her paw in greeting.

My smile widens. "I've never talked to a lion before," I send to her.

"I've never talked to a princess before," she says and lets out a deep purr. She bows her head in my direction. Gently, I take my hand and run it through her long, soft fur.

"The pleasure is all mine," I send to her and step back letting up on the blanket of silence.

"What did she say to you?" the lieutenant asks as Mindy lifts her head.

"She said she sends her respects to the Princess, and bowed, taking her life in my hands," I say and make sure to catch Zavy's glare.

When we are dismissed from training, everyone departs and heads back to their homes. Linda meets me on the edge of the training grounds and I follow her back to my room. Just like the day before, I clean up, not struggling as much with the shower, and change for dinner.

I pace around my room, waiting on Linda to come and retrieve me. The longer I wait, the more dread fills my veins. After an entire day with Zavy, the last thing I want to do is go have dinner with my father and then listen to Linda lecture all night.

I'm not sure what makes me decide to do it, but I slide out of my room and let my feet guide me outside the castle. I go through the side door, like I do in the mornings, and luckily find it unguarded. The training grounds are empty now. Everyone's returned home, but unfortunately for me, home isn't somewhere I can go.

I find a quiet spot on this hillside that looks down at the row of colored tents and focus on the ocean's ripples in the distance. I'll just sit here for a minute. I'll clear my head and then I'll go back before Linda even notices I'm gone.

"Are you waiting on someone?"

I glance up and see Max standing behind me.

"More like avoiding," I say and turn back to my view of the training grounds. I become very aware of the fact that I'm wearing a light pink dress and crystal flats; clearly clothes that don't belong at the training grounds. I silently curse Linda for only filling my closet with garments meant for royalty.

I expect Max to leave, but instead, he lowers himself into the grass next to me.

"What are you still doing here? Didn't training end an hour ago?" I question.

"For you, maybe. Seems like it never ends for me," Max says, dropping his voice.

I glance at him sideways. I hadn't noticed how tired he looked before. He picks a piece of grass and twirls it between his fingers.

"Who are you avoiding?" His green eyes catch my stare and I look away.

"My father," I say through a tight jaw.

"What happened?" he asks, as if my father has only done one thing wrong.

I shake my head, keeping my thoughts inside. I'm sure my father wouldn't want me complaining about him to one of his lieutenants.

I'm not oblivious. I can tell my father is trying to paint him, Cooper, and I into looking like a united royal family.

"You seem to be making great progress with your gift," Max says, changing the subject when he realizes I'm not answering his question.

I let out a heavy breath and lay back into the hillside, letting the tall grass fold around me.

"I've had some really good teachers," I say and I catch Max crack a smile.

I look at him, tracing his silhouette with the setting sun. He pulls another piece of grass and works on trying to tie the two blades together.

"Tell me something about yourself," I say.

He glances down at me, and then turns his eyes back to his blades of grass.

"Not much to tell," he deflects.

"Oh, come on! I feel like everyone here knows all about me."

"Well, you are the savior," Max teases.

"Tell me who you are," I say.

"I'm a lieutenant-" Max says, but I cut him off.

"No, I already know that. I mean who is *Max*?"

It's the first time I've addressed him without his rank out loud. I watch his face tighten, his eyes clouding with something I can't quite place.

"Sorry, Lieutenant Max," I correct. "I probably shouldn't have been so informal."

"You can call me Max," he says, and the setting sun brightens his green eyes as he looks down at me. "As long as I don't have to call you Princess Adaline."

"Please, don't!" I groan with a light laugh.

The air settles around us, and we're quiet for a second. Max goes to tighten the knot on his grass and they rip in two.

"What is it?" I ask, still feeling like I may have upset him.

He tosses the ripped blades to the side and leans back next to me. He squints at the sunset, and then turns to study my face.

"When you asked who Max is, I realized I didn't know."

Though the breeze is warm, my skin prickles at his words.

"I have spent my entire life trying to get my father's approval. I've done everything for him. I have no idea who I am."

I think of Captain Brutis and I imagine he's not that easy to please. I hold Max's wide, green gaze and suddenly I see past the uniform. I'm not looking at a lieutenant, but a young, seventeen-year-old boy.

"It's never too late to find yourself," I whisper.

The corner of his mouth turns up, and I catch his eyes glisten. "I'm working on it," he says equally as soft as my whisper.

"You know, I don't really know who I am either," I offer and my smile matches his. "The savior, a princess, an Alterken," I list off my titles. "None of those feel quite right. A girl who lost her first fight in front of the entire army? Yeah, that sounds more like me."

It's a joke and we both laugh about it, but a bit of it hits too deep.

"Weren't you and that girl supposed to be friends?" Max asks and

I know he catches me roll my eyes.

"Not anymore. I don't have any friends now."

"You have one."

My gaze flutters up to his. Max bites his bottom lip, and his eyes study my reaction.

"Who? You?" I joke and my smile widens.

Max tosses his head, looking away and I catch the red blush rise on his cheeks. I sit up, coming back to his level.

"Do you mean that?"

Max's eyes lift up and lock on my wondering stare. His smile softens and his words are so genuine they make my chest ache.

"I do."

I'm not the type to let people in. I like my walls and Zavy has proven why I shouldn't trust people, but Max is forcing me to fight all of those instincts.

"Adaline Sagel!" a woman's cry echoes behind me.

I curse under my breath. I've been gone too long.

"I need to get back," I say.

Max stands first and lends me his hand, I take it, and he pulls me to my feet.

"Long night ahead?" he asks, noticing the dread in my voice. He carefully pulls a piece of grass out of my hair, and his fingers brush against my cheek.

"Just dinner with the family and hours of Linda lecturing me on how a princess should walk, or sit, or eat, or whatever." I huff a frustrated sigh.

"Adaline!" Linda yells again.

Max takes this as his cue to let me go. "I'll see you tomorrow," he says before turning and heading down the cobblestone road, away from the training grounds.

I trudge through the grass and find Linda leaning against the doorframe I had slipped through earlier. Her face is as red as the setting sun.

Linda scolds me all the way to the banquet hall, reminding me that we are on a schedule at all times. The meal is a simple soup with buttery bread. The more of the meal I eat, the closer we are getting to another night of royal classes, and the thought causes me to eat as slow as possible. When we reach the inevitable end of our dinner, I know I need to do something other than sit in a room with Linda lecturing me late into the night.

"I'd like to see what you plan to do with the civilians that aren't going to fight in the war," I say at the end of our meal as Linda is arriving.

I'm more interested in what's going to happen to Molly. Everyone else from our group, besides her and Toby, will surely be returning to Dather, but she is too young and defenseless. I know most people would want Molly out of here, so I need to be sure she's going to be safe.

"Linda," my father nods, welcoming her. "Please arrange to take Adaline and Cooper out tonight for their royal lessons."

Linda glances down at the stacks of papers in her hand and she presses her mouth into a thin line.

"There's too much we need to discuss before tomorrow," she says, flustered that my father has asked her to change the plans.

"It will be all right," my father says, trying to keep her calm.

Linda seems incredibly annoyed at the idea of wasting time, but motions for us to follow her. "So, you want to know what's going to happen to the rest of us?" Linda asks. She drops off her large stack of papers that I'm thankful to be avoiding. We exit the castle and load onto the back of a small wagon pulled by two fierce black horses.

"I just want to know what will be happening here. I want to make sure this island will be secure."

The wagon starts to pull out of the castle and work its way down the winding stone roads. We pass through the town square where the stage had been set for my Welcome Ceremony. The square is quiet tonight, except for some distant music. I don't see hardly anyone out. Just a few shadows sliding behind the buildings.

"It may seem like a hasty approach, but we've been planning this for years," Linda explains. "Everyone who has chosen to fight will be going to Dather."

We've made our way out of town and I see us come level with the ocean.

Cooper nods next to me. He's been helping them plan the war so I assume he already knew this. The horses begin to pull the wagon along the coastline.

"No one will stay here to defend?" I ask, shocked. The wagon starts to slow as we pull up next to a rocky cliff that towers over us. The sand stretches from it and goes out to touch the blue water.

"Our strategy is to hide, conceal ourselves." Linda moves from the wagon and Cooper and I follow her. She walks up to the base of the rocky wall and places her hand lightly against the cool stone. There's a soft click and I watch as she pushes against the stone. It swings in like a door. I never thought about what gift Linda has. I assume now she has an enhanced sense of touch.

"These are the Libertas bunkers," she says and her voice echoes in the dark tunnel.

She moves her hand along the wall and the lights above our heads flicker on. They illuminate the long stone tunnel that stretches back as far as I can see. Along the stone walls, on either side, are tall metal doors. Right now, they are all propped open. The air is thin in the empty, underground tunnel.

Linda leads us into the nearest room and the clicks of our feet echo down the chamber. The room surprises me. A lush, soft carpet is laid down on the floor of the room. It's one large square space. There are two couches and a small end table on the right half of the room, and on the left there's a large wooden dining table with four chairs around it. Back on the far wall, sets of bunk beds are in one corner, similar to the ones we used in Sard. In the other corner is a large, regular bed. There's a multitude of closets and cabinets for storage around the space.

"The bunkers are empty now, but we'll begin moving people in soon. Each family will be assigned their own room," Linda says from the doorway.

It's nicer than any bunker I could have imagined. "What else do you have down here?" I ask, turning to Linda. "Will everyone just stay on lockdown until the war is over?"

"Follow me," she says and motions for us to walk with her. We make our way deeper into the tunnel and pass numerous other rooms identical to the first one Linda showed us. The tunnel stops and splits at a crossroad. We turn to the left and after a moment, Linda opens a door on the right side of the tunnel. Inside are rows of wooden desks that are similar to the ones on the training grounds.

"School will be taught on a regular schedule," Linda explains. "We have multiple rooms and will divide by age."

I start to feel my tension ease away, knowing the living conditions are comfortable, and Molly will continue to get an education.

"We're going to try to make this as comfortable as possible for the children," Linda assures me again.

My eyes scan the classroom and land on the green board on the front wall. In faded chalk, I see the words *Ms. Essie.* "She's staying?" I turn to Cooper.

"She asked to, we need a teacher," he explains.

"Libertas has teachers," I argue.

Cooper puts his hand on my shoulder. "Not enough since most will go with us in the rebellion."

I let the silence hang in the air and finally say, "She did always want to be a teacher."

My eyes brim with tears, remembering her and her sisters laughing together one night on our journey here when Essie told me her dream was to be a teacher. I wish her sisters were alive to see she did it. I decide not to say anything more about Essie staying because I'm happy she won't be on the battlefields. She signed an agreement to serve Libertas in this war, and I'm glad she found the safest way to do that. I'm sure some of the people who stay here won't be happy about it, but if they aren't fighting either they can hardly complain.

"Show her the kitchen," Cooper nods and leads me from the classroom. We walk back toward the crossroad in the tunnel and continue in the other direction.

"These rooms," Linda says, and motions to the sides of the hall lined with doors, "will all store food. Each chamber is designed around what it will hold. Some are kept cool for meats, and the grains room will be kept dry." I nod and we come upon a double door at the end of the tunnel. Linda pushes through them and I'm led into a massive kitchen. "This is where all the food will be prepared. We'll have a team that will plan meals, one that will do all the cooking, and finally, one that will deliver food to either the rooms or classrooms.

"It looks like you thought of everything," I say and we walk back to the crossroad of the tunnel. "And this way?" I ask, pointing down the last strip of the chamber.

"Command Center," Linda says. "We'll communicate with your father and the Commander Crymm at all times."

"And training," Cooper adds. "They'll be training everyone down here in the basics of their gifts and combat in case they are ambushed."

Linda sees the hesitation and concern on my face. "She's going to be fine," Linda says softly, talking about Molly.

"Can I see her?" I ask with a shaky voice. Linda nods and leads us out of the bunker and onto the wagon. We are taken toward one of the counties and stop outside a large stone house.

"She's been staying with the Mills. They take in a lot of kids who may have come here without their parents or whose parents may not have survived the journey."

I scan the tall building with warm golden light glowing out its windows. We walk up the stone stairs and Linda knocks lightly on the yellow wooden door. A tall woman answers with short, thin, brown hair.

"Princess Adaline. Prince Cooper," she says, surprised to see royalty on her doorstep. She drops into a low bow and gestures for us to enter her house.

"We're not really," I begin to say, always so quick to deny the title I will hold in less than twenty-four hours. "Not yet," I say softly and we enter the woman's home. "I just wanted to check in with Molly," I say, explaining our visit.

"Oh, of course," she says. "She has gotten along with the other children very well." She leads us down the narrow hall and into a large dining room where five kids sit around a large wooden table.

"Adaline!" a young voice squeals. I watch as Molly leaps from her chair and clings to my side. "Hi Molly," I say and gently squeeze her back.

"I heard you're a princess now!" she says, excited.

I laugh. "I will be tomorrow."

"What are you doing here? Am I leaving?" she asks and I see worry flash in her eyes.

"No, I just wanted to check in and make sure you're okay," I explain.

"Oh, I'm having so much fun. These are my friends," she says and gestures to the other kids. I scan their shocked faces, equally as surprised to see the prophesized savior in their home.

"What are you working on?" I ask and stand to follow Molly back to her chair.

"Homework," Molly mumbles and I crack a smile.

"They have you in classes?" I ask and she nods.

"I haven't ever been to school so I'm a little behind everyone, but I'm still having fun."

I laugh and just sit with her, helping her with her homework. After a while, Linda gives me a glance that says we've overstayed our visit.

"I think I've got to go," I say softly and Molly's wide eyes look to mine.

"Thank you for bringing me here," she says and hugs my side again.

I look from her to the other kids sitting around the table. She really has gotten to start over. She's making new friends and she has a real family. I know that I need to let her go, let her be a part of this new life they've given to her. I can't come back and see her, to remind these people how different Molly is from them. I trust the

Mills to take care of her now.

"You may not see me for a while because I'm heading back to Dather in a couple of days," I explain and kneel to be at her height.

Tears fill her eyes, but I can tell she's fighting to hold them in. She's trying to be stronger than a ten-year-old should have to. I know that feeling all too well.

"You'll stay with the Mills and they'll take care of you." I pull Molly into another tight hug because I don't want her to see me cry.

When Linda, Cooper, and I leave, I finally let the tears fall. We ride back to the castle in silence and my thoughts are filled with Titus. I wish I could have saved him too.

Chapter 14

I don't remember much of the ride back to the castle. Linda decides we've done enough for tonight and doesn't continue our lesson any further. I can tell she's a bit wary of doing this. Our coronation is tomorrow and we don't know the first thing about it, but she decides there will be enough time tomorrow to discuss it.

She drops me off at my room and tells me she'll be by in the morning. I'm told to get lots of rest because a princess should not look sleep-deprived on the night of her coronation.

The air in my room feels heavy and even though it's the most spacious room I've ever had, I feel like the walls are closing in. I pull open the two glass doors to my balcony and hope the fresh air will help. There are two cushioned chairs in either corner of the balcony and I take a seat in one. The cool air from the ride back and sitting here on the balcony has helped my mind drift from Titus, but my heart still has a small ache in it.

I look out into the dark island night. I haven't taken much time to enjoy the view from my new room since I don't spend much time here. From up on the mountain that the castle sits on, I can see the descending island side. I look over to the left and can see the majority of the training grounds, and to my right, I can barely make out the homes where my traveling group is staying. Stretched out in front of me is a beautiful garden. Flowers of every color bloom on the full bushes and tall plants. There's a small fountain in the center where a soft trickling of water echoes. But the fountain is no comparison to the roaring ocean.

Just beyond the garden, the level ground drops off into rocky cliffs and a thick forest of palm trees. Over the tops of the trees, I see the ocean, roaring with white foaming waves. Even from up in the castle, the sound is magnificent.

I close my eyes and lean back into the chair, letting the lullaby of waves settle my mind.

Clink

My eyes bolt open at the sound of something hard hitting the wall above my head.

"What?" I ask to no one, just as another small stone flies up over the edge of my balcony and hits the castle wall.

I rise and lean over the railing of the balcony. A tall boy stands in the shadows, dressed in black from head to toe. I watch him step forward into the moonlight and see that it's *Max*. He raises his finger to his lips, telling me to stay quiet, and motions for me to come down to the ground.

I look over my shoulder, into my stuffy empty room, and jump at the idea of leaving. I teleport down to Max's side, and when I appear, he clamps a hand over my mouth before a flash of light blurs my vision. The next thing I know we're standing in the town square.

"Are you trying to kidnap me?" I ask and step back from him, but his kind eyes show his intentions are not that.

"You left willingly," he says. "I thought you would like to experience a night out in Libertas before you're sworn in as the Princess."

I glance around the deserted town square. The shop doors are locked tight and the windows are dark. Something tells me Libertas doesn't have a lot going on at night.

"A night out?" I question.

Max extends his hand to me without offering an explanation. I debate about refusing it, but curiosity takes over. I place my hand in his and he leads me toward the shops. We turn down an alley that runs between the bakery and the seamstress and maneuver around the clutter of bikes and crates. At the end of the alley is a tall cement wall lining the backs of the stores. I think this alley is a dead end, but there is a thin gap between the buildings and the cement wall and Max begins to slide into it.

"Okay, now you have to explain. I'm not going back there otherwise," I say, finally letting my common sense speak.

"Listen," Max says.

I let the quiet night ring in my ears.

"With your gift, reach out," he instructs.

And then I hear the music.

Max sees my eyes widen. "Come on!"

Together we slide between the buildings and the cement wall

until we come to a wooden door. Max pushes the door open and I follow him into the back of the store. I've lost my bearings on where we end up, and can't remember what shop this could be. The room is dark, except for a single lantern hanging next to a black, metal door.

"This is the best place to be any night in Libertas," Max says, but the dark, musty room isn't too convincing. "Well, not here. There." He gestures to the door.

I approach the black, metal slab and try to pull it open, but it doesn't budge.

"You're not in the system yet," Max mumbles and slides his hand onto the door handle. At his touch, it clicks and he eases the heavy door open.

"Who has a party behind a locked door?" I ask.

"Someone who doesn't want authorities knowing about it," Max says and he begins descending the staircase.

Behind the door are steep, stone steps, and at the bottom hangs a single light. I pull the door closed behind me and follow him down. I'm beginning to feel like this may not be somewhere I'm supposed to be, and when we reach the bottom of the stairs I start to hear the music growing louder.

I continue to follow Max down the short cement hall. At the end, two heavy blue curtains hang closed. The thumping in the ground shakes harder with each step. When we reach the blue curtains, I feel like the drumming is shaking my whole body. Max parts the curtains and pulls me in.

The first thing that registers to me is the blaring music. It has a deep beat that shakes the whole room, and its melody is high and sharp. I've never heard anything like it. Next, the lights, flashing in every direction, coming from all corners of the room. They change in colors and shoot rays across the space. Then, I see the people. So many people. There are red velvet couches lining the two side walls and placed next to various clear tables. Some people sit here, enjoying a golden liquid in their small glasses, but the center of the room is a sea of bodies. All of them are dancing and shifting to the beat of the music.

"This is the Underground Kingdom," Max says, his voice barely overpowering the music.

"And it's hidden underground because," I question, my voice straining to be heard.

"Your father's curfew regulations," Max says, looking at me like I should have known that.

"I'm not sure I should be here," I say as some of the dancing bodies let their eyes linger on me.

"You're not a princess yet," Max says, a wild grin spreading on his face.

Linda would throw a fit if she knew I was here. But Linda doesn't know, and what Linda doesn't know won't kill her. Max lifts his hand again, waiting for me to accept his invitation. My lips press into a thin line and I glance around the room again. I'm sure one fun night out wouldn't be all that terrible. So, I take his grasp and he pulls me deeper into the room. He leads me to one of the empty, plush, red booths. I take a seat and lean on the clear glass table. A server appears instantly, asking what we would like to drink.

"Your usual, Max?" he asks, but Max shakes his head.

"Just water tonight."

The server nods and turns his attention to me.

"Water's fine," I say, following Max's lead.

The server nods and two glasses of water appear on the table, something only someone with an enhanced sense of sight could do.

"Let me know if you need anything else," he says before teleporting from sight.

I raise the cool glass and sip on the water, letting the ice cubes bob around inside.

"What's your usual?" I ask Max, curious now.

He grins and says, "Grape Berry Syrup."

My eyes narrow, unfamiliar with the name. I assume it's a specialty drink here in Libertas.

"You know, you should try it," Max offers and glances around the party, looking for the server. Something tells me he probably won't find him.

"Oh, I don't like alcohol much," I mumble softly, and I think my words may have gotten lost in the music.

"There's no alcohol in it," Max says, surprised at my comment.

I feel my cheeks blush red. I had just assumed.

"You've tried alcohol?" Max asks and he raises his eyebrow curiously.

"No," I admit and shake my head. "We didn't waste money on it," I explain, remembering how we lived payment to payment while my father was there, and with very empty stomachs when he wasn't. "Those who did, though, weren't much fun," I say, taking another sip of my water.

Max peers at me over his cold glass, his gaze wanting me to explain.

"My father got into a fight with a guy leaving a bar once," I say. "My father, Cooper, and I had gone out for ice-cream. One of the very few times," I add. "And this burly man stumbles out of the bar right into Cooper, knocking his ice-cream to the ground. My dad was so angry," I say, remembering him yelling about how he had saved that money for weeks. "And the drunken man punched my father right in the face."

"No," Max says, shocked.

I nod and take another sip of the water, the memory leaving a sour taste in my mouth.

"Completely ruined that night and my father never took us out for ice-cream again. So, I don't have the best opinion of alcohol and what it does to people." I set my glass down and lean back into the plush fabric. "What about you?"

Max shakes his head hard, finishing off his water. "I've tried it, but I don't have the stomach for it."

"So what do you do here?" I ask, gesturing to the room.

"You get to be someone else," Max says and I tilt my head, wondering what he could mean. "On the training grounds, I'm a lieutenant. I'm leading people into a war." He swallows hard. "But here, you can relax. No one is looking to you to make any hard calls.

I can have normal conversations and dance like an idiot to bad music, and no one cares."

A laugh escapes my locked lips.

"What?" he asks through a wide grin.

"You dance like an idiot?" I ask and tilt my head toward the dance floor.

He laughs and rolls his eyes softly, wishing he hadn't said anything. "I'll definitely need some Grape Berry Syrup if you're going to try to get me out there."

Just as the words escape his mouth, our waiter teleports in front of us, holding two fizzing purple drinks. He places them on the table and vanishes.

Max raises the glass in the air, preparing to make a toast.

"To dancing like idiots," he says and I raise my glass to his.

"To dancing like idiots," I repeat and the clink of our glasses rings.

I put the fizzing drink to my lips, the purple bubbles tickling my nose. Its sweet scent makes my head pound. I take a sip of the Grape Berry Syrup and squeeze my eyes shut at the insanely sweet glaze.

I hear Max laugh at my reaction. "Pure sugar," he says, taking another swig of the drink.

"I've never tasted something so sweet," I admit, and even though I'm not sure I like it, I keep sipping the drink.

When I've emptied the glass, my head spins in a rush of sugar. Max and I are both laughing hysterically for no reason, and soon find ourselves out on the dance floor. We mix and fold into the crowd of people. The deep beat and ringing melody twist and turn the bodies on the dance floor. I understand what Max means by getting to be someone else. Even with so many people around me, I feel like there are no eyes on me. Hidden in the sea of bodies, I just let go of the war and my soon to be royal title and let myself become the music.

Max stays by my side, always. He's sure to never leave me alone in the mix of unfamiliar faces. His skin brushes mine every once in a while to remind me he's here. After moving through the crowd we find ourselves washed out on the edge of the floor. Here, the room is cooler and I suck down the refreshing air.

I let my eyes scan the edges of the room, trying to take in every detail because after the coronation tomorrow, I'm sure I'll never get to come back here. When my eyes sweep past the royal blue curtains at the entrance to the room, they lock on Alexander's green stare.

What's he doing here?

The curtain shuffles and Zavy steps in behind him.

What's he doing here with her?

Max steps closer to me and I see his gaze has found them too. I turn and pull him by the arm, back into the sea of bodies. I don't want to let Zavy and Alexander ruin the first good night I've had since getting to Libertas.

I force my mind not to jump to conclusions and just keep getting lost in the melody of the music. Unfortunately, Alexander seems to want to do the exact opposite and immediately comes to find me in the cloud of bodies.

"What are you doing here?" he yells over the music.

"I brought her," Max says, stepping up to Alexander.

"You came with Zavy?" I ask, and Alexander tries his hardest not to roll his eyes, but I see the annoyance on his face.

"No, Essie, Albert, and James were all invited too, but Zavy and I were the only ones from our group who wanted to come," he explains.

"Why would you want to come?" I ask, not thinking this to be the place I'd find Alexander. He seems to be searching for an answer but instead lets out an exhausted sigh.

"I don't know, I guess I shouldn't have." He pauses, glancing back at the curtain door. "I'm just going to leave," he says, turning away from me.

I feel a pang of guilt in my chest for being so quick to judge him, and I grab his wrist.

"No, you should stay." I offer a soft smile.

He deserves to have a night out just as much as I do. Plus, now that I know he didn't come here to be with Zavy, my frustration has faded.

I turn to Max and say, "Get him one of those Grape Berry Syrup drinks and let's celebrate!" I scream over the rising sound of music.

The three of us down the purple, fizzy drinks and lose our stiff selves. We forget about our titles and destinies and just dance like idiots.

Max gets overly excited when the next song comes on and tells me to follow his lead. Around us, the crowded wave of bodies organizes itself into multiple rows and then everyone begins to dance in unison. This must be some kind of popular Libertas dance because everyone seems to move effortlessly in sync. It doesn't take long for me to pick up the steps. Alexander and I fall in line with Max and our row begins to flow in unison. Stepping forward and back and clapping to the beat of the music. It's the most fun I think I've ever had.

My joy doubles when I see Zavy sulking on a couch on the side of the room, watching the rest of us. I notice she's sitting next to another girl with light brown hair. It takes me a minute to place her. It's the girl I sat next to in my first lecture in enhanced sense of sight. She looks equally as dejected from the party. Good, the two of them can keep each other company.

The crowd roars in applause and laughter when the song ends. It's so loud no one hears the sirens on the street until the patrol is already in the room using enhanced sense of hearing to make their voices boom, ordering for the music to be shut off.

The music clicks off and a low hum takes its place. For a second the world freezes. Us looking at the patrol, the hum of the sound boxes, and then, like a timer going off, the crowd erupts in chaos.

"We need to get you back to the castle," Max says, pulling me deeper into the room. My hand grabs Alexander's wrist and I pull him with us.

At the back of the underground room, where the wall appears to be solid, Max presses his hand against the stone. At his touch, I hear a faint click, and a section of the wall swings in.

Alexander and I follow Max into a dark, cement tunnel and he

196

pushes the stone door back in place.

"This way," Max says, and takes off running down the stone tunnel.

It's tight, my shoulders almost grazing both walls. Dim, white lights buzz above our heads, giving off just enough light to let us move forward.

"Wait," I say, and the two stop running. "Just teleport us to the castle," I say between deep breaths of the dusty air.

A grin spreads on Max's face. "Why? This is more exciting." He turns and takes off running again.

It registers to me that this is part of the fun, the adventure of tonight. So, Alexander and I keep running behind Max, letting our racing hearts fuel our feet.

We reach a stone staircase at the end of the tunnel, climb it, and emerge back in the alley behind the stores. I'm definitely more turned around now than before and have no clue where we've come up, but I continue to follow Max.

In the distance, I can still hear the sirens of the patrol. Max weaves through multiple back allies, and eventually, we come out on the main cobblestone pathway that leads up to the castle.

"That was crazy!" I say, finally letting my voice ring out now that we are far enough away from the center of town.

"I knew you'd have fun," Max says and we begin to walk back toward the castle.

"We won't get a lot of nights like this," Alexander says, always quick to bring me back to reality.

"Right, you'll be a princess this time tomorrow," Max adds, and he gives an obnoxious turn, pretending he's wearing a large gown and showing off his crown.

"Don't remind me," I mumble and I wish I could postpone the coronation.

Maybe sometime in the past I may have thought the idea of being royalty could make my life perfect, but it's just another title. It's another role people are going to be expecting me to play.

When we make it back to the castle, Alexander breaks off from Max and me and continues to walk toward his home. He glances over his shoulder, seeming hesitant to leave me with Max. I know he probably still thinks Max was the one who volunteered me for the ring, so he's still not trusting him.

Max and I walk to the base of my balcony in silence and the night air seems to become colder by the second. After the shock of the party being interrupted and running from the authorities, the buzzing high from all that sugar has worn off.

"Thanks for tonight," I say softly.

Max grins and says, "You're welcome."

He glances away from me, and his eyes look like they are searching for something to say.

"I can't imagine what you've had to go through to get to this day," Max says, deciding on his words. "And I know the days ahead are only going to get worse. I just wanted to give you one good night to hold onto."

His green eyes shine in the moonlight and his words send a wave of heat across my skin.

"Thank you," I say again and take his hand in mine.

There's a passing of warmth between our grasp, and I really do see Max as a real friend.

"I guess now that tonight's over, we have to go back to playing our roles," I add softly.

The corners of his mouth twitch up into a small smile before he steps back, letting our hands fall. "Better get back to your royal chambers, Princess Adaline," Max says, winking playfully at his use of my royal title.

My lips spread into a grin and I laugh as I dip into a poor curtsy, not nearly as ladylike as I'm sure Linda will want. "See you tomorrow, Lieutenant Max."

He gives me a strong salute and we sink back into our titles and our roles.

Chapter 15

I wake in my large elaborate bed and see the sun tracking along the wall. Tonight I will be a princess and somehow it feels like that will change me in some way. It's just a title though, I won't be any different. Linda has one of the servant girls come by to let me know I can dress casually for this morning. There's no training today, because of the coronation, and I'm told I'll get to spend my day off getting the grand tour of the island with the rest of my traveling group.

I get up and dress in the most casual clothes I can find. Unfortunately, I don't have anything casual enough for my liking. I settle on a plain blue dress that hits at my knees and my training boots. After Linda scolds me for my choice of footwear and makes me change into shimmery silver flats, she escorts me to breakfast and goes on about how excited she is to show me all of Libertas.

She says the island is small enough that we'll get to see the entire city today. While I know that the island is small, Libertas is not. They've just built up on the small island. Today will be the first time I'm back with my entire traveling group since we had dinner the other night. As hard as I try to tell myself that there isn't a separation between me and the rest of the group, I feel it anyways. The royal title I'll receive tonight won't help either.

After a quick breakfast with my father and Cooper, I follow Linda out in front of the castle where Zavy, Toby, Mio, Cinder, Alexander, Essie, Albert, and James are waiting. We all load onto a large wooden wagon that is pulled by two jet-black horses. Zavy immediately befriends the Communicator that is controlling the horses and sits upfront with him. We are taken down to the main square of the city where our Welcome Parade had led to. As we ride along the cobblestone pathway, memories from last night resurface. I smile, imagining Max and I walking back to the castle after the patrol had ambushed the party.

Today, there is no stage set up in the town square and no crowd looking to praise the saviors. A few people wander along the brick paths going in and out of the different shops. You would have no idea a party was busted here late last night.

Linda lets us get out and walk through the square. Most of my group branch off on their own to explore the shops. I think Alexander may stick by my side, but Albert and James pull him away, excited to finally see him. He gives me an apologetic smile over his shoulder and they disappear down an alley.

I drop my eyes to my feet and find the stone pathways to be very interesting. There are different names carved into each stone. I wonder what they mean as I walk along them, taking in the history of the city.

When I come to the end of written stones, there are blank ones that continue down the alleyway. I find myself outside a small and quiet shop. It's off the main stretch from the square, so no one seems to have wandered into it today. I slowly push open the door and the store's old wooden floors creak beneath my shoes. It's dark, the only light coming from the old windows arched over the front door. Dust hangs in the air, glittering in the rays of white light seeping in from the storefront.

"Can I help you?" I turn and see an older man come out from a back room. "Oh, miss Adaline, my apologies."

"Hello, I'm just looking around," I say. "What do you sell here?" I ask, scanning the store to find it full of absolutely everything I could think of. There's jewelry, blankets, bags, and so much more.

"We sell enchanted tracking items," the storeowner says. By the look of confusion on my face, he adds, "These items have been charmed. Through the power of enhanced sense of touch, you can always find these. You pick the item and we'll add the tracking sense."

"So you pick things you lose easily?" I ask and he nods.

"Or things you want to keep track of," he offers. I walk through the store, digging through the piles of items that have ended up here. "We also do it on items you bring in. A lot of this is resale items that people are getting rid of."

"I like it. Everything has its own story," I say and imagine what Alexander would think of this place. He would be in here for days, scanning items to learn where they came from. I could do it too, but that's where his gift is the strongest.

I make my way back to the front of the shop and a glint of light catches my eye from the back of the bottom shelf. I bend down to pull out a ring with two keys on it.

"Those probably should have been thrown out. I don't know what they go to anymore," the older man mumbles to himself as he walks up to me.

"They don't have to go to anything. They can still be symbolic," I say and stand up with the keys in my hand. I give them to the shopkeeper and say, "I'll take these."

He glances down and sees the key birthmark on my arm. "Oh, I understand."

I follow him to the front of the store. "Can you make one traceable by me and one by Alexander?" He nods as he removes one from the ring.

"It'll just take a minute." He turns and I watch him head into the back room of the shop. When he emerges, he hands me two keys, each on their own chain. "I thought it may suit you as a necklace."

When I take the cool metal of the key traceable by me, it feels as though it has always been a part of me. I place them into the pocket of my dress so I can surprise Alexander with them later.

I look up shocked and stumble with my words, "I'm sorry, I don't have a way to pay for these."

He cuts me off saying, "Don't worry about it. Thank you for leading this rebellion. This is the least I could do for you."

I thank him again and leave the shop. When I make my way back to the center of the town square, I see that it is flooded with people, much more than when I arrived. They're mostly kids. I find Linda by our wagon, watching the crowd.

"What's going on?" I ask, and she smiles looking at the young children.

"They brought the schools out to view the names," Linda says and gestures to the labeled bricks beneath our feet.

"What are they?" I question.

"Everyone who has ever resided in Libertas," Linda says. "I think the children are here looking for some of the names that they've learned about in their classes."

A young girl approaches me and peers up with bright blue eyes. "Ms. Adaline, where's your stone?"

I feel my cheeks flush with heat. "I don't have one," I say.

Linda nods next me, like she's just come up with the idea on her own. "We should do that today," Linda offers. "Let's get the rest of the group together and find some empty bricks for you to sign."

Linda moves through the crowd and I stay close on her heels. I notice the young girl has decided to shadow us. We find Alexander peering into the bakery with James and Albert. The three of them are trying to decide what delicacies they want to eat. Mio and Cinder are at the town's library, admiring the rows and rows of books. I wave Cooper and Essie over from a stand of tropical flowers, and finally, we find Zavy and Toby quietly sifting through a small toy shop.

"This should work," Linda says at the end of a small brick path. There is a group of blank colorful bricks. I look around the alley, loving the natural vines and flowers that are artfully growing up the store's sides. With a simple touch, Linda transforms a small pebble into a round piece of white chalk.

"Who's first?" she asks and we all know our leader, Mio, should take the honor.

I've noticed we've drawn quite a bit of attention to ourselves, and many of the students and some teachers stand back, watching this moment.

Mio kneels down to the bricked path and scratches out the three letters of his name onto the light pink stone. I watch the white chalk transform into a deep carving of his name. He passes the chalk to Cinder who signs her name next to his. As the chalk moves among my team, I watch our names carve into the bricked path here in Libertas, officially claiming our residency. It's something that will outlive us all.

Two bricks are left at the top of the list of names. Alexander goes next, his name barely fitting on the light blue stone. He stands and hands me the chalk.

I kneel down next to the last brick, a pale yellow stone. I write *ADALINE* in clean small letters and watch the white scribbles turn into a deep carving. I gently run my fingers over the stone, tracing my name.

My eyes drift down the other stones my group signed and there's a swelling in my chest. My thoughts have turned to the group members we lost at sea. The ones who spent seven years of their lives to be here, right now, and those young girls who had no idea what they were getting themselves into. My eyes fill with hot tears, thinking of the graves we left on Old Libertas. Through my blurry eyes, I see a small grey brick on the edge of the alley, unmarked. I move to it and add the first letter of each of their names to the stone.

B for Bren, *S* for Sarah, *C* for Cassandra, *A* for Andy, *S* for Sam, *L* for Lilly, *M* for May, and *A* for April.

At the end of the list of letters, I sketch a small heart in the corner of the stone. I look up at my group and many of them have tears in their eyes, their thoughts have turned to them as well.

"Gone, but not forgotten," I say softly and hand the chalk to Linda.

We back away from the carved stones, leaving the markings there forever. As we go, some of the kids push forward and examine the bricks. They take turns saying they got to touch the stones signed by the saviors and the teachers make a note of this moment to put in their history lessons. I have Linda show me my father's stone and we stop at Alexander's father's as well.

"All that time, after he left me, I had thought he was hiding in the forest, or maybe dead, but he was actually here," Alexander says, rubbing his shoe on the stone.

"Mine too," I say, my father's name staring back up at me.

The history and memories fill the town and act as a constant reminder of what this island has been in the past and what it means for the future.

A small deli on the corner serves us lunch today. It's nice to be out of the castle and away from the training. Zavy and Toby keep to themselves, finding a table alone outside to eat at.

The rest of us sit together inside the deli and I finally get to be with my team again. I relax in my chair and enjoy this moment. It reminds me of the dinner we had at Leo's on the journey here. Everyone is so excited about the war and the future we're fighting for.

"Derith says I may get to be a lieutenant," Mio says, grinning confidently.

"King Derith," Linda interjects.

"I knew him before he had the title," Mio says, waving her off.

"They'd let a non-gifted lead a troop?" I ask curiously. I want to tell him I highly doubt that.

"We've been talking about creating our own unit. The non-gifted," Mio says. "I've survived in those woods on Dather for seven years. No one knows them better than I do."

"Also, none of the other lieutenants want any of the non-gifted on their troop," Cinder says gently.

"So, you all will get to be your own troop?" I ask. Somehow this seems the safer option in the end. They won't be sacrificed by the gifted lieutenants during battles.

"Yes, and there's no one better to lead us than Mio," Albert says, nudging Mio.

"If I could pick my troop, I'd choose to follow you too, Mio," Alexander admits. The room seems to quiet at his statement. Mio's face softens and he gives a genuine smile.

"That means a lot, Alexander," Mio says, clearing his throat.

"I would too, but you probably wouldn't want me. I caused you too much trouble the last time," I say jokingly and a chorus of laughter shakes the room.

"You are a pain, but you're fierce," Cooper says, glancing my way.

"You can't call the Princess of Libertas *a pain*," Linda scolds.

"I can if she's my sister," Cooper says and the room laughs again.

"Essie, I heard you're going to be teaching," I say.

"Oh, I'm so excited, Adaline," she says.

I wait for Linda to interrupt us and remind her to call me Princess Adaline, but I think she's finally given up on the formalities.

"You are going to do a fantastic job," I encourage her.

"I've been shadowing some of the classes for the last couple of days. I think I'm really going to like it. I've requested to have Molly in my class." Essie locks her eyes with mine and gives me a soft smile. "I'll keep an eye on her while you're gone."

I had been struggling with the idea of leaving Molly behind. My mind relaxes now that I know Essie will be here to look out for her. "Thank you, Essie."

"Are you ready for the coronation?" Essie asks, changing the subject.

"Currently ignoring that it exists," I whisper across the table so Linda doesn't hear.

Essie laughs and gives a side glance to Cooper who's in an intense conversation with Mio over who could win in a sword fight. After I saw Cooper fight Paylon, I'd probably bet on him.

208

"Your brother's really nervous," Essie says quietly. "He's been worrying about it all day."

"Why?" I ask, leaning across the table so I can keep my voice down.

"He's overheard some people talking about how a non-gifted shouldn't wear the crown." Essie's eyes turn sad, her gaze going back to Cooper. "It's not fair. They've ruined this moment for him. When we were back at our camp on Dather, he talked about how excited he was to be in Libertas one day. Now he's here and all the gifted wish he wasn't."

I hadn't really thought about what it must be like for the non-gifted. They gave up years of their lives to be here and they've been completely treated like outcasts.

"What are you talking about?" Cooper asks, turning is attention away from Mio when he notices we're whispering.

"About how Adaline is going to make a beautiful princess," Essie quickly covers, leaning away from the table.

"What about me?" Cooper asks.

"Oh yes, you'll make a beautiful princess too," Essie jokes and laughs into his side. He rolls his eyes and playfully nudges her.

The conversation around the table continues, but for the most part, I stay quiet. I like to watch them all talk and laugh. It relaxes me to see the people I care about so happy.

Eventually, our group moves to our wagon and Linda continues the tour around the island. We go down many streets that are lined with homes. Each area is separated by gifts. The doors on the houses are painted to match the gifted that lives there. We move through all five counties of the island, and for the most part, they look identical with the exception of the colored doors.

We end the tour by going along the coast of the island. On the left, the mountains stretch high up into the sky with the magnificent castle tucked up in its peak, and to the right are endless salty blue waves.

When we get back to the castle, the sun has begun to set. We each head back to our quarters to get ready for the coronation. I take the traceable keys I had gotten out of my pocket and lay them on my nightstand. Back in my room, I'm met by the three young girls who prepared me for the Welcome Parade. Again, they curl my hair and paint my face until I can't recognize myself in the mirror. They have gone with a soft, glittery pink theme on my face and my hair is all pinned neatly up.

"I understand why you asked me to teach you how to curl your hair with an enhanced sense of touch," the one servant who fixed my hair says, meeting my stare.

"I'm sorry I didn't tell you the truth about my gift. I had just learned about it and I wasn't sure who I was allowed to tell," I say.

She smiles softly and shakes her head. "Princesses don't apologize to the servants."

"Sorry," I say on instinct and laugh. "I should have been honest, but I'm glad you aren't mad."

"You're all ready, Ms. Adaline," one of the other servants speaks up.

I move in front of the tall mirror in my bedroom and a small gasp escapes me. I look young and elegant, as I'm sure a princess should. As I blink in the mirror, I flash the sight of me in Kimberly and Leo's bathroom back in Sard. My skin is no longer covered in red patches, a thick layer of cream paint covering them. My hair is free of knots and not a single piece is out of place. The pink glitter compliments my green eyes well, making them look wider and more wise than normal.

I follow my team out of the bathroom and take a seat on one of the velvet couches in the center of my room. The girls present me with the deep, royal blue gown I'll be wearing tonight. The top starts dark black and slowly fades at the waist into the deep blue of Libertas. As they move it in the light, the glitter-covered gown seems to move on its own, like a roaring wave. I put on the gown and find it surprisingly light for the pounds of glitter it must have. It's easily one of the most beautiful dresses I've ever seen.

"The black is for Alterken," the girl who did my hair says, explaining the meaning of my gown. "Everyone will represent their gift's color somehow tonight."

Once the girls decide that I am presentable, they quietly dismiss themselves. Soon after they leave, there's a soft knock at my door and I think maybe one of them had forgotten something. I hurry to the door and pull it open, but I'm shocked to see Commander Crymm on the other side.

Chapter 16

"Commander," I say and stiffen a little.

"Princess Adaline, may I come in?" she asks.

"Of course," I say, stepping to the side to let her in. I quietly close the door behind her and join her on the couch in my sitting area.

"You look lovely," she says, her eyes surveying the work the girls had done.

"Do you need something?" I ask bluntly.

Commander Crymm lets out a sigh and rests her arms on her knees. "Can you be honest with me for the next few minutes?"

Her question catches me off guard.

"Of course," I say quickly.

"Do you want to be a princess?"

"No," I answer before I can second-guess myself. I'm surprised when I see the corners of her mouth curl up into a smile.

"Do you want to be the savior?"

"No," I answer again.

This time, Commander Crymm's mouth drops a little. "What do you want to be?"

I open my mouth, hoping to keep my quick responses coming so I don't overthink what I'm saying, but I realize I don't have an answer for her.

"Adaline?" she urges me softly. I notice she's dropped my royal title.

"I want to be happy," I say softly. "I want to be free. I know that's not what you meant by your question, but it's the truth."

Commander Crymm nods and she leans back into the couch. We're quiet for a moment and it looks like she's trying to gather her thoughts. "When I heard you speak at the Welcome Parade I thought I had a real fighter to work with."

Her use of the past tense worries me.

"Then, I saw you lose in the ring against that gifted with the enhanced sense of hearing and I had thought we got it wrong." She pauses and meets my stare. "A savior shouldn't lose to a simple girl with an enhanced sense of hearing. Especially someone who had no real training except for a few hours that morning."

My words catch in my throat. I want to defend myself, and tell her that Zavy and I were friends. I didn't want to fight Zavy. For some reason, I feel like arguing that point may make me look even weaker.

"And now, with the coronation, I can see that glittery dresses and pretty jewelry have distracted you. As your commander, I need to know where your head is." Commander Crymm's voice has grown very serious.

"I told you, I don't want to be a princess. This is just for show," I say, grabbing onto the last comment she made.

"Why should I believe that you are truly the savior?" Commander Crymm asks.

I move to show her my key birthmark, but she raises a hand to stop me.

"That mark does not mean you are the savior. It means you were chosen by destiny to become the savior, but it does not make you one."

I feel my blood burn under my skin. I've sat here and let Commander Crymm speak and undermine me. I am not weak and I am not distracted by glittery dresses.

"I am the savior because all of my senses are enhanced. I am stronger than anyone on this island. I have more power than even you," I say, my voice sharp. "I am the savior because I know right from wrong. I know that what King Renon is doing is wrong, but I also know that the hatred the people of Libertas have towards the non-gifted is wrong. I am the savior because I will not stand still. I am making a change."

I press my lips together and keep my face frozen. Commander Crymm studies me for a second. I don't know why, but I want her approval. I feel the need to have her believe in me so I can believe in myself.

"Perhaps you are the savior," she says and I feel my frustration cool, but it's short-lived. "It's time that you start acting like it, though. You let others walk all over you. You're laying low in your lectures, and you're not demanding respect from the lieutenants.

You're average and forgettable."

I feel hot tears sting my eyes. I think Commander Crymm may notice that her words have upset me because she softens her tone.

"I don't mean this to be harsh. I am trying to help you." She lays a gentle hand on my knee. "I didn't become the commander of the entire army by being average."

"Have you been telling Alexander this?" I ask, my voice quivering. "He's their savior too and we've been performing the same in our trainings."

She shakes her head. "Adaline, surely you don't need me to spell this out for you."

I'm silent, forcing her to do so.

"Alexander's presence alone demands respect. He already has everyone's belief. He's a strong soldier; fearless and courageous. It's everything they believe a savior would be. As a young girl, you must understand that you have to work twice as hard to prove yourself. I know I had to."

I nod, understanding what she's saying. "It's not fair," I admit softly. "I am just as strong as Alexander."

"No, it's not fair, but it's the truth. I sat where you did once. I was overlooked, but I had a fire burning in my chest. I wanted to make a change and to stand for something. No one wanted to listen to me, so I had to prove myself. Not just once, but time and time again. I had to give them no choice but to see me."

I study Commander Crymm for a second, and for some reason, I think of my mother. I think of how she would probably be telling me the exact same thing if she were here now. She was so strong. I know she could have helped me find the same strength inside of me. I was once terrified of Commander Crymm, but now I know I have nothing to fear.

"I understand," I say and the tears that burned the edges of my eyes pull back. Saviors don't cry.

"Good. I know you have it within you, Adaline," Commander Crymm says. "I should be going. You have a long night ahead of you."

I stand and lead her to the door, trying to find the right parting words.

"Commander?" I ask as I pull the door open.

"Yes, Princess Adaline?" she says, using my title again.

"How did you know that you had done it? How'd you know that you had everyone's respect?"

She walks out into the hall and turns back to me. "I don't know if I do." Without explaining, she turns and moves away from my room.

Her words do not give me much comfort. Could there really be people out there that don't want her to be in charge? Are people wishing someone else was leading them? Before I can unravel the conversation I just had with Commander Crymm, Linda appears outside my door.

"Oh good, you're ready," she says, checking something off on the paper she carries. "Follow me."

Linda escorts me to Cooper's room, and I find it to be identical to mine. His dark blue suit is paired with a white tie and cuffs. I wonder if white is to signify the non-gifted.

Linda sits us down and begins explaining the schedule for the coronation, but since we are the first princess and prince to be appointed for Libertas it's more or less being made up on the spot. When she finishes the overview for the night, she leads Cooper and me outside the grand ballroom where I waited with Alexander before our Welcome Ceremony.

I feel the familiar nerves return at the idea of being on display for the entire country again. I haven't gotten used to the idea of hundreds of eyes peering up at me. Tonight is even more important because it is a historical event for Libertas. The first princess and prince will be crowned. Yes, it's necessary to get things like this in order before the war, in case anything were to happen to my father, but that doesn't mean I'm any more ready to do it. Cooper seems to have the same nerves as I do. I watch him unbutton and button the white cuffs on his shirt repeatedly.

"How long do you think this will take?" Cooper asks with a shaky voice.

"You're going to be fine," I say, trying to calm him, but my voice shows my own nerves.

"I don't know, Adaline. I'm a non-gifted taking a throne on an island of gifted," Cooper says.

I had thought about it, briefly, when Essie had mentioned it at lunch. I remember the council didn't even want the non-gifted to stay here. They only agreed so they could have more bodies in the war. My father has taken it a step further by putting a non-gifted on the throne, but it's his own son. Surely the people of Libertas understand that. Cooper isn't just any non-gifted. He's a natural-born leader. He deserves this role.

"Cooper, you deserve this more than anyone else," I offer and give him a small smile. "The people of Libertas will understand that."

Cooper gives an unsure shake of his head. "I hope you're right."

Linda appears again to let us know that it's about time for the ceremony to begin. She reminds us of the main points for tonight's schedule and tells us that we should enjoy every second of it. Easy for her to say, she's going to be safely out of sight in the shadows, making sure the night plays out perfectly. She wouldn't brush it off if she had to sit on the stage and accept a crown in front of the entire population of Libertas.

As the seconds tick by, I find my nervous hands running along the glittering gown, trying to busy themselves in the passing seconds. Some of the glitter has rubbed off onto my sweaty hands so I stop messing with the dress. When I lift my hands to dust off the glitter my eyes land on my key birthmark. A princess, and a savior, and an Alterken, I repeat the list in my head.

In a matter of days, I've inherited all three titles. I feel the weight of their importance settle on my shoulders. A princess wouldn't slouch, so I stand a bit taller. An Alterken wouldn't be afraid of a few prying eyes, so I release the nerves bubbling in my chest. A savior wouldn't be intimidated by one night of glittery dresses and royal music, so I stop thinking about running away from the ballroom. I am stronger and steadier now that I have become my titles. Maybe I haven't become them, but I can pretend to be them, and that helps.

When the grand doors are pulled open, the ballroom erupts in cheers as the royal music rings overhead. The walls are made to match our outfits. On the right side of the stage, curtains hang that fade from white to blue, and on the other side, it fades from black to blue. Behind my father's throne is a wall of windows with similar curtains fading from yellow to blue for my father's gift of enhanced sense of sight. Through the room, everyone stands near their color-coordinated tables as we slowly parade to the stage.

We take our spots on either side of my father to match the walls next to us, and the room quiets as everyone takes their seats again. My eyes find Alexander first, sitting at a table cloaked in white with our traveling group. I notice a small table cloaked in black was set for him, but I know he's not one to sit alone, and I don't blame him. I'd rather sit down there with Mio and Cinder than up on this stage.

My father stands and welcomes everyone to our coronation. I find Zavy in the back of the room at a table covered in green, looking like she'd rather be anywhere but here.

The ceremony begins by my father introducing myself and Cooper to the room. He talks about the days we were born, our home, our history, before going into his own credentials as our father, and reiterating that we are his children, the rightful owners of our crowns. When introductions are over, my father pauses while two captains I recognize from training step on stage, each holding a crown on a plush fabric plate. Captain Brutis and Captain Carter stand at the side of the stage and my eyes hang on the silver crown meant for me.

"Ladies first," my father says. "Adaline, please step forward."

I stand and while my legs feel wobbly, my breathing is smooth.

"Repeat your oath after me," my father instructs and I nod. "By blood, I am this role," his voice echoes in the room.

I repeat the words, my voice not nearly as powerful as my father's, but it still commands respect.

As I say the words, I can't help but think how wrong they feel. My blood wasn't made for this role. It was made to be a quiet girl living in the fields of Garth where I'd make ray berry pie with my mother and go on adventures with my father and older brother. Where I would have watched Titus grow up.

"But I belong to this position by more than blood."

Do I? Because my blood feels less and less like my own.

"I will protect and lead you."

How can I protect a whole country when I couldn't protect my own mother and brother?

"I will fight for you, and with you."

This is true, but I fight more for those I've lost and I hope I never have to add to that list of lives I've seen fade.

"The gifted will rise. A new age is upon us," I chant out the familiar Liberats saying that Linda taught me just minutes ago and it feels awfully disingenuous.

The crowd repeats it back to me and I watch Max's father take a step forward with my crown. He lifts the thin, silver band from the felt, its finish so reflective my own green eyes stare back at me. Deep blue gems are embedded around its face. Slowly, Captain Brutis places it on my head and its lighter than I thought it would be.

"Congratulations," he says, only loud enough for me to hear, and when I lift my head I see his face is much softer than it is on the training grounds.

I don't know why he seems to accept me and is nice to me when I lost my first battle in the ring. I assume Max may have put a good word in for me, and it's odd to imagine Max and his father talking about me at the dinner table.

While he seems to be on my side tonight, I won't forget what happened on the first day of training. Someone did volunteer me for the ring and I still think it may have been Captain Brutis.

The crowd applauds and I take my seat at my father's left side. Then, Cooper stands and goes through the same oath that I went through, and this time, Captain Carter places a crown on his head. When Cooper receives his crown, it's different because he is a born leader, and I remind myself he's one of the only reasons we survived the journey here. While he may not have a gift to fight with, when the playing fields are leveled out and gifts are stripped away, he'd beat me in battle any day.

He's also actually been living his whole life for this single moment, whereas I seem to have fallen into the role. The crowd applauds again, but they don't seem to be nearly as loud for him. I do find many people out around the tables that refuse to clap. It must be frustrating to watch a non-gifted take a throne in their safe haven. The look on Cooper's face tells me that he is actually excited to be in this role, honored even, and he doesn't notice the few disapproving nods in the crowd. My father orders for the feast to be served and a large table is brought up on stage for the royal family to eat at. The plates are filled before us with cooked meats covered in rich sauces, and an endless amount of greens on the side.

I scan the room as I eat and see most people are happy, accepting the night's events. I assume most of them are just excited for a free meal and could care less about the historic night. I notice Zavy doesn't touch her food, and refuses to even acknowledge me through the entire meal.

I thought I'd be sadder to lose her as a friend, but I guess that's how I learn she was never really a true friend. We were fools to think that the seven years I spent in prison could be ignored and we could go back to the way our friendship was. My shifting eyes find Max at one of the yellow tables, sitting next to his father. Becoming friends with him has helped with the loss of Zavy. He catches my wandering eyes and gives me a soft nod. I smile back and let my eyes continue to scan the room.

When we've all finished our meals, the kitchen staff comes through the hall and clears everyone's dishes. Music encloses on the space and people move to the center dance floor to celebrate the night.

"The party's for you, you should go celebrate," my father says to both Cooper and me.

After being on stage and put in a spotlight in front of the entire country, the last thing I want to do is go down and be social, but I know my father is right. My brother and I stand and make our way down from the stage.

My first instinct is to go and find Alexander. As I shuffle my way through the crowd, I leave Cooper behind. A familiar hand closes around my wrist as I slide by a figure in a black suit with a bright yellow pin on his chest. I turn, half expecting to see Alexander, but am welcomed by Max's light green gaze.

"Congratulations," he says as I turn to him.

In the tight crowd, our bodies press a lot closer than I'm used to, but I'm not uncomfortable. I've spent hours of training with him, and last night's adventure seems to have brought us even closer. I'm becoming more and more drawn to him.

"Thanks," I say, taking a deep breath and I realize his scent has become familiar to me as well.

Max's fingers lightly rub my wrist. At his gentle touch, warmth spreads up my arm.

"May I have the princess's first dance?" The corner of his mouth twitches up carefully.

I lean into him, placing one of my hands on his shoulder and taking his hand in my other. Max pulls me deeper into the crowd and we dance around the sea of people. It's not like last night, though. Tonight we dance like an elegant princess and a disciplined lieutenant. It's the same formal dance we had shared during my Welcome Ceremony.

"How does it feel to wear a crown?" he asks over the music.

"It's lighter than you'd think." I laugh softly. I clear my throat and for some reason I confide in him. "I'm not sure it really fits," I say and I hope that he understands what I'm getting at. He nods and his hold on my waist gets a little tighter as he tries to comfort me.

"It'll start to feel better. The focus is going to move from the coronation to the war overnight." His soft reassurance steadies me a little and I'm happy he didn't judge me for taking an oath when I didn't agree with what I was saying.

"When I was appointed a lieutenant I questioned if I actually deserved the role," he says as his eyes scan me. "You are beautiful tonight," he says, quickly changing the subject.

I feel my cheeks flush with heat.

Behind me I hear Alexander add, "She is, isn't she?"

I step away from Max and turn to see Alexander. He gives Max a look of judgment before pulling me into a quick hug of congratulations.

"Do you mind sharing our Princess?" Alexander asks, twirling me out of the hug.

Max nods and turns away in silence. I watch as he sinks through the crowd and out of sight. I glance back to Alexander and he bows to me as the music changes to the next song.

"May I have this dance?" he asks, acting very proper.

I smile and position myself in front of him. I take his hand in mine and he pulls me close.

We glide together and Alexander says, "So you can like Max, but

I can't like Zavy?"

My cheeks flush red again.

"So you do like Zavy?" I question, turning it back to him.

"No that's not what I meant," he starts to say. "Do you like him?" he decides to ask, rather than go back and forth with me about Zavy.

Out of instinct I quickly deny him, but then add, "I've never really thought about it."

"I didn't think you'd leave me so quickly," he says.

"I didn't leave you, I can't be with you," I correct him. After a moment I add, "I don't need a relationship with anyone. I was just appointed as the Princess of Libertas and we are leaving to fight in a war in less than a week. That's what I'm focused on."

He eases out a playful sigh and lets the matter fall away, knowing who I like is a complicated topic.

"Technically you're a prince too," I say softly.

His lips part in a sad smile and a broken laugh leaves him. "You have a funny sense of humor."

"Do you think we should tell anyone yet?" I ask softly. With the war getting closer I feel the weight of the secret multiply.

"I think we've got enough going on," Alexander blocks. I notice we've glided to the outskirts of the dance floor. I pull him to the side of the room so we can talk more privately.

"That information could affect this war," I say, but Alexander seems to only want to deflect me.

"It doesn't change anything, Adaline. My mother and father swore me to secrecy. If they thought it was important, they would have told your father."

"What if King Renon knows?" I ask and this catches him off guard. "If we go into battle and he announces who you really are in front of everyone we'll lose the trust of all these peoples. If we even have any," I add under my breath because I really don't know who will truly follow us. "Even worse, my father could lose their trust if the king didn't know who he allowed to lead the rebellion."

"We don't have to do this right now," Alexander says and it comes across as almost begging me to let him deny his true past for just a little longer.

"Before we leave for the war, we have to tell my father," I say sternly.

I don't want to push Alexander, because this is his secret, but deep down I know if we don't get the truth out, it will come back to curse us. I wonder if my father already knows though, since he is a Future Holder. I know they can't truly control everything they see in the future. It comes to them in flashes and maybe this has never presented itself to my father. I suppose, though, if it hasn't come up, then maybe it isn't a factor in the outcome. I'd rather be safe than sorry.

Alexander rolls his eyes at my command and I watch the muscles in his neck tense, trying to hold back his words. "Whatever you want, Princess," he says under his breath. He turns away from me and disappears into the crowd. My cheeks flush hot at his remark, but I'm determined not to let him ruin tonight.

For the rest of the evening, I talk with many of the citizens from

Libertas. Some kids call me their superhero instead of their savior. Many of the teens that I talk with will be fighting alongside me in the war. Some of them I remember from training, but I hadn't done a great job of getting to know any of them. I tended to stick to Alexander's side through most of the training. He's abandoned me after I had confronted him about his true past again. I don't blame him, and I don't see him for the rest of the evening.

I do spend quite a bit of time with Mio, Cinder, James, Albert, and Essie, learning about their transition to Libertas. Like Cooper, they have been a part of planning the war. Their roles line up with what they did back in our camp.

Mio and Cooper have been planning tactics and placement of our troops with the other captain's input as well. Cinder and Essie have been sorting medical supplies and living essentials like sleeping materials, extra clothes, and even organizing the weaponry. James and Albert have been coordinating with the kitchen staff to plan what food we can bring and what food we'll be able to find on Dather. And on top of all this, they have been training in combat with swords, knives, and even archery since they may need to fight. Essie doesn't talk much about her new role as a teacher. I assume she doesn't want to say anything when the rest of us will be going to fight.

I keep an eye on Molly, watching her dance with a young boy in a stiff black suit. He has a brown pin on his jacket for his sense of enhanced taste. I remind myself to let Molly enjoy her second chance here, and keep myself from going to her. She should get to be a kid.

Albert and James ask me a hundred questions about training. They want to know everything I can do as an Alterken. More than once they ask where Alexander is tonight, but I keep deflecting the question. Essie compliments my dress and she tells me how much fun Cassandra and Sarah would have had tonight. I remember they used to always pretend to be princesses when they played dress-up. They would have enjoyed the large, elaborate event.

Essie's eyes drift from me to someone coming up behind us. I turn and see that Cooper has found us on the side of the room. He approaches us, a grin spreading across his entire face.

"The crown suits you well," I say when he reaches us, happy that he hasn't let the few disapproving individuals ruin tonight.

"I'm trying not to let it go to my head," he breathes, nerves and excitement still in his voice.

"Try a little harder," Mio jokes and laughter spreads through the group.

Mio and Cooper have gotten even closer since they've been working together in Libertas. He was really a father figure to him out in the woods for all those years. Cooper's relationship with him seems a lot more natural than with our actual father, but we're all still adjusting.

"Mio tells me you've been keeping busy while I've been training," I say to my brother and he nods.

"I was actually talking with Aiden, the Commander of our air fleet, and I'm going to start training to fight with them."

The images of Cooper running around our tiny, broken down

home with his toy airplanes comes back to me. "You've always wanted to be a pilot," I say, remembering his childhood dreams.

"I guess some things come full circle," he concludes and I can tell he's holding back his excitement to finally achieve his dream.

"Oh, you become a prince and suddenly the air fleet wants you to fight with them," Mio grumbles. "You were supposed to be on my non-gifted unit."

"I know, but I've sat in on the last couple of trainings, and I really think that's where I'm meant to be," Cooper says. Mio and Cooper go back and forth playfully bickering with the other. While I am happy for Cooper, I wish he wouldn't be out in the battle. Out where danger and death are imminent. But how can I stop him when my father and I will both be fighting? Maybe it's in our blood to be fighters, but maybe we've never known to be anything else.

When the ceremony comes to an end, my father asks Cooper and me to stand up front with him on the stage. The applause seem to go on forever. Finally, the three of us take a low bow and leave the banquet hall. Even as a Princess, Linda still escorts me back to my room.

"Your royal lessons will pick up again tomorrow night," she says before turning to leave.

I walk into my room and feel the weight of my title melt away in the silence. I place my crown on the small velvet stand that's been set in my common area before getting myself ready for bed. I remove the sparkly gown and work away at the thick makeup, each minute looking less like a princess and more like myself.

Chapter 17

I'm dreaming. I don't know how I know this, but it's clear to me that the world around me is not real. I think it's because I've been here before.

It's the night of the Welcome Ceremony.

I wander around the edges of the room, looking in on the crowd. The night seems to be glitchy or not quite steady. It jumps in fast-forward around me until the moment I see Zavy lightly kiss Alexander's cheek.

It freezes here, forcing me to remember this moment. Then, the scene changes. The floor beneath my feet disappears and I fall through a dark void until I crash onto a dusty, dirt floor. I pull myself to my feet and I'm in the arena out on the training grounds. Fear begins to overcome me, and then I see Zavy take her place in front of me. At my feet there's a glittering light. I look down and see my heavy sword from the journey to Libertas. Somehow I know our gifts won't work in this dream arena so I pick up my sword and face Zavy.

She holds her own slick, metal sword, trading in her usual bow and arrows. She wants to make this attack close and personal. She charges me and as she approaches, my brain quickly processes what I want to do. *Should I try to reason with her? Do I fight as hard as I can?* Zavy doesn't leave me much of a choice. She swings her long, slender blade at my neck and I'm forced to raise my sword to deflect the blow. She's quick to swing a counter-attack, and my only choice is to keep deflecting her moves, but for some reason, she's stronger than I am.

Her next strike is so powerful it knocks me to the ground and my sword flies from my grasp. I roll on my back, trying to get up, but Zavy's foot stomps on my chest, pinning me to the ground. I try and fill my crushed lungs with air. Zavy positions the sword's tip against my throat. And then, she *smiles*.

I feel the blood drain from my face and I'm sure it's ghostly white. Zavy moves to shove the sword through my neck and as it breaks the skin, I rocket awake.

I take in deep breaths of the night air and a sweat chills on my skin. When my eyes adjust to the darkness, I'm startled to see shadowed palm leaves hanging over me with white stars gleaming behind them. *I'm outside.* I stumble to my feet and turn around frantically. I'm in a thick patch of woods. My arms and legs are covered with streaks of mud and there's dirt pushed deep beneath my nails.

Light peers through the trees. A row of yellow glowing windows lies a few feet away. I squint and realize it's the row of homes my traveling group is staying in. My blood turns cold when I realize I've woken up in Zavy's backyard.

"Finally, you're awake."

I snap my head toward the sound of her voice. The underbrush cracks beneath her feet as she walks out from behind a thick cluster of trees. Zavy's jet-black hair shines in the moonlight.

"What's going on?" I ask as she walks closer to me, my mind racing to understand what's happening.

She stops a few paces away and sits on a fallen tree. "Well, isn't it obvious? I've just kidnapped the princess of Libertas. *The Savior.*" Her voice curls distastefully on her last words.

"Why? What do you want with me? What are you trying to prove?" I ask, trying to keep my voice steady.

I brace myself against a nearby tree, my eyes darting around the dark forest. Something isn't right. How could Zavy have broken into my room and brought me out here?

"I'm proving that you aren't as powerful as you want people to believe. You think you have everyone fooled, but not me. You don't even believe in yourself," Zavy says.

I swallow hard. She's right. I've been denying my roles and trying to pretend to be them for days now. I look at Zavy, my best friend since I was five. We used to be on the same side and I wish we still were. With everything else going on right now, fighting with Zavy is the last thing I want to do.

"I'm sorry I intervened with you and Alexander," I say, my voice weak. "I didn't mean to upset you, Zavy. I was just shocked, and-" I pause. "And I still have feelings for Alexander," I admit. "You know what he means to me," I say, remembering our journey here and how I had confided in Zavy when Alexander had gone missing. "I need him."

Zavy's eyes narrow into gleaming black slits. She stares at me for a moment, letting the sounds of the woods fill our conversation. And then she starts laughing, tossing her head back and forth.

"You think," she begins to say over her laughter. "You think all of this was about *Alexander*?"

My face cools, the blood draining away. If that wasn't what she was mad about...

"You are so naïve," Zavy says, her voice edging with anger.

She rises and crosses to me with a brisk walk. I sink away from her until my back is pressed against a cluster a trees with nowhere else to go. She closes in, her face inches from mine, and I can feel the hatred radiating from her.

"We get to Libertas, and you become royalty in seconds," Zavy hisses. "Everyone is supposed to bow to the almighty Adaline, the Savior of the Gifted."

Her voice grows louder, her words shaking her skin.

"But no one knows how little you actually did to get us all here. If it weren't for Mio, Cinder, Cooper, or me, you never would have made it here. We all bring you here, and then we get cast aside and forgotten about."

She presses her lips together, surveying my face.

"And on top of all of that," Zavy says, her voice dropping to a chilling whisper. "You get your father back. You have a family, power, and people bowing at your every move." She stops, looking to me for a response.

I want to feel sympathetic for Zavy. I want to apologize for how things happened when we got here. But years of bickering and arguing with her growing up causes my next statement to come out without thinking about it.

"You're *jealous* of me?"

Zavy backs away from me, my words shocking her. I don't miss the color drain from her face, but anger quickly fills its place.

"I will never follow you, Adaline. You are not my savior. I will not bow to you."

She turns and walks toward her home in the distance. Her feet freeze, and she turns back to me. Her temper has cooled, and a sly smile falls across her face.

"How do you think I managed to get you out here, Adaline?" she asks, tilting her head to the side. "I obviously couldn't have done that by myself."

Her words make my skin chill.

"I'm not the only one who doesn't believe in you. There are more like me that will refuse to let you lead us. We may want the same thing, King Renon off the throne, but that doesn't mean we agree on how to achieve that."

She turns sharply and disappears into the forest. As much as I didn't want to fight Zavy, she's chosen her side. She is going to make my life as the savior as difficult as she can. As hard as I'm trying to convince people to follow me, she's working just as hard to get them to follow her.

Once the woods have fallen quiet again, panic fills my veins. I need to get back to the castle. My first night as a princess and I've already broken so many rules. I drag my heavy feet through the canopy of trees, back toward the castle. I stay hidden in the forest until I've cleared the view of the houses and come into the open grounds of the palace.

Here, at the edge of the forest, is the little garden I had seen before leaving with Max the other night for the party. I walk through it and admire the tropical flowers growing around me. When I come to the small fountain in the center, I'm surprised to see little glowing white lights in the water. At first, I think it's the reflection of the stars above me, but these lights glow brighter than a reflection. They move in the water, creating rings of light as they swim around. There's a very soft humming that seems to be coming from the water, pulling me closer.

My mind becomes numb to the humming and, not knowing what I'm doing, I slowly dip my fingers into the cold fountain. There's a sudden jolt of white light that fills my vision and then a loud laugh from a little girl screams in my head. I rip my hand from the cold water, snapping myself out of the trance of the humming.

I notice an engraving on the stone ring of the fountain. *MEMORY GARDEN* is carved deep in the rock. Curiosity replaces the panic in my veins and I gently dip my hand back into the water. After the flash of white light fades, green palm trees swim into view. I see my younger self running in the woods with Cooper chasing me. My high pitch laugh fills the memory and then it changes.

Now, I'm in Ms. White's classroom, at my old wooden desk with Cooper sitting behind me. The older kids in the class are making fun of me as I draw small sketches in my notebook. They yell in annoying voices about how I don't belong in their class and how I should have stayed back in my grade. Cooper stands and I watch him punch the largest kid right in the nose.

"Leave my sister alone," he says.

Before the memory shifts, I catch a glimpse of my notebook sketches. *A key.*

The next memory is my father's birthday, the familiar night that is captured in my photograph. Except the frame of us moves after the photo has been taken. Cooper and I tumble off the couch and grab our toy swords. Of course we had been playing right before our mother had wrestled us together for the picture.

Again, the memory shifts, now to the town square. I'm surrounded by my classmates and kids from other classes that I didn't know very well. We are at the Garth Music Festival. Everyone is invited to attend and a variety of people get to play for the town. I stare off in the distance at the tall palm trees swaying in the breeze, wishing I could be under their safe canopy instead of in the crowded town square.

There's a lovely piano solo being performed by a boy I can't see from my seat in the very back of the crowd. The song he's playing captivates me and I feel drawn to the player. I stand up on my toes to see who it could be. Before I can see the, memory flashes white again, moving on to the next one.

I feel as though these memories appear to me in chronological order, getting closer and closer to now. The next memory is in the field of daisies. Cooper and I walk through them, picking some to take back to our mother.

I place one behind my ear and say, "I'm the daisy princess."

Cooper rolls his eyes and says, "That would make me a daisy prince."

"I wish I were a princess," my small voice groans as I wipe my hands on my dirty clothes.

Then, another flash of white and I expect to see something from the prison, but instead, it jumps all the way to the night on the old Libertas when Alexander woke me to eat.

"Stay," I hear myself choke out.

"Always," Alexander says.

The next memory is so recent I feel it deep in my chest. The Welcome Ceremony. The haunting dream returns as a memory this time, and as Zavy kisses Alexander's cheek I rip my hand from the fountain's cool grasp. I breathe heavy, like I had just finished a long sprint. My mind feels jumbled, and I'm a bit dizzy. Some of those memories were so long ago I had completely forgotten they ever happened. Others were too recent to forget.

I blink hard, trying to settle my racing mind. *What is this thing?* I know I probably shouldn't have been messing with it. I scan the castle grounds to see if anyone had been watching, but it's so late I doubt anyone else is awake right now. My tired eyes land on the castle and I know I should be getting back. I slowly step away from the fountain and exit the garden.

I tell myself it's probably best to stay away from the magic water. It leaves me feeling sad, and a bit scared, not understanding the power it holds. When I get back to the base of my balcony, I'm about to teleport myself to my room when I hear the sound of a piano coming from the lower floor of the castle.

In front of me are two large, glass patio doors, and one is cracked open. I push my way inside and slide into the dark foyer. I don't think I've been in this part of the castle before. The white marble floors stretch out in front of me with a dark blue carpet running down the center of the hall. As I move along the velvet strip of blue, the sound of the piano begins to grow louder.

It's a beautiful melody of six notes, repeated on a deep scale. I turn to the right, into a hall that branches off from the lower foyer, and continue to follow the music. Halfway down the hall, golden yellow light bleeds out of the cracks of a small, wooden door. Quietly, I pull the door open and gaze into the warm glowing room.

Velvet blue carpet floods the small space. Along the walls are mystical abstract paintings. No definite pictures, just a blending of colors. In the center of the room is a large black piano. He sits with his back to me, perched on the small wooden bench. I watch his fingers effortlessly float along the white keys, the same six-note scale blending together seamlessly.

"I didn't know you played piano," I say softly.

Alexander turns over his shoulder and glances at me standing in the doorway, letting the music hang in the air. His cheeks look a little raw, like he had been crying a while ago, but the tears are gone now.

"Princess Adaline, out of her chambers this late at night," Alexander teases and turns back to the piano.

His voice is softer than when we had spoken at the coronation. He begins to play the six note scale again and the music feels like it's sinking beneath my skin, its melody consuming me. All thoughts of Zavy and the memory garden fall away. My head relaxes, always so at ease when I'm with him.

I pull the wooden door closed and cross the room to the piano. I lean against its shiny black finish and watch Alexander's hands dance with the moving keys.

"Did your mother teach you how to play?" I ask and the music suddenly stops.

Alexander tilts his head like he doesn't know what the right answer is. "She took me to my lessons, but neither her or my father can play," Alexander says dropping his hands from the keys. I know he's also saying that he got his musical ability from his real family.

"Will you teach me?" I ask lightly, trying to steer away from talking about his true past again.

He slides to his left and gently pats the wooden bench. I take a seat next to him and look eagerly at the white keys. Alexander stretches his hand out to the keys in front of me and plays a simple pattern of four high notes.

"Now you try," he instructs.

I lift my hand and position it as Alexander had done. When I play the four notes, they don't sound nearly as light or magical as Alexander had made them sound.

"Not so aggressive," Alexander says with a light laugh. "Softer," he explains.

I play the four notes again and keep myself from pounding the keys with each strike.

"Better," he says and lifts his hand to the keys in front of himself. "Now we'll play them together."

He begins to play the deep six note scale. He looks at me and nods, telling me to start playing. Softly, I play the pattern of four notes and the song begins to form.

"Good. Make up your own pattern with those notes," Alexander says.

He continues to play the low scale and I accompany it with a random pattern of the four high keys. The music fills the room and swells in my chest. I know we could probably use our enhanced sense of touch to control the keys into playing themselves, but there's something more magical about creating the music yourself.

The notes seem to speak to me, telling me which ones to hit next. Something shifts, maybe Alexander changes the scale, and I feel the song come to an end. I lightly press each key one last time, ascending with Alexander's scale until the last high note softly sings.

In the drawing silence of the finished song, I feel the air around me buzzing with the energy from the music. Alexander's hand ends gently next to mine, his fingers warm against my skin. I suddenly realize why the melody was so consuming. I've heard it before. Just moments ago actually, at the memory garden. It was Alexander who was playing that day at the Garth Music Festival.

I look up from our touching hands to his magical green eyes, so close my nose brushes his. The energy in the air from the music feels like a heavy gravity pulling us closer together. My eyes flutter from his green gaze to his lips. I can feel my heart pounding hard in my chest and my throat tightens.

Just as I'm about to kiss Alexander, I abruptly stand up, reality flooding back to me

"I'm sorry, I shouldn't," I start to say, but I can't think of any words to fill the silence. I take a step back from Alexander and the piano, trying to pull myself out of the energized air. I can't do that. I know I can't let my feelings take over.

Alexander's face falls sad for a brief second before he shakes his head very slightly. He pulls the black wooden cover over the keys and stands.

"I should be getting back," he says softly and makes his way to the door.

When his hand lands on the doorknob I speak up. "Were you crying before I came in?"

He drops his hand from the knob and turns slowly to face me, but he doesn't raise his eyes to meet mine.

"I had left your coronation early," Alexander says.

"Because I asked you to tell everyone the truth," I say, but it sounds more like a question.

Alexander nods and says, "I went home." He stops short, and I see the words get caught in his throat. "You just don't understand how frustrating this all is," he finally says and I see his eyes fill with fresh tears.

"Well, tell me about it," I say forcefully and cross to him. "I'm in this with you, you can talk to me."

He shakes his head and pulls back the tears. "You won't understand," he says coldly.

"I will," I offer and I suddenly realize how much time has been spent on me, my feelings, and what I want.

"I'm the savior too, but I always feel so overlooked," Alexander admits. "Cooper gets appointed a prince, and Max has all your attention, and I feel forgotten."

My emotions mix in my chest. There's a pang of guilt for him feeling forgotten. I know I haven't done the best job checking in with him. And the fact that Zavy said something similar makes me realize it even more.

But is he really saying he's upset he wasn't appointed a royal title? I don't even want mine and Alexander is upset he didn't get one.

"You're upset you're not a prince?" I ask, but the disgust in my voice is not well hidden.

"I am a prince," Alexander corrects and I feel my skin chill. "I am the heir to the throne," Alexander says loudly.

"Dather's throne," I say and raise my voice. "The one we are fighting *against*."

"You don't get it," Alexander complains. "I gave up a chance at being the next king. I'm fighting against my real brother, hiding from my sister, and being overshadowed by Cooper and Max." The air settles and he pushes the wooden door open. "I miss when it was just you and me," Alexander adds softly, and then he disappears into the dark hallway.

His words begin to fit in my head. When we win this war and dethrone King Renon, my father will take his place, followed by Cooper. Alexander is removing his family from power so mine can take over. But no one else knows that. He can't be mad about how others treat him. But I know. It's me who should have been acting differently. I'm just friends with Max, but Alexander is jealous of him because there's a chance for more there, not that I would pursue that. But Alexander and I have no chance at all.

I run out after Alexander, and meet him in the foyer by the double glass doors. "I'm sorry," I say and he turns to face me. "I'm sorry everything has been about me and Cooper. I'm sorry it upsets you that I'm friends with Max. I'm sorry you aren't able to tell anyone about your past, having to live a lie. I'm on your side, Alexander, always." I take his hand with the key-marked wrist in mine. "We are both the saviors," I add. "We *are* in this together. It is just you and me."

His face softens and his eyes smile to match the curl of his lips. He pulls me into a quick, tight hug. "Thank you, Adaline."

When he pulls away and slips out into the night, I catch the emptiness return to his eyes. He's still upset, but he's trying to hide it, to just let it be. My gut tells me to go after him, but my brain keeps repeating the reality of our situation. I have to let him get over it on his own. I can't keep throwing myself back at him and letting my heart control my actions. I am his friend, and I would give anything to protect him, but I have to do it from a distance.

I debate about finding my way back to my room, but decide to teleport up to my balcony. I watch as Alexander shrinks further from view until he's hidden by the tall trees.

When I go into my room, I lock the balcony doors behind me, I toss and turn for the rest of the night, not ever fully finding sleep. My mind seems to always want to return to the heavy energized moment between Alexander and I, right before I let reality back in. I had never felt air like that before, and the bumps on my arms make sure I don't forget the feeling any time soon.

Chapter 18

The next morning I meet Linda outside my room in my training outfit like any other day. However, when we get to the training grounds, I'm quickly reminded of how things are different. Many people greet me as Princess Adaline now, or they just silently bow, not thinking they are worthy of speaking to me. I find Max shortly after Linda leaves me and I'm thankful he won't treat me differently. Alexander is already with him and his bright green eyes meet mine. There's no trace of sadness or the tears from last night.

I debate about telling him what happened with Zavy last night, but I decide not to. I don't want anyone to know what she did. I can take care of myself. If anyone finds out, it'll just make me look weak and vulnerable.

"Welcome to your last day of training," Max says when I meet them.

My eyes squint, confused. "We have two senses left," I say.

"Sense of Taste won't take more than a couple hours to get through," Max says and begins to lead us toward the brown tent on the far end of the training grounds. He laughs to himself at his comment, clearly undermining the gifted in enhanced sense of taste. "After lunch, you'll go to training in enhanced sense of touch and Alexander will come to training in enhanced sense of sight."

"And tomorrow?" I ask.

"Tomorrow you get to show us what you've learned in the ring."

My eyes can't help but float in the direction of the stone coliseum.

"Afterwards, all the trainees will be assigned to the lieutenant that they will follow in the war," Max continues to explain. "Then, there will be unit preparation, where we will learn the strength of those working with us, as well as getting our first assignment from the War Committee."

"The war is that close," Alexander says, more to himself.

Max leaves Alexander and me at the brown tent and when we enter, we find it mostly empty. There's only one classroom on the right side with rows of empty desks. An older man comes towards us and introduces himself as Lieutenant Baxter. I connect the name back to my royal lessons, remembering Linda telling me he is one of the oldest lieutenants here.

Very few people are born with an enhanced sense of taste. It was known as the rarest gift until Alterken was discovered. It's also the weakest as there's only one real thing you can do with this gift, be a Consumer. It's mostly used for tracking, just like touch. You can pull information out of things you eat. This is an extremely easy transition for Alexander to make. I find it more difficult than tracking with touch and don't see the real purpose of it. Still, we spend the whole morning tasting different foods and trying to tell Lieutenant Baxter who bought the food, where it came from, and when it was made or picked.

After one of the more boring mornings, we break for lunch and join the ten other people who are here, training in this sense. I find that I, like many others here, don't have much of an appetite after training all morning. Alexander and I take a seat next to a younger girl who reminds me of Molly.

She notices Alexander and I aren't eating much of the berries or meat we've been served all morning in the lecture and says, "Want me to teach you a trick?"

I look at her surprised. She's one of the few who has treated me normal today. "What kind of trick?" I ask, curious.

"You can use your gift to alter the way food tastes. So you can eat that fruit, but make it taste like ice-cream!" she says, demonstrating by eating one of her berries and I assume it must taste like ice-cream. "Just recall the taste as you eat the berries."

I take one and eat it, but find it still tastes unappetizing.

"Try again," she says, laughing at the bland expression on my face.

I take another berry and this time I pair it with a memory of myself and Cooper eating ice-cream, one of the rare times we went out to have some. Suddenly, there's a rush of creamy vanilla spreading across my mouth. My eyes widen, and while I'm still chewing, I say, "That's so good!" forgetting all the manners a princess should have.

"What's your name?" I ask and she tells me it's Ziphler but most people call her Zip. I eat the rest of my meal, turning the taste into ice-cream and the rich meatloaf from Sard. "Why weren't we taught this in training this morning?" I ask Zip.

She replies, "Baxter finds it more of a novelty act than a skill to be trained in."

I laugh and think about how I'm more likely to use this than tracking when it comes to sense of taste.

"Will you stay here and continue training after we leave for the war?" I ask her, remembering the bunkers Linda had shown me a couple of nights ago.

She shakes her head hard. "Absolutely not, I will be going to fight with you."

My eyes widen. "You're just a kid, they wouldn't let you go fight."

"I'm fourteen, just old enough to be allowed to go," Zip says proudly.

My mouth feels dry. She's only two years older than Toby. We can't send kids into this war. We can't possibly need bodies that bad. The numbers quickly run through my head and my heart drops. Dather's army is probably already twice the size of Libertas's so we do need bodies, but this isn't right. Especially kids with an enhanced sense of taste. Their gifts won't do anything in the war.

"I want to go, Princess Adaline," Zip says, seeing the emotions on my face. Before I have time to answer, Max appears over our table.

"Ready to move on to your last sense?" he asks, gesturing for

Alexander and me to follow him. As we leave the tent, I glance over my shoulder at Zip, carelessly still turning her berries into ice-cream.

Max takes me over to the orange tent first. As we walk, he already starts explaining sense of sight to Alexander.

"I'll work with you today, try and get you through the most important parts," Max says.

Alexander nods, but he doesn't look too thrilled to have to take orders from Max.

Lieutenant Linx, who worked with Alexander the first day of training, meets me outside the orange tent. I had misjudged his tough demeanor, and he's actually a great teacher. He asks if I already know anything about sense of touch and I tell him Alexander had given me a few pointers. I show him what Alexander has already taught me and he's very impressed. I jump over most of the lessons for a Sensor and we move onto a Transformer.

We focus on how to fight with the ability and Lieutenant Linx teaches me the most common tactics, but truly the possibilities are endless. I'm shown how to turn the arena dirt floor to ice like I had seen Darin do my first day of training. Lieutenant Linx also teaches me how to transform a small handheld knife into a long, deadly sword just by touching it. This is a bit more challenging because my instinct is to just use my enhanced sense of sight to try and do it, but Lieutenant Linx constantly lectures me that sight is for controlling not transforming.

We don't spend much time on the theory for an Aeros, those who can master using weapons. Instead, we go straight into sword fighting. Lieutenant Linx leads me out of the orange tent and onto the training grounds. Each of us picks up a sword and positions ourselves across from the other. We begin to take easy strikes at the one another, always deflecting the other's swing.

"Let your hand become the sword," Lieutenant Linx says, as we continue to flip our swords back and forth with one another.

He repeats that a few more times, but I don't know what else to do. I try squeezing the grip of the sword harder, but it's still my muscles controlling the weapon, not my gift.

"Let your hand become the sword," he says it again, and again.

My own voice begins to repeat it in my head. *Let your hand become the sword.* Sweat breaks on my forehead and I grit my teeth, frustrated and exhausted from spending so much time going back and forth with our swords.

I squeeze my hand in a tighter fist and then something happens. It's so fast I don't register it. I flip the sword back, hard, knocking Lieutenant Linx's weapon to the ground.

"That's it!" Lieutenant Linx says, retrieving his sword. "Your gift will control the weapon, allowing you to make all the best movements."

"I don't know how I did that," I say, looking to my sword.

"Sense of Touch is very difficult to master, Adaline," he says, and I don't miss that he didn't use my royal title.

I'm suddenly reminded of the day we found Alexander's mother, Marin, on the old Libertas. We had been attacked by those vines and I had fought them off with my sword. That feeling of the weapon taking over then is the same as how I felt now. I've already used this part of my gift and I didn't even know it. Lieutenant Linx and I go back to tapping swords and I beg for the gift to take over again, but I can't get it to come.

"That's all right," Lieutenant Linx says, dropping his tired arm to his side. "It was a good start. Some people take years to ever see it work for them."

As we walk back into the orange tent, I see Toby out on the training grounds, his sword gliding in the air perfectly. I wonder if what Lieutenant Linx said is true, or if I'm just no good at this one.

Finally, the last point he teaches me is the theory behind being a Controller. You have to keep contact until you get as strong as Paylon. You focus on their brain and try to make the body do what you think.

"We won't have you practice using it today because most people can't do it. It truly takes a dark side or a real surge of anger to be able to call that kind of power. Paylon is one of the only people to truly master this gift," Lieutenant Linx says, leading me to the entrance of the tent. I don't need to be reminded of the strength and darkness in Paylon's powers.

Since I came to him already knowing how to use the powers of a Sensor, Lieutenant Linx says we'll end our lesson early today. He suggests that I go to the ring for the rest of the afternoon and view some of the fights.

I leave the orange tent, my mind and muscles exhausted. I see some people are doing ring training this afternoon, as Lieutenant

Linx had suggested. I glance over and watch someone with a yellow marked training suit for enhanced sight fall over screaming from the shirking in her ears. I don't have to guess the person she's fighting is Zavy. I know that feeling all too well.

I move my gaze from the struggling girl to the line of tall palm trees behind the training grounds. They call to me, and I don't mind getting away from the ring. I move toward them, and further away from the castle. Immediately, I'm swallowed into a silent world except for the birds and occasional snap of a branch. The trees stand up around me and the air smells thick with dirt. Already my muscles relax, feeling protected in the canopy of palm trees.

"Where are you going?" I hear Alexander's familiar voice call out behind me. I turn and watch him appear in front of me.

"Teleporting or invisibility?" I ask and he laughs but doesn't answer. Instead, he asks me again where I'm going.

"I'm not sure," I admit, thinking back to the girl in the ring. "I just didn't want to sit there and watch that."

"I saw," Alexander grumbles, equally as sick as I am. "So, just wandering?"

"Just wandering," I repeat.

Alexander and I walk together down the sharp slope, deeper and deeper into the woods, and we share what the other learned in the afternoon's training.

Ahead I see the trees begin to thin out as we approach the other end of the forest. There's a soft sound of rolling waves coming from up ahead. Alexander and I exit out of the forest and onto a soft, white sand beach. It's small, just a hidden patch that meets the water.

"Our own private beach," he says.

My eyes soak in the gorgeous sight around us. I've never seen anything so beautiful. The blue ocean water foams as the waves come to shore, and the tall palms and volcanic rock surround the little beach, making it feel secluded. The wall that surrounds Libertas towers out of the water in front of me. Tall stilts raise the wall above the water to let the waves move freely into the cove.

I take off my training boots and socks and run straight for the ocean. Alexander is calling my name behind me, but I'm already knee-deep in the cool water. It stretches out in front of me forever, and there's so much blue. I turn back to Alexander and see he's taking off his shoes and socks and he tentatively sticks his feet in the water. I take my hand and splash a wave of water at him.

"Come on!" I say, and my voice sounds so young and light. I look up to the sky and fall back into the water, letting the salty blue ocean surround me.

My head comes up for air and I see Alexander has retreated to the beach.

"It's too cold," he says, dismissing me.

It's shallow here, and I sit on my knees in the ocean, letting my chin graze the top of the water. I stare out at the horizon, through the stilts of the wall, for a long time, just letting the sounds of seagulls and waves fill my head.

Eventually, I get up, go to the edge of the sand with Alexander, and enjoy the infinity of sparkling blue in front of us.

After a while of silence, I ask Alexander, "Are you nervous about the ring tomorrow?"

"Terrified," he admits. "I've never used only my gift to fight in combat."

"You can use weapons if you want. The gifted in taste have to. They can't fight with their powers," I say, squinting at him through the setting sun.

"I doubt they'll let us. They want to see what our gifts can do." He runs his hands through the loose sand, letting his words settle.

I'm quiet because I know he's right. "Do you want to practice?" I say, an idea coming to me. I gesture around us and stand up. "We have our own private ring right here." I see the hesitation on his face and say, "We'll just practice different scenarios, not actual fighting."

I reach out and pull him to his feet. We move and stand on opposite sides of the beach. "You be an Alterken, and I'll use my enhanced sense of sight," I say, choosing the gift I'm most comfortable with. "Ready?" I ask and he nods. In a blink I make myself appear invisible. "What do you do?" I say as I take steps toward him.

"I use my enhanced sense of touch," he says, dropping to touch the loose sand and throwing it up in the air. As it falls back to the ground he's able to see where it falls and hits me instead.

I bring myself out of being invisible and say, "Good, but now what?" I say as I start to lift Alexander up into the air. Quickly he makes himself invisible and falls to the sand.

"You can't control me if you can't see me," he says and suddenly he kicks my feet out from underneath me and I fall back into the sand. Alexander comes back into view and says, "Easy."

I laugh and say, "All right, I'll be the Alterken. Choose your sense." He pulls me back up and we take our starting positions again.

"I'll do sense of hearing," he says, and a chill creeps up my neck. Before his shriek can reach me, I blanket myself in silence to block him out.

"You're going to have to do better than that," I say and a smile fills my face.

I take off sprinting towards him. With each step, I use my enhanced sense of touch to send a shaking pulse through the Earth and watch as he struggles to keep his balance. I look up and suddenly a large bird flies across my path knocking me back a few steps. I drop my silent wall for a split second, shocked, and I'm hit by a shriek that causes me to keel over, almost nauseous.

Quickly, I pull the silent cover over me and communicate up to the birds, trying to make my voice louder than Alexander's. I need something that hearing can't do.

My eyes lock on the shining blue water. With my enhanced sense of sight, I lift up a wave and tower it above us. The look on Alexander's face solidifies that he's out of ideas just as I drop the water on him.

"You won't have water in the ring," he says, drenched. The force of the water has knocked him to his knees.

"Why not?" I say and spin around. "We're on an island surrounded by water."

"How do you get it without seeing it?" he asks, trying to prove his point.

I pause and look up into the sky above us. "The weather," I say. "Control the clouds, have them bring you the water."

"It'd be hard," he admits, saying exactly what I'm thinking.

I stare up at the clouds and wonder if a part of my powers could control the weather. *How would I do that? What sense do I use to get that to work?* What I'm learning is that the possibilities are endless with these gifts. Every situation will be different, there's not one thing we can do that will always work. You have to be quick and judge your opponent and your surroundings. Being a gifted is more than relying on magical powers. You have to be knowledgeable, resourceful, and fearless. The gift is useless if you aren't smart enough to use it.

Alexander slicks back his wet hair, still trying to catch his breath. I walk over to him, my shadow stretching across the sand.

"Again?" I ask, pulling him back to his feet.

"Again," he says.

For the rest of the afternoon and deep into the sunset, Alexander and I take turns using our gifts on the other. It helps prepare us for the mentality that we will need in the ring, but it also helps train us further on using our gifts. We've run nearly every scenario we can think of, but I'm still nervous for what will happen tomorrow. When the orange sun starts to slip away and hints of stars peek through the hazy evening sky, Alexander and I take a seat in the cool shaded sand.

"Can I ask you a question?" I turn to Alexander and his green eyes meet mine.

His eyes scan my face, trying to figure out what I may ask. I can sense some hesitation. I haven't brought up his outburst last night, the secret we're keeping, or our almost kiss at all today. I think he may be worried I'll say something now and ruin the somewhat normal day we've had. He breaks his stare from my face and decides to let me ask.

"Sure," he says, dropping his hands and leaning back into the sand.

"What happened in your test? The one we took when we got here to determine our gifts." I watch his eyes turn distant as it comes back to him. He wasn't expecting me to ask that.

"Do you want me to tell you or show you?" he asks, shifting in the sand.

"You can show me," I respond.

Alexander takes my hand in his, and they fit together seamlessly. With sense of touch, he sends the memory to me. There's a flash of white light, just like when I touched the water in the memory garden. I pull my hand from Alexander's grasp.

"Lieutenant Linx didn't show me how to do that," I say. "You can show someone else the memories in your head with an enhanced sense of touch?"

"It's not a fighting tactic. I'm sure Lieutenant Linx didn't want to waste your time," Alexander says shortly. He stretches out his hand to me again and I gently place mine back in his familiar grasp.

After the flashing white light I see Alexander come into view in front of me.

"How much do you remember?" I ask as the memory starts to take shape.

"I relive it almost every night." He swallows at the thought of this reoccurring nightmare. I understand because my test is the same for me. Alexander's standing in a dark room. Immediately, the scene shifts green with his night vision.

"I used that in my test too," I say as I continue to watch the memory unfold in front of me.

When the night vision is turned on, we see that the floor has giant craters that fall to what I can only imagine would be his death. Alexander carefully makes his way around the craters and to the door on the other side of the room. With sense of touch, I watch him obliterate the steel door. I flinch at the loud explosion. I feel his strong, coarse hand in mine and realize how deadly it is. It's alarming how I find comfort in something that could in fact kill me.

The test continues as Alexander walks out into a hallway flooded with water. The lights are on out here, so the green film fades away.

"Did you know where you were going?" I ask and watch Alexander pick up his pace through the sloshing water.

"I was tracking him," he says as he watches the vision in his own head, just as transfixed as I am. I hear a boyish laugh echo through the walls of the hall.

"Sense of hearing," I offer and I feel Alexander nod next to me. He continues down the hall until he comes to a single door. Again he obliterates it with his touch.

On the other side of the door, the blue sky stretches for miles and a long wooden swinging bridge hangs tied to the doorframe. Alexander steps out onto the bridge and we see the drop is into a shallow river full of large boulders. Out in the center of the bridge is King Renon and I take in a sharp breath. In front of King Renon, tied up as his prisoner, is me. The other end of the bridge ties to the entrance of the castle back in Dather. Two guards on the far side of the bridge cut the ropes that Alexander is trying to use as handrails and they fall limp to the rushing creek below. They don't move to cut the bridge itself because King Renon roots himself in the center.

"Let her go," Alexander's commanding voice rings through the crisp wind.

"Alexander," King Renon starts and gestures around him. "Welcome home." Alexander's muscles are tense in his neck as he slowly tries to make his way down the bridge.

"Why didn't you just teleport us out of there?" I ask, getting caught up in the memory.

"I couldn't," Alexander reminds me. I watch the rest of the memory unfold as Alexander tries to run down the shaking bridge.

Boards break beneath his feet and in the memory I yell, "Alexander stop!" At my cry, he freezes just a few boards away from me.

"Adaline, I'll save you," he says, but I shake my head.

"You can't save me."

At my confession, King Renon puts his hands on my shoulders

and shoves me toward the creek below. A shriek leaves me and I grab onto the side of the swinging rope bridge. King Renon turns and walks towards his two guards at the castle. Alexander grabs my hand, like I had done for him in my test.

"I have to let go because I'm you're weakness," I say and my grip with his loosens until we slip apart from one another. But where my test ends his continues for just a second more. He stands up to face King Renon, watching the smile on his face grow with his brother's pain, and that's where the image freezes.

"That's where it ended?" I ask and open my eyes to see what's in front of me and not projected in my head.

Alexander let's go of my hand and says, "Yes, that's when the serum wore off and my doctor removed the sensors."

We're silent, letting the air grow heavy between us. It acts as a cool shock, reminding us why it's so important that we get our emotions under control. Something as powerful as an Alterken can be defeated with the blinding feeling of love. *Heart versus mind. The ones we love most will always be our biggest weakness.*

Chapter 19

It's late in the evening when we finally decide to head back toward the castle.

"Do you have your royal classes tonight?" Alexander asks as we climb back up through the woods.

"Yes, I think Linda has a lot in store for tonight," I say and the realization that we leave for this war in a few days hits me in the chest. "I have to live to actually use the information she's given me," I say and the sickness of it creeps under my skin.

After a pause of silence, Alexander says, "We will survive this."

I nod, but I don't picture a life on the other end of this war.

"One day at a time," I say, trying to drill it into my mind, so I stop letting the fear of the unknown take over.

When we break out of the blanket of trees, the training grounds are deserted. We walk past the empty tents in silence, letting the sounds of past memories and history of the grounds fill our heads. I can't keep my gaze from being pulled to the ring, sitting and waiting for whatever tomorrow will bring. I catch Alexander getting caught in its grasp and I steal his words. "We will survive this."

He breaks his stare and gives me a soft smile. "They won't let us die, right?"

I give a fake laugh and remember the feeling. "They'll let you come pretty close."

I part from Alexander and head into the castle while he makes his way to his home. When I get back in the castle, I walk to my quarters to change out of my training uniform. Linda is waiting at my door, her face resembling a pale, white stone.

"Where have you been?" she asks, her voice hissing like a snake.

"Training," I respond.

"You were not," Linda says sharply, emphasizing each word.

"With Alexander. We went on our own," I say, my explanation jumbling in my head. "I'll change and we'll go to dinner. We're still on time."

"Adaline," Linda says my name, but I've already moved around her and closed the door behind me.

I quickly change out of my ocean-soaked training outfit and find a comfortable shirt and pair of shorts to wear. I want to wash the seawater out of my hair, but I don't want to risk putting Linda even further behind in her schedule. I know how she likes to keep everything moving on time. I fix my hair up into a clean tail and decide it's good enough for now. I exit my room and Linda's cool white face has turned an angry red.

"Linda, I am capable of walking myself to dinner." I huff, turning down the hall, but she follows me anyway.

"I'm sure you are, Ms. Adaline," is all she offers to me, but her voice sounds like she's talking to a little kid.

I stop and turn to her, the frustration of being treated like a child finally bubbling over. "Are you trying to keep me from finding something or going somewhere?" I ask. "Why are you always overseeing my every move?"

Her eyes shift, obviously caught off guard by my direct outburst. I watch her eyes search the hall, looking for the right words. "We need you safe," she says, and lightly turns me around to continue walking. "Not everyone wants you to be the savior. Not everyone believes. We just need to be sure that you are safe."

I hadn't told her or my father about the night Zavy kidnapped me. Neither of them know someone volunteered me for the ring. I didn't want them to know that people didn't believe, but it looks like they can see it anyway.

"And who's going to protect me in the war?" I ask bitterly.

"We need you to get to the war. Then, it's your job to keep yourself alive," Linda rambles back to me.

I realize there's only one way my father would know these things have been happening. Of course a Future Holder would know. I press my lips together and take in her words. "What has my father seen?"

"I can't tell you that, Adaline," Linda says as we approach the dining hall.

My father is standing at the door to greet us. The disapproving expression on his face lets me know he's overheard our conversation. "Don't ask questions, Adaline."

"You do know I can see the future too." I huff and storm past my father. Cooper is sitting at the long dinner table by himself and I find my seat has been set across from him.

"Except you weren't taught how to," Cooper adds.

I wince at the comment, remembering the first day of training. My one day of training in sense of sight was cut short because Zavy had sent me to the healer's tent.

My father closes the grand dining room doors and takes his seat at the head of the table.

How ironic, the one part of my gift my father doesn't want me to be able to use I missed out on.

Then it hits me, cold in the chest.

It's not ironic at all, it's strategic, and it was done on purpose.

He sees the realization cross my face.

"You volunteered me that morning?" I ask, the words dry in my throat. His enhanced sense of sight may be strongest in seeing the future, but he can still use it in other ways.

"Knowing what comes is a burden more than a gift," my father says simply, and he and my brother begin to eat their dinner.

"It's hypocritical to say that and then control my life to get me down a specific path," I say, disgust filling my veins. I lift my fork and pick at the food in front of me.

"You'll understand when you have kids," my father chuckles like this is a joke.

I roll my eyes, annoyed with the parental saying until I realize he would know if I have kids. His eyes meet mine and he knows where my mind is going.

He lays his fork down and adds, "I didn't mean anything by that, Adaline."

I try to respond, but I can't get my mouth to form the words crawling on my tongue.

My father takes a long drink of his water before saying, "This is exactly why I didn't want you trained on this. There are hundreds, even thousands, of different futures. And anything as small as that," my father points to Cooper just as he sneezes, "Could change everything. I've seen you with kids, without kids. You can't know the true future. Don't get consumed in the possibility of knowing a future that you can't control. I just want you to live, Adaline."

I break my gaze from his and finish my dinner. He's right, there's no use in knowing the possible futures when you have no control over them. None of us say another word until Linda comes to get Cooper and me for our royal lessons.

When we stand to leave, I turn back to my father, and in his eyes, I see that he knows what I'm going to say, but I say it anyway.

"Then let me live."

Linda lectures Cooper and me deep into the night, acting unaware of the fact that I'll be fighting in the ring first thing tomorrow morning. I absorb everything she says, but my mind is still focused on the fact that my father is trying to live my life for me. I can't believe I had thought Max's father would volunteer me. The person I should've been blaming has been next to me all along. There's no lack of trust with the people of Libertas, just with my father.

Since we arrived, I've been fighting myself on whether or not I can forgive my father. I thought we had been making real progress in rebuilding our relationship, but tonight has reminded me why I can never trust him again. My father only cares about one thing; following his visions and controlling the future.

I can't decide if I'm mad at my father for keeping me from learning how to see the future, or if I'm mad that, as twisted as volunteering your daughter for the ring is, he did the right thing. I'm reminded how I felt when I had my mother's journal, always wanting to know if I'm making the right moves. Getting rid of that constant desire to know isn't as easy as burning the journal this time, because now the power is within me. I can't just cut it out and remove it.

Linda lectures mostly about what our roles will be after the war. Our goal is to take control of Dather and claim the island. Once we do that, we'll have to establish rule over everyone in Dather and here on Libertas. She focuses on how Cooper and I will be out in Garth and Sard after the war to help restore order. My focus will be to bring the gifted together and find their place in our new society, while Cooper focuses on the non-gifted.

She says it's perfect that we have one of us that's gifted and one of us that's non-gifted, because we will be a symbol of how the two types can work together. I roll my eyes, not forgetting how the people of Libertas wanted nothing to do with the non-gifted, and some of them are still angry someone with no powers sits on the throne. Her naïve words don't fool me. When we win this war and take back Dather, she will be the first to make sure the gifted get the upper hand in the new society we create. She ends the lecture by going over all the banquets we'll have. She lets us know she's already busy planning the first royal event in Garth. I get annoyed almost immediately because Linda focuses her attention on the fact that we have won this war before it's even begun.

Our night of royal lessons finally comes to an end after Linda tells us how the next five years of our lives will play out. I walk back to my room, dragging my tired feet. Linda silently follows behind me. She stays a few steps back after my outburst earlier. As we walk, a door in the hall swings open, and my father steps out. There's a small, black leather book tucked under his arm.

"Oh, it's just you," my father mumbles. He turns and goes back into the room, leaving the door ajar.

We walk by the room and I peer inside. I watch my father lay his book on a deep, red table and move to turn off the lights. His eyes meet mine as I pass the slightly open door and they look very tired and sad. Perhaps the weight of this war is hitting him a little harder tonight.

He probably sees the same dreariness in my eyes as I think about the million ways I could mess up in the ring tomorrow. The million ways I could prove to everyone that I am not a savior. I'm not meant to be a princess or to be a leader.

When I get back to my room, I slide inside and click the door shut behind me, not bothering to say any parting words to Linda. I move through my nightly routine in a cloudy haze, showering and untangling my wet hair before getting into my bed. It's not until my head is pressed into my dense pillow that something begins to turn in my mind. It's like a photo coming into view. Slowly, all the details fall into place and I sit up alarmed.

My mind recalls when I had seen my father just moments ago. That wasn't any regular black book on his desk. That was a Future Holder's journal. I leap out of bed and race to my door. I don't let my brain have any time to think, I just move. I crack open the door and find the hall empty. I silently slide along the walls in the hall, making my way back to the room my father was in. I don't even give myself time to put on my shoes, and my bare feet press into the soft, blue carpet.

I find the room easily, and no one crosses my path. When I reach for the doorknob, I find it stiff. *Locked.* That won't be enough to stop me. I call up the brief memory where I had glimpsed into the room and teleport myself through the door. When I open my eyes, I'm surrounded by darkness except for the moonlight streaming in from the tall windows. I press my hand against the dark door behind me and feel for the switch on the wall. When I flip on the switch, a soft yellow light floods the room.

I spin slowly, unable to believe what's in front of me. Both walls are entire bookshelves. Deep, dark brown shelves stretch from the floor to the ceiling, and they are covered with little black Future Holder journals.

There must be over a hundred of them in here.

I reach up and pull one from the shelf nearest me. When the soft leather book finally rests in my hand, my common sense steps in. *Do*

I really want to see the future? I can hardly stop now, the temptation is too great.

The lock on the cover doesn't even faze me now that I've been trained in my enhanced sense of touch. Effortlessly, I flip the lock off the cover, and now nothing stands between the future and me. Slowly, I peel back the cover of the book, and written on the first page is... nothing. *Nothing?*

I flip through the journal and find every page is blank. I drop it to the ground and pull another from the shelf. Again, I flip it open and find it blank. I pull two more down and discover the same thing. I'm so frustrated that, yet again, my father is keeping me in the dark. I throw the last journal on this self across the room. It barely misses a tall stone statue in the corner of the room and hits the floor.

Of course my father would enchant his journals just like my mother had done, only telling me what they want when they want to. I pick up the journals I had dropped to my feet and line them back on the shelf. I cross the room to the one I had thrown and pick it up.

When I turn to take it back to the shelf, I get a closer look at the stone statue. It's odd, not very magnificent to be in a castle. It's a slender, grey slab that rises to my waist. It looks like the podium in the council room, but smaller. On top of the statue is a flat rectangle of stone. The shape of a square is carved deep into it. My eyes flip from the statue to the journal in my hands and I realize the square in the statue is just the right size to hold the open journal.

Quickly, I pull the journal open and lay it in the square hole on the statue.

I jump back, shocked at what appears in front of me. An image of my father and mother dancing in my old living room plays out in the center of the room. I can still see the shelves of books through them, their image thin and transparent. It's a projection of what my father had written.

My stomach turns over and tears fill my eyes. My mother looks so alive. Her smile is so wide, and tears fill her eyes from laughing so hard while my father continues to spin her around the room. I reach down to the journal and flip the page and the projection changes to the two of them sitting in an old classroom. I keep turning the pages, seeing different shots of my mother and father. This must have been one of my father's older journals. At one point these were visions of the future, but now they're a reminder of what the past might have been.

I grab another off the shelf behind me and swap it out on the podium, dropping the first one to the ground. This one is filled with visions of them and a baby boy. *Cooper.* And in every single vision, his eyes are a deep caramel. He was always destined to be a non-gifted. I begin to move faster through the journals, just seeing flashes of the scenes inside them. I continue to pull the journals off the shelves and drop them to the floor when I'm done with them.

I find journals about Cooper in school, me being born, and my father beginning to work with Libertas. There are ten journals full of visions of my father and me in the woods when I was little. A lot of what I see I have no memory of. These are all the different ways my life could have played out. The day my father's group was ambushed and the night he fled is here. And there are hundreds of pages on the prison. So many things he had foreseen. The server in the prison, Alyssa, giving me those books is here too. The hardest for me to watch are the ones with Titus. I miss him so much. I would give anything to have my little brother back.

The day I escape the castle is here as well, but it's here in a hundred different ways. Every single one shows me escaping with my mother and younger brother, except one. Out of the hundreds of visions, one of them saw their deaths, and that was the one that came true. There were ninety-nine other ways that day could have gone, all of them with my mother and brother living, except one. My father had lied when he said he didn't know they would die. He saw it right here. Perhaps he was just hoping one of the other ninety-nine possibilities would play out.

I continue to work through the journals. Now, nearly half of them are strewn across the floor, the shelves left bare. My movements are hurried and frantic. I have no time to organize my thoughts or actions; I just keep flipping through journals. I don't know what I'm looking for, or if I'm even looking for anything. I lose count of how many times I watch the different aspects of my journey play out. I skip a lot of them because I don't care what could have happened, it already did.

I've completely wiped this side of the room clean of journals. I go to cross the room for the other shelves, when my eyes land on the black journal on the desk near the tall windows. My father's sad and tired eyes come back to me. He had been writing in this journal right before I saw him. I reach for it and I feel the nerves creep through my adrenaline. I finally stop my frantic thoughts and movements and look at the journal. Whatever is in here brought my father to tears. It's something that hasn't happened yet, and it scares me to know what that could be.

I move back to the podium and open the journal to the very last page. The projection that comes from the podium is hard to make out. It looks like grey smoke billowing in the room. As the image comes into focus, I see what was the castle back in Garth. The sky is an ashy grey and dirty smoke rises from the rubble of the castle.

The war.

A dark figure of a girl comes into view through the smoke. She's stumbling through the rubble near the edge of a cliff, clearly weak. When I see the stiff brown braid flip over her shoulder, I know it's me.

My eyes focus on the projection and everything else in my view fades away. I watch as my projection continues to stumble through the rubble, looking so lost and broken, edging dangerously close to the edge of the cliff.

"Adaline. You foolish, little girl," a voice says in the projection, so weak it's hardly audible.

Then, my projection turns, her eyes widening. I can't see who she's looking at, but I feel the fear on her face course through my body.

"No!" I watch the projection of me scream, and then the vision starts to shake.

It rumbles and the ground beneath my projection's feet cracks and splinters. An earthquake shatters the cliff-side and I watch myself crumble away, getting sucked off the cliff and crushed in the falling stone.

I take in a sharp breath, feeling my heart stop for just a second, tightening in my chest. The projection freezes and fades away. When the image is gone, my father's horrified gaze in the doorway comes into focus.

I have no words, my mind still stuck in the projection. "I die?" I whisper.

"Adaline, what have you done?" my father's voice roars, taking in the hundreds of journals spread across the floor.

"I die?" I repeat.

"What do you think you're doing?" my father yells, his voice growing louder.

It's strong enough to pull me from my shocked state. For the first time, I see what a mess I've made.

"You tried to keep me from seeing the future. I had no other choice," I say, stumbling over my explanation.

"Do you see why I did that?" my father asks, anger still shaking in his voice.

"I'm going to die," I say again, but this time my voice is stronger, and it sounds less like a question.

"That was one vision, Adaline," my father says, and he begins to move through the room to pick up the journals. "By now you should understand how many different ways the future can play out," he adds, throwing his hands out to gesture to the thousands of pages of visions.

"I'm sorry," I say, my voice shaking on the edge of tears, and I run from the library of journals.

I go back to my room in a hurried walk, trying to believe what my father is saying. He's right; there could be thousands of different outcomes for me in this war. But what I also learned tonight, is that it doesn't matter if there are a thousand different ways where I don't die, there is always one where I do. And sometimes, that's all it takes.

Chapter 20

I awake the next morning feeling less rested than I did when I finally made it back to my room. I laid there for hours just repeating to myself that my future isn't defined. Any little detail could still change the outcome. After I said it enough times, the fear and nausea had finally faded away and I found sleep. I've managed to get the idea of dying out of my head. I need to worry about what I have to conquer today. If I can't survive this ring, it doesn't matter what my father saw in his vision.

I get dressed in another training outfit and carefully braid my hair over the top of my head before tying it up in a high tail. I take a moment longer in front of the mirror, over analyzing the pink heat on my cheeks, the swimming of my wet, green eyes, and the knots in my stomach. Today is going to be a nightmare, and I feel the thing I'm scared of most inching closer.

A small breakfast is delivered to the common area of my room. I take what my stomach can hold from the tray and eat on my balcony. Already, I see the groups of people coming in for today's training and I know I should head to the arena soon. When I leave my room,

Linda is nowhere to be found. I debate about waiting for her; maybe she's just running behind schedule. But somehow I know she's not coming. Linda is never late. I take it upon myself to go to the training grounds, finding that I surprisingly miss her company. *This is what you wanted.* Even though the ring is inevitable, I try to take small steps and draw out the walk as much as I can.

When I get out to the training grounds, I see the massive crowd filing into the arena. I fold myself into the crowd and try to hide in the sea of bodies. It's no use though, because everyone moves away from me, creating a path for me to go down to the front of the stands. Max meets me there and has me sit in the front row of the yellow section. I notice Alexander across from me, sitting with Lieutenant Linx in the orange section. He offers me a smile, but I catch his fingers twitching at his side, the only sign of his fear.

"Nervous?" Max asks me, but my thoughts are so far away I almost don't hear him.

"Yeah," I admit, shaking myself from my thoughts. Commander Crymm's comments about needing to prove myself have been echoing in my head.

"You've already done this once," Max says, trying to make me feel better.

My mouth is dry and I keep my eyes locked on the dirt floor. I keep running each paring in my head. If I get a Sensor, how do I react? What if I can't get that part of my gift to work? Will they make me fight until I lose?

As my mind races, my eyes catch some movement on the arena

floor. I pull myself from my thoughts and focus on the ten captains filing into the ring. *It's beginning.*

Max's father, Captain Brutis, speaks first. "Welcome to our final day of training before this war becomes our reality."

I hear most people cheer, but I join the few who swallow with the realization that many of us will be dead soon. However, Max's father continues with his celebrating tone. "Not all of you will get to train in the ring today. The focus will be on you all learning something by watching others fight."

No one is surprised. We have all been either looking forward to or dreading this day all week. But Max's father says it anyways to bring some theatrics to the ring.

"Today we will finally get to see all that our Alterken saviors can do." His voice seems to echo the globe. "We've never seen an Alterken in real life, so I think we will all get to learn something new today. Both of them will take on a sense. The captains have pre-determined who will fight each sense. Since Adaline volunteered to take the ring once already." He pauses and my stomach turns at the word *volunteered.* "Alexander will get three assignments and will start us off."

The crowd cheers as he slowly enters the ring. The muscles under his training uniform ripple with intensity. His dirty blonde hair flips slightly in the island breeze. His tan skin glows in the tropical sun. But his fingers continue to twitch. His green eyes meet mine and together we take in a deep breath.

His voice enters my head, saying words only I can hear, "If I start to lose, look away. I don't want you to see me get destroyed. That's pathetic."

I send a cackling laugh back to him and the corners of his mouth turn up. "You don't need to impress me," I push back to him.

The captain from smell speaks, "Alexander will face Lexi from sense of smell."

A lean girl stands and moves into the ring. I recognize her from the first day of training. She was victorious. Alexander and Lexi meet in the center to bow before taking their places on either side of the ring. Captain Brutis places a black flag behind Lexi for Alexander to try and get, and a red flag behind Alexander for Lexi to try and grab. *Get the flag, Alexander. Don't waste time showing off your strength. Do what you need to do and get around her.*

The crowd cheers and counts down to one and immediately Alexander is knocked to the ground with the toxic smell from Lexi's powers. Many around me breathe in sharply, shocked for him, but I don't miss a beat, knowing we trained on this yesterday.

I watch as he searches for the memory of the two of us back on the boat the night we left Sard. We agreed that this memory would be our scent blocker, because of the natural smell of saltwater. Slowly Alexander stands. But Lexi is stronger than Alexander because she's trained this part of her gift all her life. So, Alexander knows he'll need to weaken her. With sense of sound he sends a shriek to her and she crumples under the blow.

With her stream of poison weakened, Alexander uses sense of sight to levitate up into the air and grab the black, Alterken flag. He lowers himself back to the ground and lets up on the shrieking sound he was sending to Lexi. The crowd explodes at the first Alterken victory of the day. A sweat breaks on his forehead, but I watch his muscles fall and relax. It's the first time anyone has seen someone use sense of hearing, sight, and smell all in a matter of minutes. Many of the whispers can't believe what they just witnessed.

The captain from sense of touch returns to the ring and announces that I will be battling next. The eyes around the ring flick toward me, every single one excited to see what I can do. On shaky legs, I stand and slowly make my way to one side of the ring. I take in a deep breath and wait to see who they have thought to pair me with.

"Adaline will be battling Park from sense of touch."

I scan the orange section and watch the largest of the group rise. He is two of me tall and his uniform seems to be splitting at the seams. I can hear the whispers spreading through the crowd. With his intense size, they don't think I stand a chance. Sense of touch is also one of the most powerful gifts. It can do the most damage. We meet in the center and go through the formalities of the ring before taking our positions under the opponent's flag.

As the crowd begins to count down, I run my training with Alexander through my head. I can't keep the corners of my mouth from turning up into a smile. When they hit *one*, I immediately lift Park up into the air. He can't use his gift if he can't touch anything. The strongest gift can be defeated so easily. He lashes his arms in the air, desperately trying to get ahold of something to use as a weapon.

Effortlessly, I make my way up the ring and grab the black

Alterken flag without breaking a sweat. I catch the smirk on Alexander's face. I know he wanted the easy pairing. I lower Park back to the ground, his frustration obvious. The cheers from the crowd are encouraging. I have proven myself, but I know what Commander Crymm would tell me. *Now prove yourself again.*

Within a matter of minutes, my first round is over and Alexander takes my place in the ring again. The captain from sense of taste enters the ring, bringing up his fighter, Trix. A guy with a similar build to Alexander's enters. When the two get through their ring formalities, Trix is allowed to select a weapon for this battle since taste can't be used in combat. Alexander will fight without a weapon, even though I know he prefers to fight with one.

Just like sense of touch, taste is one of the easiest to defeat. The crowd knows this and many dismiss the fight all together. I'm sure this is the same reaction every time someone from sense of taste is called to the ring. As the crowd hits *one*, Alexander freezes Trix with sense of sight and easily claims the Alterken flag. I'm realizing these are match-ups that probably never happen in the ring because it is clear who has the advantage.

I take my place in the ring, one last time, and my gut tells me I won't get another easy pairing. Ever since Zavy beat me, the whispers haven't stopped. Everyone wants to see the rematch and the captains won't disappoint. I watch the captain from sense of hearing enter the ring to call up my opponent.

Linda's words from last night come back to me. *Not everyone wants you to be the savior. Not everyone believes.*

I know I have to win this battle to solidify the trust of the army. This is when I prove myself. I've been pretending to play my role, my title never fully feeling real. I can't pretend anymore, I have to be the savior.

"Our next fight will be Adaline against Zavy, from enhanced sense of hearing." The green section erupts in cheers as Zavy stands and graciously moves to the ring. Every part of her bleeds arrogance. She shows no sign of fear. She actually looks excited and honored to be chosen to fight for the gifted of sense of hearing. We meet in the center of the ring and bend into a deep bow.

Her voice fills my head and she says, "I'm winning this one way or another."

We pull out of the bow and the wicked grin splitting her face turns my stomach. Without responding, I take my place on the opposite side under the green flag. As the crowd cheers and counts down, my heart beats with their voices.

"Three!" *beat beat* "Two!" *breathe in* "One!" *breathe out.*

As I let the air out, I immediately blanket myself in silence, knowing she'll use her shriek tactic first. I've practiced this defensive technique with Alexander, but Zavy is stronger. I can still faintly hear the shriek and know I can't let down my shield. I have to break her before she pushes past my silent barricade.

I drop to the ground and with sense of touch, I pull dirt tornadoes up from the floor. As they whirl toward Zavy, I split the ground and large cracks snake across the floor, threatening to split open into a cavity. Zavy closes her eyes and curls on the ground, trying to keep as much of the dirt out of her eyes and lungs as possible. I know the only other tactic she could have is to pull in an animal, so when Mindy the lion pounces into the ring at Zavy's side, I'm not surprised, but fear still creeps in.

The lion's eyes have gone completely black. Zavy has filled her head with commands to attack. My heart quickens as the lions stalks toward me, ready to pounce. *Think Adaline, think.* I try and push the fear away and call back to my training. I can't blanket Zavy's shriek and overpower her voice in Mindy's head at the same time. She's too strong in sense of hearing. I need to pull in another gift.

Just as Mindy launches herself, I teleport to the right five feet and barely miss the blow. Before Mindy can pounce again, I make myself invisible. When I do this, I let go of my dirt tornadoes and they fall in a cloud of dust. The lion tosses her mane as she spins around, trying to find me. Zavy's eyes widen and she knows the battle is slipping away from her.

That's when the distant shrieking that was trying to break my silent wall changes to a song. Zavy focuses hard, begging the music to be louder in my head. I'm so confused by the sudden change, I find myself *trying* to listen. I let up on the silent wall, wanting to place the music. It's the Welcome Ceremony. It's the moment Zavy kissed Alexander's cheek.

I'm so distracted I forget to keep myself invisible. Just as the memory of the song hits me, Mindy the lion attacks. Her heavy paws crash against my side. I scream in pain, her claws digging into my leg. *I can't believe I fell for that.* I hear the crowd gasp, shocked at the lion's attack. Zavy knows her song made it into my head, confirming my wall of silence is gone. She flips the music back to her shriek and my head pounds.

You can't lose. Get in control.

I squeeze my hands into tight fists, grind my teeth together, and build my silent wall back up. I fall invisible again and pull myself to my feet. In the manufactured silence, my ears ring. Blood runs down my leg, marking where I stand.

Max's training echoes in my head. *Visible or invisible you are still a solid body. You can still be hit.*

Mindy's eyes see the blood, and she knows where I stand. I need to move. I try and run as fast as my wounded leg will allow. I watch as the big cat turns her nose to the sky, trying to smell where I am.

I keep pushing myself, ignoring the pain in my leg and the ringing in my ears. *I'm going to win this.* I climb up to my flag, feeling the victory within my grasp. I close my hand around the handle of the black flag and I know I've done it. When I bring myself back into the crowd's sight, I'm standing atop the ring with the Alterken flag in my hand. I let out a slow breath as my heart pounds.

I try not to get excited, but can't help the widening smile as the crowd cheers. I knew I could beat Zavy. Her face draws stiff when my victorious eyes see her crumpled on the ground. I notice even people in the green section applaud, their belief restored. I carefully make my way back to the ground, limping on my clawed up leg, and two healers run to me.

"We need to get your leg fixed," one says, trying to lead me from the ring.

"No, I'm fine. Fix it here. I want to see the last battle," I say, watching as Mindy and Zavy are ushered out of the ring.

She tosses a nasty glare in my direction before melting back into the enhanced sense of hearing section. The healers nod, not daring to question the Princess of Libertas. I'm led back to my seat in the section of yellow. I prop my leg up and the two healers work together to fix the deep gashes from Mindy.

Alexander takes his place in the ring for the last paring. I watch as Captain Brutis enters the ring and we know sense of sight is the only group left.

His voice calls out, "Alexander will battle my own son, Max."

The crowd cheers and I clap as Max enters the ring. I realize I've never seen Max use his gift in combat since we've been here. I do know training Force Lifters is his specialty, but to be a lieutenant, you need to master all of the other abilities in your sense.

The two make their way to the center of the ring. Alexander approaches from the left, his broad shoulders rolled back, and his tan skin slick with sweat. Unlike Alexander, Max has little to no muscle, but I know that means he's spent all his time training his gift and not building brute strength. That may be his weakness in the war, but in this battle, it makes Max that much stronger.

When the two dip into their low bow I see Max's mouth move, speaking to Alexander. I use my gift to listen to their words and catch Max say, "How about we say winner gets the girl?"

Alexander's eyes tip up to Max. "She's here to train, not play games. She's not a prize."

Max's normally calm nature turns and his voice is filled with a sour edge. Alexander is just fueling him with the power he's going to need to win their battle.

"Then let's just say the loser has to stay out of the way. Unless you're afraid you'll lose," Max says.

Alexander smirks and the two pull out of their deep bow. "You shouldn't be making bets when you know nothing about an Alterken."

A soft smile falls on Max's face and his next words creep into my heart. "That's how crazy I am about her."

Alexander's smirk is wiped clean and a stone expression replaces it. The two turn and take their places under the opponent's colored flag. I watch the two men my heart confides in get ready to shred the other to pieces. I know Max and I established a quick friendship, but I didn't realize how he truly felt about me, and I'm not supposed to know. I shouldn't have been listening.

Like Alexander said, I'm not interested in being in a love triangle, but as the crowd begins to count down, I realize I don't know which one I'm rooting for. When the crowd reaches *one,* the first thing Alexander does is turn himself invisible. We trained on this yesterday, sense of sight can't control what they can't see.

The soft dirt on the arena floor puffs up in little clouds where Alexander's invisible self is running. I watch Max concentrate and follow the clouds of dirt with his eyes, and suddenly, Alexander begins to become visible again. It's glitchy, just showing spots of Alexander, but soon he crashes to the ground. Max can now control the parts of Alexander that he sees. I've never seen someone with an enhanced sense of sight pull what's invisible and make it visible again.

Max begins to crumple back as Alexander sends a shriek his way. With Max weakening, Alexander goes back to flashing in and out of visibility. It's hard to watch the two pull at one another. Every step Alexander takes, Max tries to use sense of sight to pull him down, and then Alexander responds with a wave of shrieks to shake Max off.

Alexander knows he needs to do something else. I watch as he beats against the ground, sending ripples through the dirt to knock Max over. When he falls, Alexander uses this as an opportunity to throw Max up in the air with sense of sight. I watch Max go higher and higher and I think Alexander is hoping Max will fall and break every bone in his body, but then realize Alexander's just distracting him. Max will need to focus his energy on saving himself and not fighting Alexander.

As Max begins to fall back toward the ground, he uses his gift to teleport himself safely to his feet. I expect him to come back to the arena floor, but instead, I see him appear under the yellow flag where Alexander is already waiting. He knew that's what Max would do.

When Max comes into view, Alexander attacks from behind and pulls him into a headlock. He knows that Max can't do anything with Alexander behind him and out of sight. Alexander presses his hand onto Max's forehead and suddenly, Max's head falls limp in Alexander's arms.

Alexander's controlling him.

The gasps through the crowd at Alexander's powers don't go unnoticed. I'm reminded of my brief lesson in sense of touch yesterday when I was told controlling someone's mind took a dark-minded person, nearly impossible to do. The lieutenant had used Paylon as an example of one of the only people to master it. I swallow, thinking of someone besides Paylon who has that much hatred and anger. For the first time, I see a part of Alexander's brother, King Renon, show itself.

Alexander teleports himself and Max's brainwashed body to the other side of the ring with the black Alterken flag. Alexander takes the flag in his hand before releasing his control on Max and waves it victoriously. The crowd goes crazy. Every person in the arena stands, clapping and whistling for Alexander. They have never seen someone powerful enough to control someone's mind that easily.

I stand and clap with the crowd, even when the healers tell me not to, but the devastation on Max's face pulls at my heart. The two are brought down to the center of the ring to be inspected by another group of healers and the cheers never seem to end. What the people of Libertas view as incredible strength in Alexander's power, makes me nervous. I tell myself he's strong enough to use the powers of a Controller because he's an Alterken, not because he has evil flowing in his veins.

Alexander and Max exchange a brief conversation, but I don't listen in time to catch what they say. The two exit the arena floor and the captains return to the center, the applause carrying over to their reentrance. I take my seat again and the healers working on my leg have finally finished repairing the gashes Mindy had made. My skin is still sore, but other than that, my leg is as good as new.

The entire mood of the ring has changed to complete adrenaline after seeing how powerful Alexander and I truly are with our unique gifts. It makes me feel unstoppable, which could arguably be the worst feeling to have going into a war.

The captains quiet the crowd and Captain Brutis begins to speak. "Sight fell to Alterken as well." He shoots a judgmental gaze at his son who drops is head, upset he disappointed his father. I wish Captain Brutis wouldn't be so hard on him, and I almost say something, but when he continues to speak I lose my words in my throat.

"Our last battle today is one we are all excited to witness. Alterken against Alterken." The cheers of the crowd are deafening.

Alexander and I are ushered into the ring.

Part 3: The Storm

Chapter 21

My body swells with a mix of emotions. There's excitement at the thought of fighting with him, like we did yesterday, but there's a sickening feeling of knowing one of us will have to lose. One savior will be named more powerful than the other. We're both pretty beat up after the other matches. The healers worked nicely on my leg, but my body still aches. The crowd in the arena cheers so loud my eardrums throb. I stare across the dirt floor at Alexander and notice his fingers aren't twitching with nerves anymore. The captains place one black Alterken flag for us to fight over. We take even steps toward the other and meet in the center of the ring. Alexander and I bend into a deep bow, following the formalities of the ring.

"I guess we'll see if we've gotten our emotions in check," he says and I'm reminded my gift won't work on him if I lose myself in my feelings.

But a dry laugh escapes me because I know my emotions won't get in the way today. In battle, where his life is truly in danger, maybe. But today, on this island, he's just another competitor.

"I'll let you win if you want," I offer to him, for only us to hear.

His warm laugh fills my head as we take our places. "Fight back. I want to see how much destruction we can cause."

The crowd begins to count down and when they finish, Alexander and I explode in a mix of powers, each countering the other. The fight begins to blur together, a blend of powerful senses taking over the ring. We flip from being invisible to visible across the arena. The fight moves from the dirt floor to up by the flag, until one of us knocks the other down. I send ripples through the ground and he sends cracks. A pulse of shrieks and silence fills the air and bit by bit, with my sense of sight, I pull together an entire lightening storm above our heads, sending dangerous bolts of electricity into the earth.

The battle stretches on and on. The ground of the arena is obliterated with an abundance of rocks and craters scattered around us. Many people in the front rows back up to give us more space. I watch as some of the captains try to repair the destruction we've done to the stands, wrecked by shots of power that got away from us. This battle is becoming more about endurance. *Who can outlast the other?* I know if I let it get much further Alexander will always outlast me from his training in the Dather army.

I'm going to need to distract him. I just need one moment with his guard down to get past him and to the flag. I remember how Zavy had done something similar to me, and I fell for it. Maybe he will too.

Alexander moves to place his hands on the ground, and I know he's going to use his enhanced sense of touch to whip the rocky ground again. With his focus on his enhanced sense of touch, I know he's abandoned his sense of hearing, and that's when I send him the melody of the beautiful song we had played on the piano just two nights ago.

The melody lands in his mind with his hands just inches from the dirt ground, and he freezes, thinking of the moment we almost kissed. It gives me the one second I need. I teleport myself from across the ring and to his side. Using sense of touch, I land my final blow and crush Alexander into another crater. Then, I teleport up and grab the single Alterken flag.

The crowd cheers again, as if this wasn't the sixth battle they've seen today. I pull Alexander from the crater and the healers make quick work of fixing the ribs I'd crushed.

"Interesting tactic," he huffs.

"Guess we know whose emotions aren't under control," I joke, trying to catch my breath.

He gives a small smile, but it's clear he's in pain from the fight. His eyes seem a bit distant and I know he probably hates the fact that I beat him. I don't want this to cause the people of Libertas to think I'm more powerful than Alexander, because it's not true. I think back to how he had controlled Max's mind and it's obvious which one of us is really the strongest. He's been able to use his gift to do more than I can so far in training. I only beat him because I outsmarted him. I relied on intelligence and I used Alexander's weakness against him. His gift is stronger, but my brain is faster.

But didn't I use Zavy's tactic? When she did it to me, I found it manipulative. When I did it to Alexander, I thought it was strategic.

Alexander and I are escorted to the edge of the ring so the healers can continue to examine us. They can't have us going into a war already injured, so they take their time to find every possible flaw to fix. As they do this, the captains return to the arena floor and encourage the loud, thunderous applauds from the stands to continue. It's incredible, the amount of energy and excitement buzzing in the air. It's the fuel we needed to motivate them for the war. Fear will kill this rebellion faster than King Renon's army, but we have given the people of Libertas something to believe in.

I have given myself something to believe in.

The captains release the crowd of trainees for lunch as the healers finish pulling Alexander and me back together. They've moved the lunch tables out from the individual colored tents and onto the training grounds, with food set on tables around the clearing.

After we have been released by the healers, we pick up our own lunch and find a table to ourselves to eat at. Since our fights in the ring, more of the trainee girls have taken notice of Alexander. I catch groups of them whisper and stare at him throughout lunch, but it's easy to ignore them when he seems to only notice me.

"You did a good job today," Alexander says between mouthfuls of food.

"We both did good," I offer.

I search Alexander's face to see if he's going to mention what Max had said to him.

After a moment, I decide to just ask him myself. "What did Max say to you in the ring?"

His green eyes lock on mine. "What do you mean?" he asks after swallowing.

"He said something to you before and after the fight," I question, not trying to say too much. I don't want him to know I was listening.

Alexander drops his eyes and says, "He was trying to set a prize for the winner of our battle."

"So what did you win?" I ask softly.

"Nothing," he says flatly before adding, "He was just trying to get in my head."

I nod and let it go, but something in Alexander snaps. He drops his fork to his plate and looks at me with a hard and stern gaze.

"He likes you," he says bluntly. "He wanted to bet on you. The loser had to step back and not try to build a relationship with you. I told him I didn't want to be a part of that."

My cheeks flush red and I know I should deny what Alexander just told me or at least act surprised.

"But you already knew that," Alexander huffs, shaking his head.

"Not entirely," I stumble. "I didn't catch what you both said at the end."

Alexander stares at me for a minute, his lips pressed in a thin line. "He said it was a good thing we didn't shake on it." I keep my gaze down at my lunch but I feel Alexander turn his eyes toward the table Max is sitting at. "So, what are you going to do?" Alexander asks and my cautious eyes lock back with his.

"I'm going to fight in this war. I'm going to bring freedom to people who will otherwise die."

Alexander nods, knowing I was going to say this. It's the truth, but it's beginning to also feel like an excuse.

The horns ring out, signaling the end of lunch. Lieutenants work their way through the groups of tables to tell us to head back to the ring for some announcements from our captains and Commander Crymm. Alexander and I stay together and find ourselves sitting in the front row of the section for enhanced sense of sight. The ten captains return to the center of the ring and motion for the crowd to quiet.

When my father and Commander Crymm enter the ring, everyone in the arena stands and bends into a low bow for their king. When we take our seats again, I feel the skin on my arms tighten. My father and Commander Crymm would only be here if they had something important to announce.

I haven't seen my father since our encounter last night. He doesn't show any of the signs of sadness or exhaustion that I saw when we were in his library of journals. He's putting up a strong front for his army.

The sight of him brings up the vision I had seen of my death, but I quickly push it from my head. I can still control my own future.

"Training has now, officially, come to an end," my father says and his words echo in the arena. What I hear instead is that the war has officially arrived. "You will be assigned to your troops and you have the afternoon to learn about the members of your team. We leave for Dather in just under forty-eight hours."

The silence that follows his words is a slap of reality. *This is it.*

These are the last hours we are guaranteed life.

"Each captain will have a team of lieutenants to direct, and each lieutenant will have a troop to lead. Lieutenants, please come forward and shadow your captains," my father instructs and I watch as the lieutenants who have been teaching us all week stand and move to the arena floor.

My eyes fix on Max as he moves to stand by his father's side. He still looks rough from his battle with Alexander and his father still gives him a disappointed glance.

That's when my father says, "We will also be appointing two additional lieutenants to lead a troop of their own."

My father doesn't have to say our names. Everyone turns and stares at Alexander and me. We are ushered to the center with the other lieutenants and are told we will be leading a troop together under the direction of Captain Brutis. The other lieutenants and captains drop to one knee as Commander Crymm approaches Alexander and me.

"It is my honor to congratulate both Adaline and Alexander, and promote them to lieutenants," Commander Crymm says. She steps forward and pins a shiny, black tie on mine and Alexander's ragged training uniforms.

When she clips the pin to my shirt she leans in. "I think you have just proven yourself to be the savior, Adaline."

My eyes catch hers as she pulls back and I remember our conversation before my coronation. I have forced the people of Libertas to believe in me, to believe in a sixteen-year-old girl who spent half her life in a prison cell. I have just defeated a trained soldier. No one would question my strength now.

Commander Crymm gives us a short bow and says. "You will lead Libertas proudly, and you will be our key to victory."

Her words crawl across my skin. So much of the success of this rebellion has been placed on our shoulders. I think back to the massive power Alexander and I each possess. We are the secret weapon, something King Renon will not be expecting. *We are the key.*

My father gives each lieutenant a piece of paper with the names of the trainees that are assigned to them. One at a time, we read the names and spread out across the training grounds to discuss our future as a team.

Alexander and I have one of the smaller squads, even with two of us leading. We are assigned two people from each sense and I'm more than pleased with who we get and who we don't get. Darin and Lexi, the two that battled the first day are in our troop. Darin's younger brother Luis is also with us from sense of touch. Lexi walks with her partner from sense of smell, Sam, who I remember from my brief training with them. We get a set of red-haired twins from sense of hearing and I remember them obsessing over Zavy; Cecelia and her brother Fawn. They're the oldest members of our troop, and I worry I may run into issues trying to give them orders.

I'm not very excited about our two from sense of taste, Zip and Jennie. It takes me a minute to place Jennie, but then I remember her from the day I was tested. She had been sitting next to me in the waiting room. Both of them are young girls who I wish didn't have to go into the danger of a war. Finally, we are assigned two guys from sense of sight. I don't remember them from my training, but they say their names are Luke and Tryle. They both are built to fight in combat as well as with their gifts, and I know they will be a strong asset to our team.

In total, there are ten in our squad, then Alexander and myself. I note that Zavy was assigned to a lieutenant from enhanced sense of hearing and I hope our troops' paths never cross. We go around our team and introduce ourselves to the others. Alexander and I admit quickly that we don't know the first thing about leading a troop, but we will work as a team to figure it out.

"What's your best advice for fighting troops from Garth?" Zip asks us.

"Know how to fight with your hands," I say. "Too many times you'll find they are immune to your gift and you'll need to be ready. With the growing technology and knowledge on the gifts, it's more than likely going to be an issue."

Not too many people look comfortable with my answer so we decide to spend the rest of the afternoon practicing in combat. We'll need to create drills on how the senses work the strongest together, but I know physical combat is where our team is the weakest.

The rest of the troops seem to be jumping right into practicing with their gifts, so the combat training grounds are empty. Everyone partners up with the matching gifted they came with and runs drills. We start with sword fighting and I show them some defensive and offensive swings they can practice on each other. I partner with Alexander and we both draw two practice swords from the selection they have. Alexander and I stand across from each other and clash the metal together. Left, right, low, high, repeat.

"Did you know you could control people?" I ask as we keep running the drill.

"I knew it was possible, but I hadn't done it before," he says. "What do you think is going to happen in the next few weeks?" Alexander asks, changing the subject.

"I think a lot of people will die," I say honestly, but not loud enough for others in our troop to hear. "I think we will win," I add softly and punch another strike with the sword, my arms shaking.

"I think we will win too," Alexander agrees, deflecting my swing. "And then what?" he asks.

"From my understanding, we take control of Dather. My father will rule there as he does here," I say and raise my sword to meet Alexander's attack.

"And what will you do?" Alexander asks, sweat dripping down his face as he swings again.

"Whatever a princess does," I say, remembering all the different plans Linda already has for me. "I hope I can just live," I admit and for a second I let myself wonder if my home is still there, abandoned like we left it. Could I ever really go home? Would I want to be there without my mother and Titus?

"You'll probably live in the castle," Alexander offers, almost reading where my thoughts were going.

"The view will be a little different this time," I joke. My breath catches in my throat, my father's vision forcing it's way to the front of my focus. *The view will be much different this time.*

Behind Alexander I see the group of captains making their rounds with my father, talking to each lieutenant. When I see them come our way, Alexander and I drop our swords and wipe the sweat from our faces.

"Lieutenant Adaline, Lieutenant Alexander," they greet us.

"We have the first orders for your squad," Captain Brutis, our direct superior, says and hands us an envelope. I break the seal and Alexander and I read the orders.

"We're recruiting?" I ask, offended. The order says our troop will be traveling to an island that is similar to Libertas to bring in more forces.

"Not exactly," my father explains. "Xavin is a neighboring island that many gifted from the other islands have fled to. Similar to us. It's a smaller community, just fifty or so. You will go and collect them, and meet up with us in Dather." My father points to a set of numbers on the order paper. "Those are your docking coordinates for Xavin and Dather. We will be waiting for you just outside of Sard with your next move."

I nod, understanding our squad's job. I had thought we'd be thrown into battle immediately. I'm almost insulted to find out we are put on this task, but then I realize why we were selected. Of course the saviors for the rebellion should be the ones to collect more soldiers. They will need to trust us and want to follow us, just like the people of Libertas needed to. It'll be much easier to bring them on board if Alexander and I are there in person.

"There's one more thing," my father says, dropping his voice. "There's a valuable object on that island, guarded by the gifted that have been living there."

"What is it?" I ask, sensing the edge in my father's voice.

"You'll find out when you get there. I hope it brings you some closure, Adaline."

A rumble of thunder not too far off interrupts my father. I glance up seeing the grey clouds rolling in.

"Looks like a storm is approaching," Captain Brutis huffs, his gaze following mine out to the dark clouds.

"Dismiss your team early today. We don't want them stuck here in the rain," my father says before moving around us to deliver the rest of the orders to the other lieutenants.

Alexander and I have our troop circle up and we explain to them what our first orders have been. Unlike me, they don't seem upset to be taking on this safe task. I know, since Alexander and I are the most powerful gifted, we will be in the heart of the battle. I should be thankful we'll start easy. We dismiss them from the training grounds so they can get back home before the rain starts. Many of the other teams have also dismissed for the night. My father has already headed back in the castle, and I know Linda won't be coming to get me, so I start heading in that direction on my own.

"Linda's not escorting you anymore?" Alexander asks, noticing her absence.

"I asked her not to," I say, even though it was more of a demand.

Alexander nods and we part from one another, me heading for the castle and him heading to his home. The air is eerie as the storm grows nearer. I glance up at the thundering dark clouds above, ready to drop their rain to the ground. The air has turned warm and sticky, thick in my throat. Just as the rain is unleashed from the clouds above, I slip into the castle and out of its grasp. But even in the stone fortress, the loud thunder shakes the floor beneath my feet.

Chapter 22

My spoon rattles in the empty glass bowl on the table after another low rumble cracks in the sky. Cooper and my father continue to eat their dinner, but my mind has turned away from the food.

"Heard you destroyed the ring today," Cooper says, not looking up from his plate.

My eyes shift to my father, even though I know Cooper is talking to me. "How has training been going with the air fleet?" I ask, ignoring his comment about the ring.

He shifts his head a little as to say it's been all right. "The storm cut us short today," Cooper says a bit annoyed. "Heard you brought lightning down from the sky," Cooper adds, returning the conversation to the ring.

Again, I glance toward my father, and this time he looks up to meet my gaze. "I did," I say through a tight throat. I don't want to talk about the ring, but clearly Cooper can't understand that.

I continue to shift in my chair; incredibly uncomfortable in the shimmering crystal gown Linda made me wear. Tomorrow, I will be having a private dinner with the highest-ranked personnel on the island. It's the first royal dinner Linda has prepared for us. Commander Crymm will be there, along with the other captains and lieutenants. I'm supposed to be using tonight as practice.

"Sit up straighter," Linda calls from the other end of the dark, wooden table. Her narrow brown eyes catch even my slightest slouch. I let a heavy sigh escape my lips and I sit up in my chair.

My feet throb in the tall crystal heels she forced me in. I could hardly walk out of my room in them, stumbling along the wall for support. Linda still seems to be upset about my outburst yesterday, and she's surely taking it out on me now.

From across the table, Cooper snickers at me. His stiffly pressed, black suit fits him well, but his crown has fallen crooked on his head. Linda doesn't miss a beat, quickly fixing it on his head before returning to her chair at the end of the table. Lucky for me, my hair is braided around my crown and it helps me hold it steady on my head.

Another deep rumble of thunder sends shudders through our glass dishes. Suddenly, someone pushes open the main door to the dining room. They race in, gasping for breath. Linda looks like she's going to lose her temper at the intruder, but my father's motions quiet her. He stands slowly, his shocked face locked on the visitor.

"What is it?" my father asks.

"The storm," the man says, taking in a deep breath. "Sir, you need to sound the Retreating Bell."

I turn to my father and see his shocked face has turned to stubborn anger.

"I can't," my father says, but the visitor is persistent.

"Sir, I beg you. Come and see for yourself." I watch as the visitor turns and leaves the dining room. My father moves around the edge of the table and hurries to follow him. Cooper and I share a quick glance before jumping out of our seats to run after them.

"You have not been dismissed," Linda roars, upset that her practice dinner has been interrupted.

Neither Cooper nor myself sit back down. I rip off the heavy heels, not able to keep up in them. I carry the shoes in my hand as I run after my brother and father barefoot.

When I reach the balcony that Cooper and my father are standing on, I lose my breath in my throat. There's an overhang on the balcony that keeps us dry, but the rest of the island is soaked. I look at the bricked path that twists and turns down the mountain and into the center of town. Water rushes down the path, making it look like a river.

"Sound the bell," my father says softly. Then, he turns in a hurry and rushes back into the castle, yelling to the nearest servant. "Sound the bell!"

I step out further, grasping the railing of the balcony with my empty hand for support. The sky is a mix of black and grey clouds, glowing white with the occasional jolt of lighting. But what my father is most afraid of lies out in front of me.

The ocean.

It's a mess of wild ripples, foaming white waves stretch the height of the steel buildings in Sard. Even from up here in the castle, they reach eye level. The shore is already a foot underwater, leaving a thin stretch of sand as the island's coast. Soon, all of Libertas will be devoured by the sea.

From a tower above my head, I hear a low tone ring out. It's slow and deep, echoing through the pouring rain. People wander out of their homes in a confused haze, staring up at the ringing bell. For a moment, through the sheet of white rain, the island balances in a frozen minute of confusion. Then, the swarms of people start pouring from their homes and into the river roaring down the street.

"We need to go, now!" my father commands, pulling Cooper and me away from the balcony.

"Where are we going?" I question, running to keep up with my father. He hurries down the wide staircase, toward the front of the castle. Linda joins us there, two black horses standing at her side. I stumble back from them, startled to see they aren't tied to a wagon like usual.

"Cooper, come with me. Linda, take Adaline," my father says and I watch as he pulls himself up onto the back of one of the black stallions.

"Where are we going?" I ask again as Linda helps me up onto our horse.

"The bunkers," she says and takes her place behind me, straddling the horse.

She gives the horse a soft kick and a strong command. He begins running out into the rain. I glance back and see Cooper and my father's horse following ours. The pounding rain chills my skin almost immediately. The crystal gown does little to keep me warm and I've had to pull it up to my knees to even stay on the horse.

To my amazement, Linda doesn't mention how unladylike I look; my hair falling from its braid and my heavy shoes dangling in my hand. Perhaps she understands this isn't the time to be ladylike. On the backs of the horses, we move much faster than we ever would in a wagon. The horses race through the deep water on the paths, easily maneuvering around the running people heading to the bunker.

When we reach the shore, I know we're almost too late. The ocean's tide is coming in so far it strikes the stone door to the bunker. Linda and I slide from the horse's back and shove our way through the crowd of people gathering outside the bunker door, waiting for Linda to let them in. She slams her hand on the door, and it clicks beneath her touch. She pushes in on the door and flips on the white buzzing lights of the tunnel.

"File in! Find a place along the tunnel to sit. We'll assign rooms later," she yells as the flood of people chaotically run into the bunker and out of the pouring rain. My father, Cooper, and I help escort people into the bunker in shifts, trying to find somewhere for them to wait in the tunnels. I quickly realize there aren't enough rooms for everyone on the island. These bunkers were made for those who weren't going to war, not for the entire population of Libertas.

"We'll leave the door open for a few more minutes," my father instructs to Linda.

The flood of people has finally made it inside, but in the case of a few stragglers, we wait as long as we can. The sheets of rain soak the entrance to the tunnel and small cracks of water crawl back along the stone floor. The citizens of Libertas are soaking wet, leaving puddles where they sit. The wind howls through the tunnel, sending bursts of cold, wet air over the group. Many of the people are shivering and have asked for blankets or spare clothes, but we tell them they have to wait until we see what we can distribute.

"Are you okay?" A tight hand grasps my wrist. I turn and see Max, soaking wet and still in his training uniform.

"Yeah, I'm fine," I say, happy to see he made it here okay. "Does this happen often?" I ask.

Max shakes his head, drips of water escaping his short brown hair. "We've never had to sound the bell," Max says, peering out the entrance at the roaring dark clouds. "We've had practice drills, but I've never seen a storm like this."

I remember Cooper's comment about my lighting from the ring and my face goes pale. "Did I cause this?" I ask, the thought registering. "I had brought down the lighting in the ring. I didn't mean to call on an entire storm."

"I don't think you could have created this," Max says, but the screams of a young girl overpower his words.

"Adaline!" Molly screeches, running to my side. "Adaline, my friend isn't here. She went back inside our house to get her cat, but she isn't here." Her high voice echoes through the wet tunnel.

I don't even give myself time to think or respond. I drop the crystal heels to the ground and run out into the storm. My bare feet sink into the wet sand as I struggle to run to the Mills's house.

"Where are you going?" I hear Max call out.

I glance over my shoulder and see he's following me out in the rain. "Go back!" I yell over the thunder, squinting through the sheets of rain.

"I'm not leaving you out here!" Max roars, flinching from the bright strike of lighting.

I don't want to waste any time arguing so I turn and continue running through the soaked beach, Max at my side, until we get to the cobblestone paths. I head toward the Mill's home, trying to remember the way from the night Linda brought us there.

"Hello?" I scream out. "Hello, is anyone out here?"

Max joins me, calling out into the sheets of rain, but our voices are easily drowned out. When we make it to the Mills's home, the front door hangs ajar. I rush in and yell out again, "Hello? Is anyone in here?"

"You need to leave the house now!" Max yells.

We decide to split up and Max runs upstairs while I check the kitchen and the dining room. Scattered on the table are sheets of school work and empty dinner plates, left behind in a hurry.

"I found her!" Max calls and his voice floods my veins with relief.

I meet him at the bottom of the staircase, a little blonde girl in his arms. She rests her head on his shoulder, a matted, brown, stuffed cat grasped in her tiny hands. I follow Max out of the house and we splash through the deep water. I pull up my long gown in one hand to keep from tripping on the slick crystals.

When we get to the coastline, we are nearly knee-deep in the sea.

There's a line of gifted at the bunker entrance, using an enhanced sense of sight to hold back the water from flooding in as best they can. The current in the water is hard to walk through, trying to pull Max and me out to sea. When we reach the entrance to the bunker, I'm breathing so heavy my chest aches. The gifted help Linda push the heavy door back in place and the tunnel shakes around us when it closes. Immediately the sounds of the storm are blocked out and the eerie quiet tunnel, filled with everyone's panicked breaths, makes my skin crawl.

"What were you thinking?"

I expect it to be my father that scolds me, but I'm shocked to see it's Alexander.

"She got left behind," I start to say, still trying to catch my breath.

"Did you drag her out there?" Alexander asks Max, disgust in his voice.

I watch as Max lets the girl down and she runs to find Molly. "No, I went out after her to help," Max says, his voice harsh.

"I'm fine," I say, turning my back on both of them.

My father, Cooper, and Linda are leaning against the entrance to the bunker, taking in the number of people in the tunnel and the lack of rooms we have.

When I reach them, my father looks at me, pressing his lips together. I know he wants to yell at me for running out into the storm, but for some reason, he decides not to.

"We need a plan," my father says, his voice low. "We've got an entire population buried in the side of a mountain, soaking wet, and we're on the brink of a war. We have to gain some control of this situation."

"We should start with dry clothes," I offer. "The last thing we need is for people to get sick down here."

Linda nods, agreeing. "We've already started stocking the bunker, so the rooms all have at least two or three sets of clothes for each of their occupants."

"All right, elderly and kids first," my father instructs. "Then, we'll assign rooms, starting with the highest-ranked captains and lieutenants."

"And when we run out?" I ask, knowing the Mills and some of the kids I trained all week with won't be ranked high enough to get one of the rooms.

"We'll deal with that later," my father says dryly.

He leads us toward the rooms and we begin to empty out the clothes that are stored there. It's nothing fancy. It honestly reminds me of the prison uniforms we wore back in Garth. There's at least a variety of clothes; short sleeve shirts, thick long sleeve sweaters, thin knee-length shorts, and long soft pants. But everything is a muted shade of grey. I had expected some sort of color distinguishing the type of enhanced sense. Max and Alexander offer to help, but my father has them join the rest of the crowd. He not only wants to take control of the situation, but he also wants to maintain his hold of power.

Thankfully, we do have more than enough clothes to go around. I'm happy to trade in my crystal gown for the thick, long sleeve shirt and pants. Linda almost screams when I drop the gown, my crystal heels, and crown into a wet puddle in the corner of the tunnel. She scoops them up and hurries off with them, trying to keep some sort of normalcy down here. Once everyone has changed into their dry clothes, we begin the hard task of assigning rooms.

"Rooms will be given out based on residency rank," my father says.

I watch many unfamiliar faces drop, knowing they are nothing more than the common citizen.

"We are turning classrooms, training rooms, and storage rooms into overflow areas. It won't be comfortable, but hopefully it's just for tonight. We'll wait the storm out and reevaluate our situation tomorrow."

At the mention of the storm raging above our heads, there's a low rumble of thunder that feels like it's in my chest, reminding us we are at its mercy tonight. Commander Crymm and three other highly ranked captains get the first room. Max and his father get the next room, paired with two additional captains. This continues until all of the captains and lieutenants, Alexander included, have received their own rooms.

Of course my father, Cooper, and I are given a room, though I'd rather give it to Molly and her friends. I'm not surprised that the non-gifted members I traveled with aren't lucky enough to be granted a room. Not only that, but none of the other gifted want to stay with them. I bite my tongue and keep from causing an outbreak. We are limited on space, can the gifted not see that? Essie offers her classroom and that's where they go. The Mills and the kids they've taken in move into another classroom. Somehow we all do find our places. It won't be comfortable, especially for those without a bed or blankets. There were some extras down here in the bunker, but not enough.

Linda had already stocked some food, so we won't starve. Not yet, anyway. Most people decide not to eat. They're not hungry, their stomachs full of nerves. As a constant reminder, the thunder above continues to rumble on. I find myself walking aimlessly around the now empty tunnels, not wanting to lock myself up in our room for the night.

I help Linda distribute some dry cookies to the kids who have found their appetite after getting comfortable. It's not Molly's group, but that's probably for the best. I've already drawn enough attention to her today, after running out into the storm at her simple plea. I would have done it for anyone, I think, but I don't know if that's entirely true.

I find my father in the command room. There are large monitors, like the ones from the testing facility, hanging all across the walls. Big, black boxes sit at each one, a mesh material covering their front. When the next crack of thunder is released, I breathe in sharply. The rumble sounded like it was right in this room.

"I'm listening to what's going on out there," my father says. He looks deeply into one of the black boxes. He allows his eyes to shift my way and notices my confused expression. "They're speakers. Technology created in Sard that we've stolen over the years. When we sounded the bell, I turned on my connecting monitor back at the castle so I could keep track of how the storm is progressing."

Another crack of thunder roars, like a whip, and I jump.

"Doesn't sound like it's gotten any better," I offer. "I was wondering," I begin to say, allowing my thoughts to process, "did I create this storm from what I did in the ring?"

My father gives his head a confident shake. "No. Your gift only acts when you have intent. You can't accidentally make something happen with your gift."

My father seems confident my mix of powers and loss of control in the ring had nothing to do with the storm raging above us, but I'm not so sure. He knows far more about gifts than I do. I understand what he means, I do have to tell my gift what to do and since I didn't tell it to unleash this monster of a storm, then it must not be coming from me.

Chapter 23

Listening to the constant cracks of thunder and pounding rain has done little to help with my nerves, so I decide to leave the command room. I walk back toward the quarters that were assigned to the royal family and hear the sounds of shoes splashing in puddles up ahead. I stop at the crossroads of the tunnel that leads to the storage units and classrooms. Max is walking toward me, his face stiff. When he sees me, he tries to force a smile, but his eyes still look cold.

"What are you doing?" I ask, my voice echoing down the tunnel. It cracks, but I try to make it seem playful, not nervous.

"Just checking on my mother," Max says, meeting me where the tunnels cross.

"You've never told me about her," I say. I glance over his shoulder. He's coming from one of the overflow storage rooms. Why wouldn't she be staying with him in his room?

"I don't see her very much," Max tries to offer as some sort of explanation.

I'm not sure how to respond. I'm afraid I may say something wrong.

Max's face suddenly changes to a confused squint. "Adaline, do you even know how this island operates?"

My cheeks flush red. "Yes? Different types of gifted are put in their counties. You either train and fight or you run the community on the island."

"And if you don't have the same gift as your parents?" Max asks.

I hadn't thought of that. Most people keep the same enhanced sense as their family, but not always. Especially if your parents have different enhanced senses from each other. There's no telling what, or if, you'd have one. I assume anything is possible. Max leans against the stone tunnel wall and slides down to sit on the cold floor.

I sit next to him and ask, "They can't live in that county, can they?"

Max shakes his head. "My father has an enhanced sense of sight, but my mother has an enhanced sense of taste."

"So, when you were born you stayed with your father?" I ask.

"I went back and forth until I turned fifteen. Then, you have to stay within your county. I can't believe you didn't know that. You are the Princess, right?" Max asks, but his tone is lighter.

Still, my cheeks blush an even brighter red. "Well, it doesn't make Libertas sound all that great," I admit. "Linda knows I had a hard enough time accepting the division between the gifted and non-gifted. She probably knew I wouldn't agree with the segregation on the island."

"It's just always been this way," Max says, analyzing the society here in Libertas.

"That doesn't mean it's right," I say, feeling myself getting more irritated. "This is what we're fighting for? A world where we divide everyone up based on their powers? Discriminating against the ones with no powers? How is that any better than what King Renon is doing?"

Max is quiet, considering this for a second. "I don't know if it's better, but it's certainly not worse. At least this way no one is being locked away and used for their powers. Everyone still has a life to live, and they get to be in control of it."

I shake my head and stare down the wet, dark tunnel. "That's not good enough," I say under my breath.

"So, will you not fight with us?" Max asks, and I feel his stare burning into the side of my face.

I turn to him, scanning his light green eyes, his pale face, and thin shoulders. "I will fight, but I'm hoping we'll do better when we win." I pause, seeing his eyes grow brighter. "I am the princess. One day I could even be the queen, and I will be the change."

"All on your own?" Max asks and his thin lips part in a smile.

"Will you help me?" I ask, tilting my head.

"Princess Adaline, I will follow you to the ends of this world," Max says softly.

The corners of my mouth twitch up into a smile and my eyes wander his face until the sound of whispers breaks the silence. I turn and see Zavy and another girl walk out of a room at the end of the hall. Zavy's eyes find me quickly and they immediately stop talking. The two walk by Max and I, heading toward the food storage rooms.

When they pass us, I realize I recognize the girl Zavy's with. She was at the party beneath the store.

"Who's Zavy with?" I ask Max once they have gone into the food storage room.

"That's Lilliana," Max says. "She has an enhanced sense of sight. We trained together until I got appointed to be a lieutenant."

When Max says this, I remember her from my brief training the first day. I let out a hum, wishing I didn't care that Zavy has found someone else to be friends with. A door suddenly slams near the front of the bunker, and I snap my gaze toward the noise.

"Help!" A voice calls out. "Commander Crymm is gone! Someone help!"

My father comes running by Max and me, heading toward the screaming. We scramble to our feet to follow after him. Many people have cracked open their doors, leaning out to hear what's going on.

"Commander Crymm is gone!" The voice yells out again. I see it's Captain Marc who was sharing a room with her.

"What happened, Captain?" my father asks.

I watch as Captain Marc's mouth hangs open. His eyes bulging, shocked. "I don't know," he says, looking around the bunker. "One second, she's saying she's going to lie down for the night, and then she said she had to go and," he stops, the words catching in his throat. "She just vanished."

"She teleported out of the room?" my father asks and Captain Marc nods.

"She went out in this storm?" I ask.

"No, she must be somewhere in here," my father says. "Commander Crymm!" he yells, heading down the hall. He continues running the length of the bunker until the chilling truth sets in. *She's not in here.*

"We have to go get her!" I say and head toward the entrance of the bunker. Alexander emerges from a room at the end of the hall, stepping into my path.

"Adaline, you can't," Alexander says. He doesn't stop me, but my feet freeze. His concerned green gaze begs me not to fight him on this.

I feel the eyes of hundreds burning into my back, waiting to see what I will do. I turn around to the other faces in the bunker and see they agree with him.

"None of you want to go out there to look for her?" I ask.

"She could be anywhere," my father mutters. "I don't know why she would go out there, but I'm sure she'll find her way back or she'll find somewhere to take shelter."

"Captain Marc, you're sure she didn't say anything else?" Max asks, but the captain shamefully shakes his head.

"I'm sorry, Lieutenant, she didn't." The silence that fills the tunnel is feeding the fear I'm starting to see in the faces leaning out of their rooms.

"Everything's fine," my father says, running a nervous hand through his hair. "Back into your rooms, please," my father commands, giving an exhausted wave of his hand. Slowly, people sink back into their rooms and click their doors closed.

Alexander comes to me and says softly, "You can't keep running out into storms for everyone, Adaline."

The muscles in my face are still tight with frustration. My heavy gaze hangs with him for a moment before turning to my father.

"We could hear her through the speakers, right?" I ask, trying to find some kind of action to take.

"If she's near the castle, maybe," my father starts to hesitantly explain, but it's enough for me.

"Can she hear us? Could we call out to her?" I ask, my mind racing and trying to figure out the different technology I had seen in the command room. Surely the speakers could work both ways.

My father gives an unsure nod. "Again, she'd only hear it if she were near the receiver I turned on. In this storm, it will probably never reach her."

"But it's something," I say and take large strides back to the command room.

My father dismisses Captain Marc and him, Max, and Alexander follow me. In the command room, the sounds of rain and rumbling thunder continue to scream from the black boxes.

"You'll never hear her," my father begins to say, but I raise my hand, stopping him.

"You won't let me go out there to help, so I'm going to do whatever I can from in here. How do I talk to her?" I ask.

My father lets out a heavy breath and walks over to a small black remote with a little speaker in it. "Push this button," my father says, clicking a red button on the side of the black box. "And speak into the mesh circle." He hands the radio to me and adds, "If she's close to my receiver, she'll hear it and we'll catch anything she says back."

"Commander Crymm, can you hear me?" I ask into the radio. The room seems to balance on a pin, but the only response we get is another earth-shaking rumble of thunder.

"Commander Crymm, this is Adaline, can you hear me?" But the black speakers around us continue to only spit out sounds of the rain and whining wind.

"She's not there," my father says.

"Not right now," I say, and I take a seat on one of the metal stools along the wall of speakers. "I'll keep trying every couple of minutes. She may go there."

"You're going to stay in here all night? Adaline, you need your rest," my father tries to lecture me.

I ignore him and push down the red radio button again. "Commander Crymm, can you hear me?"

"I'll stay with her," Alexander says, laying a comforting hand on my father's arm.

"I can stay, too. Maybe we can take turns trying to contact her," Max adds.

"You don't have to," I begin to say, but Max and Alexander have already moved to sit on the other stools in the command row, each listening to the speaker nearest them.

"Just pass the radio down. We'll trade off every hour or so," Alexander offers.

I look at Alexander and Max's faces, seeing they think this is never going to work, but they are willing to try. *For me.*

"It's hopeless," my father scoffs beneath his breath, heading to the door. "This is the Commander of our Army we're talking about. She can take care of herself. You three aren't helping her any."

"But it's better than doing nothing," I say coldly.

My father lets out another heavy sigh before leaving the command room.

"Commander Crymm, say something if you can hear me," I speak into the radio. *Please say something.*

A crack of thunder roars through the black speaker box, the pelting sounds of rain play on an endless loop, and the howling wind sings a haunting melody. But there's no response from Commander Crymm.

I hold onto the radio for the first hour, repeating the same call out to her. I pass it to Alexander next, when I finally get tired of hearing myself speak to the storm. He holds onto it for a while, trying different messages to reach Commander Crymm before letting Max have his turn.

It's been nearly three and a half hours now, probably one or two in the morning. She hasn't returned to the bunker yet, and I wonder where she could be in the storm. What drove her out into its wrath? Max hands the radio back to Alexander after barely mumbling his last few attempts to reach Commander Crymm.

My eyelids have been growing heavy and I see Max has resulted to resting his head on the cool metal counter. Alexander slouches forward in his stool, the radio lightly grasped in his tired hands. He clicks the red button again, repeating her name with his dry voice through tired yawns.

My heavy head hangs low and, as hard as I try not to, I give in to sleep. Just for a second. I close my eyes and my mind begins to drift. The storm has seemed to quiet, the rain acting as a soft lullaby.

Screaming shrills fill my ears and my head snaps up. Max has fallen back off his stool, startled by the loud screeches. *How long have I been asleep?* Alexander snaps his head between the speakers and me, not believing the sound coming from them. The screams are not human. They do not belong to Commander Crymm. Again, the ear-piercing screech comes from the black box. *It's the monster eels.* I know that sound from the worst day of this journey, when half my team was killed during their attack.

"Go get my father," I say, snapping my attention to Max, still shocked and sprawled out on the floor.

"What is that?" Max asks, his voice shaking. His wide eyes flash between the roaring speakers.

"Just go get my father," I yell, panic taking over.

Max fumbles to his feet before running out of the command room.

"They sound like they're on the island," Alexander says.

"Unless the island is so far underwater that the ocean has reached the castle," I say, drawing out my words while I try and understand what this could mean.

The sound of running feet echoes down the bunker tunnels and my father and Max appear in the doorway.

"What is it?" my father asks, but I don't have to answer.

The eel lets out another screech, this time accompanied by a lower roar. There's more than one. The color drains from my father's face. His boat was attacked by these creatures too. He knows how destructive they are.

"The water must be nearly to the training grounds by now," he whispers harshly.

"You still think Commander Crymm didn't need our help?" I ask, standing forcefully, knocking my chair to the ground. "We should have gone to get her!"

"I didn't know how bad it was," my father says, frustrated with himself.

"Well, if she hasn't drowned already, these monsters will surely finish her off!" I yell at my father. I know it's not his fault, but I don't know what else to do.

"Are we stuck in here?" Max asks cautiously. He seems to be stuck on the fact that we are currently underwater.

My father stiffly shakes his head. "The storm will pass and the water will draw back out to sea. We'll get out, we just have to wait."

"But what's going to be left out there?" I ask. The winds and rain had already done so much damage. I saw it when I ran out to get Molly's friend.

"You need to calm down," my father says, forcefully taking control. The shock of hearing the eels has worn off. Now he's very aware of the situation we're in. "All three of you are dismissed. Go."

"No," I say, offended he's shutting me out.

"Adaline, I'm not going to tell you again. Get out!" He raises his voice, eyes bulging with anxious anger.

My mouth hangs open, searching for words of protest but they don't come. In a confused shuffle, Alexander, Max, and I exit the command room. My father slams the door behind us, sealing the sounds of the storm and the creatures inside.

"Now what?" Alexander asks.

I swallow my fear, knowing we only have one option. "Now, we wait."

The early morning passes at a crawl. I eventually go back to my room, but can't find sleep for more than a couple of minutes. Every time I get close to sleep, the screeching eels find their way into my dreams. Alexander, Max, and I keep the information about the eels to ourselves, so we don't worry the rest of the group. When the time for breakfast arrives, Cooper and I help Linda take a small amount of food around to the different rooms. She says it will be good for them to see our faces, but I know my drained face with dark bags under my eyes will do little to keep them calm.

After breakfast is distributed, I meet up with Alexander and Max outside of the command room. Unfortunately, waiting is not easy to do. My father hasn't come out all morning. I hold a single roll and a pouch of fruit in my hand to deliver to him for breakfast. Linda said she would do it, but I'm hoping I can catch an update through the speakers. Alexander and Max couldn't resist the opportunity either. I raise my hand to gently knock on the thick metal door when it suddenly springs back from me.

My father's thin, grey face looks down at me.

"Breakfast," I say weakly and hold the small meal out to him.

"It's over," my father says, his voice scratchy. He walks around me, toward the front of the bunker.

The bread and fruit fumble from my hands, landing on the nearest counter. I turn to run after him. "What do you mean? The storm's over?" I ask, my tired body finding some energy. Alexander and Max jog and fall in line with me.

"The eels drew back hours ago in the receding water. It's been quiet for the entire morning," my father says, but it feels like he's trying to convince himself.

When we get to the entrance of the bunker, he lays a light hand on the stone door. He hesitates to open it, and suddenly, the sounds of small clicks ring against the door. He drops his hand and stumbles backward, but the clicking continues.

Alexander's face squints at the noise. "It sounds like hail," he says. While it's rare, we've had a few hail storms in the colder months in Garth. Maybe only twice in my entire life.

It grows louder, pounding against the stone door until it eventually stops. None of us says a word, waiting for the silence to be broken with more clicks, but it doesn't. My father lifts his hand back to the door, now severely shaking. When he pushes it open, bright light pours in through the cracked opening.

My father leans into the door and, with the help of Max and

Alexander, pushes it open through the thick, damp sand. The sound of waves instantly floods the tunnel. The white grains of sand reflect the blinding sunlight up at me and I have to cover my eyes until they adjust. I realize, though, that the sand is much too bright. It's too reflective. I step out into the scorching sun, the air thick with humidity. I expect my feet to sink into the soft sand, but instead, I step on something hard and hot. When my eyes adjust to the bright sun, I finally see them. Scattered across the beach are hundreds of small metal keys.

Chapter 24

At first, no one says anything. We just stare out at the sandy beach with scattered keys reflecting the sunlight. Slowly, I bend down and pick up the one I had stepped on. It's old, there's brown rust coating parts of it, and it's heavy in my hands. I run my fingers along the key, amazed by its detail. The top of the key is a twisting of metal that forms a perfect, little crown.

What we had thought was hail, was actually keys.

My father stumbles over to the key nearest him and examines it. Alexander crosses to me and I silently hand him the one I had picked up. With the loud tapping of raining keys and pushing open the bunker door, a crowd has begun to form at the entrance to the cave. They stand at the edge of the bunker, not sure if it's okay to come out.

"Do you know what this means?" I finally ask my father, breaking the silence.

He squints hard, still turning the key over in his hands. "I-" he stops, trying to force some explanation to come to him. "I don't know."

"Can you get any information from it?" I turn and ask Alexander.

He closes his hand in a tight fist but shakes his head. "There's nothing there."

"Well, it has to mean something!" I say, raising my voice.

I pick up another one from the sand and examine the new key. My stomach tightens. "It's the same," I say softly and show Alexander. We each compare the keys in our hands and my father comes to our side, his key having the same twisted crown on its top. "They're all the same crowning key. This means something!" I say and my eyes search the other's faces. They all look at a loss for words, no explanation making sense.

For the first time, I look up past the beach covered with keys and see the rest of the island, what's left of Libertas, anyways. Hardly any homes still stand. Single walls that were once houses topple over onto one another. The stone pathways survived though, and the castle still stands. Seaweed and green moss hang from the stone peaks of the towers. The slimy stuff also coats most of the island. I realize that the keys are not isolated to the beach. They scatter up the stone pathway and into the rubble.

"I don't know what to do with this," my father says, pulling my attention back to the heavy metal key in my hand. "But we are supposed to leave for the war tomorrow."

"We can't go tomorrow. We aren't ready," I say, shocked as I see my father's attention turn from the keys to the war.

"We're out of time, Adaline. We have to move tomorrow or Dather will be impenetrable," my father tries to explain to me.

"We barely survived the night. Everyone is tired and hungry," I argue, but my father's face remains unchanged. "We don't even know where Commander Crymm is," I say under my breath, so I'm not overheard by the growing crowd at the mouth of the bunker.

My father's eyes shift, but I know he won't change his mind. He turns his attention to the gathering group. "We have survived the storm, but we need to be ready to move tomorrow morning," my father says, raising his voice. It echoes back through the tunnel for everyone to hear. "First, we get our home cleaned up. Go to your houses, shops if you own one, and collect what is left. If you are staying behind, we will move you into your permanent bunkers tonight. Everyone going to the war will spend the night in the castle if your homes were destroyed in the storm."

My father pauses, letting his orders sink into the crowd. Many seem shocked we will still be leaving for the war tomorrow, but not as shocked as I was. I'm reminded they've spent their whole lives planning for this war, for tomorrow. They, like my father, don't want to let anything delay what they've worked so long for.

"If you find yourself needing something to do, help those around you. We are all one island, together. The gifted will rise. A new age is upon us!" He thrusts his fist into the air, chanting out the lines I remember from my coronation.

The roar of the crowd repeating the words floods out from the tunnel, and I find myself chanting the words with them, thrusting my own fist into the air. If there's one thing this journey has taught me, it's that fear and self-doubt will be your biggest weakness. If we're going into war tomorrow, then we are going together, chanting for the new age, and helping each other get there.

The crowd begins to flow out of the bunker and towards what used to be their homes. The sight reminds me of one of my training days. Everyone looking exhausted, but happy to be tired. My father begins to use his enhanced sense of sight to pick up the hundreds of keys.

"What are you going to do with them?" I ask.

"Keep them stored in the castle until I know what they mean," he says. He moves away from us and works his way further up the coastline.

"I could use your help here," Linda calls from behind me. She must sense my confusion on what to do next. Alexander and I follow Linda back into the bunker while Max excuses himself to go help his father find the remains of their home.

"We'll need to get these bunkers cleaned and stocked for the move tonight," Linda explains as we walk to the first row of rooms.

Now empty, the bunker balances in a silent bubble, causing all of our footsteps and words to echo in the chamber. We split up and comb through the rooms that were left behind in a hurry. All the bedding is sent to be cleaned. Most people changed this morning into their now dried clothes from before the storm, leaving the grey uniforms piled on the floor. I send them with the bedding to be washed.

Once all the rooms have been stripped down, I meet Linda and Alexander by the classrooms. The desks had been stacked in the corners to make more room, so we work together to reset the classroom. Afterward, I help Linda take inventory of the food storage rooms.

"We'll need to restock," she mumbles, digging through a bin that had held apples this morning.

"Where are you planning to get enough food?" I ask as I finish counting the loaves of bread on the shelf nearest the door.

"We have more storage under the castle," she says, standing up from her empty fruit bin. "I'm sure the gardens have been wiped clean now, though. We're lucky we harvested yesterday before the storm hit."

We head back toward the front of the bunker and Linda explains how the different gifts, like enhanced sense of touch and sight, can help grow the food supply carefully. She doesn't seem too concerned with it. Alexander meets us outside the bunker after doing a final sweep of the empty rooms.

"Can the two of you go to the castle and bring me more food and clothes to stock in the bunker? Cooper can show you where it's at."

We agree and head towards the main bricked path that leads to the castle.

"Are you doing all right?" Alexander asks when we're far enough down the coast.

"I feel out of control," I say and take in a nervous breath. "I just feel like we're being pushed into the war. It's just happening so fast."

"Nothing has changed, Adaline," Alexander says. "With or

without the storm we'd still be leaving tomorrow."

"I know," I say softly.

"Hey, don't forget our first orders are just to go to Xavin," Alexander says.

I feel my nerves ease away. "Right," I say, remembering our troop's first task. "We technically still have another day or two before we'll be back in Dather."

We make it to where the cobblestone path meets the sand and we start to climb through the rubble. I do feel better, now that I'm reminded even though we leave for the war tomorrow, I will just be traveling on a boat to a neighboring island.

"I'm glad they have us leading a troop together," I say and look at Alexander.

He gives me a side glance, his light green eyes bright in the morning sun. "I am too," he says and lays a gentle arm around my shoulders. "I like our troop, too," Alexander adds, nodding his head. "We've got a good group of fighters."

"Except Zip," I say and roll my eyes. "I wish we didn't have anyone that young fighting. Especially since she's defenseless."

"Better that she's with us then. We probably have the best chance to protect her," Alexander offers.

I'm quiet as I process this idea. I glance at Alexander through the fallen pieces of my brown hair. He's so much calmer than me. Maybe calmer isn't the right word. He's just sturdy. He was trained for war. Where I get hung up and anxious about things, he has already adapted to them. I mention the abrupt leave, and he reminds me we have other tasks than just battle. I get worried about Zip on our squad, and he tells me we'll protect her better than any other team. He doesn't let anything faze him.

Again I say, "I'm really glad they have us working together." Alexander is my rock. He's the one who has been with me every step of the way. From the very first night when he helped me escape the castle.

"There you two are!" I hear Cooper call. He hurries to us, climbing over a pile of loose debris. "We're trying to clear off this debris so the horses can help move people down to the bunker. The water never reached the stables by the castle."

I glance over his shoulder and see the groups of gifted are using enhanced sense of sight to lift the rubble out of the way. Some, even as young as Toby, try and lift the smaller planks of wood. Alexander and I turn back the way we came and make quick work of cleaning off the path, leaving heaps of soaking wood on the side of the stone street.

Cooper shuffles along the edges tossing small pieces of wood with his hands. We help clear the rest of the main path that leads to the heart of town. Alexander and I are approached with many grateful handshakes and the horses begin to trot back and forth from the town to the bunker, taking what little items people have found with them.

"Cooper," I say, crossing to him while he still tries to pick up and toss stray pieces of wood off the path. "Linda wants you to show us where the storage rooms are at the castle. She needs us to start stocking the bunker."

"Yeah, sure! I can show you," Cooper says, wiping sweat off his forehead. His hands are brown with mud from the wet wood and he smears a bit on his face.

As we continue toward the castle Alexander and I continue to move the fallen debris into heaps at the side of the road. Some small pieces I miss, Cooper grabs and tosses over his shoulder.

As we approach the castle, its entrance just a few paces ahead of us, I see a hump of black fabric on the first marble step. My father stands over the pile of dark material, his face as white as the stones on the castle. When we get closer, I see a small white finger poking out of the black cloak.

My steps come quicker and I run toward the castle entrance. When I get there, I lose my breath in my throat. My shaking hand raises to my mouth to cover my horrified reaction. I stumble back a few steps and Alexander is there to catch me. I lean into his side, tears reaching the edges of my eyes.

Commander Crymm's translucent face stares up at me, her eyes wide. I don't have to ask, I know she is dead. One hand lies limp, poking out of the black sleeve of her nightgown. The other is tightly closed around a metal band. My father bends down and pulls it from her cold fingers.

I find my breath, and take in a shocked gasp. *A crown.* The tears in my eyes have pulled back, shock now taking over. I lift a shaking hand and my father passes the crown to me.

I rotate it, looking at it from every angle. It's made out of keys.

The entire crown is a puzzle of keys.

My father lifts Commander Crymm's other hand and pulls out a small metal tube she had concealed in her grasp. It's no bigger than a fingernail. My father twists it and one end separates from the other. He pulls out a small piece of paper that's rolled into a tiny scroll. Carefully, he unrolls the parchment, his eyes taking in the words. After a moment, he reads them out loud. "To the future Queen. To the prophesized Key." My father looks up from the paper, to the crown, and then to me.

"She came out here to get you a crown?" Cooper asks.

"I've never seen that before," my father says. "I don't know where she could have gotten it."

"None of this makes any sense," I say, my voice tight in my throat. "The keys, the crown, Commander Crymm, none of it!"

"Sometimes you don't get the answers that make sense," my father says. "You need to get back to cleaning up," my father adds, seeming to forget what we just found.

"We can't go to war tomorrow without a commander," I say. I don't want to do anything without Commander Crymm to help guide me. "We are a mess. We are not ready."

"We will not be delayed," my father yells, his voice sharp with anger. He turns sharply, heading into the castle.

My mouth hangs open, looking from his shrinking figure, to Commander Crymm's glossy eyes, to the crown of keys in my hands.

"To the storage units?" Cooper asks gently. He doesn't wait for us to respond and heads into the castle himself, careful to step around Commander Crymm. My feet move to follow him, my brain not telling them what to do. He leads us back into the castle, through the grand entrance, under the arching staircases and past the banquet hall and council room. When we reach the slim staircase that leads up to the residence floor, I finally find my voice.

"I'll be right back," I say and hurry up the staircase.

My grip tightens on the crown and I take the steps two at a time. When I reach the landing, my feet are quick to carry me to my room. I slip inside, noticing the blue carpet is actually quite dry. The ocean must not have gotten any higher than the base of the castle.

Once inside, I cross the room to the little podium. I gently place the crown of keys onto it and step back. I know what my father meant when he said he was going to leave the keys until he knew what they signified. We can't get every answer right now. And sometimes, it may not even be the answer we want. I spin on my heels and hurry out of my room and back toward the staircase.

I'll leave the crown there until I can figure out what it means.

When I reach Alexander and Cooper, I've tried to push all thoughts of the keys, crown, and Commander Crymm away. Keep moving forward, Adaline. You have to keep moving forward. You can only deal with what makes sense, with what you can control. *Keep moving forward.*

The hallways around me begin to look familiar and I realize we're heading toward the underground chamber where the testing rooms are located. We file down the wide, stone staircase, into the basement of the castle. Cooper doesn't take us too far into the chamber, entering a room on his left. It's a narrow hall with large white doors on the left-hand side, and it looks like the hall splits open into another room at the end. Cooper pulls open the white doors, they let out a sucking noise, and I'm hit by a burst of cold air. When we file in and Cooper closes the door behind me, my hair falls limp with the absence of the breeze.

"The air seems awfully thin," I say, my voice feeling weak in my throat.

"Sealed so the food will last longer," Cooper explains.

I scan the room, taking in the shelves overflowing with food.

"We just harvested yesterday," Cooper says. "We'll load up these wagons and the horses can take them down to the bunker."

Alexander, Cooper, and I load two large wagons with food to last through the next several weeks. It's a bit unnerving because I realize we don't know how long this war will last. Will we arrive on Dather and order King Renon's surrender in one day, or will we fight across every inch of land between Sard and Garth? We could be fighting for days or months. Perhaps years, but I'm not sure we have enough bodies for that.

I realize why my father is so adamant about pushing forward with our schedule. We always have to be on the offensive in this war because Dather's forces will always outlast us. For every one of us they kill, we have to remove three of them. That's not something you can do being on the defensive.

After we load the giant wagons with food, Cooper has us push them forward into what he calls the loading hall with a large metal door that stretches from the floor to the ceiling. Once here, he pulls another set of giant white doors closed. In the loading hall is another door to my right, and to my left it seems the hall opens up into another chamber.

"This way," Cooper says, directing my attention back to the door to my left.

He leads us into the neighboring room, but the air is not sucked thin in here. Stacks of the grey bunker uniforms spread around the room. We even find spare bedding to replace what had been removed from the bunker this morning.

"They aren't all that attractive," Cooper says, holding one of the grey shirts up to his chest. "But it was quicker to make hundreds of the same thing,"

"I actually think it's nice to see that they aren't separated into the colors of their gifts," I admit and begin piling in stacks of clothes into a third wagon. Once full, we roll this wagon into the loading hall as well. Cooper flips a large switch on the wall and the metal door begins to climb toward the ceiling, revealing the outside world.

"We'll get the horses now," Cooper says, leading us down the loading hall, toward the open chamber I had noted earlier.

As we pass the wagon full of fruits, Cooper plucks a shiny red apple from the top.

"These are the Libertas stables," Cooper announces as we turn into the chamber.

Ten or so large, powerful horses stand in different wooden stables and mounds of hay coat the floor and pile up in the corners of the room.

Cooper holds up the apple to one of the jet-black horses. After investigating the apple with its wet nose, the horse takes a large bite out of the fruit. "He's a bit stubborn, so he needs a little extra motivation," Cooper says, patting the thick neck of the horse. "You two can talk with them, so you shouldn't have a problem. We'll need three to pull the wagons." Cooper turns and begins to lead the black horse down the loading hall, pulling another apple from his pocket to persuade him.

Alexander and I each find a horse to take back to the wagons. I pick out a light brown horse near the back of the stables. She looks calmer than the other animals and I'm hoping she's also more willing to help. I've only ever used this gift to talk with Mindy, but find it easy to persuade the mare. These horses are probably used to having the gifted talk with them. I remember the boy from the Welcome Parade, and the tour into the city before my coronation, was a Communicator that had led the horses.

"I need your help pulling a wagon," I send to the horse. She just gives a low bow and begins to make her way toward the wagons.

Cooper straps our horses to the wooden wagons and helps me mount mine. Pulling the wagon of clothes behind her, we make our way down from the castle and back toward the bunkers. The morning sun has reached its peak and I know it must be nearly noon by now. The rumbling of my stomach reminds me I didn't eat any of the breakfast this morning and now it's time for lunch. When we reach the bunker, Linda tells us we can leave the horses and wagons for her to deal with.

"Your father called for an emergency training session," Linda grumbles and rolls her eyes. "As if we all don't have enough going on. You three better hurry up to the training grounds, you're already a bit late."

We jog back up the bricked path to the training grounds, seeing some fellow trainees are still making their way there too. Clearly, the others are still being informed of the emergency training and we aren't the last to arrive. The training grounds didn't hold up well in the storm, however. All the tents have been ripped and blown down. The ring is the only thing standing unbothered, but the crowd isn't heading toward the ring.

They are filing into the side entrance of the castle.

Chapter 25

"What do you think this is about?" I say under my breath.

I scan Cooper and Alexander's faces, but they are just as confused as I am. My father emerges from the door and sees us as we cross to him. He looks stressed.

"Cooper, you're needed at the air fleet training," my father instructs, not even bothering to say hello to his son. He turns sharply and leads Alexander and me toward the castle, clearly a man of business right now.

"What's going on?" I ask as we enter the castle and make our way down a dimly lit hallway. "Linda said something about an emergency training?"

My father doesn't answer. Instead, he gestures to the grey steel doors that are pulled open to our right. We file in and I notice everyone from our regular training sessions is here. The room is much larger than I had expected. It's nearly the size of the ballroom, but no fancy curtains or lush blue carpet decorate this room. Cool grey concrete paves the entire space, meeting the rough cement walls on all sides. Sickly white lights glow overhead, reminding me of the testing room. My eyes first land on the walls of weapons to our left. The options range from swords, to bows and arrows, to tridents, and spears. There are so many different weapons that line the walls, some I don't even recognize, their lethal points and sharp edges forming into different deadly blades.

Stretching down the center of the room, is a long table piled high with food. There's a large variety of sandwiches and fruits, but my eyes seem pulled to the sweet desserts at the end of the table. Clearly, the castle's kitchen was untouched by the storm.

"Before we get into our final training session, I thought we'd serve lunch," my father announces, releasing us to take what our plates can hold. No one complains about being offered the delicious treats and while we eat, my father prepares us for what we'll need to get accomplished in this final training session. Alexander and I take a bit of everything from the table and I even slip an extra bright yellow cookie on my plate.

"I wanted to call this training together, first to make a hard announcement," my father says, hushing the casual chatter in the room. "Commander Crymm is dead."

Alexander and I already know this, and when I scan the other faces in the room, I can tell many of them are not surprised either. They look concerned, but I don't think any of them expected her to survive the wrath of that storm.

"We will have a ceremony for her tonight. She may not have led us in this war, but she devoted her life to preparing us for it." I watch as my father crosses to the center of the room, scanning the hesitant faces staring back. "Originally, Commander Crymm and I were going to be leading together, but now I will bear that responsibility myself. I know this news may be weighing heavily with some of you, but you can not let this falter us. We have to continue moving forward. We have to win this war."

In the room, many people nod and I slowly see the emotion here shift from upset and mournful, to pride and power.

"The gifted will rise! A new age is upon us!" Max yells out, throwing his fist in the air. Everyone in the room, myself, Alexander, and my father included, repeat the words back, the chant echoing off the cement walls.

"Now, we are here to cover one important subject," my father says after the echoing of the chant passes. He waits to see if anyone will offer him his answer. "Hand-on-hand combat," he finishes. "In this war, it will be inevitable, and you all need to be ready for that. For those of you who were at the residency hearing last week, you'll remember Adaline had talked about the rocks that keep King Renon's army immune to your gifts."

A lot of people in the room look uncomfortable at that statement. Using their gifts to fight is all they know how to do. I realize it's our army's biggest flaw. They have missed an important step. My father's face looks pained as well. He knows he's set us up for failure when it comes to hand-on-hand combat. I know they've trained on it. I've seen them using the weapons on the training grounds, but not nearly as seriously as they should have been.

"Do you know what weapon you fight with best?" he asks,

directing his question to a sea of blank faces. "Is it a sword? Maybe a bow and arrow? What about a spear?" he gestures to the long wall of silver weapons. "Today you find out, because you're out of time. We go to war tomorrow. Your troops and tasks have already been assigned to you, but now we need to know what weapons and gear to give you. Your lieutenants will be observing today's training to help decide what weapon you'll be assigned."

After we finish our lunch the table in the center of the room is cleared. Servants I've seen silently moving throughout the castle the last couple of days enter with containers full of spare training uniforms. We all change and prepare ourselves for one final day of lessons.

Alexander and I lead our members to the front of the training hall where they spread out into two lines, facing each other. My father has everyone start with swords because that's what we have the most of. Those who feel uncomfortable with that weapon, or prove better with a different weapon, can rotate through the other options. All of the lieutenants line the edges of the room and watch their teams run drills with their swords. Right from the beginning, I know half of my troop will need something else. Their strikes are too wide and sloppy. They leave themselves completely open to enemy attacks. *But what would fit them better than a sword?*

Max's troop lines up near mine and I catch his wild glance wander over to my group. I know I could ask for his advice. He's been training with these people his whole life. Before I finish processing the thought though, Alexander says, "Lexi would be much better with a bow. Her hands are quick enough to pull arrows, she just doesn't have the upper body strength to wield a sword."

I watch as Lexi's arms shake, raising the sword for the counter-attack in the drill. Alexander has spent the last two years working in an army; he'd know exactly what weapons to recommend. I glance over at Max, letting the idea of needing his help go. Alexander and I can handle our own troop. Still, Max's eyes tend to wander over to my troop, curious with what I'll have to work with.

"Zip may be better with just a knife," I say under my breath. It's more of a joke because every other weapon is far too large for her, but Alexander nods, seriously agreeing.

"No, you're right," Alexander says. "If we could get her a set of throwing knives, she could probably do some real damage."

After my father ends the sword fighting drill, we separate into weapon assignments around the room. We send Lexi over to the wall lined with large bullseye stripped targets to try a bow and arrow. Zip goes with her, but we have her try throwing knives. We haven't been able to figure out Jennie yet, so we have her stick with Zip for now. They're about the same size, but Jennie seems a bit too timid. I find it hard to believe she'd be able to hurl knives at her enemies.

The two redheaded twins, Cecelia and Fawn, as well as Luke, stick to sword fighting. Tryle is strong with his sword but claims he'd be better with a trident. His wandering eyes haven't left the weapon since we started today's training. Sam and Luis take to throwing spears and Darin, unimpressed by any of the weapons, makes comments that he'll just find a way to use his gift and settles on a sword. But while everyone else takes to practicing in their assigned weapons, Darin practices transforming his sword with his gift, proving he'll have unlimited options for his weapon. The sword shifts to a small knife, to a long spear, and back to a slim sword in a matter of seconds.

Alexander and I make our way around the training room, checking on our other members. Tryle surprises me, twirling the long trident with ease like it weighs no more than a stick. Lexi is great with the bow and arrow. Alexander was right about her quick hands. Her aim isn't the best, though. While she does make contact with the target every time, the arrows tend to land in the outer rings. Zavy steps up next to her and sends her arrow right into the center of the target. Just to show off even more, she sends two more into the targets to the right and left of the first one. She's the last person who needs special weapon training. She was always going to be assigned the bow and arrow.

Alexander and I move on before either of us engage with Zavy. The smacking sound of something hard on the target further down the wall pulls my attention. Zip has just hurled a knife into a perfect bullseye.

"Nice job!" Alexander says, watching her throw another knife. This one sticks just a bit above the first one. "How do you feel about using the knives?"

"I like them more than the sword," Zip admits, twirling one knife slowly in her fingers. She snaps her arm back and sends the knife whizzing through the air, and it lands deep in the target.

"What about you, Jennie?" I ask, noticing she hasn't tried throwing her knives yet.

"I don't know," she says, hesitating. "Maybe I should just stick with the sword."

"No, the swords are too big for you," Alexander says.

"Try this," Max says, walking up from behind me. He offers me a soft smile as if to say he'll handle this. He hands her a wooden stick with a short linked chain on the end. Attached to the chain is a metal ball with spikes.

"The flail will be too heavy," Alexander says, but Max shakes his head.

"This one is made extremely light," Max explains.

Jennie takes the flail in her right hand and flips her wrist back and forth, trying to get a feel for the weapon. With her rhythmic turns, the spiked ball on the chain picks up speed, making tall arcs in the air.

"Much better," Max says, an approving smile spreading on his face.

"All right, next matter of business," I hear my father call out. Silence settles over the room with the final smack of Zavy's arrow sinking into the target. "Endurance training. Strength training," he says and I watch as the ten captains come through the main entrance, wheeling in wagons full of rubble from outside.

Max's father uses his enhanced sense of sight to arrange the pieces of jagged rock around the room. He begins by placing them like stepping stones across the floor. The other captains add on by piling cement blocks into a shallow tunnel or short hurdles. The pieces come together around us and I realize they've created an obstacle course.

"We'll call in each group one at a time to complete the course. Lieutenants, this will also be a test to see how well you can lead. No gifts can be used. This is strictly physical endurance."

"Of course, this will be a contest," Captain Brutis says, placing the last large cement block on his towering mountain of stone, nearly touching the ceiling of the room. "The team who completes the obstacle course the fastest will receive a treat tonight."

We're all escorted out into the hall to wait to be called in. Luckily we aren't the first to go, so we have some time to strategize. Down the long stretch of hall, many of the other troops are huddled together, coming up with their best course of action.

"We'll just follow you, right?" I hear Zip ask, pulling my focus back to my team.

"Alexander and I can lead," I say. "I think it may be smart to go in with pairs, that way someone is always helping you through."

"I agree," Alexander says and begins to match up our troop members, trying to balance size and strength. Lexi and Darin, once enemies in the ring, are now paired together and placed at the end of the line. "You two will make sure no one falls behind," Alexander instructs.

"Lieutenant Max," I hear my father's voice call out of the training room. "We're ready for your troop. Adaline and Alexander you will be next."

Max's troop files into the training room behind my father and we take their place waiting by the doors.

"Don't you have this pang of guilt in your chest?" I ask Alexander under my breath. He gives me a curious side glance that asks for an explanation. "Our army's commander just died and they want us to play some game? Complete some silly obstacle course?"

"It's training," Alexander says shortly.

"If that makes you feel better," I mumble.

He turns to me, staring as if the words he wants to say are written somewhere on my face. "What does being upset and mourning Commander Crymm's death do? There's a time and place for it, but the time for training is now." He turns his attention from me to the army filling the hall in front of us. "Fight now, mourn later," he says softly.

His words make my skin tighten. I had said something similar the night my mother and Titus died. *Run now and mourn later.* I've been out of the prison for nearly three weeks, and I still haven't stopped running. I have barely given myself that time to mourn everyone I have lost. Alexander's eyes meet mine and I give him a small nod.

"Fight now, and mourn later," I agree.

We continue to wait for a few minutes. Maybe it's longer, it's hard to tell, but eventually, the door to the training room opens and Max leads his troop into the hall, sweat glistening on his forehead and a breathy grin wide on his face.

One of his members lands a congratulatory hand on his shoulder and a couple of the other members clap and give enthusiastic whistles, clearly happy with their performance.

"Good luck," Max says as he passes us, making his way down the hall with his troop behind him.

"Adaline, Alexander," my father calls from inside the training room.

We enter, our troop following behind us in our assigned pairs. Somehow the room looks even more destroyed since I had seen it originally. My father, along with the ten captains, sits on a balcony that overlooks the obstacle course.

"You will begin there," my father says, pointing to a pathway of rubble stepping stones.

I scan the rest of the course, trying to plan my moves in my head. The stones are far apart, but it's manageable. After that, is a tunnel that stretches a couple of feet. I'll need to crawl on my stomach to fit. Then, there's a stretch of hurdles made of soaked, old wood. Past the line of hurdles is the mound of rubble Captain Brutis had built, nearly touching the ceiling. That's where most of our time will go, trying to climb over it. After that is another shallow tunnel and a series of stepping stones towards the end of the course.

"A few additional things," my father says, pulling my attention from my planning. "You will all need to complete this course carrying the weapon assigned to you." He nods toward the wall next to us that has the large variety of weapons hanging from it.

Alexander, myself, Cecelia, Fawn, Luke, and Darin take swords, Lexi finds her bow and arrow, and Tryle picks out the trident he's been attached to. Finally, Zip finds herself a pair of throwing knives and Jennie picks up her flail.

We take our positions at the start of the course, Alexander and myself at the front. I place the sword in the belt at my hip, the feeling familiar to me. My eyes focus on the stones spaced out in front of me. It shouldn't be too bad, the worst part is no one behind me can move forward if I don't. I position my feet, ready to launch myself at the first stone, when my father speaks again.

"One more thing," he says, giving a slight wave of his hand. The scattered rubble on the floor amongst the stepping stones shifts and forms into two stone statues. "We will be popping up targets throughout the course. You have to attack them as you go. Any you leave still standing will result in a ten second penalty. And remember, there will be no use of gifts." He pauses, letting the last additions to the rules sink in before saying, "Begin."

I push off the ground with all the strength my legs have and I launch myself to the first step. When I land, Alexander is close behind me. We share a quick glance before jumping to the next stone and then the next one, our troop following behind us. The rubble to my left raises into a loose form of a statue. I pull my sword from my belt and slice it through the chest, watching the stones return to a pile of rubble again. My natural movements with the sword have come back easily to me.

We continue to throw ourselves from stone to stone. As I take my next leap toward the end of the stepping stone maze, a statue forms in mid-air in front of me. An arrow from behind whizzes past my ear and drives into the statue, bringing it back to a pile of rubble and out of my path. I glance over my shoulder at Lexi who has already pulled and launched another arrow at a statue up by our next challenge, the tunnel. Now across the maze of stepping stones, we freely sprint to the opening of the tunnel.

"I'll go first!" I say to Alexander and before he can object I throw myself flat on my stomach. I dive into the dark tunnel and crawl across the rough gravel. I find it much easier to just pull myself along the rocky ground, the light at the other end growing larger as I get nearer. When I pull myself out of the tunnel's end, I'm coated in a dusty, grey powder. Alexander is close behind me and we work together to pull Luke and Zip from the tunnel after us.

"You two should go ahead," Luke says. "Zip and I will help the others."

Alexander and I don't hesitate, knowing the mountain of rubble coming up will be tedious and we aren't doing any good standing here waiting on the rest of our team to get through the tunnel. We turn and head toward the mountain of concrete, but first, need to get past the wooden hurdles.

Alexander takes the lead, having no problems. His muscular legs launch him well above the hurdles. I take off at a sprint, hoping my speed will help me make it over the wooden beams. It's not as impressive as Alexander, but I am able to get over most of them. A few I have to use my hands to stay above the beam, but I make quick work of them.

Behind us, Sam and Tryle are through the tunnel and are heading for the hurdles. We have a good system. Everyone is moving forward. We haven't been delayed. After I get over the last hurdle, Alexander and I cross the fifty-foot clearing up to the mountain. As we take off down the concrete stretch, more rubble rises into statues around us. Together we pull our swords and send them through the necks and heads of the rock statues. Alexander covers our right and I cover our left. We do relatively well, both very effective with our swords, but I soon realize there will be more than we can handle. When five statues form instantly to my left, far too many for my one sword to fight off, a long spear launches past me, driving through all five statues at once. Sam is quickly at my side, pulling the spear from the rubble.

"Let's keep going, Lieutenant Adaline," she says and urges me forward.

When we reach the base of the mountain, I glance back to check on the rest of my troop. Zip and Luke are working together to pull Lexi from the tunnel and I'm sure Darin will be close behind. That's the end of our line. Everyone else is taking on the hurdles, easily knocking down the statues that get in their path.

"Let's go," I say to Alexander and we begin to climb. We work together, carefully trying to find the quickest and easiest way to the top. Unfortunately, the two don't seem to work together. The jagged edges of the rubble, hard on my hands, cause a sharp pain and I fear it could draw blood. One wrong step and I could slice my leg or arm open.

When we get about halfway up the mountain, I hear a large crash come from below us, and a child's scream rings out. With my hands tightly gripping the stone, I glance down over my shoulder.

"Zip!" I call out when I see her limp on the ground. Wood from the hurdle she must not have cleared piles on top of her. I feel my grip loosen, wanting to go down to help her. Alexander's hand clamps on my wrist as I'm about to let go.

"Adaline, Darin's got her," he says. His grip tightens on my wrist, the only sturdy thing keeping me on the mountain.

As if to reassure me, I hear Darin yell, "I have her!"

Alexander tugs lightly on my wrist, pulling me up. I grit my teeth and work against my instincts to go to her rescue. That's why I have a team, I remind myself. We make it to the top of the rubble mountain with no other delays and I give myself a second to glance back at my team, carefully following the path Alexander and I mapped out for them. Darin is at the end of the line, carrying Zip on his back, her small arms locked tightly around his neck.

"Now down," Alexander says, continuing to help me forward.

Down should be easier, but I find it trickier. I try to climb down, but I can't see where I'm trying to place my feet. After about halfway I get frustrated enough to roll on to my back, thinking I may be able to shuffle and slide down. But when I go to move my right foot to the next slab of rock, the rubble falls loose and I'm thrown off balance. I drop hard into the jagged rock, feeling it dig deep into my back, and then I'm sliding, rolling, falling down the mountain. My arms, face, knees, drive into the rubble before I land hard on my stomach, finally reaching the bottom.

"Adaline!" Alexander screams from above me.

I try to tell him I'm okay, but I struggle to even fill my crushed lungs with air. There's dust coating the inside of my mouth and a metallic taste lingers on my tongue. My eyes crack open and I see the red bloody droplets under my face, dripping from my mouth. There's a sound above me of loose rubble and sliding feet. Alexander is being too careless, trying to get to me. But he has better balance and strength to keep himself upright. He manages to make it down to me quickly, jumping the last couple of feet.

"Adaline, are you okay?" he asks and I feel his familiar hands searching for my injuries. He pauses at my foot and I can tell by the increasing throbbing pain coming from my ankle that I've probably sprained it. His hands find the gashes on my arms and the bruises on my knees. Tryle, who was behind Alexander, reaches him next.

"We'll need to carry her the rest of the way," I hear Alexander tell him.

No, please don't. We'll surely have the slowest time now. Can't they leave me behind? Call me a casualty to the course and finish without me? Please don't move me.

When their strong hands roll me on to my back a pain shoots down my spine and I take in a sharp breath in shock.

"It's okay, Adaline. I've got you," Alexander says, locking his green gaze with my tear-filled eyes.

I squeeze them shut with the growing pain. *Please just leave me. Don't pick me up.*

But the words don't make it out and against my hopes, Alexander lifts me up into his arms and he starts moving again. The pain is so strong, pounding through my veins, that I start to lose sense of my surroundings. I can tell that Alexander has definitely slowed down his pace. The tunnel passes in a blur of grey rubble and dark shadows. It takes them forever to slide me through, careful not to cut up my back any more than it already is.

When they reach the last stretch of the obstacle course, a final maze of stepping stones, Alexander sends Tryle first and holds me cradled in his arms. The stones must be closer together because Alexander is able to step, not jump, from each one. When my heavy head rolls to look ahead of us, I see that Alexander has sent Tryle to fight the stone statues growing from the rubble. He pierces them with his trident, sending them back into rocky piles. I hear Alexander's heart begin to pound faster, my head close to his chest. His arms throb and I feel his legs grow more wobbly, but he keeps pushing himself forward until he lands on the final step and crosses the finish line.

He sets me down against a wall and props me up so I can watch the rest of my team work their way toward the finish line, now all at the final maze of stepping stones. But what I see, instead of the faces of my exhausted troop, are the captains' faces above on the platform looking down at the broken spectacle in front of them. Captain Brutis actually lets out a loud bellowing laugh at our performance. My father's eyes are cold, disappointment written all over this face.

We are supposed to be the most powerful troop here. We are the saviors. I don't have to ask anyone, I know we'll be the worst performing team in the entire army.

Chapter 26

Once everyone has run the course, we file back into the training room. Conveniently, I'm able to lead my troop into a back corner, hopefully where no one will see us when they announce our horrible performance. I'm back in perfect condition after the healers took care of me. The ten captains and my father stand on the balcony overhead, waiting to announce the troop that won. Just by the look on Captain Brutis's face, I know it has to be Max's troop. Embarrassed and frustrated with myself, I tune out everything around me. After such a powerful representation in the ring, I've taken steps backward.

"Adaline, relax," Lexi says, leaning up to whisper in my ear.

I turn over my shoulder and scan the faces of my troop. They give me reassuring smiles and pats on the back. I don't know how many times I had to hear them say that my fall was an accident and that it could have happened to any of us, or if I had been allowed to use my gift it never would have happened at all. I'm glad my troop doesn't think less of me, but unfortunately, I'm my biggest critic.

My father confirms my suspicions, announcing that Max's team completed the course in the fastest time. At the front of the crowd, I see his members lift him up into the air, chanting congratulations. Thankfully, they decide not to announce last place and I'm spared the embarrassment.

"The ceremony for Commander Crymm will begin shortly," my father says and a hush falls over the room. "The funeral will take place on the coast. We would like you all to march in the procession."

Captain Brutis steps up next to my father. "Her army should lead her," he says, raising his hand to point toward the exit. "Please, change out or your training uniforms and head toward the main entrance hall of the castle to line up."

My father dismisses us with the wave of his hand and the crowd begins to shift, flooding toward the exit. There's a mix of emotions in the crowd around me as we line ourselves up in the main foyer of the castle. Many of the older members seem very reserved. I know they probably knew Commander Crymm the best. I'm sure her loss is hurting them. I've only known her for a few days, but she did make a lasting impression. She cleared Molly to stay, giving her a second chance. She believed in me when no one else did. She understood me and this mess of a situation better than anyone else.

The younger members chat amongst themselves as if they are lining up for a parade, not a funeral procession. I bite my tongue to keep from scolding two younger girls who are more concerned about a rumor they heard that there's a send-off banquet tonight. That's not what's important right now. I'm about to snap at them when I stop myself. They're just kids. Don't force them to grow up faster than they should have to.

What I would give to actually be a normal sixteen-year-old girl. If I wasn't here in Libertas and I wasn't a princess, I'd have just finished school. Maybe I'd work somewhere in Garth. I did love baking with my mother. Maybe I could have worked at the bakery with Essie's mother. But my train of thought stops. No, that never would have happened. If I lived a normal life in Garth, I would have been tested at the age of ten for my gift. King Renon would have enslaved me and turned me into a Lost Soul. I would have spent my whole life as a brainwashed slave.

That's what the war is about. Fighting for a better world. A world where no one is put in chains for what makes them different.

"Adaline, this way," my father says, pulling me from the crowd. "You'll walk with me and your brother."

As we move to the back of the funeral procession, Linda meets us halfway. "This will be more fitting for a princess," she says, lifting her arms wrapped in glittery black gemstones. I see Cooper come out of the crowd and notice Linda has already wrestled him into a crisp jet-black suit. His hair is gelled back and the silver crown is balanced on his head.

"You can change in here and I'll go get your crown," Linda says as she leads me into an empty room.

"Can you get the one with keys?" I ask. She tilts her head a bit confused. "You'll see it up there," I say.

I softly close the door and change into the long, black gown, thankful to get out of the torn training uniform. Linda has folded a pair of silver flats into the dress and I'm relieved she's given up on the heels. The dress reaches the floor, a waterfall of black diamonds. The neckline is a mesh black lace that climbs up to my collarbone. It looks like a feathery necklace.

When Linda returns she helps me place the crown of keys on my head. "It's magnificent," Linda says examining the way the light reflects off of it.

"Commander Crymm died holding the crown. I don't know why she faced a storm to get it, but I want to wear it tonight in her honor," I explain to Linda as she leads me to my place next to my brother.

"I think that's very fitting, Adaline," Linda says.

As she turns away, Cooper explains how the procession will work. Right before we begin, Linda returns with Alexander and places him in front of me. He hasn't been given any fancy clothes or medals to carry, but he is the other savior and we should be presented together on the eve of this war. Cooper falls in step next to me, and my father hovers behind us. After my father, the ten captains stand at attention around the silver casket, designed to keep the island from absorbing her gift.

At the sight of the casket, I take in a sharp breath. I don't know why, but the weight of Commander Crymm's death didn't hit me until now. There's a deep engraving on the casket of the symbol for an enhanced sense of sight. I hadn't even known that was her gift. She had all my respect, fear, and admiration, and I never even saw her use her powers. She didn't need to rely on her gift to convince me to follow her. Her strength, confidence, and intelligence were all it took. I hope I can make her proud. I hope I can be that powerful one day.

The army forms in long lines, ten across, and too many to count out in front of me. They pull open the castle doors and we move forward in a stiff, slow march. Those with an enhanced sense of hearing send a low trumpet tune out across the island. For a while, the only things I register are the crunching of the rubble beneath my boots and the haunting song.

When we reach the beach, everyone else in Libertas, the commoners not going to fight, stand in huddled crowds around a wide hole that's been dug in front of a shiny white slab of marble. There are other headstones next to it and they stretch back into a shallow field. I stop scanning the stones, closing off my mind from counting them. Now is not the time to fall back into old habits. I don't want to know how many have died here and never saw the change we're all fighting for.

As the funeral procession ends, we line ourselves along the water's edge and wrap around the area. Alexander is the last soldier to fall in line, closing the ring around the graveyard. Myself, Cooper, and my father take our places behind the white headstone. The sight of the three of us, dressed in royal garments, crowns resting on our heads, is a symbol of unity and strength. After last night's storm and the sudden death of Commander Crymm, I know it's what the people around us are looking for. The ten captains finally approach the grave, bringing up the end of the processional.

When they reach the hole, the casket is slowly lowered inside. I try to keep my focus on the waves of the ocean, so I don't have to hear my father talk about losing Commander Crymm. Each captain takes a few minutes to say something, whether it's about how she trained them or how they knew her as a child. I try and block it all out, begging this to end. I never have done well with the dead. I don't know how I'm supposed to feel. No matter what washes over me, I feel like it's wrong somehow. After all ten captains speak, my father steps forward again. Commander Crymm didn't have any family or children, so the tribute to her is relatively short.

"The most important thing we can do is move forward," my father says, the tropical breeze blowing his royal blue cape around his shoulders slightly. "We have spent nearly a hundred years talking about wanting our freedom, multiple decades planning it, and now, tomorrow, we begin to take it." There's a wave of nods in the crowd. "Those of you not fighting have already moved into the bunkers. Tonight, I'd like us all to be together one last time."

My eye catches the movement of the two girls who had been talking about the rumor of a banquet earlier. They look giddily to one another, excited to have been correct.

"We will have one last gathering in the bunkers tonight to celebrate our time together and what we are beginning tomorrow. We don't know what the war will bring, but I do know we have tonight." My father steps back as the crowd gives a respectful and excited round of applause.

Then, the captains lead the crowd toward the bunkers, letting the royal family come in last. As I wait, my mind twists my father's words. We do know what the war could bring us, I correct in my head. I know it could bring my death. I know it probably will bring my death. He's a Future Holder, surrounded by other Future Holders, and yet, we all want to stand here and say we don't know what the war will bring. Surely we can have some sort of idea or some sort of guess. Isn't there a certain outcome that happens more than any other in everyone's visions? My mind stops racing. There probably is a certain outcome, and the fact that my father isn't sharing it is a sign all in itself.

When I enter the bunkers, I'm shocked by their transformation from this morning. Small twinkling lights are hung down both sides of the hall with tables and chairs spread underneath them. People begin to find empty seats to claim and my father escorts me and Cooper to the long table in the center of the crossroads. Here we join the other ten captains and our army fills the tables in the halls branching off from us.

Alexander finds a table in the back with Mio, Cinder, and his mother and father. As I take my seat at the main table, Linda slides behind me. "Don't forget, sit up straight."

I guess she's getting her royal dinner after all.

The food is served from the kitchen and the waiters carefully maneuver down the packed hallways. Casual chatter breaks out around me and I feel the energy of the nation shift to celebratory. Our last night together. I try and push away the war, the death of

Commander Crymm, and the vision of my own death. *Enjoy tonight, Adaline.* You may never get another like it. No, I correct myself. I know I won't get another night like this. Never again will all of these people be together. Even if we win the war, there will be casualties. Nothing will ever be the same again. *Tonight will never come again.*

My mind relaxes and I start to enjoy the food presented to me, eating every last bit of it because I know I won't see a full plate again. I converse with the other captains about how growing up in Libertas was like and I even let myself laugh at their stories. Even Captain Brutis has let his guard down, sharing an embarrassing story about how he lost his first ten battles in the ring during his rise to Captain.

I notice many of the adults have been drinking a clear, bubbly liquid, each glass bringing out more hilarious stories. When the waiter casually offers me a glass, I'm quick to turn it down. As fun as tonight may be, I'm not looking to lose control of myself altogether.

The evening shifts from the dinner to a party as the tables are cleared and music floods the stone tunnels. The only things that remain from the meal are the clear bubbly drinks. Captains and lieutenants I've never even seen smile now twirl together in a loose rhythmic dance. They know this may be the last time they ever dance. Maybe even the last time they'll ever hear music like this.

In my elegant black dress, I stick out in the crowd. Easy to spot with the glittering lights reflecting off the black stones, and the crown of keys balanced high on my head.

"May I offer you a drink?" a voice forces out behind me in a very tight accent.

I spin in my dress and see it's Max. He holds out the glass to me in a low bow. He stands and leans in to whisper in my ear. "It's only water, I swear." I take the cool glass from him and he adds, "I found if you keep hold of a full glass, the waiters will stop offering the alcohol to you every other minute."

"That's awfully clever," I say.

The music continues to swell in the tunnel. It's not the ballads I'm used to hearing at the banquets, but more similar to the night Max took me to the party under the city. The beat shakes the floor, thumping inside my head.

"To one more night of fun," Max says, clinking his glass with mine.

After that moment, the night moves in flashes of pulsing music and dancing. After two or three songs I feel the need to get out of the crowd and find some fresh air. Max and I make our way to the entrance of the bunker where the door has been slightly propped open to let in the cool breeze.

"Oh, I'm so sorry," I say, bumping into a girl who had been standing just outside the door. "Oh," I say and step back.

The girl had been kissing a boy, the crown on his head crooked.

"Adaline," Cooper says when he sees my shocked face. My mouth hangs open, frozen somewhere between being embarrassed for interrupting and wanting to make my older brother squirm.

The girl pushes her hair behind her ear and I see that it's Essie.

"Oh!" I say again, louder this time. A smile spreads on my face. "I didn't mean to interrupt," I say, back-peddling into the bunker, laughter escaping me.

"Adaline!" Cooper calls after me, but I hurry back toward the party. I see Alexander coming toward me and yell, "Alexander, you are not going to believe what just happened!" I feel the need to tell someone what I just witnessed and I don't know if it's because I want to embarrass my brother or if the giddy energy of the night has in fact taken over. "Essie and Cooper were kissing!"

Alexander's draw drops. He makes a bewildered, over-the-top, surprised face. "Really? Essie and Cooper? I never would have thought."

I hear Max clear his throat from behind me. I had forgotten he was there.

"I was just going to get some fresh air," Alexander says, gesturing toward the opening of the bunker and ignoring Max.

"Better not," I say with a grin and a large wink. "Dance with me?" I ask Alexander and offer him my hand.

For the first time, Alexander acknowledges Max, locking his gaze with him over my shoulder. The two communicate in silent stares.

"I should actually be going," Max says, pulling back from us. He melts into the crowd and out of sight.

Alexander places his hand in mine and we fold back into the sea of people. This will be the last night I won't have to worry about his safety. The last night I know I can just enjoy being with him. After a couple of songs of twirling through the crowd, the music slows and my hands position themselves on Alexander's shoulders naturally.

"Commander Crymm would love that you wore that crown tonight," Alexander says, brushing his fingers lightly on the side of my head.

"I thought so too," I say.

A moment of silence passes between us as we move to the slow melody. *Could this be the very last dance I ever have with Alexander?* My mind sends flashes of the vision of my death through my head. I feel my throat tighten and my eyes burn with salty tears. Suddenly, a wave of fear floods my veins and I find my breath stuck in my throat.

This probably is my very last dance with Alexander.

I stop suddenly, my wet eyes meeting his. He notices the tears I'm holding in and his face becomes concerned. I throw my arms around his neck and pull him into a tight hug. I feel his strong arms wrap around my waist, pulling me close.

"You're my best friend, Alexander," I say into his shoulder.

I pull our hug even tighter, squeezing my eyes shut as the tears threaten to fall. Alexander has been by my side for everything I've been through since the prison. From the moment he picked me up on the rocky path outside the castle, to helping me run from Paylon. When he risked his life as a decoy so I could save Zavy, and when I found him in Leo's storage room. The night he trusted me with his past and never left my side when I recovered from the eel's attack. *After everything that has happened, Alexander has always been there to catch me when I fall.*

"You're my best friend too, Adaline," Alexander says into my hair. He holds me tightly, helping the anxiety and fear that rushed through me fade away.

"I'm sorry," I say. I let out a breathy laugh and wipe the tears off my cheeks, stepping out from our hug. "I don't know what came over me. I just had this thought that this would be our last dance ever." I trail off, my hands still shaking.

Alexander lays a gentle, steady hand under my chin. "We'll have many more dances in the future." He tries to give me a reassuring smile, but I know he doesn't mean what he's saying. He knows he can't promise me that, but I nod anyway. The slow music fades out and a quieter melody takes its place. I notice the crowd has thinned out considerably and many people are turning in for the night.

"Let me walk you back to the castle," Alexander offers.

Before I follow him towards the exit of the bunker, I take a moment to just stand still, to take a breath and not move. Then, I turn, slowly in a circle, taking in the entire space. I want to remember this night forever. *The last night we were all happy.* I memorize the feeling of the crowd, the twinkling lights on the wall, and the melody of the music. I look down at my feet, marking this spot in my head. *The spot Alexander and I danced for the last time.*

Chapter 27

Alexander drops me off at the main doors of the castle and says the homes they built for them weren't damaged in the storm. When I get to my chambers, I slip out of the silver shoes and sparkly gown, thankful to take the costume off. I place the crown of keys back on its podium, feeling better now that I had a chance to wear it. I take my last real shower, removing as much dirt and sweat as I can with the various soaps. I gently untangle my hair and find the softest shirt and pair of shorts tucked away in my enormous closet.

I crawl into the large bed, wanting it to swallow me whole. Sleep is so incredibly important right now, especially with the journey we will begin tomorrow. But after an hour or so passes with no sleep, I give up and start pacing my room. I ruffle through my closet, taking in the gowns and sparkly shoes that will never get worn, left here until maybe after the war.

At some point this afternoon, someone delivered a black backpack to my room for me to take on the journey tomorrow. Inside, I have two additional black training outfits that have been tailored to include the velvet black collar for my new rank as a lieutenant, a thin blanket, and packs of nuts and dried fruit. So, I'll always have some food in case of an emergency. That's all I'm probably supposed to bring.

The old pack from our journey here and my sword sit in the corner of my room, untouched until now. I move my sword next to the door so I remember to take it tomorrow, and I salvage a few items from my old backpack and add them to my new bag. I pack the ripped photo of my father. I'm glad Titus is remembered here, but I wish my mother could be too. I take the gold coin from the guard who helped me escape the castle, and I pack the green rock that keeps the non-gifted immune to the gifted. I don't know when I may need it, but it's better to have it just in case.

On the cord that ties the necklace together are spots of red blood. Could that be Codian's? Or Cooper's from when he fought Paylon? Maybe it's Paylon's blood? *So much blood.*

"Kill me," Codian's voice still echoes in my head.

I shove the necklace deep in my bag and remind myself that those losses won't be for nothing.

As I'm making the third round of my room, I notice the two silver keys laying on my nightstand that I had gotten from the store in town. My brain jumps at the idea to do something other than pace my room. I pull on a thin jacket and shove the keys into my pocket. Once I'm out on my balcony, I teleport down to the ground and follow the trail from the castle until I find myself passing through the rows of houses where my team lives. Sleeping, I hope. *Like I should be.*

I walk up the stone path to Alexander's home and knock lightly on the door. I hear soft footsteps on the other side, making their way to the front of the house. He opens the heavy door and the warm yellow light glows behind him. He has a soft, grey t-shirt on and long, cotton pants.

"Couldn't sleep either?" he asks, though his voice sounds groggy. I shake my head and he moves to open the door wider, letting me in.

"I actually brought you something," I say and we take a seat together on the couch in his living room. "When we were in town the day of my coronation, I got these," I say and I pull out the two keys hanging on their chains. I hand one to Alexander. "They're traceable," I explain and place mine around my neck. "In case we get separated, I can always find you and you can always find me." My voice breaks at the thought.

Alexander rubs the metal key between his fingers. "Thank you," he says and looks up to me, tears hanging in his eyes.

"Are you scared?" I ask and he nods his head. He was putting up a good front earlier but now, in the quiet of the night, those fears have surfaced.

"It's worse for us because we have an idea of what we're walking into," Alexander says and he places the key around his neck. "It's hard to leave when you know you could be safe here," he admits.

"But we're more prepared now," I offer and take his strong hand in mine. "We're going to win this war. We're going home," I say and a smile splits on his face.

"When did you become the brave one?" Alexander jokes.

"I'll be brave for you and you'll be brave for me," I say.

Alexander reaches for my other hand and squeezes it. "I couldn't do this without you, Adaline."

"I think it's crazy that we didn't even know each other a couple of weeks ago," I say.

Our memories being altered has been a sensitive subject, but now I feel like it's behind us. I've really connected with him. If it wasn't for him being my weakness, I know I would have fallen for him already too.

"Do you want to know how I know we're going to win this war?" I ask.

"How?" he questions.

"Because we're together."

Alexander smiles at that. His wide, goofy grin that I love so much. "You're absolutely right," he says. We're quiet for a moment as Alexander twists the key around his neck. "Symbolic," he huffs.

"I thought so too," I agree, looking at my key. "How can we be the most powerful people on this island but I feel the most ill-prepared for this war."

"You're not alone," Alexander exhales. "At least we aren't walking straight onto a battlefield tomorrow."

"Just taking the first step toward one," I mumble.

"You took the first step the night you escaped the prison," Alexander says, and it hits me that he's right.

I realize I've probably overstayed my visit. We need to be resting for tomorrow.

"I should get back," I say and the thought of pacing my room again makes my heart drop.

"I'd offer to let you stay, but I don't think that's such a great idea," Alexander almost whispers, his voice so soft.

"Yeah, we don't want them to think the Princess is missing the day we go to war," I breathe out and stand.

Alexander walks me back to the front of his house, each quiet second making my heart beat harder. I wish I could stay here with him. I don't want to be alone tonight, but I'm out of time to get my feelings in line.

"Thank you for the necklace," Alexander says as he pulls open the front door.

"That's our job," I say, and turn to face him. "Keep the other alive, no matter the cost." My heart tightens at my words. *Even if the cost is heartbreak.*

Alexander nods and I take off down the dirt path and back to my room. The cool and dreamy night air seems to have pulled a haze over my mind and as soon as my head hits my pillow, sleep finally finds me.

When I awake the next morning, I change into the black training uniform I had laid out last night. I twist my hair into a single braid, throw my backpack over my shoulder, grab my sword, and meet my father and Cooper in front of the castle. We are taken down to the docks where we arrived just over a week ago and find many of the troops are organized and ready to depart.

The group of commoners staying behind in Libertas has woken early to send us off. They stand in a huddle outside the mouth of the bunker where they'll be sealed in until this war is over. They wave and applaud the soldiers as they take their places in line with their lieutenants. When Molly sees me arrive at the docks, she sprints across the beach, throwing her arms around my waist.

"Be careful, Adaline," she says, her words muffled by her tight embrace.

I pull her close and stroke her thin blonde hair. "I'll be just fine, Molly," I force myself to say calmly. "I'll be back to get you when we win the war."

She steps back from me, tears streaking down her young cheeks. I wipe them away and force myself to smile. "No crying today, okay? This is the beginning of a new age for everyone."

She nods her head, sniffling back tears. "I'll see you soon," she says, her voice quivering.

"I'll see you soon," I say softly and stand back up. She turns and makes her way back to the crowd at the bunker.

That'll be the last time I ever see Molly.

Stop. I can't think like that. It would mean I'm accepting the vision of my death. I can change the future. I will make sure that doesn't happen. I will come back for her.

Just as dawn tracks over the wet horizon, troops are escorted onto their assigned boats. Nothing fancy for most of us. I know Libertas has a Navy Fleet, just like they have an Air Force, but few ships in comparison to troops.

Most of us get small motorboats, like the one I came in on, where you rely on the sail and wind just as much as the motor.

Alexander and I exchange a silent greeting, the keys on our necks reflecting the early morning light.

"Did you want to say goodbye to her?" I ask Alexander softly. I see his stare is on Molly, his only real family besides King Renon.

"When we win the war, I'll tell her everything," Alexander says, his words stiff.

We escort our troop to our assigned boat, 312. It's almost double the size of the other vessels. When I turn and see Max leading his troop down the dock I understand why.

"Lieutenant Max," I say as he approaches Alexander and me.

"Looks like we have the same orders. Xavin?" he asks and I nod.

"Boat 312?" I ask and a cool grin spreads on his face.

My mind wonders if fate really assigned us together, or if he organized this. He had been paying close attention to my troop during yesterday's training. I know if I had been taught to see the future, like my mother and father can, then I would already have known about this arrangement. I'm reminded Max once told me he had to master all aspects of his gift of enhanced sense of sight, and I wonder if he'd teach me. Just to spite my father's protective grasp, I'll be sure to ask. When it's time for our troop to pull out, my father and brother give me a quick goodbye.

"We'll see you tomorrow in Dather," my father says. He's trying to keep his strong front, leading an army on his own was not how he planned this.

When Cooper gives me a quick hug, I say, "Don't forget to tell Essie goodbye." I feel him laugh against me as he pulls away.

"Sail straight," Cooper says, backing away from me.

"Fly high," I say, watching my brother turn to join his air fleet.

Alexander, Max, and I file onto our boat last. Max takes the lead on undocking the boat and starting our departure since he's sailed on these ships his whole life. Most of the crew is quiet as we set sail into the early morning sunrise.

"Should be a relatively short trip," Max says, meeting Alexander and me at the rear of the vessel. "We'll be there early tomorrow morning. Rations for meals are organized in storage compartments below the ship."

"Is there anything we need to do before we get there?" Alexander asks.

Max shakes his head. "Everything should have already been organized."

"Are the people in Xavin prepared to fight in a war?" I ask.

"I'm not sure they're even prepared to see our faces," Max mumbles.

"What do you mean? Do they not know we're coming?" I ask, confused.

"Some of the gifted have seen them in the future," Max explains. "They believe they play a major roll in how this war will turn out."

"So we are going to Xavin based on a vision?" Alexander confirms and Max doesn't respond.

"Let's get the breakfast rations out," I say, trying to escape the tension between them.

When the sun has fully risen, we divide the food for breakfast. It mostly consists of fruits and oats. Most people entertain themselves with things they brought with them, card games or books. I make my rounds to each of them to try and make connections with my group, but more so to stay away from the tension between Alexander and Max, now doubled in our small quarters. Everything has to be a discussion from who orders the ship directions, to who cleans up the breakfast mess. They're mentally and emotionally draining.

I'm taught lots of Libertas's classic card games and they tell me what it was like to live in Libertas. Most of them were born there, but some were brought over. The redheaded twins, Cecelia and Fawn, made the journey with my father. They say it was one of his last.

After school, they all attended training at night. Children in Libertas learned all the same things we did, but they didn't have the fear of being taken in as prisoners looming over them. They had an annual summer parade where the best of the training groups would parade through Libertas doing tricks for the crowd. Most of the people in Libertas joined the army. They felt it was their duty to defend the place they found safety at, but some just wanted a place to live, to be a shopkeeper, and to raise their gifted children.

It's odd to think that a gifted could try to live a normal life, but someone has to grow and gather crops. Someone has to teach and look after the kids. There has to be healers and there has to be builders. We can't all fight.

By late afternoon, long after we had our dinner rations, I find myself laying on the front of the ship watching the rosy pink clouds float above me, or maybe I float below them. They scatter through the sky, streaking across the deep setting sun. I figure Cooper and the rest of the air force will be up in the clouds somewhere. To me, the clouds look flat, two dimensional. But I wonder what they look like up there. How tall are they? Are they their own form of rolling hills, or peaked mountains? What's it like to fly, to be up that high?

By nightfall, Max decides to take the first watch. We spread out on the floor of the boat, unpack our thin blankets, and use our bags as pillows. No one seems to have trouble falling asleep but me. I toss and turn on the hard wooden floor until I've worked up a large knot in my neck. I eventually give up, knowing that, just like last night, I won't be able to force my mind to quit racing. I move and take a seat next to Max at the front of the boat.

"Can't sleep?" Max asks.

I shake my head and ask, "Would you teach me how to see into the future?" I see the hesitation mist over in his eyes.

"Your father has us on strict orders not to," Max admits.

I take his hand in mine and beg. "Please, I want to be as ready as I can for this war."

His hands are softer and smaller than I thought they would feel. My first thought is they are not Alexander's hands, but I don't let go until Max lets out a breath and agrees. Ever since I saw my father's vision, I've had an urge to know if it's going to be true. If I could see into the future, maybe I could see a different outcome, or I could see how to change it.

"It's not what most people think," Max says. "You can't see the future because it's constantly changing. Like, me teaching you this, will no doubt change the future. We don't pick what we see. It just comes in flashes."

"What do you use it for, then?" I ask.

"Events that are happening now. If you get really good, you can use it to know your opponents move before they make it. You'll be able to see things closer in the future more accurately. Like a hundred things may affect tomorrow, but only two things will affect the next few minutes."

I nod, understanding. "So how do you call for these flashes?" I ask.

"For beginners, we have you close your eyes," he starts explaining and I follow his instructions. "For me, I count backward from one hundred until it kicks in."

"Out loud or in my head?" I ask, my eyes squeezed shut.

Max laughs and he says, "In your head, please."

My cheeks flush as I laugh. I begin to count in my head, backward from one hundred, my numbers returning easily to me. When I get to fifty-three, a shot spills across my eyelids like a movie screen. I'm sitting on the boat with Max and everyone else is asleep.

"You learn quick," he says and his hand closes around mine.

Our eyes lock and he leans closer to me. The moment our lips would meet my eyes jolt open and I'm not looking down on myself, but into Max's green gaze. My heart beats fast in my chest, not understanding what I had just seen.

"Did it work?" Max asks, his eyes searching my flushed face.

I nod and try to slow my heart.

"You learn quick," he says and his hand closes on mine.

Just like I had seen.

As he leans in to kiss me I say, "Wait."

"Sorry, I shouldn't have," he stumbles over his words, trying to find what he wants to say. "I really like you, Adaline. I feel like we've just connected really well." He stops to let me speak, but my words are caught somewhere in my throat. "But you like Alexander," he huffs trying to fill my silence.

"I don't know what's right," I say and his glassy eyes lift to mine. I want to just tell him it's him my heart wants because I want him to be happy, but I don't know if that's true. "Until I know what is right, I'm just here to fight this war. To free the gifted. To change Dather."

"The stars won't align for us," Max says. "But I won't stop trying. Adaline, you're not like any other girl. You're a warrior. You can make decisions and stand true to them. You have lived through the unimaginable time and time again. Your beauty is simple and true." The compliments flood from Max and my heart falls for each and every one of them. "Don't count me out, Adaline," he finally says before standing to move to the front of the ship.

I look out past where Max had been sitting. In the distance, I see a dark shadow on the midnight blue sky, the outline of an island starting to form. Slowly, we float toward Xavin and my mind tries to straighten itself back out to.

Remember the war and where we are right now. Stop wondering how it would have felt if Max had kissed you. Stop trying to decide between him and Alexander.

I keep telling myself this until finally I just stop thinking altogether. The sounds of salty waves are the only thoughts to process in my head.

Chapter 28

By early morning our boat pulls up to a worn, wooden dock, much less magnificent than Libertas. Our teams unload from the boat and take in the bare island. Where Libertas had rocky mountains jutting from its surface, Xavin only has rocky hills. We begin to follow a small, dirt path over and around the hills of black volcanic rock. On the opposite side of the island, I see a thick jungle, like the one on the original Libertas. Its deep green trees stretching high into the air. But before the jungle, a couple yards ahead, I make out small blue tents propped along the base of a hill.

"Not as luxurious as we had it," Max says back to me as we close in on the circle of tents.

We stop a few paces outside of their camp, not wanting to intrude. A few thin faces stick their heads out from inside the tents, and then an older man begins to make his way to us.

The greying man embraces Max, Alexander, and I in a tight, unexpected, hug. He is extremely skinny, like those who were imprisoned with me in Garth, and I wonder how survival has been for them out here. However, if it's been hard, he doesn't let it show.

He is grinning across his entire face. I've never seen someone have so little but be so incredibly happy.

"You came from Libertas?" he asks, his voice quivering with age.

"We were sent to bring you with us to Dather," Max explains and the old man nods.

"We are ready to fight with you," he slowly thrusts his old boney arm into the air and gestures as people start to come out of their tents. There's about thirty of them in all. Most are my father's age, with just a few being closer to my own.

"We thank you for your support," Max says, shaking the man's thin hand.

I suppose they were expecting us after all. But when I look at the thin bodies walking out from the tents, I'm not sure why we even bothered to come to get them. They won't have the strength or endurance to fight in a war. I bet none of them have even held a weapon.

"My father said you have been protecting an item here that I am to retrieve," I say, peering at him.

His face lightens and he suddenly pulls me into another tight hug. When he releases me, his eyes are shimmering with tears. "You're Rosa's daughter?"

My heart clutches at the mention of my mother.

"Yes," I say, my voice sounding airy. "You knew my mother?"

The man nods. "I have spent my life guarding her secret so that I could one day give it to you."

He turns quickly, moving toward the tents. We follow the old man into his camp and he takes us around and introduces us to the others. All of them are from different main islands, like Hamni and Sone. They explain how my mother had organized this group to protect whatever she left behind.

"We were much stronger when this all began," Juse, the older man who approached us, explains. "It's been over a decade now, but I'm glad you have finally come for us."

Juse stops in the center of the camp where a large boulder sits. He looks to me, a weary smile lining his face.

"You'll need to use your gift to retrieve what she left. If you are truly Rosa's daughter, it will reveal itself to you."

I look from Juse to the large boulder. Alexander and Max stand on either side of me, waiting for me to move first. With my gift, I slide the large boulder to the right and a cylindrical metal lid reveals itself.

I approach the lid and grip the metal lip engraved in the center. I hinge it up toward the sky and a shallow dark cavity sits below it. The morning sun now illuminates a long, skinny wooden box inside the cavity.

I reach inside and pull out the box. The idea of my mother being the last person to touch this, over ten years ago, makes my heart beat faster. Now I know what my father meant when he said he hopes this brought me some closure. He wanted me to finish something my mother had started. I've been longing for her journal, but now he's given me something else of hers. Something so important she's been hiding it here all this time.

There's a square metal lock on the box. I examine it and see that there isn't a hole for a key. I glance up at Juse, who is still watching me closely. He nods toward the lock, and I realize *I'm the key.*

I take the metal lock in my hand, it vibrates against my skin, and then pops open. I toss the lock aside and pry open the wooden box. Inside is an old roll of parchment. I take out the document and begin to reveal its secrets.

Alexander and Max kneel next to me, trying to get a better look at what was hidden in the box. They each take an end of the parchment, and once it's fully unrolled, Alexander gasps next to me.

My eyes fly across the document, black ink bleeding all across the page. It looks like a map, but I'm not entirely sure of where.

"What is it, Alexander?" I ask, glancing up to see his expression has grown excited.

"It's a map of King Renon's castle," he says.

My eyes fly back to the parchment and I begin to see it too. Ballrooms and royal chambers are sketched out across the paper.

"I lived there for seven years," Alexander says, examining the map closely. "There are dozens of entrances on this map that I never knew existed."

He points some of them out to me, and I realize why he never knew they existed.

"They're secret entrances. This is how we are going to ambush the castle!" I look between Max and Alexander, my blood pumping fast through my veins. "This is how we win the war."

"We need to get this back to your father immediately," Max says, moving to roll up the map. "They can't move forward without this."

I nod, agreeing. Max hands me the rolled parchment and I tuck it safely away in my bag. I glance up and see that we have drawn quite the crowd over us.

"Please, pack what you want to take with us. We need to leave here soon," Max instructs.

Most of them don't have more than a small bag to bring with us. Juse, the leader of the group, invites us for breakfast before we depart for Garth. It's nothing more than coconuts and berries, with a few pieces of meat from an animal they've found in the jungle. We're told the meat is a luxury since today will be historical.

We eat our share of the meal and explain to Juse that we have food on our boat they can have, but most are content with the meal in front of them. They're full with what their stomachs are used to. I ask why they haven't used their gifts to construct a bigger home here, but they explain many of them don't know how to use their gift. Just like on Dather, you are enslaved for having a gift on Hamni and Sone. No one there is teaching them how to use their powers. I nod, understanding how hard it is to do anything with this gift with no instruction.

After the meal, Juse explains that they need to perform a ritual to the island and tells us we can join them.

I'm hesitant at first, knowing we should really get started on our journey to Dather, but I can tell this is something that's very important to these people. Juse leads us further into the island, toward the thick green jungle. Just outside the tall forest of palm trees, a river runs out and towards the coast.

Those of us from Libertas hang back and let the others move in towards the river. Most of them don't have footwear on, but those that do, remove it and they all walk into the shallow waters of the river. An older woman in the front of the pack, next to Juse, begins a low hum that is picked up among the group. There are some people who harmonize with the sound, creating layers and depth to the song. Then, in unison, they all begin a slow dance. They move together lifting every arm and turning all their heads in unison.

"They come from a different world than we know," Max says softly.

"What are they supposed to be doing?" I ask, confused at the scene in front of me.

"I think they're thanking the island for its resources that helped them survive," Alexander says, joining the conversation.

"They think the island cares that they dance barefoot in the river?" I ask, though it's a rhetorical question.

"Everyone has their own beliefs, I suppose," Alexander says simply.

The ritual continues to stretch on for most of the morning. When the humming finally stops, the group walks together, up the river, and to the base of the jungle where they wander around, placing their palms to tree trunks and mumbling words of gratitude to the island. Their tribute to the island is intriguing, but all I can think about is we could be halfway to Dather by now.

Finally, Juse leads the group back towards where we've been

huddled, all of them looking very at peace with themselves. He tells us that they are now ready to go and I bite my tongue from adding a comment about how late we're going to be.

We lead them down to the dock and onto our boat. Some are eager to get on, but some take another minute to say goodbye to the island. It may not have been as magnificent as Libertas, but it was a place of freedom for many of them.

Now with the extra bodies, the boat is filled to the maximum with many people having to sit on one another. And to fates amusement, I end up directly wedged between Alexander and Max.

"How long to Dather?" I ask, looking at the crowded ship.

"Tomorrow evening," Max says and the dread of a hot and uncomfortable ride sinks in.

At first, the ship is full of loud conversation. Everyone is excited to be making our way towards the war, but as the day drags on into the early evening, the group sits in almost complete silence now that the adrenalin has sunk away.

"What do you think our next orders will be?" I ask Max and Alexander. Neither has an idea or they don't want to say something so the other can counter them.

"It's hard to tell," Max finally offers. "I'm sure we'll need to approach the castle."

Alexander joins in with, "It'll depend on where Dather's troops are when we get there. I'm not sure where their defense will start and how much ground we'll gain before the fighting begins."

I'm reminded this isn't Alexander's first time being a part of an army. "You've fought before, right?" I ask, bringing up Alexander's past with the Garth army, from before we fled to Libertas together.

"Once before, in the annual Allignmass battles," he says.

I nod, remembering how full the castle was during those weeks. Each surrounding army would send the best group of soldiers they had to take on the current reigning champions, which was always Dather. By random draw, each army would face off against each other in the coliseum where my mother died. This tradition dates back to the very beginning of our world, since the asteroid shower. Dather has never lost a battle and has always kept control over the neighboring islands. I wonder, if another island had been given the power, would life for the gifted be different?

"For most of the battles I sat out," Alexander continues to explain. "I was among the youngest in the army and they were rotating us through the fights."

Alexander's eyes grow distant, as I'm sure the memory is playing in his head. I expect him to push the memory to me so I can see, but I'm not sure I would want to. "It was the last battle of the Allignmass. Sone against Dather, and Commander Paylon put me in."

Just at the mention of Paylon's name, my skin goes cold.

"I had sat on the sidelines and watched the massacre, but nothing would prepare you for being in it. It's a different kind of fight. You aren't allowed to use your gifted prisoners in the Allignmass battles, so it was all combat. Simple swords for most of the fight. I pulled back and watched the men around me go at each other's throats like a game. A Sone soldier impacted me in the back of my armor and I crumpled below him. I rolled to my back and looked up, hoping to beg for my life, but I knew from his blank stare he didn't care if my blood ran cold. He wanted his sword through my neck. They're a different breed, men who want to fight."

"Clearly you didn't die," Max barks coldly, pulling from Alexander's story.

Alexander hangs his head for a moment before locking his eyes with Max. "No I didn't, but he did."

The meaning of his words balances in the small space of air between the two men, tight on my face.

"I don't think you know what it feels like to kill someone," Alexander's voice cracks and I feel every ounce of pain he does, remembering Codian and all the soldiers' lives we ended to get to Libertas.

"Nothing you do will prepare you for that," I say softly, pulling my eyes up to the ocean. "You'll always remember the first," I add, knowing the guard I killed the night I escaped the prison never saw it coming. He didn't even know it was his last moment alive.

For the next hour or so, no one says much. When dinner comes around, we shuffle and unpack more of the rations. With the food out and our stomachs filling up, people are more willing to socialize with each other. Alexander and I sit with a group from Xavin and we talk about the gifts they have. The pair we sit with explain that no one was tested for their gift; it's just something they discovered by accident as children. They kept it hidden from the patrol on their islands long enough until making the journey to Xavin.

With hardly anything to do onboard to keep us busy, I find myself wanting to use what I've learned in Libertas to teach those from Xavin how their gifts work. I hope that, maybe, even this short training will help them in the war, though I know they will need much more than this. I try and partner up everyone from Xavin with someone from Libertas and we work on the easiest parts of their gifts. The people from Xavin are impressed with how well trained everyone is, seamlessly using their powers. The youngest of the group catch on the fastest, but I'm pleased to see everyone is at least willing to learn.

Soon, night begins to creep into the sky and Max and Juse volunteer to take the first watch. There's not much room aboard to spread out and sleep, so we do our best to prop ourselves around the edges of the boat. Alexander and I take our seats on the bench at the side of the boat where we've been most of the ride.

I lean back and watch the sky shift from burning orange, to lover pink, and deep dreamy purple. The stars speckle the sky until we've been swallowed into almost complete darkness. The others on the boat are still restless, and somewhere on the opposite side, one of our members from Libertas begins to sing the song I had heard back at Mio and Cinder's camp. The one my father taught everyone he brought to Libertas.

See this city in all its horror
Let us leave this tyrant power

Through the woods and across the waters
Walking where our fate desires.

Gather now, sisters and brothers
Listen to our journey's travels.

We've traveled long, we've traveled far
Left behind what we know
Here we sit strong and steady
And off we'll go when we are ready
We'll travel long and travel far
Until we reach our new home

Many will leave, few will arrive
Whatever we face, we will survive
We've seen each other at our worst
But in the end, we'll be the first

Gather now, sisters and brothers
Listen to our journey's travels

We've traveled long, we've traveled far
Left behind what we know
Here we sit strong and steady
And off we'll go when we are ready
We'll travel long and travel far

Until we reach our new home

And so they're here to sit and wait
For a queen to accept her fate
Our current king will crumble away
And the queen shall find her way

Gather now, sisters and brothers
Listen to our journey's travels

We've traveled long, we've traveled far
Left behind what we know
Here we sit strong and steady
And off we'll go when we are ready
We'll travel long and travel far
Until we reach our new home

After three rounds of the song, they've taught our new travelers how it goes and a chorus of their voices ring for a fourth and final round. When the song ends, everyone turns and begins to settle in for the night. A song that was once sung on a journey to flee from Dather, now echoes through the night on our way back to the island.

Chapter 29

Max shakes my knee lightly and my eyes break open. Alexander's soft, black shirt presses into the side of my face. I slowly sit up and stretch out my muscles. It's still dark and Max lets me know that it's my watch. I gently lift Alexander's arm and unwrap it from my shoulders. I should wake him, because it's his watch too, but I let him sleep a little longer.

Max finds an empty corner on the far end of the ship and settles in for what's left of the night. Every once in a while, I reach out with sense of smell in search of the creatures that took half of my traveling group on my way to Libertas, but I find the waters completely empty for miles.

When I'm sure that we have nothing to worry about, I close my eyes and begin to try and call something from the future, something that can maybe prepare me for what's to come. It takes longer for the vision to form this time. I get to almost thirty before my eyelids are filled with a blinding white light.

It slowly fades into an old road that has green weeds growing out of the tan stone. Tall trees line the left side of the path and a field stretches out to the right. I'm not sure what they are growing, it looks like corn. Straight ahead, down the road, tiny specs of white float in the air. This vision is different than the other because I'm seeing through my own point of view instead of looking down on myself.

"Dandelions," a muffled voice from behind says, but it sounds like it's echoing through mud.

I connect the name to the pieces of fluff in the sky. We aren't moving forward, just looking straight ahead, and nothing changes until the scene fades away. There's an odd familiarity to it when I come back to myself, like I had seen this before, but I figure that's how this is supposed to feel.

At the first hint of light, Alexander stirs next to me. He processes the time of day and rolls his eyes.

"You were supposed to wake me," he says softly.

"Why? To stare at nothing?" I say. "We all need as much sleep as we can get," I add. "You're welcome."

He lets out a breathy laugh as he stretches out his arms. "So, nothing exciting happened?" Alexander asks.

"No, I've just been trying to use my gift to see into the future," I admit and Alexander's eyes widen.

"Will you tell me how to do it?" he asks. "Max wouldn't teach me the day I trained with him. He said we didn't have time to go over it then."

"It hasn't proven to be useful, yet," I admit but explain to him how it works. He tries but can't get anything to come.

"The future wants to remain a secret," he says. "What have you been able to see?"

"Of the war? I'm not sure. I had one vision of me at a stone road, but nothing happened," I say and the conversation falls silent. After I toss the idea around in my head, I finally speak the words out loud. "I saw one of my father's visions though, in one of his journals."

The sounds of waves lapping at the side of the boat fill the dark early morning. Alexander feels my body tense next to him, my skin going cold. "What did he see?"

"At first, I wasn't going to tell anyone because it's just one vision. I know it shouldn't mean much." I feel myself rambling and stop speaking.

"What did he see?" Alexander asks again.

I dig my nails into my hand, fighting the nerves inside of me. I stare at the ocean across the boat, knowing I can't look at Alexander when I say this. I swallow hard and force the truth to form.

"He saw me die."

The words come out very soft and dry. Alexander doesn't say anything and I force my gaze to his.

Alexander's face has gone pale. He's bright green eyes search mine to see if I'm going to say anything else.

I decide to walk him through the vision. "I was stumbling through the smoking rubble of the Garth castle towards the edge of a cliff," I pause, seeing the vision still flashing in my head. "I heard someone yell at me, but I couldn't place the voice. Whoever it was, did something to obliterate the ground beneath my feet and I collapsed with the cliff, getting crushed in the destruction," I whisper.

Alexander seems to push the shock away and finally finds his voice. "That's just one vision."

"I know, that's what I keep telling myself too." I take in a deep breath and push away the nerves.

"I won't let it happen, Adaline," Alexander says, putting his arm around me and pulling me close. "I promise you, that won't happen."

I feel better now that I've told him. I know Alexander would do everything he could to save me, as I would for him. "I don't want anyone else to know," I whisper, pulling away from Alexander to look him in the eye. "I mean it, Alexander. If any of them find out there's a vision of a savior dying, it'll only drive more fear into the group."

"I agree. It's not something we should advertise." After a minute of silence, Alexander adds, emotion quivering in his voice, "This is why I can't risk having a relationship with you, because I can't watch you die. I need to be able to save you, Adaline."

His words go straight to my heart and it throbs in response. This is our biggest fear coming true. Before, we had just been talking about needing to save the other theoretically. Now, we actually know there's a future where I die. I know I need to change the subject before I start crying, so I latch onto the first thing that comes to mind.

"Do you remember our first night after we left Sard?" I ask, trying to turn the conversation away from the vision.

I don't want to talk about it too much because the more we talk about it, the harder it is to try and forget about it. Alexander nods his head, understanding I'm trying to change the subject.

"We had asked each other questions to get to know the other."

"Yes, would you like to know more about me?" Alexander boasts, helping to break the tension, and I laugh.

"If you're willing to answer my questions," I say.

"Ask away," he offers, shifting to get comfortable.

"What's your favorite childhood memory?" I ask.

"Wow, you're already asking the hard questions," he pretends to be stressed and runs his hand through his hair.

My body shakes with suppressed laughs, trying not to wake our sleeping troop.

"My last Christmas with my mother and father together," Alexander says and I smile, remembering how we celebrate the ancient holiday carried here from the world before ours. "The night before, we were decorating the tree my father and I had picked out with crafts my mother and I made. I didn't know Renon was my brother at the time, so when my mother asked me what I hoped Santa would bring me and I said a little brother, you can imagine her reaction." He pauses, letting the memory fill his head.

"What did she say?" I ask, trying to picture Marin stumbling around her kid's Christmas wish.

"She said I better hope for a puppy instead," Alexander says, laughing at the thought. "We spent the rest of the night taking old pillows and cutting them open to spill the fluff all over the floor to replicate snow. It was like I could pretend I was anywhere else in the world. Somewhere it was cold enough to get snow. It's my favorite memory, because Christmas time was always my favorite time of the year, and that was our last Christmas together." He pauses before turning to me. "Was Christmas a big celebration for you?"

I nod and say, "As big of a celebration as my parents could afford to make with three kids."

"Well, now that you're a princess, you can have as big a Christmas as you want," Alexander jokes.

I nudge him and we laugh, but I know we're both thinking it only counts when we win this war.

"Okay, your turn," I say and add, "But you can't repeat questions."

He nods, thinking for a minute before he asks, "Do you really believe that everywhere else in the world was destroyed in the asteroid shower?"

I tilt my head slightly, thinking for a moment. "Yes and no," I answer. "Yes because I don't think that anyone survived it that didn't make it to the islands, but no because I believe those places are still there, they're just deserted."

"I think about that a lot," Alexander admits.

"A world outside of this one is tempting," I agree. "What are we going to do with King Renon when we win this war?" I ask, and it's not a question about Alexander, but one that's been sitting in the back of my mind.

"He'll be executed, I'm sure," Alexander mumbles, knowing he is technically talking about killing his brother.

"I think it's what the people are going to want," I say hesitantly.

"I don't want him alive, but he is your only real family, besides Molly."

"I don't see it that way," Alexander says bluntly. "He brought this on himself." He pauses a moment, then tries to lighten the conversation again and says, "Does that count as your question?"

"No," I say, smiling up at him. "Did you ever really like Zavy?"

The smile that spreads on his face tells me he finds my jealousy or curiosity funny.

"That night in the hall, after the dance. Did you kiss her?" I ask, remembering the silence that filled the hall when Alexander walked Zavy to her room.

"No, of course not," he says, his wild green eyes laughing at me. "But if I say yes, and you stay jealous, will you like me even more?"

My cheeks blush. "You're just going to say no? You're not going to explain?" I push, avoiding his shot at me.

"I never liked her like that," Alexander starts, clearing his throat and leaning further into the side of the boat to stretch out his legs. "When I handed you off to Max, for that dance, I had moved off the dance floor and ran into Zavy standing by herself. She asked where you were and I told you were being swept away by one of the guests. She asked if I'd dance with her, so we didn't look like outcasts, and I said yes. Partially just as friends, and partially because I was jealous you were with him." Alexander's eyes land on Max's sleeping form across the boat.

"And then she kissed you on the cheek," I say, remembering how the sight made the room spin under my feet.

"She did," Alexander says nodding. "Then, after you ran off the stage, Zavy came up and thanked me for the dance. I told her I was heading to my room and she said she'd walk back with me." He pauses taking in a breath. "When I dropped her off at her room, she didn't kiss me. She asked if I wanted to stay with her for the night, like messaged it into my head."

"She didn't," I gasp, never even imagining Zavy would try something like that when she knew my feelings for Alexander.

Alexander nods his head and says, "Obviously I told her no. I wasn't even thinking about Zavy. All I was thinking about was how upset you had looked and how I was going to make Max pay for whatever he had done. But it turned out I was the one who had hurt you."

He looks at me with damp eyes and takes my hand in his.

"I'm sorry for hurting you."

I drop my eyes from his and my heart flutters in my chest.

"And I'm sorry for Zavy too, because we know she'll never apologize."

A breathy laugh escapes me. I lift my eyes back to his and say, "Thank you for apologizing." A moment of silence lingers before Alexander asks if it's his turn to ask a question and I agree that it is.

"Do you really like Max?" he asks softly.

I take a minute and let my eyes scan Max across the boat.

"I think I could," I admit, considering the idea. I look back to Alexander and see the hope in his eyes pleading that I will choose him. "I can't choose you, Alexander," I say gently. "I will not have you die because I couldn't keep my emotions in check."

"But does it feel wrong with him?" Alexander tries.

"It feels different," I correct. "I haven't let myself completely fall for either of you and I don't plan to until this war is behind us."

"But if you had to choose right now?" he asks.

"Right now?" I say and Alexander nods his head. "I'd choose Max so I could ensure I could save you in this war." Alexander's lips press together in a tight line and I understand how he feels. I want him to pick me, even though I also want to count on him to save me.

"Maybe we're not meant for more," Alexander says. "Lieutenants leading the same troop. Partners in this war." After a pause, he adds, "I still want you to choose me, but I know it's more complicated than that. You should be with Max."

"What?" I ask, confused by his change in viewpoint.

"If you die in this war, I don't want you to die in a love triangle with me and him. Be with him and be happy," he says, trying to be okay about the words he clearly doesn't want to say.

"I'm glad I have your approval, but I'm not rushing into a relationship before going into battle," I say.

Alexander puts his arm around my shoulders, letting me sink in next to him. "I think you'll always do what you want to, no matter what I say."

I laugh and agree. "You'd probably be correct." We sit there for the rest of the early morning and watch the sunrise, the sky slowly fading to life like stage lights warming up.

The boat is a mix of excitement and nerves, knowing we'll be in Dather by the end of the day. Everyone has woken up and we pass out fruits and oats for our breakfast.

"You were born in Libertas, right?" I ask Max as we go around and clean up breakfast. I remember it coming up in training once, but I hadn't gotten a chance to really talk to him about his life.

"I was. My father was friends with your father when they were younger. He said they were in the same class in school. When he had heard people were being moved to Libertas your father helped him. It was your father's first trip alongside King Marvin."

"I didn't realize they had so much history," I admit. " I wish I had more time with my father to hear stories like that, but there's simply no time with the war looming over us."

"Are you nervous to be back in Dather?" Max asks and we take a seat on the edge of the boat.

"I'm not going to lie, it does almost feel like I'm taking steps backward," I admit.

"But this time you have an army behind you," Max adds.

"I'm glad we're going back to fight, and not just running and hiding," I say. "But I also am terrified to see some places and people again." I pause and think about Paylon and the castle in Garth. Then I ask, "Do you know what your next steps will be? What's your troop's next move?"

I had asked him this yesterday, but I'm not entirely sure he told me the truth. I had the feeling he just didn't want to say anything with Alexander there.

He looks at me curiously before asking, "Do you know your next move?"

"No," I admit.

"Then what makes you think I know mine?" Max asks

"Because you didn't seem all that surprised to see we were on the same task yesterday." He hangs his head for a minute to hide the growing smile.

"So maybe I do know my next steps."

"And?" I question him.

"And I'll be working with you and Alexander for at least the next part of this war," Max explains.

With this information, my skin seems to relax and my anxious energy evens out. I had begun to think when this boat docked in Dather and we went our separate ways, I may never see him again. He's one of the only people from Libertas who seems to like me for me. Not because I'm an Alterken or I'm the chosen savior. He's filled the void that Zavy left, but the more time I spend with him, the more we do feel closer than friends.

"So what's our next step?" I ask, ready to hear where this journey will take me next.

"Our troops will begin with our focus on Sard. If you cut off the resources, you shorten the war from months to days. After that, we'll be moving toward the capital. We aren't sure what will be in our path on the way there, but we'll meet up with other troops before moving in to take Garth."

Max and I continue to talk about what the journey ahead could be and planning what we would do if this or that happens until we've covered every *if this* statement we can imagine and the sun starts to break back down toward the ocean.

Alexander's letting Max have all my attention today. After our conversation last night, I'm not surprised. He's been busying himself with the other members of our troop and using his gift for small tricks and practice. The people of Xavin have never heard of an Alterken, and they can't believe what he's able to show them. Alexander walks towards Max and me and nods at something behind us.

"There it is," he says.

Max and I turn and I can barely make out Dather growing in the distance. I scan Max's face and see the first signs of fear fill his eyes.

"Bigger than you thought?" I ask.

"Much," is all he says. Libertas was magnificent in its own way. While the island was small they built up. Dather is almost three times the size of Libertas. "You can see the castle all the way from out here," Max adds, turning around to take it in.

I squint and see the peaks of stone stretch to the sky from the center of the island.

"A castle or a jail cell. Depends which way life took you," I mumble.

"If we can see them, they can see us," Alexander says.

"We should cloak ourselves in invisibility," I say, processing how to do that. "The three of us can probably manage it together."

Max nods and stands, following my train of thought. "Everyone," he says, immediately silencing the boat. "We are getting closer to Dather and need to conceal ourselves. We will blanket the boat and ourselves, making us invisible with the help of our members from enhanced sense of sight. When we get closer, those of you with enhanced sense of hearing will make sure our arrival is silent. We need to go in as undetected as possible."

Everyone begins to shuffle around the boat to get into position. Alexander and I take our seats at the very tip of the boat along with Luke and Tryle. Max moves to the rear of the boat with the members from his troop with an enhanced sense of sight.

"When we become invisible, you're not going to be able to see the boat, those around you, or yourself. Stay absolutely still until we dock in Dather," Max orders, and the group gives a silent nod. After a second, I see the boat and our troops fade away as we slip from view. I sit facing Dather and watch its details get more defined the closer we sail toward it.

Everything around me is water, like I'm floating above it, but I know that I'm not floating. I can still feel the wooden beams of the boat below me. I take my hand and slowly run it up and down the crack between the boards to remind myself what's real.

In the cloud of invisibility, I feel the familiar grasp of Alexander's hand in mine. I can't see him, but I can feel him here with me. Reminding me I am not alone. Reminding me what is real.

Chapter 30

Our boat sails just outside of Sard, and around a bend in the island. We bypass the city by a couple of miles to avoid any guards they would have stationed there. When we pull onto the shore, I glance over at the tall buildings in the distance and remember the first time I looked up at them. A terrified nerve crawls through me now when I see them, so much different from the first time I saw Sard with so much admiration and amazement. The more I know the more scared I am. Sometimes knowledge is not power, it's weakness, and it reminds me of my father's lecture about seeing into the future.

We dock our boat on a small, muddy bank, where the tall forest of palm trees touches the ocean. Since we are outside the city, the use of our gifts will go undetected by the security system they have set up there. Alexander and I begin releasing the cloud of invisibility and slowly the boat and troops come back into view.

"The lieutenants will go first. Everyone else stays here," Max instructs, climbing through the crowd from the back of the boat. Alexander and I drop ourselves over the front edge and into the soft mud below.

"They all docked here," I confirm with sense of touch, reading the soft mud for who came through earlier.

Alexander nods, getting the same information. "No struggle. An easy docking, like they had planned. They took themselves and the boats this way," Alexander points toward Sard and deeper into the jungle.

"Let's survey the area," Max says, leading Alexander and me deeper into the thick palm trees. The forest is quiet and undisturbed. After we're sure the area is safe, we head back to our troops.

"I think we're clear to move," Max agrees and motions for the others to come onto shore.

Our troops drop down from the sides of the boats, many of them never being on an island other than Libertas. Alexander and I help the older members from Xavin off the boat while Max organizes our next moves. The Trackers and Sensors group together to follow the path the rest of our army took yesterday. When everyone has stretched out and finds their balance on land instead of water, we begin our hike.

In two tight rows, we move together with Alexander and Max leading the group followed by the Trackers and Sensors. Our soldiers with an enhanced sense of touch carry the boat and shrink it down to half its size just by transforming it. Darin tries to argue that he could make it small enough to fit in his pocket, but we don't want to run the risk of it expanding back to full size. At least this way, they can stay in control of it.

The burning heat that haunted my last few days in Dather still remains, soaking my uniform with sweat. I sip on my water as we walk, but I'm careful to not drink too much. I'm not sure how far they went before setting up our camp. Every once in awhile, I hear someone from Xavin stumble in the back of the group and I have to stop and help them up. They're quick to thank me and continue on, but I just keep wondering what benefit they will be to us in this war.

We hike for about half an hour when we start to lose their trail and I know we must be getting close. They couldn't erase their scent completely, not in just two days, but I know they'd be sure to cover the trail closest to camp. A few paces more and we suddenly emerge into the chaos of camp. The silent forest is now filled with conversation. I realize they have a wall of invisibility up to protect the camp and a barrier of silence keeps them well hidden, and we have just passed through it. Cooper and my father stand ready to greet us and I know the troops watching the camp must have sensed us coming.

"Glad you found us," my father says, embracing me in a quick hug before moving to greet Juse, the leader from Xavin. Cooper shows our troops around the camp. I take a minute to examine the complexity of the massive community they've set up. They worked fast in the last two days. Many tents have been propped up around the camp, two or three per troop. Cooper explains everyone will be staying at camp for a few days while we get a bearing on our surroundings. As far as they know, King Renon doesn't know we've made it onto the island. The longer we can keep that a secret, the more surprised they'll be with our first attack.

I notice lookout posts are built high in the trees around the circumference of the camp, a platform every five feet or so. Each post has three gifted stationed on top of it. There's one to keep us invisible, one to silence the area, and one to make us untraceable, while all three simultaneously track the surrounding area for intruders. Most people are housed four to a tent except the lieutenants and captains. We each get our own to call home, even if it's just for a few days.

Once everyone has been assigned a tent and they begin to move into their temporary shelter, I ask Cooper if I can see the lookout posts. I'd like to know what kind of vantage point we have from this area. Cooper leads me up one of the platforms that faces north.

The lookout post sits so high up I'm level with the tall palm leaves. Up here, the air is much thinner and the noises of the woods and people's voices fade away. I spin around, taking in what we can see from here. The blue ocean is what I notice first, looking back the way we just came.

I turn to the right and see Sard's steel buildings glistening in the distance. It's not far from us, maybe a day's hike. I feel a bit nervous at the idea that we are so close to Sard, but that is the point of this war. We can't win by hiding in the woods and demanding change. We have to go into the city and fight them up close.

I keep turning, scanning the tops of the trees that rise and fall over the mountain ridge until I stop, frozen. The nerves I had when I saw Sard multiply across my skin, and I think I may be sick. In front of me, up on the steep hill in the center of the island, the Garth castle peeks out of the trees. I can't see the town from here, but I know it's below the castle at the base of the hill, and the house I use to live in is somewhere over there too. *That's where this war will end. With that castle in ruins.*

We've arrived relatively late in the afternoon, but they have waited to serve dinner until we arrived. Before dinner, many of us change out of the uniforms we left Libertas in and clean up in the creek that runs through the center of camp.

There's a huge clearing on the far end of the camp that is being prepped for dinner. I can tell this will be a multi-purpose space for last-minute training and additional planning for the war. The gifted have turned our boats into large wooden tables with benches to sit at. The lieutenants and captains are seated front and center of the group and the rest of the troops fill in wherever they can get a seat.

It's a bit different than the traditional way of Libertas, where we were always divided by the type of gift we have. It's more unified this way, which is exactly what this army needs for the war we're about to fight in.

I'm thrilled to see some familiar faces preparing dinner. Albert and James have taken to their old roles of cooking the meat over a couple of large fires, while Cinder works with some additional members to hand out various handfuls of berries, including the familiar ray berries. The people handing out the food aren't used to serving others, as many of the servers from our past banquets are tucked away safely in the bunkers on Libertas.

When the meat is done cooking, it's also distributed to the group. While I'm sure they had a big catch, once it's divided among an entire army, it isn't much. Still, in the first days here they've already shown surviving off the island won't be a problem.

"You've adapted well," I say to my father who sits across from me. Alexander nods next to me, agreeing.

"We've theoretically been planning this war for decades, so I'd hope we'd be ready," my father jokes.

When we've finished eating, the kitchen crew moves to clean up and Captain Brutis stands to announce he's put together a surprise for us. The crowd hushes each other and silence settles around the camp in anticipation as to what has been organized. Max's father invites Zavy and Lilliana, the girl from enhanced sense of sight that seems to have replaced me as Zavy's best friend, to join him. At the mention of Zavy, I feel my skin harden into a shield of armor, always on guard when she's near.

"Two of our own want to showcase some abilities and tricks that they can perform with their gifts for our entertainment," Captain Brutis says. The broad description pulls in everyone's attention.

"We are here tonight because two very important people have come to lead us in this long-anticipated war." Lilliana smiles and gestures to Alexander and me. "We want to share some of the highlights from the last week to celebrate you both being a part of our Libertas culture." Scattered members of the army applaud and the girl continues speaking. "Tonight, we celebrate and thank you for coming to our aid."

Her and Zavy step off to the side and when the applause has died down, I'm suddenly looking at myself and Alexander in front of me. But not entirely. It's faded and I can see through ourselves and at the trees behind us.

"It's like a projection?" my father mumbles trying to make sense of it and it reminds me of how I viewed his journals.

I understand that Lilliana is projecting the image, and Zavy will be controlling the sound. The first clip they project is our arrival to Libertas, and then clips from the residency council.

I watch my projection stand and say, "Just know that without any of them, there is no me, and there is no key."

It's word for word from that day. I remember it so clearly. Then they show moments from the Welcome Ceremony and dinner. It's odd to watch it back knowing that I was mentally fighting the news that Alexander and I had to change the relationship we thought we were moving towards, but we look happy and excited to be there. The next few shots are a mix of training and I'm relieved the only shot from my first day in the ring is when my father volunteered me. They conveniently leave out the fact that Zavy beat me in the ring. I know it's probably killing Zavy not to show that. They probably made them leave it out to make sure no one falters in their belief of the saviors.

Suddenly, there's an odd projection from a dark night. In the distance, Alexander and I are illuminated by the moonlight. It's the night I snuck out of the castle and I remember Zavy sitting on the porch, watching us. My cheeks flush red at the whispers of the crowd. My father shoots me a scolding look, but I see the smile he's trying to hide.

Then, it's more clips from training and shots from the final day in the ring. Even though I lived it, I'm in awe by the immense power that Alexander and I show through each pairing. With each Alterken victory, the troops around us cheer. I can feel the passion and drive in the army rise. This is a successful motivational tactic and the feeling of support and belief in the troops continue to grow.

The final shots they show are from the coronation. I watch as I recite my oath as the Princess of Libertas and receive my crown from Captain Brutis. Then, they show Alexander and I dancing around the room.

Over the music and the dance, Zavy projects my voice. "Technically you're a prince too," I say.

Suddenly my blood runs cold, remembering what we had discussed that night.

I watch Alexander's response play out. "You have a funny sense of humor."

The whispers have already started, trying to understand what I said. Then, the scene changes to just moments later when Alexander and I had moved off the dance floor. When we thought we were talking alone.

"What if King Renon knows? If we go into battle," Zavy continues the dialog and I feel the air get trapped in my throat. "And he announces that you're his brother in front of everyone," the gasps in the crowd make me feel like I'm suffocating. "We'll lose the trust of all these people. If we even have any."

The shot glitches away and with my wide gaze, I catch Zavy's wicked grin.

The commotion in the group rises and Zavy amplifies her voice above everyone else. "This is who you're following?" The commotion dies down to listen to her proclamation. "We are preparing to fight a war to dethrone King Renon, and his own brother has been *spying* on us all this time." The glares our way scrape down my skin. "Alexander's blood is not *pure*, it's tainted *evil*."

Lilliana plays the battle scene where Alexander controls Max's mind and it drives her point even further. I force my eyes to look away from the projection and find Max. He sits at the next table over and must feel my gaze because his light green eyes find mine. A muscle in his neck throbs with anger at Alexander's secret. But his eyes are wide and sad, and I know that's meant for me. The group begins shouting and proclaiming they can't believe what they just saw. Many start chanting that they won't follow someone with the same blood as King Renon.

The scene around us is mass chaos. All the confidence I had built up, disposes itself. As my breath slowly comes back to me, Zavy's voice fills my head with words only I can hear.

"I told you I was going to win this one way or another." Her wicked green eyes lock on mine through the uproar of the group.

I beg my heart to beat again, for air to fill my lungs faster, but shock has frozen me. Zavy has just destroyed every bit of trust Alexander and I built with these people. She has exposed him as

King Renon's brother and made him look like the enemy. Hot tears burn at the edges of my eyes. I can't believe she just did that. She has turned all of these people against me in a matter of seconds.

If this war wasn't going to kill Alexander or me, then our own army will.

END OF BOOK TWO